Exile

Book Two of the Phenderian Series

Mark L Porter

ISBN:10: 0615767982
ISBN-13: 978-0615767987

DEDICATION

To LaWayna, for all of your support and encouragement

CONTENTS

Mark L Porter

Mark L Porter

Lands Of The Great Beyond

St B

Waston

Walse

Bodash

Glendba

Donga

Kresh

Idlosa

Richba

Stobela

Ghalcadia

Bowenda

Hitrenda

Valdo

Gealdo City

Gestiqfelg

Sienda

Vienda

Kimpriatelg

Bortegestia

The Isle Of mosa

Strgight Of Mosa

Iclania

Meyda

Derentia

Lostenda

Phenderia

Phenderia City

Ponican Ocean

1

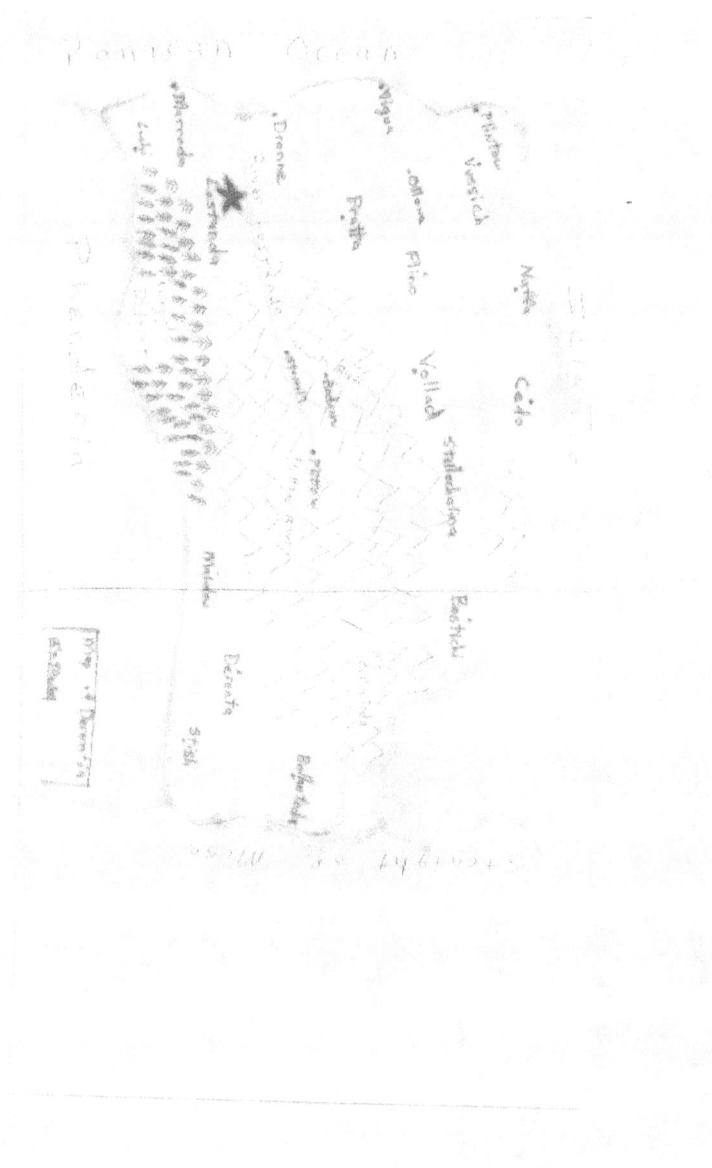

Preface

From 'The Dialog of History' Chapter 20 Page 418 – 433

Library of the Tribunal, Eutheria

And the Great Sorcerer Rustaph stared off to the west towards the great Armies stationed there from the ten kingdoms of the West. Each one of them displaying their individual colors to represent their Kings. Pike men with their pikes standing tall, gleaming in the bright light of the early afternoon, running drills Rustaph knew would not be drills tomorrow. Archers practicing with bails of hay for the events of the coming day while swordsmen worked with one another. The tent of the commanders stationed directly at the center of the great mass of humanity, strategizing the best way to annihilate the meager forces to the Lands of the East. It would be a short battle. The West outnumbered the East easily two to one with better trained men, more explosives, more weapons, and a central leader to fight around.

The East was not well run or unified. All of the twenty-six kingdoms had their own leader, each unwilling to allow a central figure to order around its people. There was a language barrier as well. With eighteen different languages and no one except Rustaph who could speak them all, it was impossible to unite them under one ruler even if they would have stood for it. Rustaph had to try in spite of this.

"I am glad you could all join me here." Rustaph stated in his opening comment, "We have a great task to undertake today. As you all can see, we have over five hundred thousand of our enemy's soldiers assembled at our doorstep here in Granwik. They want our surrender, and they want it unconditionally. I think we may need to agree to this."

"No!" It was King Vloriate of Qalthoe, a man of around fifty with dark hair and dark eyes, standing to make his point, "We cannot accept their offer. They wish us to be enslaved as farmers to feed their kingdom's families and Kings. We have been free people ever since the beginning of time. We can settle for nothing less today."

Cheers rose from the voices of the other twenty-five Kings or representatives to Kings around the tent. All of which were in agreement with King Vloriate.

"Normally I would agree," Rustaph continued over the din, "but after assessing the two sides, we not only appear to be smaller, weaker, and less prepared, but we are also divided. Your stubbornness as leaders has kept our forces apart while our enemy has unified itself under one leader, and an intelligent man at that. King Woopan of Hitrenda has all of the ten kingdoms solidly under his command. We have pockets of untrained and undisciplined soldiers waiting to be slaughtered. You have to see the only hope for your people is to accept their terms and negotiate afterwards. If this meager army, which you have assembled, goes out there, they will all die, and you will have given the West a clear path to your people and your lands."

"Why do you doubt our chances?" asked Yorbatha, Chief advisor to King Rhonnafik of Vorastan, "Our men are great and highly motivated. It's their families who would suffer if we were to lose tomorrow. Men under such motivation are equal to six of an attacking force."

"Because they will be cut down before they ever get a chance to fight a Westerner." Rustaph was holding back his anger, trying to save these people from themselves, "The West has more archers, arrows, catapults, pikes, lances, and horsemen than we do. We will be mowed down before their swords and lances can reach a Westerner. Those catapults you have seen will send out a mixture of explosives meant to spray up to a hundred feet in all directions. Men will burn to death before they can fight. After reducing our forces from a quarter of a million men to around one hundred thousand they will send in the horsemen to shred most of what's left. Then the foot soldiers will attack, approximately four hundred thousand against fifty thousand. We will be annihilated."

"You speak as a traitor." King Uberresh of Bishada announced, "Even if the battle were to go as you have described, our fifty thousand men would not stand for the Western Army to advance. We would mow them down and afterwards we, the East, would be able to send our conquering forces into the West to loot and pillage, demoralizing them once and for all. I tell you all, at the end of the day tomorrow, we will stand as the victors and the West will have to bow down to us finally."

Cheers and laughter were all the ears close by could hear from the tent of the Kings. Onlookers watched as the great Sorcerer Rustaph exited the tent. Concern on his face, he entered into his own tent at the opposite end of the staging grounds. Sitting on a low bench he opened a book on his table and studied it carefully.

It was a map of the Island of Mosa. He knew he had only one more chance for peace, a direct meeting with Feachen the Twenty-eighth, the Wizard of the Western Kingdoms. He located him at the cave on Mt. Bollantoda at the center of the Island. Pulling in his energy, he moved his spirit outward and in a flash was inside of the same cave as Feachen.

"My friend," Feachen walked towards Rustaph to meet him at the center of the cave, "come sit. I see we have much to work on."

"We do." Rustaph agreed, "The rulers of my lands seem to believe they can defeat the West in battle."

"Oh my." Feachen's eyes widened in awe of the situation. His heart sinking as he was made fully understood of the gravity of the situation.

"I know. The fools believe they can withstand the West's Armies and then invade themselves to loot and pillage your Kingdoms." Rustaph paced through the study of his oldest friend.

"What do we do?" Feachen asked, "This is what has the West in an uproar to begin with. The arrogance of the East and the unruly taxes they place on the most staple of exports. That is what has the Western leadership poised in the direction they are in."

"The West has been ignoring the needs of the East for hundreds of years, Feachen." Rustaph defended, "We do have the best farming land, and we do export most of our foods to the West."

"Because your lands produce far more than your people need." Feachen replied, "Your people starve because your Kings can make more money by exporting your food supply than feeding the people they are responsible for. It is simple greed and abuse of power."

"I agree, we have our differences," Rustaph acknowledged, "but right at the moment, we stand on the brink of a larger battle than we have ever had in the history of any of our lands."

"What can I do?" Feachen earnestly asked.

"Can you talk to King Woopan?" Rustaph asked, "If he keeps his attack from happening, I could try to persuade the Kings of the East to negotiate with the West. Maybe a treaty can take the place of war."

"Even if he would listen to me," Feachen sighed, "I'm afraid he is driven by the people at this point. They are tired of shipping all of their wealth to the East just to have the luxury of eating."

"Then I may have to step in." Rustaph stated.

Feachen looked to his old friend helplessly, "And I would have to try to defeat you."

"I am far too much for you." Rustaph revealed.

Feachen nodded, "I know, but I would have to try nonetheless."

Rustaph placed a hand on Feachen's shoulder and acknowledged, "I do not cherish that thought."

As the two made the sobering reality, Rustaph faded out to return to his tent in the plains of Granwik, reattaching himself with his body and standing to see his two Adherents, Falsdor and Pazlin.

"How did it go, Master?" Falsdor asked.

"Not well," Rustaph stated, "even though Feachen agrees this battle is stupid, he is bound to help aid the West should the need for him to step in present itself."

Pazlin looked at his Master, "Then what do we do?"

"You two are not to do anything." Their Master ordered, "You are nowhere near ready for an undertaking of this proportion. I am not sure I am either, but I have to do something."

Falsdor and Pazlin walked behind their Master to the edge of the cliff overlooking the valley the Western soldiers were camped in.

Rustaph drew in energy to project his voice far out onto the plain below at the attacking army, "King Woopan, Generals, and all belonging to the Armies of the West, please listen. You will not be able to attack tomorrow. I will not allow it."

A great roar of laughter proceeded up the cliff walls towards the three standing at the top. The Kings and Advisors of the East were seen assembling behind Rustaph at a pace of fifty feet. Rustaph turned to his Adherents, both appeared to be sympathizing with their Master's position.

Rustaph continued, "I will give you something to think about." Drawing in more energy than he had ever drawn before, he pressed upwards on the surface of the ground under the feet of the opposing forces directly under the leader's tent. A hill started to form, breaking the poles of the tent and causing it to crash to the ground.

King Woopan turned with hands on hips to speak to the Eastern Sorcerer, "Make me heard throughout the entire region as you have done for yourself."

Rustaph accommodated the foreign ruler to hear, "Is this what we have to see upcoming, cheap magical theatrics? We are discussing war, yet you amuse us with a slight of hand, a mere inconvenience, a hill, a mound of dirt? That is the best the great Sorcerer Rustaph can do? I can have a brigade duplicate it in a day with a few shovels. This is what we should fear?"

"I can do far greater," Rustaph supplied, "should the need arise. Return to your homes, all of you. There will be no battles, no conquerors, and no invasion. Turn and leave, you have until sunset to remove yourselves from Eastern lands."

"We do not need to wait until sunset." King Woopan announced, "We will invade in the morning. You will lose, and all of the lands of the East will be ours. No more begging for reasonable food for our children. No more high taxes lining your Kings pockets, and most of all, freedom for the West to live a lifestyle without fear of knowing how we will eat tomorrow. We will attack, and you will be defeated. If you wish to surrender we will accept, but we will take your lands, all of them."

Rustaph left the edge of the cliff to talk with the Kings of the East once more, "Do you see what your greed has done?"

"No," stated King Vloriate, "you are being lied to and duped. Let them come. We welcome them to die here."

"And if you are wrong, it will be the end of the East." Rustaph added, "Your women will be raped, your riches plundered, your children murdered. Are you willing to risk all of that as well?"

"There is no risk." King Vloriate replied, "We know what we are doing."

"I will save you from yourselves then," Rustaph told them, "but only for the innocent people you are trying to kill." With that he turned as the monarchs of the East laughed at him for his ignorance of leadership.

Pazlin stopped Rustaph short of the cliff, "Master what is going to happen?"

Rustaph sighed, "That would be up to them."

"You return, oh great Sorcerer?" Woopan mocked with a bow.

Rustaph again sighed and stated, "This is your final warning. Turn and go home."

"You bluff," Woopan defied, "Generals, assemble your men. The invasion starts now."

"Very well then." Rustaph, the greatest Sorcerer the world had ever seen, drew in as much energy as he could take, pressing himself to the limits of destruction. Then releasing and using himself as a tunnel for more energy, he passed all he could grasp through to move the ground under the great army amassed below him. The ground shook and cracked, trembled and opened. Many tried to stay on top of it, but all within sight where buried under the shifting land, crushing them and all around them to death as it did so.

The Kings of the East stood ecstatic at the great loss suffered by their enemy. Cheering and laughing, great cries of joy filling the entire camp of the army of the East. Looking onward they saw the great mountains rise up in front of them until nothing of the West or the soldiers could be seen.

"What have you done?" Feachen the Twenty-eighth appeared to cry over the thunderous noises, "You know we are not to impose ourselves onto the human world! You have doomed my people!"

Exhausted and weak, Rustaph, being held up by his two Adherents, explained, "I have set things right. The East and West are cut off. Your soil is fertile from the rotating of the soils from this region to theirs. Their rocky, bleak, and useless land is now able to produce great harvests in many areas. You have no need for us, and we no need for you."

"Except for the fact," Feachen reminded him, "that we are left without an army to keep your greedy monarchs out of our business." Feachen turned to the quarter of a million men behind Rustaph. Watching the clouds roll in and the winds rise up, Rustaph, Falsdor, and Pazlin saw the lightening strikes, multiple and swift. Each had a purpose, and each had deadly accuracy. The Kings and Advisors where the first to be struck down.

After they were no more, the army running about in disarray was slaughtered by the electrocuting volume of the storm being fed by the Wizard of the West.

"Stop!" Falsdor drew in energy to force Feachen to withdraw his attack, but Feachen was far superior to the Adherent. Sucking the energy back out of him and using it to fuel his storm, Falsdor found himself caught. He had no way to break himself free, and Rustaph was too weak to aid him.

He tried anyhow.

The three connected together, all weak, all strapped into their fate. Nothing could have saved them now. Pazlin stood watching as his friend, his Master, and the Wizard all disappeared from sight. Rustaph and Falsdor died from the energy. Feachen gasped his last as his spirit returned to his cave on the Island of Mosa.

Pazlin listened to the quiet. In the spot where there had been three quarters of a million men only moments before, there was now just charred ground, blue sky, and tall mountains.

Weeping, Pazlin drew in energy from the air around him, and in his agony, he erased the memory of the East from every living inhabitant and book on the western side of the newly formed mountain range.

Chapter 1

Violta felt the familiar presence of the boy wizard, Chessington, as he stepped within reach of the mental capacity coming into the Woods of the Doltists. She had felt him only once before, even then for only around a twenty-four hour span, but remembered him quite distinctly for his mind already was changed by his ability. She felt seven others accompanying him this time as opposed to the four who were with him the last. She smiled knowing the group had succeeded in finding the others they had been looking for. In hindsight she had known he would. The books the Queen had read to the members of his group had always alluded to this, but now with it upon them, she was relieved to know it had truly come to pass.

She touched the mind of Queen Rhyshena, 'Shall I go to meet them, Your Majesty?'

The Queen replied, 'That would seem proper. I will send Wahldor to meet up with you there as well.'

As Violta sped off in the direction of her charges, she looked deeply into the mind of the young wizard. *This must be Violta?* She felt him ask.

Startled at first, she then replied, *Yes, you have learned to recognize my mind?*

Chessington thought back to her, *It would seem so; although, I don't know how I could have learned this without ever being shown.*

It is of no matter. I will be to you in a few moments to lead you all back to Queen Rhyshena's court. The small green Doltist returned to him.

Chessington turned to the rest of his traveling group. Sir Ghalkin, Chief Tutor to Prince Palton and the unofficial leader of the Royal Phenderian Council; General Vastion, Commander of the Army of Phenderia; Sir Malden, Royal Court Librarian and Head Advisory of all legal matters in Phenderia; Sir Bansinghaim, Royal Champion to the Prince as well as his personal bodyguard; Gurlig, a simple town drunk from the logging town of Lorning; Preda, the seven year old cousin to Chessington; and Prince Palton, heir to the Thrown of Phenderia after the King and Queen, his parents, had been lost at sea.

"Violta just told me she'd be here in a moment to take us to Queen Rhyshena's court." Chessington informed them.

"I'm new to this," General Vastion admitted, "who will be taking us where to see whom?"

"Violta, a small green Doltist who's their head a the military," Malden deciphered, "is takin' us ta see Queen Rhyshena, Queen a the Doltists, at her court in the center a the Woods. Try ta keep up."

"I still ain't fond a bein' here." Gurlig added, unease showing all over his face, "It ain't fer normal folks."

Chessington replied, "You'll be a little more uneasy in a moment when she arrives. She will tell you what you're thinking before you say it. She's around three-feet tall and covered in tree moss."

Sir Ghalkin raised his eyebrow, "Even for this last week, that sounds far fetched, but I don't doubt you."

Bansinghaim laughed, "I will never doubt anything again. How long are we to be in these woods, boy?"

Chessington shook his head, "I have no idea. Queen Rhyshena controls everything in here."

Malden grimaced, "Ain't that the truth. That old girl 'll make ya pull yer hair out."

Ghalkin raised an eyebrow, "Infatuation, Malden?"

"Ain't the word I'd a used." Malden corrected, "Rude, offensive, pompous, pretentious; those 're better words."

"You just described yourself," Bansinghaim grinned, "and remember she heard that."

"She already heard it when I thought it the last time we was here." Malden stated, "If she's gonna be in ma head, she's gonna know a lot a stuff I believe. She don't like it, she can get out."

Vastion kept it going next, "Seems she's gotten under your skin."

Malden was saved by the sight of Violta standing on a rock fifteen feet in front of them, "Welcome back. Queen Rhyshena has requested me to guide you back to her court. We are all pleased to see your safe return."

Chessington spoke for the party, "As are we. Thank you for your hospitality. We hope to be on our way soon, but would be pleased to confer with your Queen before leaving."

"Very well put," Violta nodded, "even if it is not from your heart, it is always nice to hear pleasantry. Please follow me. We should be to Queen Rhyshena's Court just at the start of evening meal. Royal Knight, please try to acknowledge our customs, as we cannot allow you to observe yours."

"I understand," Bansinghaim nodded, "I don't like it, but I understand."

"What was that about?" Vastion asked the large Knight.

"They have an annoying custom at their meals," Bansinghaim answered, "no meat."

Gurlig looked puzzled, "What they eat then?"

Bansinghaim finished, "Grasses, barks, roots, and leaves. I could lose many pounds here if we stayed too long."

"Yeah," Malden added, "'bout a hundred years."

True to her word they pulled into Queen Rhyshena's court just around the approach of evening meal. Vastion, Ghalkin, and Gurlig were amazed at the regal stature of this court. They could see where the throne was, even though it was actually a tree, and the ring of firs closing it in to give the feel of a gathering place with the focal point to the front where the Matriarch presided.

Queen Rhyshena was as tall as the rest of the Doltists, but you knew once you saw her she was their leader. Her stature made you respect her, and her diminutive size was never an issue when dealing with the Queen. "Chessington the Twenty-ninth, it is good to see your return as well as your friends."

"The Twenty-ninth?" Vastion questioned.

Malden shrugged, "Long story. Fill ya in later."

"Thank you for receiving us again, Your Majesty." Chessington bowed, not really knowing what he should do; although, propriety would say he did the right thing.

"To answer your groups most pressing question, you will spend two nights with us and leave the next morning. You will be leaving here at the opposite end of the woods and traveling to Mount Bollantoda, the highest peak on the Island of Mosa. There you will all go to the upper cave, visible from the ground. There, like here, you will be free to use the energy without detection as long as you are inside the cave as was Maldo the First. You must go there as Chessington the Twenty-ninth will learn something new about himself."

"An' if we don't?" Malden interrupted.

The Queen looked into his face, "Then you are doomed to fail the world to misery."

"Not much choice." Malden finished his original thought.

"No," the Queen agreed, "you seem to feel your quest only is reflected upon Phenderia. This could not be farther from the truth. As we speak, your enemies are poised to invade Derentia as well. We have felt the presence of their armies building at the borders close to our own Woods. We have even heard the mind of one of their leaders, the ones you refer to as the Robes. They are to press to Lostanda, attack the same as they did in Phenderia City, and remove the monarchy. Iclania will follow."

Sir Ghalkin seemed puzzled, "Why? Who are these people? And most of all, why the Island of Mosa?"

"I can answer your questions in order," the Queen replied, "but first we eat."

Vastion was now seeing why Malden was so annoyed with Her Majesty, "You must be joking. You have the answers to some of our most key questions, and you choose to tease us with this?"

"See," Malden grinned, "an' I don't think she knows how ta joke."

Ghalkin scowled at the pair, "After we eat will be fine, and thank you again for your hospitality."

The group followed Violta, and now Wahldor, to a side clearing, where it was obvious the Doltists used this gathering area for festivals and meetings associated with food. They were directed to sit on the ground next to the Queen to her immediate left with Violta, Wahldor, and two others in that order proceeding from her right.

The meal was far more proper than the few the five remembered from before. A bark and leaf mixture was the main course, wild potatoes and onions, and a raw spinach salad. Doltists served the Queen, then the group starting with Prince Palton first, and Chessington served second. Then to the amazement of all, Preda third.

Reading their thoughts, Queen Rhyshena smiled and explained, "As knowing a bit about the future, we see how lives can possibly turn out. You will find out in time, if all goes accordingly, we were correct to serve a small girl with a future monarch and a royal wizard."

"Explain." Malden questioned.

"It would change things if I do." The Queen dodged the question, "I will, however, start to explain the answers to the questions you have posed. First, the question was why. This is the oldest reason in history, power, unmatchable power."

"How can taking a farming and lumbering kingdom," Vastion asked, "plus a neighboring mining country to it's north, and even north of that a frozen wasteland where the people can't even be outside for the three most extreme months of the year, be empowering to anyone?"

"Because," the Queen explained, "three days journey by ship due west of the mouth of the Lostanda River is an anomaly, a Phanthow. A sea hole, which is something that defies all natural laws and exists in spite of this. At the bottom of this Phanthow is the area of the beginning source to the Energy you have all just learned about. Books in your enemy's libraries tell of the one or ones to occupy this area controlling every ability the energy can offer. They also believe they have a map of how to get there. To my knowledge, it would be the only one."

"How is that possible?" Chessington wondered, "I know I'm very new to this, but it doesn't seem like the sort of thing you can take away from someone after they know about it."

The Queen shook her head, "That I do not know either. My assessment would be the same as yours, but your enemy at least believes differently."

"So who is this Enemy?" Malden asked.

"They belong to a country farther away than you have knowledge of." Queen Rhyshena spoke, "A land across the Great Beyond and larger than all of the area you know about."

"They got a name?" Malden was proving he had little patience, "It'd be easier 'en just referrin' to 'em as the enemy for the rest a our lives. However short that may be."

The Queen replied, "Chiloe, an entire nation ruled by a single noble. Lord Maldifren, as he is referred to, is the military ruler, dictator, and judicial system for the entire Empire. His ancestors have already exterminated whole ethnic groups in his own lands and seek to do the same on this side as well. He has limited ability with the energy, but his chief adviser, a Sorcerer of no equal named Pazlin, is aiding him until the time is right to stage his own political overthrow. For now Maldifren is in charge of the Chiloes, but the day will come before too long when Pazlin will in one way or another have eclipsed him and rule with a more evil heart than even Maldifren."

"So how do we combat this great evil force," Vastion wondered aloud, "with a wizard of a weeks experience, four politicians, a reformed drunken lumberjack, and two children?"

"First off," the Queen announced, "you all have more buried deep in you beyond what you have stated. Second, the ones who foretold all of this from the beginning of Pazlin's reign are assisting you as well, or you would not have reached this stage of your journey. And third, you will gather more to your band starting when you leave these woods. When you do leave here, you will be nine strong and not eight."

Sir Ghalkin, looking for clarification, asked, "Is it truly necessary to add to our numbers? Should we not stay small enough to be able to out run or elude our enemies and not draw attention to ourselves. Even though we are presumed dead to our enemies, these Chiloes, should they find out we are alive we would have a need for swiftness, which too many people would inhibit."

"A valid point," the Queen recognized, "but each who will be joining you is for a reason. A reason you may never find out was important, even to the one it concerns. If a certain person is not there at an important time, you could all fail."

"How will we know who these right ones are?" Bansinghaim asked.

The Queen stated flatly, "You may not, but I assure you, they need to be there."

"Great," Malden grumbled, "clear as mud."

"You never said who would be joining us from here?" Ghalkin remembered.

"Violta will go from here with you to the end of your quest." She announced, "She is our military leader, knows many tricks and devious deceptions, and has a limited amount of her own use of the energy which cannot be detected. She can also aid in helping Chessington the Twenty-ninth refine his wizardry along the way and notify him of other areas where neither the great Pazlin nor his Adherents can detect him."

All eyes turned to look over the small female Doltist who was going to be one of them. She smiled back down the row, mostly at Chessington, and continued eating her dinner.

"She gonna read ma mind the whole way?" Malden asked.

"I'm not going without real food out there." Bansinghaim argued.

"She has no ability to see your thoughts once you leave these Woods here, Master Librarian." Queen Rhyshena soothed, "The trees and the woods themselves are the ones reading your thoughts. We are just able to read them from the trees and only these trees who have grown to accept us. As for your customs with meat, they are solely offensive to the Doltists here in this forest; although, knowing Violta as I do, she will state her opinion to you more than once Sir Knight."

"How do we know where to go after Mount Bollantoda and Iclania?" Vastion inquired.

"I know that one." Chessington answered, "I turn to my part in the book which speaks to me."

"Correct," the Queen praised, "always look to the books if you are completely lost or can find no direction to follow. As you proceed it will become more and more obvious to you all what your next steps will be. I can tell you this, finish with Mount Bollantoda and you will be turning to leave the island before you end up trapped here for the winter. You do not have the time to stay here for months on end waiting on the weather, and it will certainly not wait for you."

"We should have 'round three months 'fore the turn ta winter, even in Iclania." Malden informed.

"Yes, and you will need all of it." Queen Rhyshena started into her plate signifying the end of the evening's discussions.

Gurlig spoke to his group, Chessington mostly, "I did think a more stuff ta make fer the trip since ya can do that in here. Might have a use fer a few more items, so 'fore we get outta here remind me ta tell ya 'bout it."

"Very good point." Ghalkin nodded, "We have no Iclanian Milos to spend if need be to go there, only Dernos, and it would draw less attention if we had the local currency."

"Small problem there." Malden remembered, "We gotta have one 'fore he can make one."

"That's true, Sir." Chessington agreed, "I can't make it if I don't know what it looks like."

"That would be a problem then." Ghalkin thought about it before turning towards their newest member, "Violta, would you have a place where things are gathered, which are left behind by forest travelers?"

"We do." The small green Doltist replied, "I can take some of you there in the morning to look it over and see if there is something useable."

"Vastion looked at the petite green woman asking, "You and I should discuss your style of military here in the Woods. It could really help down the road if we knew each others capabilities a bit better."

"Very well," Violta agreed, "I have time at the present if you wish."

"Fantastic," the General stated, "how do you defend your Woods?"

"Well, mostly the trees do that." She replied, "They inform us to outsiders in the forest. We suggest to them what the person or persons should do, and they plant the idea into the intruders mind. They believe it was there idea and leave or wander around lost in the woods."

"I see." Vastion nodded, "Haven't you ever been attacked?"

"No," she spoke, "no one really wants our land. Most people have no idea Doltists exist. Even if they did, we would just have the trees change there mind."

"I got a question." Malden interrupted, "Ya say ya can talk with the trees, but what about other plant life? Bushes, weeds, flowers, ya know."

"We could," she admitted, "but bushes are stupid and some vegetation can hurt or even kill us. You know how some are used for medicines and some for poisons, well we can feel there traits as we converse with them. Many are good, yet some are terribly toxic. I think after three hundred years of conversing with vegetation, I can tell the good ones from the bad."

"Hold on," Ghalkin interjected, "you are three hundred years old?"

She straightened up her stance, "Three hundred and two actually. My mother is eight hundred and forty seven."

"How long is your life expectancy?" Ghalkin continued.

Violta looked up as if thinking hard, "I'd say around fourteen hundred years, but old Creatia is close to nineteen hundred, and the trees are telling me a male named Dorsif was two thousand and eighty one when he decomposed."

"Decomposed?" Bansinghaim asked.

"Yes," she nodded, "you must understand, we are part vegetation ourselves. If you remove a limb from a tree, it will in time grow a new one. We are the same, stab us, cut us in two, smash us into pieces, it doesn't matter. The only fatal blow to us would be from the inside out or fire."

"Poison?" Chessington asked.

20

"Exactly," Violta shuddered at the thought, "it is slow and painful, and a horrible way for us to go. Also, the ultimate crime in our society is poisoning or cutting down a tree. Neither has ever happened on purpose though"

"No one's ever cut down a tree?" Gurlig asked.

"No," she replied, "if they start, we tell them to stop."

"I can't imagine your way of thinking working after we leave the woods," Vastion had hoped for something a bit more tangible to aid them, "but I'm sure you'll have insights we don't."

The sun had been replaced by the moon an hour before their conversations ended. They were shown to the guest section, which was a beautiful area next to a stream surrounded by oaks and bushes. Soft underbrush had been laid out freshly, one for each visitor, and was remarkably comfortable, or the group was extra tired. It seemed like years ago when they awoke yesterday morning, some of them from a warm bed, the others from these very Woods.

Looking back at the peacefulness of the morning, Chessington remembered the large fireplace, delicious breakfast at the restaurant, the book store with Malden, and waiting by the fountain. It all seemed to be blotted out by the attack in Marroda, fleeing to the grove of trees outside of town, and the battle with the Chiloes. There was enough packed into these two days to complete a busy month. Now, a few short hours later, he was lying safely in an oak grove surrounded by friends, and going to learn more about his new found ability. The next day after that would start their quest once again.

Seeing all of his friends fast asleep, nodding off quickly from the riggers of their day as well, he wondered just how things would turn out. He had no idea how to defeat the powers from Chiloe nor any idea of how to imagine a Phanthow either. He remembered the feel to the mind of the invader at the battle. Could it have been Pazlin? He was certainly evil feeling. And how could you release a living human being back into nothingness? The disregard for life and others was beyond his understanding. He felt slightly what the Doltists felt towards him and his kind with their destruction of trees and animals.

Very insightful. He heard Violta in his mind, *Does it change your perception of us a bit?*

Chessington, caught off guard a little, thought back to her, *It does, but why aren't you asleep?*

Like you, she explained, *we have no need for sleep. The same as you allow the energy to freely come in and out of you is the same with us. We are refreshed, as you call it, all the time.*

We'll still be able to talk this way after we leave the Woods right, with no one able to know except us? Chessington asked.

Yes, Violta answered, *I feel that seems to please you.*

It does. The young Wizard admitted, *In the past week or so, I've gotten very lonely at night being left to myself for hours on end.*

Oh. The young Doltist woman sighed.

Chessington changed the subject, *Won't your family miss you after you leave? I can't imagine it's normal for a Doltist to leave the safety of this forest.*

They will, she continued, *I am really only close to my twin sister, and my mother understands exactly why I need to go.*

Do Doltists have what we would call husbands or wives?

She thought, *Yes, we would call them a partner. We think of men and women as equal far, far more than your culture would. We are connected by a bond which cannot be broken until decomposition starts. Then we aid the half going to make it an easier journey. We find a mate once, and we stay mated for hundreds of years.*

And your mate won't miss you? Chessington pried.

I am barely of age to find a mate. She replied, *My lifespan is only approximately a fifth of the way through. In your terms, I would be equal to a sixteen to twenty year old in your culture.*

Chessington had never though of it this way before, *We're about the same age?*

We are. She grinned to herself, knowing he could not see her, *Does that bother you?*

Oh no, Chessington tried to cover for himself, *I just hadn't thought in your terms before.*

I suppose I am going to have to start thinking in yours, too. Violta admitted, *I am not accustomed to riding on horses or carts, but I would assume my little legs would not be swift enough for your group. I cannot eat animals like you do though. That is as repulsive to me as you would be to eating another human. I will like seeing the cultures outside of our Woods though.*

You may be disappointed. Chessington could see she was ready for an adventure, *It can be less than honest and admirable.*

I have seen inside the minds of the people who come in here. She explained, *I understand dishonesty and self-benefiting behavior. Even though we do not really have that here, we do know about it. I will be eager to see it in action on a large scale.*

Chessington laughed, *Oh, you will. I'm quite sure of that. We are who we are. Even our babies know how to manipulate adults to get what they want.*

Ours too. She agreed, *We can see each others thoughts, but we still have to make our own judgments. You think we act as one enormous being, but actually we are far more individual because we can see each others thoughts.*

After a moment of silence, the Wizard asked a question of the Doltist, *How will you keep from drawing attention to yourself once you leave these woods?*

She paused for another moment and answered, *I suppose the green moss would attract attention.*

Just a bit, Chessington agreed, *although your height and weight can be explained, it would be more difficult than your moss.*

I can change it, Violta stated, *I can make it so I have skin like you. I cannot change my size, but I can change my skin, hair, eyes, that sort of thing. Will I have to dress also?*

That would be a good idea. Chessington smiled to himself, *You would draw less attention by being moss covered than undressed.*

Humans, Violta laughed, *you can kill, steal, and destroy the land, but show a body part half of your species already owns, and you are mortified. I honestly do not understand people.*

Chessington laughed inwardly, *I have no comment after that. You have summed up my people in a sentence.*

Violta laughed as well, *I will see you morning after next. I have some things to tend to before we leave here.*

I will see you in the next morning then. Chessington thought about her for the rest of the evening. How she could converse so well. How she was so tiny. How she was over three hundred years old. After a few hours of this, he noticed General Vastion, with his eyes wide open, seemingly thinking as well.

Chapter 2

The first morning for the group of nine started calm and casual. An early morning shower by the waterfall at the west end of the guest area, followed by the presentation of freshly laundered clothing, and then the gathering together for breakfast were the first orders of business. All feeling refreshed and ready for the new adventures and travels, they ate together discussing the way this day would go.

Chessington's day was planned for him. He was to go with Wahldor for more training. Prince Palton was to sit with the Queen. She wanted to understand him better, hoping beyond hope this young boy was the future for the outside world closest to her domain. Bansinghaim and Gurlig would go with a hunting party to forage for knowledge of things edible and poisonous in a forest. They would also learn about some of the benefits certain plants had to offer humans. This left Ghalkin, Vastion, Malden, and Preda to go with Violta to the area containing things from outside of the forest.

"There you have it." Violta pointed to a gully filled with former personal belongings of some of the guests of the woods, "Everything we have come across. Mostly knives and odd clothing left behind in haste. A few things we do not understand. Most we do."

Ghalkin looked at the size of the debris and sighed, "We had better start. Milos are small, round, and could be copper or pewter."

Vastion stared at the volume of waste before him, "All this was left behind? How did there get to be so much?"

"It has been many years since humans started coming into the woods." Violta explained, "There could easily be things at the bottom from thousands of years ago. We bring it here if we have no use for it, so it gets ignored. Besides, we really do not have any need for such things. If we need something, the Woods provides it."

"My my," Ghalkin exclaimed, "what a beautiful pocket watch. It does not work, of course, after being outside for so long, but I would assume it cost someone a few day's wages."

"There are quite a bit of useful things here." Vastion added, "I see a sword which must be five hundred years old at the very least."

"This is interestin'," Malden held up a very proper lady's riding gown, "wouldn't a thought ta a found somethin' like this in here."

"The stories these things must have." Ghalkin smiled, "Every one is of a person trying to leave a forest they felt lost in. I wonder how many reasons there are for people to be seeking out this place?"

Preda held out her hand, "Is this something?" Showing it to Sir Malden she continued, "There are lots of them in that old cast iron pot there."

"Well," Malden smiled, "it ain't Milos, but it is Dernos. Why would someone leave a fortune in Dernos behind?"

"They did not have a choice." Violta explained, "That story is not very old. Three men came to us from the north. They rode in and killed one of the men, something we do not like in the least. The other two, without knowing, were sent out. As a punishment they were forced to leave the thing they cherished the most. That pot of Dernos as you called them. Queen Rhyshena was very displeased."

"Don't doubt that." Malden replied, "Can't say I blame her, but I thought you guys filled intruder's brains with happy thoughts?"

"No," Violta corrected, "we can suggest, even suggest strongly, but the decisions are always up to the individual. If a bad seed decides to do it anyways, we cannot really stop them, but in the past thousands of years, there are very few incidences to have gone the wrong way."

"Here we go!" Vastion exclaimed, "A five Milos pewter coin."

"Yep," Malden concurred, "that's a real one. Good thing too, we ain't gettin' too far on our looks."

"Speak for yourself, old sport." Vastion smiled, "I've let my looks take me places."

"Before ya had yer title?" Malden asked.

The General stared at him blankly.

"Didn't think so." The Librarian added.

Vastion ignored the remarks, placing the Iclanian coin in his coat pocket for safe keeping. Turning to leave, he was stopped by the appearance of a new object he had not noticed before.

"I wonder what this thing could be?" Vastion held up a stone approximately the size of a normal potato. It was opaque for the most part, but you could see a solid red center to it through the pinkish glowing exterior around it. It had no weight to speak of, and the General was surprised it was so light.

"That is an odd thing." Ghalkin observed, "Why would you not have seen it before? It is so unique, so different, I would have pulled it out just to study it."

"It did not want you to notice it." Violta revealed, "It liked it here with the trees and the energy."

"It liked it here?" Vastion wondered, "It's a rock, a very pretty and special rock, but a rock nonetheless."

"No," Violta argued, "it thinks. It knows things. I do not know if it is good or bad, but it is more than what you see."

"Did you notice it?" Malden asked the Doltist, "I mean yer tuned inta that stuff. Why didn't ya find it?"

"It did not want me to either." She explained again, "It works on its own agenda."

"Great," Malden rolled his eyes, "leave it!"

"It wants to go with you." Violta spoke for it, "It needs to be with you for your journey."

"Our journey." Ghalkin looked at Violta.

She smiled, "Our journey."

"And the rock told you this?" Vastion asked.

"Not exactly." She conceded.

"I see." Vastion acknowledged.

Violta continued, "The trees told me that it told them. I cannot speak to that."

"Well, of course not. How silly of me to think you could talk to a rock." Vastion looked at the sky as he spoke, "Good thing the trees set us straight."

The band of scavengers seemed to get a laugh out of him, realizing they were not as in charge of things as they normally would have thought, and also to realize how fast your concept of what is possible and impossible can change. Two short weeks ago anyone claiming the things they had seen would have either been laughed out of the castle or sent to be looked after in a government sponsored institution. Things still surprised them, but they were considerably more open to entertaining thoughts of the inconceivable than they had been in the past.

"I feel we are done here." Ghalkin stated, "It is almost lunch anyhow. I will carry the pot of Dernos. General, you have the Milos piece and the rock, so I would assume we are finished here."

Vastion nodded, "I think we've touched everything in the collection. Unless we want utensils or knives, I think we're through."

They walked the few feet back to the cart placing the pot on it, as well as Violta, Preda, and Ghalkin as the driver and headed back towards their guest area.

* * * * * * *

Chessington looked over the lump in his hands trying to figure out what he saw in it. It was a hard clay like material which could be bent or even broken but was hard and difficult to bend. It had much more density than normal, and was the color of fresh blood. It felt warm to the touch, but not hot, and never cooled. He looked out at the vast acreage noticing the red spots popping up between the dirt of the field.

"So this is what gives the woods its energy?" Chessington clarified.

"Yes," Wahldor agreed, "these pockets of Maltham run to the core of the world and connect with every other place on the planet. The energy flows through it and circles the world. It connects here to everywhere you can stand."

"Would it connect to the Phanthow?" Chessington wondered.

"In theory it would have to." Wahldor agreed, "In all likelihood it would seem logical it either originated there or at least is highly concentrated at that point."

"Is that why other forces can't see into the woods because the Maltham is on the surface and not buried deep underground?" Chessington was becoming very astute to things connected to the energy.

"Yes," Wahldor agreed again, "it is the very reason. It protects us and aids us. We by ourselves have very little ability with the energy, but because of our long term exposure to it, it has become a part of us. Our species started as vegetation and over thousands of years of exposure to this energy, we have evolved into what you see today."

"Interesting," Chessington stared at the lump in his hand a little more, "what if you tried to mold it into something or fire it like you would clay or pottery?"

"For what purpose?" Wahldor asked.

"So you could create an atmosphere of energy to saturate an item with." The boy Wizard replied.

"I suppose in theory it could work." Wahldor agreed, "It has just never been tried."

Chessington pulled a larger amount of the energy out of the ground and placed it on a rock. Pulling and pushing in different areas, pressing his knuckles to the center, and pulling the sides up to form a pot. "It's not pretty, but it'll be good for what I was hoping to do. Now what to place inside of it?"

The two looked around seeing only normal objects from the woods. Chessington picked up a stone about three inches across and one inch in width, flat on the top and bottom, and placed it in the pot.

Grabbing another lump of the energy, he patted and pressed it thinner and thinner until it was larger on all sides than the opening to the top of the pot. Placing it over the top, he watched as the two pieces seal themselves together and held tightly. Making the stone inside airtight from the outside world.

"Now what?" Wahldor asked.

Chessington shrugged, "I guess we leave it until it wants to open for us."

"That could be eons." Wahldor stated.

"I suppose it could." Chessington agreed, "We don't really have a choice now though do we."

Wahldor chuckled, "No, I suppose not."

"Is there more today?" Chessington asked.

"Just one more lesson." Wahldor returned, "You need to practice speaking to the trees. They can be of great assistance to you in the future."

"I thought Violta told me she couldn't speak to the trees outside the Woods of the Doltists?"

"She cannot," Wahldor explained, "but she is not a wizard. You on the other hand are, and you can have conversations with whatever living object you desire. The only specifications are it has to be living. A tree yes, your wooden cart no."

"Anything?" Chessington was taken aback with the thought.

"Anything still living." Wahldor reiterated, "Go ahead."

"How?"

"The same way you have spoken to Violta in her mind." Wahldor explained.

"I guess I can try." Chessington closed his eyes to concentrate better and focused on a beautiful willow tree at the opening of the field back by the trail, which had brought them here.

"Hello, Master Chessington," the willow responded, "it is a pleasure to feel you here."

"Umm, hello beautiful willow tree, ma'am or sir. Umm, how are you today." Chessington was at a complete loss for words having never spoken to a tree before. He had no idea if he would offend it or say something completely inappropriate.

"You needn't feel uncomfortable, Master Chessington." The willow thought back, "I am not a judgmental tree. You may speak free and honestly."

"You seem very proper, Master Willow." Chessington asked, "Are all trees proper?"

"Most are, yes." Master Willow replied, "But some are more than others. The oaks feel superior and the pine more down to their roots, but for the most part we are a proper race. Your species seems to differ drastically this way as well."

"We do." Chessington agreed, "There was a man back at the castle in Phenderia City who knew only how to be proper. His job was to make young uncultured girls into proper ladies."

"You speak well, Master Chessington." The willow stated, "Were you raised an aristocrat?"

"No, Master Willow," Chessington answered, "I was raised in a common family and sent to my Aunt and Uncle's farm around the age of nine. There I worked the soil with my Uncle Fein to produce vegetables and grains for the markets in the city."

"You cared for plants?" Master Willow asked, "That is a fine profession. It would seem remarkable you hadn't spoken to us before."

"I had no concept of the idea before the Doltists introduced it to me." Chessington explained, "If I were to go outside of the woods and tell other humans I was speaking to a willow tree, they would laugh at me or even lock me up."

"So humans believe they are the only species with intelligence?" The willow seemed to find humor in this.

"Yes," Chessington confirmed, "wouldn't that explain most of my species actions?"

The willow agreed, "Yes, as a matter of fact, that could possibly be the only way to explain your species actions."

Chessington smiled, "I believe you are correct. I have enjoyed our time together, Master Willow. I do feel I must be moving on to the rest of my group, however."

"It has been an honor to have made your acquaintance, Chessington the Twenty-ninth." Master Willow concluded, "I should very much look forward to conversing again. I feel I have learned from you, and that is always a good and proper thing."

"Yes it is." Chessington agreed, "Thank you for listening and good day, Master Willow."

"Good day."

"Well," Chessington turned to Wahldor, "I can honestly say I never expected to do that when I got up this morning."

"You are fascinating Chessington the Twenty-ninth." Wahldor smiled, "You are human and not human all at the same time."

"That sounds funny," Chessington laughed, "but I know what you mean. I feel almost to being my own species anymore. I feel quite unique."

Wahldor sighed, "Yes, I would agree. I suppose we should return you to your group."

"Lead on, Wahldor," the boy replied, "I'd hate getting lost out here."

"I'm surprised it has not occurred to you yet."

"What?" Chessington appeared puzzled at what the Doltist was getting at.

Wahldor smiled, "You cannot get lost anymore. The trees will help you find your way now. They know you."

"But I've only spoken with one willow tree?"

"One, all, it does not matter." Wahldor explained, "Why do you think Doltists know about each other?"

"Ah, from the trees." Chessington remembered.

"Exactly," Wahldor grinned, "and by now every tree in the Woods of the Doltists knows about your conversation with Master Willow. Any one of them would converse with you if you asked them to."

"I have to start the conversations?" Chessington asked.

"Oh yes," Wahldor replied, "a tree would never start a conversation with us unless it was important. They do not think you being lost is important. They know how to get you to wherever you want to go. Lost is a foreign concept to the trees. They are root bound to one spot until they decompose. Lost is only a concern to beings who are mobile."

"That does make sense." Chessington was finding it easier and easier to understand how other creatures thought with the exception of the evil presence at the battle in the wooded area outside of Marroda. His mind was far beyond his comprehension. The absolute disregard for anything except itself, he simply could not grasp.

As he mounted up and started to follow Wahldor back to the guest area, he turned to look over his shoulder one last time to see the willow which was so enjoyable for him to speak with.

* * * * * * *

"A Clover Grape ya say." Gurlig was holding a purple berry about the size of a man's thumbnail between two fingers and studying it hard trying to memorize every aspect of the large berry.

"Yes," Bradel acknowledged, "it has more of the qualities of a peach, but no pit and much smaller. The seeds are on the outside the same as you think of a strawberry, but too tiny to be seen. It can be wonderful for fevers and nausea." Bradel was the head forager for the Queen's chef and knew every property of every plant inside of these woods. He was the same size as the other Doltists, but had a dead patch of moss on his right shin. It was the only way Bansinghaim and Gurlig could differentiate him from other male adult Doltists.

"Could it be used without the medicinal qualities?" Bansinghaim asked, "Just as food I mean, or is that one solely for fevers and nausea?"

Bradel thought for a second, "No reason why you could not eat them. They are very sweet tasting, but I do not think I would eat too many, maybe six or seven at most."

"Why is that?" Bansinghaim wondered.

Bradel smiled, "Because the opposite of nausea would happen, and that is not pleasant either."

Bansinghaim curled his lip, "True."

"What else ya got?" Gurlig looked around at the other plants in the meadow.

Bradel held up a plant he had uprooted, washed in the pool next to them, and handed to Gurlig, "Take a bite."

Gurlig looked at the plant closely resembling celery, but was thicker and more dense at the bottom, and bit the top of it, "Tastes like licorice!"

"It is called fennel," the Doltist explained, "good for the heart and stomach. It also can be mashed into a paste for open cuts and used to decrease the swelling."

Gurlig stripped off a stalk and handed it to Bansinghaim. "Very nice, almost a treat in its flavor." The large Knight replied.

Bradel almost whispered, "And you can convince those with bad breath to eat it, and it will help that, too. Over here is a Rams Head Pea. It is good for your heart as well. It is excellent for giving you energy and protein at the same time. You as meat eaters seem to require more protein than we do, so if you cannot find a small or large animal to kill, these are an excellent substitute and healthier for your bodies. They also are good for drying and storing. They can be eaten as you travel and make for a good soup, fresh or dried."

He handed a small handful to each of the men. "Eat."

Bansinghaim popped one into his mouth, "Rather hard for a plant. You do have to chew it."

"Oh yes," Bradel agreed, "swallowing one whole could get caught in your throat, also."

"Not bad though," Gurlig looked them over to memorize them further, "good taste, too."

"Here is the last one I will show to you." Bradel pulled a few leaves off of a ball shaped plant closely resembling lettuce, but the leaves were more vertical and less in a ball shape, "This is called cos. Eating it regularly can help with your circulation and the amount of health transported throughout your bodies through your human blood."

"A little bitter." Bansinghaim noticed, "Can you mix it with something?"

"Sure," Bradel replied, "anything sweet. The Queen's Chef usually melts a mixture of bee's honey and pine nuts with it. It is a big favorite for a treat that way."

Gurlig noticed a smile come to Bradel's face as he told of it.

"Because I have a good friend who tends to the bee hives." Bradel answered to Gurlig's thought, "He is a wonderful helper to the bees, and they like him. It would be hard not to. He has been working with bees for five hundred years. If bees like you, you must be trustworthy."

"How's that?" Gurlig asked.

Bradel chuckled, "If you want to find out if someone is completely trustworthy, put them around insects who are guarding something. If they let you around you can be trusted with anything."

As they headed back to the Queen's Court, Bradel led them across a beautiful clump of birch trees. "It seems your friends have found what they needed at the storage area."

Bansinghaim brightened, "Oh really."

"Yes," Bradel continued, "they found the coin of Iclania you were searching for."

"Things are looking good for our departure in the morning then." Bansinghaim added, looking forward to the next step of their journey and hoping to find an unsuspecting deer or boar to fill his need with.

"You really enjoy your food." Bradel interjected, "You think about it as much as the grain drink you enjoy."

"I do enjoy them both tremendously, Master Bradel." Bansinghaim confessed, "The grain drink maybe even more than the meat."

"We have a fermented grain drink as well," Bradel announced, "but it takes around six months to age properly."

"Sounds familiar." Gurlig smiled.

"I believe we're talking about the same thing here." Bansinghaim brightened.

"I have some back at the Court." Bradel mentioned, "I will give you a taste, and you can tell me if it is the same."

"I would be glad to." Bansinghaim replied.

"Me too!" Gurlig begged.

"Certainly, Good Gurlig." Bradel smiled at the eagerness of the pair. At this moment Bradel felt the overwhelming joy come to the hearts of both of the men he was with.

Chapter 3

The sun had been just peeking over the far horizon as the traveling party poked out from the stillness of the Woods of the Doltists. Emerging from the trail into the full light again after the few days spent in the care of the trees and the Doltist creatures who had opened up their entire village to the strange group of Phenderians. Each one of the members of the group was feeling at peace and refreshed for the next leg in their long and important journey.

In the lead was Sir Bansinghaim next to General Vastion, the best of the fighting men should a reason occur. Sir Malden and Gurlig followed them a few paces behind discussing the different things they had each experienced back in the woods. Sir Ghalkin drove the cart Chessington had produced to carry the supplies the group would need to aid and even sustain them over the courses of the next few months. Also, the cart was appropriate for Preda the small cousin to Chessington, who would be a hindrance on horseback, whether riding by herself or with someone, finding it easier to be more comfortable seated on the cart than bouncing on a horse. Next to her was the military leader of the Doltists, Violta, stepping outside of the forest for the first time in her life. Wide eyed and curious as she found herself trying to take in everything and feeling ashamed she was unable to see it all. Behind the cart traveled Prince Palton and along side of him Chessington, the boy Wizard, the sole reason any of the Phenderians in their group were still alive. At any of at least twenty points in the past two weeks, if the new Wizard had not succeeded, they would not be around to be where they are now.

"I don't believe I've ever seen a mountain before." The Prince turned to Chessington.

"Me either, Your Highness." Chessington confessed, "I've seen plenty of pictures though."

"Yes," Palton agreed, "I've seen those, too. They look huge and some have snow at the top."

"I think we'll find out soon." Chessington added, "Sir Malden was saying it should take about a week to get close enough to see it and another week through the mountains to get to the foot of it."

As the boys conversed about the adventures ahead, the females on the cart were discussing their own wonders. Looking from side to side, realizing she was doing what no other Doltist had done in history, Violta grinned and asked about everything.

"What is that?" The Doltist asked sitting on the front bench to the far right next to Preda with Ghalkin to the far left controlling the horses in front of them. Violta had changed herself to a female human form before they left the security of the woods. She dressed herself in a blue dress with a beige apron, long wool stockings, and tall brown canvass boots. She had no sooner produced the clothing then thought about why anyone would do this to themselves. She felt confined, restricted, uncomfortable, and even imprisoned by this absolutely normal custom of the person she was imitating. Why would humans submit themselves to this? She had no idea, but when told of undergarments, she flatly replied this was enough costume to get her appearing to be human, and no one would check to see if the costume was complete below the surface.

"What is what?" Preda replied.

"That over there." Violta pointed to a brick house centered inside of a fenced area next to a large barn.

"It's a farmhouse." The child answered.

"What does it do?" The Doltist asked.

"I don't think it does anything." Preda smiled at her naivety, "You live in it."

Violta seemed confused, "Why would you do that? It's so nice here."

"Well," Preda followed, "it gets really cold a lot, especially at night or in the winter time. Besides humans have to stay warmer than you guys I guess, and our stuff would get wet and be no good any more."

Violta figured she had much to learn about this outside world, so for now she would let it go and mentally digest what she had just heard.

Moving up to Malden and Gurlig, they were conversing on the things which had happened before they had met at Marroda. Things the other smaller party had witnessed to catch them up.

Gurlig was remembering the outskirts of Velso, a pawn in the invasion of Phenderia.

"Not a soul 'round nowheres." Gurlig told of, "An' the General says that ain't nobody livin' in there no more neither. Just a bunch a dead litterin' the streets that nobody cared ta clean up."

"Discustin'," Malden shook his head, "no respect fer nothin'. Lots a civilians dead, too?"

"Not a one!" Gurlig exclaimed, "From what the general says, it's just the solders, an' the folks was marched off ta the south."

Malden lowered his head, "Not sure 'tween the two what's worse. Dyin' er bein' a prisoner."

"Dyin'." Gurlig answered confidently, "Ain't no hope if yer dead. A prisoner can still escape er change stuff."

"Yeah," Malden nodded, "guess yer right."

Still further to the front were Sir Bansinghaim and General Vastion, leading the way down the trail to their first town, Maldow.

"In town around lunch tomorrow, eh?" Bansinghaim asked.

The General shook his head smiling, "Your clock seems to have three times to it: breakfast, lunch, and dinner. I was thinking about noon or shortly there after, but I suppose lunch would be the same, and yes that should be about the time we pull in."

The large Knight, seemingly unoffended, continued, "I'll feel better after we get off of this trail. After the past couple of weeks, I'm not ashamed to say, I'm a bit edgy."

"True," Vastion nodded, "Maldow is small and too much of a farming community, but two days ride further east, and we'll be in the city of Derenta, a major hub. I can snoop around and see if anyone knows anything we don't. It would be a great place to hire a spy also."

"Do you think that's smart?" Bansinghaim wondered, "It could alert the Chiloes we aren't really dead yet. I don't think we want that."

"The spy is loyal to the Derno in Derentia. They don't ask why you want to know if the price is right." Vastion explained. "Besides, these Chiloes are busy invading. We're old news."

"I'm not ready to take that kind of chance." Stated the Royal Protectorate, "In a fair fight, I feel pretty good about it. They don't fight the way I'd call fair."

"No, they don't." The General agreed, "We are doing the best we can and even have Chessington to keep the sides matched, but I'm with you, let's not provoke a fight just yet."

"Just yet?" Laughed the Knight, "When would you say the time to fight would be?"

"We'll try to get some advantages," Vastion spoke, "but I don't see the day coming soon. Chessington isn't strong enough to do it, and we have no army. Until we find out just what we're up against. We can't even start a counter attack, but we will have to fight them and defeat them to get Phenderia back."

"I suppose." Bansinghaim sighed, "I'm okay with a life on the run if I have to be, but the kids back there, it's a tough way to be brought up. I don't know, maybe it'll make them stronger, and a little more prepared if we do get the throne back."

Vastion looked up to a rock formation, "Don't let the others see you looking, but what do you make of that?"

Bansinghaim squinted and saw two men on horseback trying to stay behind a group of trees on a rock bluff overlooking them. "I'd guess we'll have company up around a corner within the next mile or so."

Vastion nodded, "My assessment as well. Ideas?"

"I remove their heads." Bansinghaim answered.

"And how many heads would that be?" the General inquired.

"I see your point." Bansinghaim frowned, "Get Chessington up here, and let's see what he can help with."

"He can't do anything without bigger enemies knowing it." Vastion reminded him.

"Queen Rhyshena said he could still do a few things though." Bansinghaim stated, "Let's find out what they are."

Vastion called for a rest as the nine member party was happy to oblige, except for Malden, "What ya got us stoppin' fer? Site seein'?"

"Bansinghaim and I spotted two men on horseback on top of the bluff behind us." Vastion explained, "My guess would be there are more who they'll report to ahead."

"I'm guessin' you're right." Malden agreed, "Now what?"

"Chessington," Bansinghaim asked, "what can you still do about this without being detected by the Chiloes?"

"I could leave myself and go check ahead." He smiled.

"Leave yourself?" Vastion asked.

"Creepy stuff," Malden shuddered, "he did it in the tunnel a few times. Made me jump ever' time he came back."

"I'll go on and send back to Violta what I see." He sat down and closed his eyes.

"I hate that." Malden stated, "Looks just plain wrong."

"I see what you mean. "Ghalkin added, "How long does this take?"

"He is there already." Violta reported, "There are six of them. I can hear everything Chessington is hearing and seeing it play in my mind. Two are very large men, the others are average. They have knives and swords, and a few arrows, but only four horses. The plan seems to be the four with horses will stand in the middle of the road. The two without will be behind us in the trees in the woods. The four on horseback will draw there swords, show us our escape route behind us is cut off, kill one of us at first to show they mean business, rob us, and then kill the rest of us."

"Wonder how many times it's worked?" Malden asked.

"The four to the front are no problem." Bansinghaim announced, "It's the two archers in the trees."

"I thought all six created a problem." Ghalkin added, "Malden and I are not fighting men. Violta would not be very handy in hand to hand combat, and the kids are out of the question as fighters."

"That leaves Bansinghaim, Gurlig, Chessington, and me." Vastion evaluated, "Four on six, poor odds at best."

"Because you're thinking like fighters instead of strategists." Violta piped in with her little hands on her hips, "We already know there will be two in the trees up ahead. We send Chessington to find out exactly where and surprise the surprisers, so to speak. We have a few arrows. Shoot first."

"That takes it down to four on four." Vastion looked more hopeful than he had, "Chessington and Gurlig aren't really fighting men either."

Bansinghaim shrugged indifferently, "I'll have two dead immediately, you keep one busy, and Gurlig and Chessington can double up on the other one. As soon as I get done, I'll help them."

Chessington returned and popped up, "The two in the trees are just around the second bend."

"So you heard our plan then." Vastion nodded.

"Every word," The boy Wizard replied, "just as Violta could see and hear where I was, I could do the same through her."

"Are you ready for the fight then?" Bansinghaim asked the boy.

"I suppose I'll have to be." Chessington replied.

Ghalkin spoke next, "I'll take the archers. I would wager I'm the best shot with an arrow of the lot of us."

Bansinghaim raised his eyebrows, "Are you sure? One miss and we have to start improvising."

"Can you hit two for two from fifty feet away?" Ghalkin asked.

"No, never much good with arrows." The knight replied, "Looks like you get the job."

"Ghalkin smiled, "Thank you, I think."

"There is one on either side of the road," Chessington told him, "The one on your left will be about thirty feet behind the one to the right."

"Alright, I had better get going." Ghalkin grabbed the quiver and bow out of the back of the cart and started off on the left side of the road slowly and quietly about fifty feet back into the woods.

"Go scout with him, boy." Bansinghaim turned to Chessington. Immediately Chessington dropped down and left himself.

After nearly three minutes had passed, Violta reported again for Chessington, "Sir Ghalkin is about twenty feet from the first one."

"He shouldn't miss at that range." Vastion laughed.

"He didn't." Violta winced. "He shot it right through his neck."

"Good idea." Bansinghaim grinned, "He can't make a sound to alert the other one that way."

"Your kind has a lot of fluid to them, yuck." Violta grimaced.

"Where is he now?" Vastion asked.

"He is getting closer to the other one." Violta seemed deep in thought and concentrating very hard, "He is stopped, aiming, and."

"And what?" Vastion almost screamed.

"Oh my," Violta cut off all communications, "That was truly disgusting."

"What?" Vastion exclaimed.

The Doltist, looking repulsed, told him, "He shot it through his eye, killing him instantly."

"I didn't think the old man had it in him!" Bansinghaim laughed.

"Gruesome or not," the General stated, "at least he saw the need to let the other ones think they had support from behind. We might have just been given the upper hand."

Chessington, popping back into himself, admitted, "He's very good with a bow."

Vastion hesitated a second or two and spoke, "Get back to your normal positions except for Chessington and Malden. You two switch to get him closer to the front."

Ghalkin reentered the group and sat quietly at the reigns of the cart, a little glassy eyed, holding them tightly. He started thinking about how he had not used his talent as an archer since he had been in his early teens. It amazed him how well he took it back up. The feel of the bow, fingering the fletching, the release of the shaft, all of these memories flooded back to the forefront from the recesses of his mind. The accident had changed his life, but he was able now to feel he could finally go back to a sport which was his greatest passion as a youth.

The group turned the corner to see four men on horseback facing them, blocking their path across the road. The Phenderian party stopped twenty feet before them, riding high on their mounts with Gurlig and Chessington to the right of the General and Bansinghaim.

The leader of the highwaymen was placed in the middle to the right and spoke in a low raspy tone, "Empty your pockets, saddlebags, and give us the cart."

General Vastion smirked, brimming with confidence, "And why, pray tell, would we do that?"

"Because," the leader laughed, "you want to. Oh now, we could kill all of ya for it, even the children and the lady there, but you seem smart enough to figure poor and alive beats poor and dead."

"So let me see if I have this straight." Vastion surmised, "Without the lady and the two children, we have six, and I see only four of you."

The leader grinned and dropped his arm to signal his archers. His grin faded as no arrows appeared. He dropped his arm again and felt a sinking feeling at the pit of his stomach.

That was when the two arrows simultaneously appeared piercing the highwaymen mounted on the far left and far right. The one to the left was pierced through the heart, and to the right through the stomach. The heart wound was fatal upon impact with the other man sent writhing to the ground.

As if on cue Bansinghaim unsheathed his broadsword and rode swiftly the short distance to the two left mounted slicing the first across the belly and wasting no time imbedding his weapon through the leader, slicing upward and pulling his sword back out as his victim was falling off of it.

"What happened to the plan?" Vastion asked in amazement, "We had this all worked out."

47

Ghalkin was now the center of attention, "I had no idea until the time arose if I could still do it. I apologize for my renegade actions, but I knew if I did not perform this way, one of us could have been hurt or killed. I am sorry I could not inform you earlier, but I simple did not know if I could."

"And if you had missed?" Vastion was more annoyed than angered, "We could have had a very large problem then."

"Hey," Malden turned to the General, "he didn't. In fact he saved our backsides. Looked damn remarkable ta me. Did any a us get a scratch? Did the kids get harmed? The old plan got us a heck of a lot closer ta actual fightin' than this did."

Violta had come down off of her seat on the cart to attend to the highwayman with Ghalkin's arrow protruding from his stomach. "He does not have much more time of consciousness left."

Vastion dismounted and walked to the dying man. "Who are you?" He asked him.

Panting and vacant eyed he spoke softly, "I should ask the same thing." He hesitated a second or two and finished, "We've been on this road for years. You all looked rich and helpless enough for six men to handle, especially with two hid like they were. Are they dead, too?"

"Yes," Vastion answered, almost feeling sorry for the man, "they were dead before we appeared."

"Just as well," He spoke, "they were good shots with a bow, but none a us would a made it a day without Sanfor. He's the brains. Was the brains."

"Are there more of you?" The General asked.

"Naw," was his final reply. He had gone from the restrictions of the body.

"Where's Gurlig?" Malden asked.

"There." Chessington answered, pointing to the side of the road about fifteen feet into the brush. Gurlig was digging.

"Bless his soul." Ghalkin stated, "We should help." With that the men, including the Prince, each took a shovel or bucket or pick, and helped dig the graves for the six slain robbers.

After an hour and a half of digging, wrapping each man in a blanket found on their horses, and properly burring them. They remounted, hitched up the mounts from the robbers, and headed further down the trail before stopping for lunch.

Chapter 4

The group felt refreshed as most had arisen the morning on the day they would ride into Maldow. Vastion and Ghalkin had built a fire for Gurlig to cook over while Bansinghaim hunted at the break of dawn. The Royal Knight Protectorate was dreaming of a large buck or a wild boar, but had to be content with six wild partridge and three nests totaling thirteen individual eggs. He also noticed the wild fennel Bradel had shown them remembering the qualities of it for heart, stomach, and even a person's breath. He cut seven plants eating half of one as he returned and saving another also remembering its value as a paste for swelling.

Gurlig cooked as the four Councilmen, Chessington, and Violta sat relaxing, taking this rare occasion to talk while the children still slept.

"Okay," Malden gazed, looking at Ghalkin, "we gave ya yesterday ta yerself. Taday ya got some answerin' ta do."

"I know," Ghalkin responded, "and thank you all for such respect. You are right, my friend." He sighed deeply, "Well, as a small boy, I started practicing with the bow at around age seven. I would practice for hours in the woods behind my parent's country home. I was dreadful. I could not even hit a tree at four paces. This went on for the better part of a summer."

"You seemed to have figured it out." Bansinghaim laughed.

"I did, yes." Ghalkin continued, "But it was my fortune and bad luck to have found a woodsman who took a liking to me. He showed me how to hold, aim, steady, and release correctly. He had been a Royal Archer in the Army and actually served at the same time as Prince Palton grandfather, the late King Rundol. He taught me about trajectory and proper care for my weapon. At the age of seven you start feeling a bit smug of yourself when you have your first adult friend and can do something which is not considered as playing. We had progressed to the point where he could throw up an apple and I could hit it at its apex. That was after four years."

"An' ya kept it a secret all this time?" Malden wondered, "Why?"

Ghalkin's face turned somber, "About three years after that, my friend the Woodsman and I were out in the woods when two undesirable men came to us with knives. I could have outrun them, but my friend was caught by surprise and held at knife point. I had my arrow notched and ready to fly, but the second was rushing me from the side. I turned and skewered him between his eyes at a distance of only three feet. I went to grab another for the man holding my dear friend, but I was too late. He had been slit across the throat, blood everywhere."

"Horrible." Chessington said.

"Yes," Ghalkin agreed, "but by this point it was him or me. I let it fly, and he received it at the heart, falling forwards immediately. I was the sole survivor of the incident. Completely dumbfounded, I returned home telling of what had happened. My father beat me severely for the talk the country folks would have about our family. We were too important to have scandal attached to us, and I had done the exact thing I had been advised not to do since I was born. I really think he would have rather I had been killed than to have me associated with a murder or killing."

The silence surrounding the campfire was deafening. "It was many years ago," Ghalkin added in, "and believe me, I am very glad it came back to me in a crisis."

"We are as well, old sport." Vastion slapped his fellow Councilman on the shoulder, standing to refill his morning tea, "No telling how it could have turned out otherwise. Are you one hundred percent recovered from your childhood trauma, or do you even know for sure yourself?"

"Oh, I believe I am fine." Ghalkin stated nodding his head with reassurance, "I am a grown man now, and I can differentiate between right and wrong. I know my father was wrong. He was a product of his upbringing, and I feel immune to it."

"Good," Vastion reiterated, "you are quite a valuable asset to have around with those kinds of skill. We can't have too many assets."

Gurlig turned to Chessington, "Ya wanna git the kids. Breakfast is ready."

"What do we have on the menu, Gurlig?" Vastion asked.

Gurlig, pointing to the fire, speaking in a rather pleased voice, "We got roast partridge, hot wheat porridge, scrambled partridge eggs with cheese melted in, an' fennel in a milk gravy."

"Sounds wonderful." Vastion complimented.

"Hold yer thanks ta Sir Bansinghaim over there." Gurlig nodded towards the knight diving into the roasted birds taking a whole one and some eggs, "He's the one thet got up early ta catch the birds, foller 'em back ta their nests fer the eggs, an' picked the fennel."

"So these poor creatures were alive not two hours ago." Violta stared towards Bansinghaim, "Until you killed them, correct?"

Bansinghaim, with a partridge leg in his mouth, replied, "Yes, pretty much. Figured with the adults gone the eggs wouldn't hatch anyways, so I traced back to where I had seen them come out of the brush towards my trap."

"Barbaric!" Violta exclaimed in a huff, eating her cereal and fennel, "No wonder your kind has no respect for each other!"

"We are carnivores, not herbivores." Bansinghaim justified, "We eat meat. Meat comes from animals. You're part plant, and you eat plants, right?"

"Completely different!" Violta rebuffed, "We do not take the life of something for our own regeneration."

"Lil' lady," Gurlig jumped in softly, "we are what we are. Some stuff you folks does seems pertty unreasonable ta us too."

"For instance?" The Doltist wondered.

"Yer superior attitude." Malden answered.

"Messin' with folks minds." Gurlig added.

"Don't forget the meat policy." Bansinghaim chuckled.

Violta stood, "We do not *mess* with human's minds, we defend ourselves. Meat is part of something that used to be alive! And we do not feel superior!"

"Then why do you take such delight in correcting *my* flaws when you have forgotten about your own." Bansinghaim asked.

"What flaws do I have?" Violta almost screamed.

"Malden laughed, "Ya don't see any flaws in yerself, but ya don't feel superior ta us. Is that what I just heard?"

Violta sat back down and ate her breakfast, fuming about how she had reacted poor manner. She was used to knowing the thoughts of the members of this group before she had to speak. Out here in the world of humans, she could not use her ability. She had to use her own wits and argue as the others did without the advanced warning of how a person was thinking. It seemed a blessing in disguise to have had this revelation with her friends rather than with a group of strangers.

Chessington sat next to Violta after helping the kids get their plates ready, Preda sitting next to him. He stayed quiet and gave silent support to her knowing she would not see their side of this, and they would never see hers.

He thought of how she appeared in human form, not the dress or clothing, but her face and hair, fair skin, soft complexion, green eyes, curly red hair, long thick eyelashes. He looked deeply into her eyes and saw the hurt she was feeling. He had never seen someone so captivating and found himself thinking of her every chance he could. Her petite features, small rounded nose, puffy curved cheeks, soft smooth chin. His favorite feature though had to be the slightly upturned upper lip. It seemed to be the defining point to her beauty. She was so small, her hands were almost like a child's, but you could see they were older.

He thought about her for only a moment when he heard her voice in his mind. *I am happy this form pleases you.*

Chessington snapped back to reality, cheeks flushing, *I apologize most sincerely!* He turned to look away, *I should have had better manners than that. Please forgive me. Will you?*

Violta giggled internally, *Of course, but you need to remember, we are connected mentally, and I have had much more practice shielding my thoughts than you have.*

Oh that's just not fair! Chessington thought back, *I'm an open book, and you get to be selective?*

Exactly. She was normally so matter of fact, but now she was flirting just as a human girl would. She felt every attraction he did, but she knew how this worked. He would be her significant other, she had already come to this conclusion. She just had to make it his idea now. After three hundred years of seeing others do this, she felt assured she could handle him as she chose.

She continued, *Since you have already let the girl know you're interested, what is your next move?*

Poor Chessington was out matched, and he knew it. Honesty would be the safest thing at this point. *I have no idea. I didn't intend for the girl to find out just yet.*

Alright, Violta conceded, *take your time. We have a long, long time to spend together, and I respect you chose honesty over deception.*

Will you do the same? Chessington asked.

This shocked Violta a bit, *You have a sting to you, Chessington the Twenty-ninth. This may be more challenging than I had expected.* She needed to be more on her toes than she had originally thought. He was more than a smitten young man. Showing he could keep his composure under fire, made her respect, and desire, him all the more.

Immediately fixing his guard internally, he knew she would still be listening, and he had to have some secrecy. He looked into her mind and figured out the safeguards she had placed to keep certain things from the front of her thinking. He righted himself both mentally and externally to keep her out.

Hey! she sent to his mind, *you tricked me!*

No, Chessington answered, *I was merely following Queen Rhyshena's orders.*

She actually placed her hands on her hips to show disgust, *How could that be obeying the Queen's orders.*

She told me to learn from you, the young Wizard reminded, *and now you have taught me a valuable lesson about the mind. Thank you very much.*

She could not help but smile as his eyes connected with hers, and they shared a moment. She felt content to sit next to him for as long as she could. She also could not hide the smile and euphoria she felt from their internal conversation.

Chessington, on the other hand, was now swimming in his thoughts. Was he the hunter or the hunted? Was she actually receptive to his liking her? He had never had a girlfriend before. He was always too busy. Anitona at the age of eleven did not really count. She had convinced him to go to sleep together in the barn at her family's farm after they had shown each other what made a girl a girl and a boy a boy. This was with feelings, and real attractions, not kids innocently playing a game. He felt like things would never be the same, and he thought it might be a good thing for him. He just was not sure yet.

* * * * * * *

Master Pazlin sat at his usual overstuffed wing-backed chair in the spacious study he had called his home for over three thousand years, sitting with his hands crossed at his chin, deep in thought. His ancient face twisted into lines as he thought of the plan to take control of Chiloe and inevitably the world. He sat thinking about how the plan would come about, needing to be in charge just before the complete occupation of the Isle of Mosa. With Phenderia conquered, Derentia about to be, and Iclania a technicality, it was a matter of weeks before these things were set in place. His adherents were in the proper spots to be able to control the generals left after the overthrow. He was not worried about what would happen if he failed. He could not fail. Maldifren was overmatched. There was no possible scenario Pazlin could think of where he could lose. These plans could have been carried out at any time within the past three thousand years, but he had no need for them to be until now. Maldifren and his ancestry were important pawns in this plan. If he had chosen to be the Emperor at the beginning, he would not have had the freedom to come and go as he pleased. He would be responsible for mundane government practices he frankly did not have the time or the desire for. He would teach them enough to make them believe they had absolute power, but he had never taught any of them one tenth of what he really knew.

He thought back to his younger days when he had first planned his take over. He planned to make Chiloe, then Jostenda, the most powerful of the nations east of the Great Beyond. Remembering before the group of mountains existed how, and more importantly why, they had come about. How Rustaph, his mentor, had used the energy to seal off the East before the armies of the West invaded. How the West had suffered great casualties then, the mountains closing in around them and swallowing them deep inside, destroying the Wizard of the West at the mountains still on the Island of Mosa, and the erasing of the East from the minds and pages of the Western civilization. He also remembered how doing this had killed his Master. He relived his feelings of withdrawal and remorse after the Great War no one knew of any longer. No one was told of Rustaph, the creating of the Great Beyond, or the evil the West was forcing on the East. The West was unified. All the tribes and civilizations consisting in them were attacking in unison, but the East could not find a leader. Each nation unwilling to be led by another. How it had almost cost them, and how it made them feel they had made the right decision after the creation of the

Great Beyond. Rustaph had done a great service and disservice to them because of this.

Pazlin had corrected it. Taking the leader of Jostenda, a good but not great general named Chiloe. He made people follow him until he was too strong for any of the other nations to oppose. Chiloe, at Pazlin's advice, conquered the smaller tribes close to them at first, and then it started on the larger kingdoms afterwards. Many had died. Many more were put to death if loyalty was not given to the new fledgling Empire of Chiloe. There numbers decreased drastically. What was once a great area, twice the size of the West with half of the inhabitants, was now diminished even further down to a small sliver of what it had been in population.

With the lands of the East now firmly under one solid ruler, Pazlin could rebuild what he had just torn down. The first order of business was to restock the supply of healthy civilians. Poor underfed people did not give the greatest chance of building a strong attacking force. Men were divided into two general fields to be placed by the government into their lifelong professions. Farming, creating more food for the population to become stronger, or military, the smarter of the men would be directed this way to organize and strategize just how things would be handled.

Women also had two directions in which to thrive. The first was in the youth houses where all children were taken ten days after birth, the second was the procreation houses where they would be given the best of the foods and the finest atmosphere. Their jobs were exactly as they sounded, to reproduce more Chiloes to the race which would one day overtake the West. The only exception to this was the Imperial Family founded by Chiloe himself. The direct descendants of the line were allowed to take wives from the children so long as the girl chosen was about to come of age to conceive. The female offspring of them were sent to the procreation houses to be given to only chosen men of upstanding quality to the Empire.

This system had made them strong for three thousand years, and now, finally, Pazlin felt they had the shear numbers on their side. His great plan was entering its final stage, and he would not let an idiot like Maldifren take the glory. Pazlin would finally vindicate his fallen mentor seeing to it that all, East or West, would know the story. Only a great leader such as Rustaph could have trained one as great as Pazlin. He himself would send the crushing blow to bend the West into submission. This victory was hard fought, long, and thankless to this point, but it would all be worth it soon enough. His vengeance would be final.

A slender robed figure walked through the door, closing it before walking over behind Pazlin, shaking him from his memories. "Yes, My Master."

"Welcome Grastock." The teacher greeted, "I think it is time for us to have a discussion about the upcoming events. Your role will be to lead the Adherents while I take care of the matters here at the Palace."

Grastock nodded, "As you wish, My Master."

"I need you to keep the other six in place." Pazlin ordered, "Bring Phosting back from Mosa as soon as you have been told Maldifren is dead. The Generals could try a feeble attempt to regain the throne. I am going to make sure they are all dead and display the bodies outside the Palace gates, next to them the dead bodies of the entire Royal Family, or better yet we will get the fool Maldifren to execute his own family. I need you and only you to track the bloodline to the third cousins. He will have every one eliminated on that list as well. I do not want anyone in the future claiming they have a right to this Empire."

"As you wish, My Master." Grastock replied.

"I have waited over three thousand years for this." Pazlin added, "I do not need a loophole after it is over to give me grief."

"I understand, My Master." Grastock agreed.

"Complete this for me and you may eliminate the rest of the Adherents after things calm down." The ancient one grinned.

Grastock found emotion in his voice for the first time in years, "Thank you, My Master."

He turned and exited his mentor's chambers, feeling power course through him. Power Pazlin was feeding to him.

Chapter 5

The traveling party entered Maldow slightly before noon noticing the stares coming from the onlookers as they traveled deeper into the small town. The stares became more apparent while the whispers started to increase. They watched all of the town's folks talking amongst themselves and not hiding the fact they were.

The General pulled over to a hitching area, which appeared to be uninhabited, dismounted, and called his entire group in tight to speak, "We seemed to have started something. I believe we should be cautious until we find out what's created this buzz."

Violta looked at him quite puzzled, "They're saying things about why did a group like us, wealthy and with more old men, a woman, and children than fighting men get through on the road. Are you deaf?"

Everyone turned to her and looked towards her, wondering at how she knew this. Chessington regained himself first to ask her, "How did you know this? Queen Rhyshena said the trees outside the Woods of the Doltists wouldn't help you read minds."

"Are you serious?" It was her turn to look at them and wonder what was going on, "They are being rather loud and rude about their conversations, do you not think?"

"I barely heard the whispers," Ghalkin explained to her, still wondering, "let alone actual words. Did you hear them word for word?"

"Of course," she stated somewhat confused, "they certainly were not trying to keep it to themselves very well."

"Well, I'll be!" Malden chuckled, "I think we can add incredible hearin' ta what's differnt 'bout Doltists than humans."

"I should say so." Vastion agreed, "What did they say, Violta?"

"Well, most were just wondering how we made it through," she informed them, "but others were asking about who we are, why would we be here, and how no one had ever seen us before. Also some very rude comments from a few men about me personally, but that is not really relevant to the group; although, they were quite pleased about how disgusting they could be."

"Men do that." Malden stared at Bansinghaim and Vastion, "I take it they understand 'bout the guys back on the highway who tried ta rob us. Guess it'd be crazy ta think we was the first ones they'd stopped."

"Yes," Vastion nodded, "maybe we should split up and talk to the towns folk all under the guise of business, of course."

"Malden and I can go to refill the water at the town well." Ghalkin started, "Women usually gather there throughout the day and have a tendency to enjoy conversation."

Vastion turned to Violta, pointing to the children as he talked, "I believe you should appear to be a nanny for the children. You look far too young to be their mother and have no resemblance to being a sister or any other family member. Also, you know mostly nothing of the world outside of the Woods, and that could get us into trouble. Besides, with your hearing you can spy on the folks walking around and eavesdrop in on their conversations."

"I understand." Violta was not at all surprised. It would be what she would have done in the same position as the General. "We can pull out a book, and I can pretend to read to them. I remember seeing a mother and child doing that before in the Woods."

"Wonderful," Vastion agreed, "Chessington and I can purchase a few of the supplies we've used so far."

Bansinghaim spoke next, "Gurlig and I will find a nice Inn with a restaurant close by. I believe under the circumstances we should appear to be high brow. What do you think?"

"I would agree." Vastion concurred, "Let's all meet back here with Violta and the kids as soon as we can." They dispersed going their separate ways once the plan had been made.

Ghalkin and Malden drove the cart to the center of town pulling up next to the well. They started pulling an old wooden bucket up to fill the barrel on the back of the cart. Feeling this would take a while since the bucket was leaking about one quarter of its contents out for every three quarters put into the barrel. "Here comes a lady." Malden whispered to his friend, "I'll take this one."

"Are you sure you want to?" Ghalkin asked.

"Yeah," Malden replied, "I'm less of a threat than you."

"And how would you suppose that?" The Royal Tutor seemed shocked at the statement.

"Cuz I'm ugly." Malden grinned, then immediately turned to the round woman coming to the well with what appeared to be her two small children "Nice day ain't it, good lady."

The woman placed herself between the men and her children, looking them over with a very reserved look to her face. "Yes, it is."

He could tell by her cautious look she was leery of the strangers who had just rode into town, more than likely for good reason, but he was going to give it a try nonetheless. "We came from Lostanda four days ago. Nice in the mountains this time a year, don't ya think?"

"I've never traveled through the mountains." The young mother opened up slightly, "Just here and Derenta, but here mostly."

"Nice town, nice little town." Malden stated looking up and down the main road and nodding his head, "It's a clean little town. Ya folks do a nice job keepin' it tidy."

"We try." The woman smiled, "You say you're from Lostanda?"

"Oh, no no no." The Librarian lied, "We're hired out a Marroda ta take the kids ta a relative in Bollantoda. After that we're ta wait 'round an' return back."

"How did you get through the road back there?" The woman asked, completely bewildered by the group being there, "We haven't had normal travelers from the west in two years. The outlaws always get them."

"Oh, those guys?" Malden turned to look back down the road as if he could see them, "They wasn't so much. Ya might want ta get the word out folks can travel that way 'gain though."

"I suppose your band of old men, a woman, and children took care of them." She asked skeptically.

"Yep." Came his reply, "I can tell ya where we buried 'em."

"Really?" She looked him over as well as Ghalkin who could only look like a proper gentleman and would never pass as a fighting man.

"Not the two a us, ma lady." Malden explained, "The other four we're traveling with. They're the brawlers, good ones, too."

She smiled a disbelieving smile to ask, "Four of you defeated a band of highwaymen who had the advantage on you?"

"Who sez they had the advantage?" Malden inquired.

"Well certainly just four men couldn't count on defeating six highwaymen with years of experience." She explained, "How did they do it then?"

"I have no idea how it happened." Malden lied, "The four a 'em rode ahead an' always came back ta get us if it was safe. One time they just didn't show up fer a while an' we figured they was doin' some business. Sure 'nough, they found six a 'em an' killed all six. My friend an' I helped burry 'em."

She ran off in the direction of the village mercantile leaving Ghalkin and Malden by the well. Entering the mercantile she interrupted the store owner, who was talking to Vastion and Chessington at the time as if nothing could have been more important than her news.

"Jophes, these two men outside just told me Sanfor and his men tried to rob them, but these guys here killed them all!" The young mother from the well exclaimed.

Jophes stared at Chessington and Vastion making things very awkward between them all. "This true?"

Vastion felt a bit concerned and was wishing Malden were there to have his neck wrung, "We were attacked. We truly had no choice."

"They all really dead?" Jophes asked, not believing his ears.

"Umm well, yes they are." Vastion admitted.

"Flonia, go get Mayor Dobbins!" The shop keeper was jumping around with no general direction to him, excited beyond belief. "Those men have been keeping people out of Maldow for years. People have been hard pressed to get by around here without anyone passing through."

"Why didn't you get some men together and defeat them?" Chessington asked.

"Look around," Jophes held his arms out, "most in this town are old men and women. The King took all the young ones for military service. In Derentia for the past five years, if you're between seventeen and thirty, you have to be in the military. Some joker tried to kill the King, so now all the young men have to protect him. It makes the rest of us an easy target."

"Did you let your King know about the trouble on the road?" Vastion asked.

"Of course, we did." He answered, "But he only seems to care about matters that will keep him alive and doesn't want to weaken his forces to save common folk."

"That sounds backwards." Vastion added.

Flonia came in to the shop with a man appearing to be of around forty-five to fifty years of age, which both Chessington and General Vastion assumed to be Mayor Dobbins.

"Are these two of the men who claim to have stopped Sanfor and his band?" The Mayor asked.

"We are." Vastion started walking over to the Mayor.

"You have proof?" Mayor Dobbins puffed out his chest.

"Well," Vastion stated, "we came down the road we hear tell of that no one gets through without either being killed or robbed."

"I'm afraid I'll need a little more than that as proof." The Mayor added, "Others have claimed to have done away with them, but they hadn't."

"I would love to take you back to their grave sites, but we'll be leaving in the morning for the city of Derenta." The General stated as a matter of fact.

"Not until we get proof." The Mayor added.

"This really isn't up for discussion, my good Mayor." Vastion was getting irritated at this point, "We have a schedule to keep, and it doesn't include sticking around here. I can draw you a map of where we buried them, but I really must insist we leave in the morning."

"I thought you might feel that way." The Mayor nodded, "Seems doubtful what you say is true since you're in such a hurry to leave after seeming like you've saved us." He went to the window to see Malden, Ghalkin, Prince Palton, Preda, and Violta surrounded by men with axes and pitchforks. "We would like to see you stay until we can verify what you claim. If what you say is true, we'll let you on your way. Otherwise you'll all hang. The last group to claim they did this was hung after three townsfolk were killed going down that road they were told was safe!"

"I guess you have us then." Vastion conceded, "You have my word. We will not leave town."

"I know you won't," The Mayor replied, "because you two and the other two we don't have yet will take us to the place you buried them. We'll dig them back up and return them to town for all to see it's really over, but if it's an empty grave, or you don't seem to remember where it was, we'll hang the four of you on the spot and return to do the same to the other three adults."

Vastion was beyond speaking to the Mayor. His face was contorted into the look of rage he was trying with all of his might to constrain.

Chessington filled the void of silence between the two men, "We should get going then, so we aren't too far behind schedule. Don't you think, Sir?"

"Very well," Vastion was allowed to get out of this current situation, "let's go then."

Bansinghaim and Gurlig were found returning to the group and filled in by Chessington as to what was going on. Vastion was still quiet, completely fuming at the occurrences of the day.

"We ain't heard Malden's side a this." Gurlig reminded him, "Could a been somethin' blown outta per portion er somethin'. How would he a known the town would do this?"

"I'm sure that's all it is," the young Wizard was trying to smooth this over, "and I can't blame them for wanting us to stick around. They seem like they want to believe us, but past events dictate this. Wouldn't you do the same thing, General?"

"Oh, don't think for one minute I'm getting sucked into that line of thinking!" Vastion whispered a little louder than he probably should have, "When I think of what we still need to do before winter here in this part of the world, it makes me dread this damned quest we've been given all the more." Calming slightly he turned to Chessington, "Can you go see how the others are fairing. It might be handy to know how they're being treated, and where they are when we get back."

"Right," Chessington agreed, "I'll check with Violta."

He immediately slumped over and the three members of the group he was with knew he was not there any more. The two town's men riding behind looked at him rather strangely as he fell forwards slightly and closed his eyes.

"It's a condition he has." Bansinghaim lied, "He'll be fine."

The two men from Maldow looked more puzzled at Bansinghaim's reply than the actual passing out of the boy in the saddle ahead of them. They kept an eye on the captured men all the more after this.

Chessington returned after only a minute or two to report, "They're treating them well. They're being fed at the Inn on the eastern edge of town where they'll be guarded the whole time, but they are not abused. I explained to Violta to tell Sir Malden and Sir Ghalkin we should be back as soon as possible."

The General nodded, but refrained from speaking, still annoyed at the circumstances.

After eight hours of riding, they stopped at the spot Vastion directed them to and proceeded off the trail to find the grave of the six men they had dug not even a full day before. The dirt was still soft and the digging was fast as there where many men anxiously awaiting the results of what would be at the bottom of the hole.

"Got one," the first man digging screamed, "he's wrapped up in a blanket."

"Pull him out!" Mayor Dobbins ordered, "Let's see who he is."

They pulled him out and found another blanket under it, then another, and another, until six wrapped carcasses were laid out in the back of three wagons, which had been brought along to carry either the dead bodies of the highwaymen or the four who were taking them there.

"Open them up." The Mayor ordered to the men standing close by.

They rolled the blankets open to see the six dead highwaymen just as Gurlig had prepared them, two with fatal sword wounds and four with the holes in them left by Ghalkin's arrows. The faces of the crowd turn joyful as they realized they could finally believe their town's nightmare was over. Cheering commenced and congratulations were given to the four men present who took responsibility for the slaying of the bandits. The Mayor walked straight to General Vastion and extended his hand.

"Anything you and your party would like is yours once we return to town." Mayor Dobbins gave to him as a reward for their heroics, "I'm sure you understand why we had to be this way."

"I do," Vastion agreed, "and I'm glad your town is safe once again, but we must return to retrieve our friends and leave tomorrow morning."

"Nonsense!" Mayor Dobbins stated, "You and your friends will be the guests of the town for at least a week's worth of celebrations. You have no idea what you've done."

"I can see you're a man who doesn't take no for an answer," The General had to get them out of Maldow in the morning. A week would be impossible, "but I have an order, and we are being paid by those children's parents. They have to be delivered on time."

"We must celebrate!" The Mayor insisted.

"I know," Chessington piped in, "we could deliver the children to Bollantoda, and then return to Maldow. We get the children there on time, and we get our heroes welcome as well."

"That suits me fine!" The Mayor agreed, "Should we set camp and return in the morning?"

Chessington froze in his tracks. There in front of him another fifty feet into the trees peering at the group, were two gray-faced soldiers, which he had remembered all too well. A new sense of urgency hit him, as he elbowed the General and nodded to the trees. Seeing General Vastion's face light up, Chessington knew he had seen the same thing he had.

"Why wait until morning, Mayor?" Vastion smiled, "The sooner we get back to town the sooner the folks there will be relieved these scoundrels are dead and they can prosper again. Also, we can get on our way and return for the celebration much more rapidly, and we'll stay on our schedule."

"True, true." The Mayor granted, seeing also the sooner they returned the sooner he could look like a great leader to his town, "You're right, Sir. Let's return tonight! I doubt any of us would sleep much after all the excitement anyhow."

"Good," Vastion smiled, "Let's mount up."

As they were all walking back to their respective mounts, Bansinghaim walked close to Vastion to ask, "Why are we pushing? We've been awake for over twenty-hours now, and we have eight more to ride."

"We'll have more than that I'm afraid," General Vastion told him, "There are at least two Chiloes in the woods behind us, and I'm assuming even more behind them. I guess the occupation of Derentia has started as well. I'd give us a week, maybe ten days, to get to Mt. Bollantoda before the entire country is completely taken. Then we'll have to figure out how to get to Iclania."

Bansinghaim exhaled hard, seeing the situation now for what it was. These people would be free from one oppression just in time for another. He knew they had no way to help them, but they absolutely had to help themselves.

Vastion leaned towards Chessington and spoke. "Get in touch with Violta and let her know as soon as we get back and they're freed, we will be leaving as soon as possible."

Chessington understood, "Yes Sir."

Chapter 6

Chessington spent most of his time out of body scouting the perimeter in a radius of between one and two miles of the traveling party in an attempt to find any sign of Chiloes. Ever since they had left Maldow that morning, they felt the pressing need to get to Mt. Bollantoda as quickly as they could. Traveling in a different formation than before with Gurlig now at the rear with Bansinghaim, Prince Palton in the middle ahead of the cart with the hunched over form of Chessington next to him, and Malden in the front along side General Vastion, they could get a good night's sleep in Derenta if Chessington's scouting report went favorably and with a little speed to them and stopping as little as possible. There was a definite advantage for him as well as Violta to have no need for sleep. Allowing the energy to freely pass though them, they constantly felt refreshed. The others needed rest and were not fairing as well.

"I understand you thought nothing was wrong with telling her back there," Vastion told Malden, "but it really slowed us down. Now almost half of us have missed a night's sleep."

The conversation at the front of the precession was going quite well with Vastion and Malden discussing what had happened back in Maldow to create the fuss, which had occurred the previous night.

"An' I'd a known that how?" Malden replied, "She asked how we got through on the road. I had ta tell a few lies, which I think they'll see through if they think 'bout it, but I couldn't just say, 'we didn't see nobody'. That'd been worse."

"We'll never know I guess." Vastion was ready to let it go.

Malden thought a moment to remind him, "Besides, if ya hadn't gone back ta the graves with 'em, we'd still have no clue 'bout how close those grey guys are."

"You are right there." Vastion conceded, "We assumed too much I suppose. I do feel better with Chessington scouting for us all the time."

"Damn right ya do!" The Librarian spoke out, "An' it's cuz a me we got the chance ta find out!"

Vastion rolled his eyes, "Don't push it, Malden."

Just behind them Prince Palton was lagging just enough to be able to chat with the three riding in the cart. "We seem to be going much faster today." The Prince stated.

"Yes we do, Your Highness." Ghalkin confirmed, "We have a need to get out of this area with greater speed than before. The last thing we want is to be surrounded by Chiloes with no way out."

"Oh, I like it, Sir." The Prince answered, "I'd like to get there as fast as we can."

"Not me," Preda exclaimed, "it's way too bumpy on these roads."

"Well, we all have to put up with it." Violta reminded her, "Sir Ghalkin is right. It would be far worse to get caught than to have a little discomfort. Besides, it is all the faster we will get to an Inn and a good rest for you humans."

"I like that." Preda agreed, "I'm tired of moving all the time. I wish we could stay put in one spot for a long, long time."

Ghalkin smiled, "I do not see that happening for a goodly amount of time. We will need to get Phenderia back before we can truly rest."

"I like it out here." Palton admitted, "No offense, Sir, but this is way more exciting then Math and Spelling."

Violta agreed, "I am enjoying the travels as well, Your Highness. I have never really imagined how things are out here. We see your lands through people's minds back in the Woods, but we never get to experience it first hand. I believe I would be the first to ever venture this far outside of the Woods in the history of the Doltist civilization."

"You've never come out?" Preda asked.

"Nope," Violta answered, "we have never needed to. Everything we have ever needed was inside the protection of the trees. We really are not a forceful or physically strong race, but we have learned to take our advantages and make them work for us."

"I should think," Ghalkin stated, "if we find our place back to a seat of power once again, we should keep your peoples profile still under wraps. Many would see the advantages of working with your Queen while others would try to take and plunder your way of life to their own personal gain. I know you can defend yourselves, but the less known about the Doltists the better for both of our races."

"I do not believe we really have anything to offer your race, we just want to live peacefully. You seem to respect that." The Doltist added.

"We do," Ghalkin explained further, "but not all humans think as we in this group. They would find a way to turn it into a windfall for their personal betterment at your expense. Remember the highwaymen we had to dispose of back before Maldow? They were ready to murder their own race for profit. What do you suppose they would do to a race who was not even their own?"

Violta thought a moment, "I see your point. Are there really many of that kind in your race?"

Ghalkin chuckled to himself, "Considerably more than we care to admit, some even within the government. Even though we are supposed to be in a position of leading the people to a better time, some officials prefer to better themselves and their own personal positions rather than the rest."

"Do they not understand a strong group makes for a strong individual?" Violta asked.

"No," Ghalkin stated flatly, "they do not."

"I cannot understand your kind." The Doltist just shook her head.

Ghalkin laughed, "I cannot either, Violta. You heard how the King of Derintia was towards the town's people back in Maldow. He did not seem to care in the least about his subjects, only his own personal well being."

"Why do the people of Derentia not change their government then?" She asked.

"You are speaking of open revolt," Ghalkin stated, "many would die, especially since the King has control of the military. Usually, as I have noticed, in history it takes around three to seven years before someone assassinates the Kings who are not doing very well."

Violta looked puzzled, "Then why would a King not try his best to keep the people happy?"

Ghalkin paused a moment to think of how best to explain it, "Because, my dear, Kings have been taught ever since they were little Princes that what they say goes and no one is to dispute it. They think even though it has happened before, there would be no possible circumstance anyone would want to do the same to them. Mostly because of the advisers who tell them how the people really feel about them already understand a Prince or King is much easier to work with if they believe they are beloved by their people."

Prince Palton looked shocked, "You wouldn't do that to me would you, Sir?"

"Absolutely not, your Highness." Ghalkin seemed offended the thought would even be spoken pertaining to himself, "I genuinely respect and care for you far too much to set you up to fail. I believe if you look at my past, I have not had a problem disciplining you or treating you as someone who needs to know right from wrong."

"That's true," the young Prince agreed, "I remember being sent to my room to clean it, and how mad you were when I wasn't doing just that after about an hour."

"I would not say I was mad," the boy's tutor explained, "I was concerned about your time commitments."

Palton leaned closer to Preda, "He was mad."

"I know all about that." Preda nodded, "I've been scolded by both my Mom and my Dad. Dad may be louder when he's angry, but Mom's the one I wanted to stay on the good side of."

"I feel secure in knowing you are turning out to be a responsible young man, Your Highness." Ghalkin started to defend his actions, "You will make a fine King one day, and I am pleased to have had a hand in it."

Violta added following this, "I hope we get the chance to find out what kind of King he will make. It seems you are on the outs at the moment."

"I wish I knew how this was going to turn out." Ghalkin admitted, "I feel as if we are doing this all one day at a time."

Just behind the cart rode the knight and the former drunk. The two men were finding an unusual friendship growing between them as their similarities seemed to give them common ground for conversation.

I find the darker ales make me more tired than the lighter ones," Bansinghaim commented, "but I enjoy the flavor of the dark far more."

"Never saw a ale I didn't like." Gurlig admitted smiling at the memory of the ales he had enjoyed. None of which he had a chance to enjoy since the sobering up back at Lorning. "Spirits er better fer my tastes. I likes somethin' that'll tingle a bit goin' down. A good rye'll make me smile. Er a dark whisky a any kinds."

"Ale let's me keep most of my wits about me." Bansinghaim continued, "In my position that's also necessary. Ah, but the women of class and society just can't compare to the women in the pubs."

Gurlig grinned from ear to ear, "Ain't that the truth. Give me a good serving wench any day a the week. They know 'bout a man."

"I could tell you stories, good man Gurlig," The Royal Knight Protectorate admitted, "I surely could."

"Ya think we got much more ta go taday?" Gurlig asked, "I ain't so familiar with Derentia as I am 'bout Phenderia."

We should be there around early afternoon." Bansinghaim was in a hurry to find Derenta also. His need for rest and food, not necessarily in that order, were gaining on him. "I know what you're thinking, and we don't have the time or the energy to close a pub tonight. I'd imagine Vastion and Ghalkin would at best leave us behind."

Gurlig saw an opportunity, "They can't. Ya heard the Queen back there in the Woods. They gotta have all a us er nobody get's through. We gotta go with 'em!"

"I prefer," Bansinghaim advised his new found friend, "we hold off on that at least for a few more days. Those two would make our lives miserable, and Malden would be no picnic either! My job is to protect the Prince. I think I'm needed more for it now than at any other time in our kingdom's history."

"Good point." Gurlig conceded, "After this'd be all done an' o'er with, you an' I 're gonna tie one on ta rival any that 'd ever been tied 'fore!"

"Deal!" the knight smiled.

* * * * * *

Master Pazlin waited until Lord Maldifren was seated on his throne in the Throne Room at the center of the Palace grounds before entering and walking past every dignitary waiting in line to present his business to the monarch. He was reminding himself again why all those years ago he had not wished to be Emperor. Soon it would not matter though. He would rule all and none would bother him again. After finding the core of the source of the energy at the bottom of the Phanthow, he would have no use for others except to praise and worship him as their leader and savior from the horrible evils of the West. He was ready to start his plan into process.

"Lord Maldifren," Pazlin spoke while the Emperor was finishing with a dignitary from the far community of Grostil, a farming community far to the west of Ruderrac, the capitol city of Chiloe, "I apologize for my rude interruption my Lord, but distressing news has fallen upon me from very reliable sources."

"Is it about the Island of Mosa?" Maldifren wondered.

"No, My Lord." Pazlin sighed, "I fear it has the potential to be far worse than any bad news from there."

"Go on, old man," Maldifren leaned back into his thrown, waiting as if enduring this trifling bit of news, "I have work to do. Look at this line and tell me your news is more important than theirs."

"I fear it is, My Lord." The Sorcerer explained, "I have caught news of an assassination attempt on your Imperial Majesty."

Pazlin paused a moment for the buzz to quiet down in the Throne Room. All inside were shocked and talking at once. The roar of the crowd was loud and uncontrolled, making it harder and harder for Lord Maldifren to hear anything except the chatter.

"Silence!" The Emperor screamed out while standing in front of his seat and pounding the ground with a large staff he had grabbed from his personal guard standing next to him, "Silence!"

Turning with newfound interest, he looked towards his advisor, "Continue, Master Pazlin."

Now he was called *Master Pazlin*. The ancient man smiled a bit, forcing it back to appear serious once more, "as I understand it, six extremely high ranking officials and officers have devised a plan to poison you this very day at your luncheon in front of all of your daily guests."

"Who," replied the Monarch, "give me names!"

"I believe, My Lord," Pazlin spoke, "it might be more proper to have your guards seal the room as all are present at the time being."

"Guards," the Emperor bellowed, "seal the room!" Twenty or so guards dispersed throughout the massive Throne Room to take there places in front of doors and windows effectively sealing the room to any and all who would care to leave for whatever reason.

"Now," The Emperor looked at Pazlin, "tell me the names of the six to be executed today on the spot."

The crowd was again surprised and talking constantly about the matters at hand. No one had expected to witness an execution when they had entered the room let alone six extremely high ranking officials and officers as Pazlin had stated.

After the crowd had been allowed to calm down, each wanting to find out who the villains were, Pazlin started his story, which was as false as could possibly be.

"My good Lord Maldifren," he started in, "it seems approximately three weeks ago your oldest son Millicom spoke with General Trakkes about how this was a time that would go down in history books as the greatest moment in all of Chiloe history. It seemed Prince Millicom did not want to be the next Emperor after the one to conquer the West, but the one who was written about, aspirations being what they are with young men."

"That is a lie, Father!" A slender man of about twenty-six stood to defend himself, "I have no idea why Master Pazlin would tell you such a lie, but I assure you that is all it is."

"I concur, My Emperor." A man of closer to fifty stood to agree with the next in line to the throne, "No such conversation has ever or will ever take place. My loyalty to you is as it has always been, to you your Imperial Majesty."

"Guards," Maldifren ordered to the two standing next to Prince Millicom, and another two by General Trakkes, "bring them to me now. Seat them at the end of my procession to await my verdict."

The two were moved abruptly to a pair of chairs seated at the end of the long line protruding straight out from the Throne.

"Proceed, Master Pazlin." The Emperor waited.

Pazlin took a deep breath and continued, "As I was saying your Majesty, Prince Millicom and General Trakkes have devised a plan to overthrow the government and kill you creating the promotion of Prince Millicom to Emperor and in exchange Millicom would take Trakkes as his chief General of the military replacing General Geddol. They needed more assistance it seemed, so Prince Millicom confided in Prince Ashicom, your third in line, guaranteeing him after the overthrow he would have Prince Frillom beheaded and move Ashicom, since they both have a common mother in Queen Lucimos, to his direct heir to the throne until Millicom produced an heir from his loins."

"Bring Ashicom to the other prisoners." Maldifren ordered to a pair of guards close to him.

"Father, I know nothing of this!" Ashicom replied as he was hurried to the seat next to his oldest brother.

"Continue." Maldifren asked of Pazlin.

"Yes, my Lord." Pazlin used all of his strength to hold back his glee, trying with all his might to appear as if an Imperial tragedy was befalling, "General Trakkes knew they would need assistance from inside the kitchen as well. He approached your Head of Kitchen, Chef Rostach, your personal Assistant, General Halbenem, and your Royal Body Guard, Flollam to aid in this attempt, promising all of them higher seats of power in the new administration."

This time he did not speak, he just snapped his fingers at a group of guards and pointed to the three newly accused men. They were brought, the same as the others, to be seated next to the General and pair of Princes.

Prince Millicom stood to defend himself, "Father, if I…"

"Sit!" Maldifren ordered, then turning to Pazlin, he stated, "I know of only one way to prove you right or wrong, old man. Its justice will be swift if you are right, and if wrong you will be executed on the spot."

The guards in the room took notice to this since none of them would feel able to kill Master Pazlin.

"I am sure your verdict will be just, My Lord." Pazlin knew it was going exactly the way he had planned.

"Bring my plate from the luncheon set in the adjoining room" Maldifren ordered. Quickly it was brought and placed in his hands. "This is the plate I was to eat from the luncheon?"

"Yes, Your Majesty." The servant stated.

"Could there be a mistake as to it being the one intended for me?" He added.

"No, Your Majesty," the servant replied, "it is the one under the golden dome, which is always designated for the Emperor. It has been this way for centuries."

"Bring me six plates." Maldifren ordered.

"Yes, My Lord." The servant moved quickly to comply with his Emperor's wishes.

The reining monarch divided his meat into six equal portions and placed each on a different plate. Personally handing one to each of the accused he stated only one word, "Eat."

Each one, afraid to do so, took the bite sized portion of beef and placed it into their mouths, all the while feeling the point of a guards blade directly at their backs.

All chewed cautiously and swallowed. The crowd waited to see the results. None of the accused seemed to be feeling ill, which allowed a cocky air to come over the eldest Prince.

"I tried to tell you father. There was never a plan to harm you that was originated from me."

The Emperor placed a piece of carrot on each mans plate, stating once again, "Eat."

As each took the small round carrot into their mouth. They were seen after approximately ten seconds gagging, foaming at the mouth, and turning instantly blue from the neck up. Each fell to the floor dead and stiff.

Lord Maldifren, Emperor of all Chiloe, turned his back on what had been six loyal men to him, two from his own bloodline, refusing to look upon them dead on the floor. He ordered over the noise returning to the Throne Room, "Remove them from my sight, and have their carcasses burned. Bury the remains outside the city gates and place a fence around it with no gate. No one is ever to go near the remains of the traitors. Today's court is adjourned." With this being said, he turned to leave his Throne Room not wishing to be disturbed for the rest of the day.

Pazlin could smile now. His plan was moving forward.

* * * * * *

Chessington sat straight up in his saddle back with the traveling party next to the Prince. The group, now noticing he was back, stopped to circle around the head of the cart to listen to what he had seen. Violta had already known, but out of respect for her new fancy, she waited for him to tell the news he had.

"I have good news, better news, and bad news." Chessington started with.

"Let's hear it, boy." Malden stated, "I kinda wanna be done today."

"Well," The young Wizard began, "first, I've looked ahead as far as Bollantoda, and I see no sign of the Chiloes. They seem to be coming from Phenderia to the south and not from the eastern coast of Derintia or from the western coast either."

"That makes sense." Vastion agreed, "They already have a base on the island, no need to attack from ship to shore again like they did with us. Please go on."

"Second," he continued, "Derenta is just ahead. We'll go over three hills in the road and see the city from the top of the third hill. It'll be about a mile and a half after that."

"Thank goodness!" Bansinghaim exclaimed, "I'm exhausted!"

"Need yer beauty sleep there?" Malden ribbed.

"I could be too tired to be held accountable for my actions, Malden." The large knight warned.

"Ya throw that around a lot." Malden noticed.

Bansinghaim laughed, "It works."

"Go on," Ghalkin pressed, "the third thing the one which was not good news?"

"Maldow fell today to the Chiloes." Chessington stated somberly, "The people were all rounded up and marched south. The town of Stish to the southeast of here had fallen two days before as well, and the people marched also to the south. I would guess they're coming north from Phenderia and taking whatever happens to be in the way."

"I would guess that would be a sound assumption." Vastion agreed, "I believe we can plainly see they are interested in the entire island of Mosa. We need to get to Mt. Bollantoda as soon as we can and have our young friend read his book or learn his lessons or whatever it is he's supposed to do, and we need to keep heading north."

"Don't get yer plans too far ahead." Malden forewarned, "Seems like the book is directin' us ta where we need ta go."

"Malden is right." Ghalkin concurred, "It has been right on the mark thus far. There would be no reason to change it now. We would be foolish to think we were not being led from outside forces."

Vastion admonished, "I'm not ready to give into magic and sorcery where good sound logic can say otherwise."

"Ya just gotta be in charge," Malden grinned, "don't ya."

"It's not that," the General defended his statement, "I just think if it told us to run off of a cliff, we should think about it first."

"I'm runnin'." Malden stated.

"Me too." Bansinghaim added.

"Not you too!" Vastion turned to the knight.

"I've seen things these books have been responsible for that I could never explain in a million years." The Royal Protectorate stated, "Until it's proven to be wrong once or even twice, I'm going with Chessington and the books and so will the Prince."

"Alright," Vastion gave in, "we still have a long way to go before we get, or if we get, as far as the mountain."

"Positive thinkin'," Malden stated, "positive thinkin'."

"One more thing." Chessington piped in.

"What's that, boy?" Malden asked.

"At the rate they're moving," he stated to his friends, "they will be in Derenta the morning after next. And their history seems to be to completely circle a town or city and close in on it."

"They have that many soldiers?" Vastion asked.

"And then some." Chessington confirmed.

"They treat their army as if it were disposable." Vastion revealed.

"They do," Bansinghaim agreed, "but what they call a soldier is more of a puppet. It seems void of personality or even thought. Fighting them back at the castle, they showed no fear, no emotion, no glee, nothing."

"That makes for a great fighting engine I suppose," Vastion admitted, "but also makes changing plans in the middle tough."

"They can do that, too." Chessington told him, "They have a constant watch on each man and can switch in an instant. What they don't have is any care for whether they live or die. It's like a plow to a farmer, if one breaks, you simply get another one."

"So what are their weaknesses?" Vastion wondered.

Chessington just shook his head, "I would have no idea, Sir."

Chapter 7

They crested the third hill Chessington had spoken of to see a town of considerable size and distance. Homes nestled on the outskirts as businesses and industrial areas were at the center of the town. Roads crossing in perfect grid lines, either east to west or north to south, none of them moving diagonally could be seen from the vantage point where the group had stopped.

Vastion called the group together to strategized, "I believe after what happened at Maldow, we should stay together. We'll need to replenish our stock on the cart and maybe pick up a few more blankets as well. Tomorrow night we'll have no Inn to save us, so we'll be camping out until we get into Bollantoda. Before then we should look into some climbing gear. Ropes, spikes, heavier jackets, and smaller water bags we can easily carry once we have to leave the cart behind. We still need to figure out what to do with the horses once the trail becomes too much for them. Then we can find a nice inn to settle into after our purchasing is through. Have I left anything out?"

"I got somethin'." Malden added, "How 'bout a book store. We got a map a Derentia, but we ain't got nothin' after that. If this country is a few weeks from bein' occupied, we better find a new country ta reside in."

"Valid point," Vastion agreed, "I doubt if we have to go to Iclania they'd have any maps there to purchase."

"Er a book fer that matter." Malden replied, "This might be our last stop in what we call civilized Mosa."

"Another ego shattering fact." Vastion sighed, "This continues to get better and better."

The group started its way down the final grade into the small city of Derenta. It was different than most towns any of the group had seen before due to the simple fact there was no major river dissecting the town. To the northwest were mountains and to any other direction were plains of farmlands. Small rivers, mostly creeks, could be spotted here and there, but no major river or tributary could be seen anywhere close by.

They entered the town beginning with houses lined on either side of the street. No one particularly interested in people they had never seen before as it was fairly common here to see travelers coming in and out. After nearly another twenty minutes of riding, they spotted a shop to the left and tethered the horses while they all went inside.

It was a general store much like any other they had ever seen with barrels of flour and sugar, shelves of merchandise, and bins of fruits and vegetables strewn throughout the inside of the one large room making up the entirety of the store.

Gurlig started gathering the supplies he knew of, which had been decreased and placed them on the counter for the shop owner. Vastion was looking at the ropes and harnesses trying to see how they could be used for harnessing humans instead of horses and oxen. He had been thinking at some points the children or at least some supplies would need to be lifted up to where they were climbing rather than strapping them to their backs.

Malden walked up to the store owner to inquire, "Ya got any good maps a places?"

"Not here," the owner replied, "I have no use for them. Anyone traveling here already knows how to get here and how to get back home. The people who live here don't travel much, so I have no need to stock that sort of thing."

"Ya know a good place we could find some?" Malden continued.

"There's a book store right down in the center of town. I think it's called *The Page*. I've never been in it personally, but others I know have. They should have something you could find."

"Thanks." Malden turned away.

"Where are you folks headed?" the owner asked.

"Oh, just here an' there I guess." Malden decided to be vague after what had happened in Maldow.

"It's just you folks seem to be looking at things to buy that would suggest you're staying around to settle, but look like you're headed off out of town again."

"What makes ya say that?" Malden screwed his face up slightly, puzzled at what had tipped him off.

"Your friend here is buying supplies to restock and nothing perishable at that." The owner explained, "At the same time your other friend over there is looking very hard at oxen harnesses. I can't imagine any use for oxen harnesses for travelers who have as many horses as you folks have tied outside."

"I try not ta get involved with those two." Malden nodded, "The one with the harnesses is always thinkin' 'bout how ta do stuff differnt."

"I have a cousin like that." The store owner nodded.

"An' the other one's just too practical." Malden stated.

"Nothing wrong with that I suppose." The shop owner replied tallying what Gurlig had brought up so far.

"Heard anythin' 'bout the road to Bollantoda?" The Royal Librarian asked, "We gotta go up that way in the mornin'."

"I haven't heard of anything unusual." The merchant replied, "A few minor robbers, but no one stupid enough to mess with a group your size."

"Good," Malden nodded, "we ain't real interested in bein' stopped, legal er not."

Vastion looked over to the shop keeper to ask, "Excuse me please, would you know of a good leather worker here in town?"

The shopkeeper thought a moment, "Gabbler would be the best around this end of town. He's just three doors down from me. He's good, been tanning and sewing leather for forty years. I'd try him."

"Thank you." Vastion nodded.

They tallied up the bill and paid the man. Gurlig, Bansinghaim, and Chessington took the items to the cart and put them where they belonged, strapping down the items which could roll or tip over. Ghalkin, Malden, and Vastion headed over to the tanners with a few harnesses they had just purchased from the general store. Violta, Palton, and Preda mostly stayed out of the way, but also looked after the horses as the older men were inside getting supplies.

Three doors down Vastion, Malden, and Ghalkin entered the tanners shop to see mostly leather items for plow horses and oxen, but also a few item for barns such as straps and leather netting.

Vastion spoke first, "Good day, my good man. I need a specific good, but I'm not sure exactly what it is."

"Hard to help you then." The tanner did not even look up, he just kept stitching together a boot strap he was to be put on the partially assembled saddle thrown over a sawhorse behind him.

Vastion thought a little more to begin stating, "I need a sturdy way to haul items straight up using a pulley and ropes. Strong enough to hold around five hundred pounds but light enough to carry without straining the horses as we ride."

The tanner got up and walked over to a leather net hanging on the wall next to the door they had just come in through. "I would guess this would be your best bet. Weighs about twenty pounds, but strong enough for five hundred pounds, maybe more. I would guess three men such as yourselves could be held up with this. I wouldn't go much more than that, but I figure you three to weigh about your five hundred pounds. The leather will stretch but shouldn't break under that kind of use. Now, if you start jerking and bouncing your load the stitching might give out, that'll be your weak point."

"How much?" Malden inquired.

"Fifteen dernos." Answered the tanner.

"My, my," Malden replied, "yer pretty proud a yer work I see."

"It took me a week to make it." He replied.

"I see," Malden remarked, "give us a minute."

The three huddled together with Vastion starting the discussion, "We do need it. Fifteen doesn't sound too bad to me."

Ghalkin spoke next, "I think I see why Sir Malden has balked at the price. We currently have only one hundred and eighty dernos left. This would take us down to one hundred sixty five and we need rooms tonight plus dinner and breakfast tomorrow. We'll be lucky to get out of here with one hundred thirty. Then we need a room in Bollantoda, dinner and breakfast there, and enough left over for a guide to the mountain, which I would expect to be at the very least fifty dernos. It is cutting us close."

Malden had an idea, "How's 'bout we climb up ta the cave in the mountain, Chessington zaps up one a those an' while he's doin' what he's gotta do, some a us could take the net an' haul the junk up?"

"Because," Vastion answered, "once we get to the cave, he can zap up the stuff we were supposed to haul up. We could be two or three nights climbing up that mountain. We'll need our stuff as we go, not once we get there. The climb is going to be the tough part. Besides we may need it to get the children up."

"That's a problem then." Malden wrinkled his brow.

Ghalkin looked at the other two, "Could we sell some of the things from the cart we do not need? Things like the pick or the extra clothes and take a chance we will not need them."

"We'd waste too much time trying to sell them." Vastion answered, "We'd need to find someone to buy them and that could take a while. We have to be gone in the morning, early! I'm not comfortable about how far the Chiloe Army is behind us."

"Well," Malden stated, "we should probably buy it here an' then buy our map book, get just three rooms an' have dinner. Tomorra mornin' we'll have breakfast out a town a ways ta save money, an' not spend anythin' more 'til Bollantoda."

"Sounds wise." Ghalkin agreed.

Vastion turned to the tanner, "We'll give you twelve."

"Thirteen." He stated.

"Sold." Agreed Vastion.

They exited the tanner's store with the net and a complementary block and tackle to support it. Placing it in the back of the cart, they all circled around to discuss their next steps.

"Let's split up and cover our next two stops." Vastion explained, "It's going to be late before we know it, and I'd like to have one night to relax before we start pressing again."

"Chessington an' I'll go ta the book store an' get a good current book on maps a the mainland." Malden stated.

"The rest of us will get three rooms and unload." Vastion nodded his approval.

Bansinghaim wondered, "Why just three rooms? I would have thought four or five if we're going to relax."

Ghalkin explained, "Our funds are not as large and plush as we had anticipated. We need to conserve now, or we might not get a guide who will be worthy to what we need. Once in the cave, Chessington can make more, but we need to get there first."

"Alright," Bansinghaim approved, "it's only a couple of days. Do we really need the book? Can't Chessington pop one up in the cave?"

All eyes turned to the Wizard, "I could make the book, but I have to see one first. We could go to the book store, and I could study the book. After seeing it, I could make an exact duplicate in the cave."

"Exactly?" Malden wondered, "Ya just need ta see it once an' ya can make it perfectly again?"

"Yes Sir." Chessington reassured him, "It's like I have no end of storage in my mind now. If I need to retain something, I can store it in a smaller space by using the energy, and I can store it outside of my mind and bring it back whenever I choose. I could store an entire library in my mind with it and pull it out at anytime, but I have to read or study the book first."

"How long would ya need ta study a book a maps?" Vastion asked.

"Probably for a while." He thought, "I would need to make sure I really looked over every square inch before I went on to the next one. I'm sure after seeing the ones back at the castle, I'd need at least an hour and maybe two. It wouldn't be like a book you read. That would take longer. A map I can do a little faster I would think."

"That'll save us lots, kid." Malden explained, "Books 're expensive."

"Good," Ghalkin added, "we should make it then. I still do not think we can go crazy and act like Bansinghaim."

"What did I do?" The large knight stated in surprise.

"Ya live well." Malden laughed.

"I have stated before," Bansinghaim reminded them, "I have a reputation to uphold. People expect me to be carefree."

"Ya do a good job." Malden finished.

"Anyway," Vastion brought everyone back to the conversation saving his friend the knight from any further embarrassment, "we'll meet back together in two and a half hours for dinner. Afterwards, Chessington can search out the surrounding area and the route to Bollantoda for grey faces and anything else that might be coming along. If we need to communicate, Chessington and Violta can talk to each other and fill the rest of us in. Any questions?"

After a short pause no one answered the call and Vastion mounted up, stating, "Alright then, we'll see you two in a bit." Looking at Malden and Chessington turn to head down a side street towards the eastern end of downtown as the store owner had instructed while the other seven rode straight ahead towards the area described as having plenty of inns and restaurants.

"So boy," Malden asked Chessington, "we got a while ta ourselves here, refresh me on just what did happen in the tunnel with the Shade ya talked 'bout? I was a little stunned the last time ya told me."

"Where to start, Sir?" The young Wizard smiled, "I guess where I saw my Uncle Fein in the wing of the castle no one uses anymore."

"Good as any spot I guess." Malden agreed.

Chessington thought a second and then started his story, "You remember the afternoon, right after lunch, when Sir Bansinghaim took Prince Palton for lessons and Sabinnes had Preda for a few hours."

"I remember."

"Well, the night before, the Prince and I went exploring through the castle and went a ways down that hallway, but we ran out of time to go to the end and had to come back. I thought I had plenty of time that afternoon to explore the rest, and besides, I really wanted to be alone to straighten a few things out in my head after the fire and all."

"Don't blame ya there son. Go on."

"Well," Chessington continued, "I found a room close to the end of the hallway with a table and chair and a couple other things in it, sat down, and thought about things. After a while, I have no idea exactly how long, I went to go back to the castle proper to meet back up with Preda. I felt a wind blow through and the door slammed shut. I tried opening it, but it was stuck really hard. I figured I'd better see if the window was too high to jump out or if I could climb down somehow when I turned around and my Uncle was standing between me and the window."

Malden shook his head, "Hard ta believe if I hadn't seen the last few days."

"I know!" Chessington revealed, "But he told me I'd see a Shade that night in my sleep and to follow him and do what he says. He didn't last very long. He told me it took quite a lot to get him there, but this was important, so he had to do it. After he faded out, the door just swung open like it was never stuck."

"Ya think these outside forces made ya stay there on purpose?"

"It must have," Chessington stated, "otherwise, I don't know how the door would have done that. My Uncle, I was ready to write off as a delusion of my mental state, but the door was really, really stuck. That's what made me think twice. Anyways, after I had returned back to the rest of you, Preda and I went to dinner. I took her back to the room and put her to bed then went back to the Library to get enough books to stay awake all night."

"That's tough ta do." Malden shrugged, "Most times books put folks ta sleep."

"Believe me," he nodded, "I had incentive to stay awake. I didn't want my mind messing with me anymore. If I didn't fall asleep, I couldn't have my mind fool me into thinking a Shade would come to me."

"He obviously did."

"Oh yes," replied the boy, "I fell asleep faster than I ever had in my life. I don't think I had been seated for two minutes when I was asleep. Then it gets really strange."

Malden laughed hard from the bottom of his toes, "Think 'bout what ya just said there boy."

"I know, I know," He grinned back. It did sound ridiculous, "but listen to this. I felt myself being pulled out of my body through the top of my head. I remember seeing myself asleep at the large table by the main door in the Library and floating away from myself."

"You're right," Malden amended his former thought, "that would be the strange part."

Chessington smiled and continued on with his story, "I floated through the hall, down the main staircase, and into the Great Entranceway. There I saw a light from an area in the wall and found out it was a hidden hallway. You remember the one we escaped through when we fled the castle."

"I remember." Malden nodded.

"I looked down the hallway, and the Shade was standing there and motioning me to follow. I had no choice. I was moved towards him just as he wanted me to. He had me follow him down a bunch of different hallways until we were at a room with a table, a chair, and a blanket over some things on the table. I removed the blanket and saw a crate. The Shade told me to open it, and I found these three books. He showed me the proper way to read them,…"

"Huh," Malden asked, "ya lost me there. The proper way ta read?"

Chessington nodded, "Yes, I had to read them in a certain order. It was impossible to read ahead or read the wrong book first, because only the parts I was to read at that moment were readable; otherwise, they were in a language I couldn't even begin to tell you where it was from."

"Okay, go on."

"Well," he started up again, "I was shown how to get back to the room by the Shade, and after I had woken up again, I was sent back to my body. That's the morning you woke me up for breakfast, and I was very strange."

"Yeah ya were." Malden remembered, "You were the strangest I'd ever seen anybody. Ya acted like ya didn't know where ya were er what day it was er nothin'."

"I'm not sure I didn't." Chessington laughed, seeing how ridiculous he must have appeared, "I took Preda to breakfast and slipped out to the

Great Entranceway. I found the spot in the wall where the tunnels started and found my way back to the room where the Shade and I had been in my dream. It was the way I had left it from the dream exactly! I started to read the first book, a fascinating history book of past kings and wizards from thousands of years ago, and I lost track of time. I ran back to the dinning hall, and you guys told me I had been gone about fifteen minutes, but it couldn't have been less than two hours. I was even more confused."

"I agree," Malden nodded, "ya were."

"Do you remember you sent me to my room to get some rest and took the kids to study?"

"Yep."

"Well, as soon as I could, I returned to the room with the books and read the entire first book to the end. Then it told me to finish reading and practice what I had read before leaving. I had to stay there for what seemed to me about two or three days, but the books had told me time outside the room was standing still until I returned from the tunnels to the castle again. I did as it said and returned after I was finished to find the whole place in the middle of the battle we all remember."

Malden waited to mentally digest what he had just heard. After a moment, he asked, "Did ya think ya were out a yer mind after ya started readin' er just 'fore that?"

"I knew I was okay after I went to the room the last time." Chessington added, "Before that I thought I was insane."

"I could see it." Malden nodded, "I'd a thought the same."

Pointing and turning his attention down the street a half of a block, the Royal Librarian announced to his new friend, "There's *The Page* right there."

They dismounted, tethering their horses by the front door. After going inside, they could see it was not a large shop, only about the size of a good bedroom back at the castle, with books shelved neatly in order of category. Finding the Geography section, they found a very nice current book on Mainland Geography and saw this was exactly what they needed. Malden browsed around the shop so as not to draw attention to Chessington staring at the same book for a couple of hours, and the Wizard started memorizing the maps on the pages in front of him.

After approximately an hour and a half, Chessington shelved the book and motioned to Malden they could be finished here. Walking out the door to mount back up, Chessington connected with Violta.

We're done with the book store. He announced, *Where should we meet you at?*

Violta hesitated a moment to answer him. Their plans had been changed. Gurlig had been arrested by the local authorities.

Chapter 8

Chessington and Malden met back up with the others, minus Gurlig, at the inn Violta had instructed them to come to. Under better circumstances this would have been a very calm and relaxing night. All were seated around the room Vastion, Ghalkin, and Malden were to have shared for the evening, but the need to have their friend returned was the most pressing need at the moment.

"Of all the things I'm sure he's done in his life," Vastion stated, "he gets arrested now for something he couldn't possibly have done."

"Did ya tell the authorities that?" Malden wondered.

"Yes," Vastion replied, "but we're foreigners here, and our word doesn't hold much value."

"Exactly what did they say Gurlig did?" Chessington asked.

Ghalkin explained, "It seems this morning around daybreak a certain shop was broken into and had a sizable amount of money, they would not say how much, stolen from it."

Chessington slumped over and left himself to go see how Gurlig was doing and what exactly the situation held for getting him back as soon as possible. He found the local precinct guarded with two guards at the front door and six other people inside. The jail itself was a set of five cells two on the one side and the other three across the hall from them. The keys were on a ring by the precinct chief's desk, and the ring held about thirty keys to it.

Reconnecting to his body back at the Inn, he awoke and told the rest of them, "He's locked up with eight guards in various places all around. The walls to his cell are foot and a half thick blocks with metal between them and no windows."

"Sounds like they know how ta keep someone in." Malden spouted.

"How do we sneak him out?" Vastion mulled around, "We're no match for eight guards, and I'm sure we don't want them chasing us to Bollantoda. The Chiloes can't be too far away. I'd hate to run from one force just to find another worse one."

"Any ideas, boy?" Malden asked Chessington.

Chessington thought of his options. "I think the one we used back at the castle would work, turning myself and Gurlig into a translucent state, which could be seen through easily."

Vastion looked to Malden, "Can this work?"

"Did 'fore." The Librarian stated, "How ya gonna open doors an' stuff?"

"I'd have to wait for them to do that." The young Wizard replied, "If I get solid enough for my hand to turn a knob or push a door open, they'd see it. It would most likely scare them seeing a floating hand opening a cell door, but it would work."

Violta, thinking the entire while about things, told the group, "How about if Chessington slips into his cell at some point, makes Gurlig see through as well, and waits for the guard to open the door to investigate. After he opens the door, they can slip out into the main room until someone opens the front door. They come back here, where Chessington and I change Gurlig into a creature, which would not be noticed as much. We leave town and resume back to normal down the road."

Ghalkin looked at the boy, "Can you do all this without being detected?"

"I'm not sure about the changing Gurlig's form part," he answered, "I'd have to check with Queen Rhyshena first before we did it."

Vastion asked, "We'd better check first. We don't want to have him here and find out in the middle of the plan we can't finish it."

"I will check." Violta closed her eyes and left much like Chessington had done before.

Malden looked over, "Great, there's two a 'em."

Violta popped back to announce, "We can do it, but he has to be changed into an entirely different species. We would have to transform him piece by piece, and it will take a bit of time. I have to do the transforming, so Chessington is not detected by the Chiloes, but he has to send me extra energy I cannot do by myself. They cannot really see what we do, like they can with humans, sort of like communicating from a human to a deer. The human would not know what he or she was looking for."

"How long?" Vastion inquired.

"We will need a couple of hours at most." The Doltist answered.

"That's no good." Vastion admitted, "The first place they'll check for him is here. We had to tell them where we were staying when they arrested him. They'll be here looking around inside of the first hour of his escape."

"Then we don't take him here." Chessington added, "After Gurlig and I are free, I call Violta to meet with us on the outskirts of town. Once there we work on Gurlig's appearance and move down the road to wait for you."

"I will take the cart with me." Violta stated, "It would be less noticeable if just one person takes a large item out than a whole group with it."

"How do you know that?" Vastion asked.

Violta smiled, "That is what we do, General. Doltists know every way of moving ourselves around, as well as things, which we do not want others to see."

Vastion sighed, "Alright then, let's do it. Chessington, don't get yourself caught. That could take more explaining than we have time for."

"Yes Sir." Replied the Wizard. He shimmered for a few seconds and seemed to disappear.

Violta walked to the door and opened it. "He had no way to get out."

Vastion just looked amazed, "Of course, he didn't. How stupid of me."

* * * * * * *

Chessington finally found someone to walk into the precinct at the north end of town, having to hurry before the door closed on him. He looked around to find the hallway he had seen before with Gurlig sitting in the center cell of the side with three cells connected to each other. Dinner was waiting outside the cells as the guards returned with the keys to give the prisoner his meager evening meal.

"Not what ya planned for dinner is it?" A fat guard asked Gurlig, "Probably thought you'd be spendin' some a that money ya stole."

"I didn't steal nothing!" Gurlig shouted, "An' ya all knows it, too."

"I see," the guard laughed, "the three eyewitnesses were wrong."

"Yep," Gurlig stated, "they were!"

The guard walked in and handed him a board with an old tough looking piece of meat on it stuffed between two slices of hard bread, which still showed the spots the mold had been cut off. Gurlig looked at it and shook his head back and forth.

After the guards walked back down the hall to the main room, Gurlig felt a hand covering his mouth and Chessington reappeared.

"Shh!" The boy slightly spoke, "I'll explain later, just go along with what I'm doing."

Before Gurlig could answer, Chessington had worked the energy to make them translucent as he had with the others before when the castle was under siege. Gurlig felt strange as he was not anything close to solid and trusted the boy knew what he was doing. It was only moments before the guard returned to heckle Gurlig again.

"Hey,…" Then noticing he was gone the panicking guard screamed, "Escape! Escape!"

The chief of the precinct ran down the small hallway to the cells, looking inside the center one, and finding no one there. "Open it, you damned fool! He has to have left a clue or something in there! You three search the precinct, the rest search the streets around here. He couldn't have gotten too far yet!"

The mad scramble ensued throughout the building as doors were flying open everywhere. Chessington guided Gurlig through the cell door and out the front of the building. They passed by the local authorities as they walked fluid and safely past the frantic police to the edge of the town and north on the highway towards Bollantoda.

* * * * * * *

At the Inn the knock came on the door everyone was expecting. Sir Ghalkin opened it to see two local deputies and the precinct chief standing there with scowls across there faces.

"What may we do for you this evening, Sir?" Ghalkin stated as a matter of fact. His practice with diplomats in his profession back at the castle made him an excellent choice to do most of the talking here. He had to make the authorities believe he and the rest of his party had no idea what was going on.

The chief paused a moment to see if information would be given without asking first, but Sir Ghalkin was more experienced in negotiations than the chief, and would not allow himself to tip his hand. "It seems your friend isn't in our custody any longer." He wanted to be vague to see what Ghalkin already knew.

Ghalkin smiled and answered, "That's wonderful! Then he can leave with us in the morning as well. You know we were quite ready to go without him, but it is better to be all intact when we leave. Where is he?" Ghalkin looked past the guards down the hall to see if he could see Gurlig coming.

"You don't seem to understand." the chief continued, "He has escaped."

"Oh my," Ghalkin's eyes widened as if this was a complete surprise to him, "how did he do it!"

"Well, ah… , we don't actually know yet." The chief explained, "We were hoping you could tell us a few things about it."

Ghalkin looked puzzled, "Why would I know anything about it?"

"Because," the chief continued, "you people are his friends. We have a good idea you, at the very least, know about it, and I could believe you all figured into it at some point."

"Those are very serious accusations, Sir." Ghalkin understood how this worked, "I believe you could ask the front desk, but we have not left here this entire evening. We will be leaving fairly soon to continue on our way though."

"No, you won't be." The chief stood his ground, "You are all required to stay where you are until he is found. I will have guards posted outside your door until then."

"I see," Ghalkin looked him in the eye, "and your grounds for our imprisonment would be for what, Sir? That you could not hold on to a single man? I believe your supervisor would be interested to hear how a man, locked in your care, could escape without someone of your caliber knowing about it. We will be leaving in the morning, without Gurlig. If we should happen to see him, we will send you word of his whereabouts."

"I order you all to stay in Derenta! You will not leave, and that is that."

"On what charges?" Ghalkin asked, "Name what we have done to warrant being detained."

"Suspicion of harboring an escaped prisoner." Replied the chief.

"Suspicion? Search our room." Ghalkin turned aside to allow him in, "Search our belongings. Do whatever you think you need to do. We will be leaving in approximately two hours from now, and you have no legal grounds to say otherwise."

An awkward silence filled the room as each was waiting for the other to baulk first. Ghalkin won this battle as the chief turned to leave, "Fine, it's true, I have no legal right to detain you, but I will be following you all the way to Bollantoda personally."

"Then we will feel safe and secure in this leg of our journey." Ghalkin nodded a final farewell to him and started to shut the door, "Good evening, Sir." As the door shut on the three, Ghalkin sighed and sat in the closest chair to him.

"Remarkable." Vastion laughed, "You ate him alive!"

"I have not had to do that for quite some time." Ghalkin exhaled mildly and looked at the floor, "I believe the last workout I had with a hostile diplomat was Rothsenee of Paldost. I believe it was approximately four years ago. The pompous moron decided Paldost was more important than the Affiliation kingdoms should be to us. I have very little patience for arrogance when it is completely foolish like that."

"So now what do we do?" Bansinghaim wondered aloud, "He's going to be all over us for quite some time."

"I think he'll get bored with us after he sees we seemingly told the truth." Vastion grinned, "He'll follow us for a while and then get tired of it and return back home."

"And once we meet up with Gurlig, Chessington, and Violta," Bansinghaim asked, "then what?"

"Then," Vastion turned serious, "we hope Chessington and Violta can do what they say with him and disguise him so no one can tell who he is."

* * * * * * *

Violta pulled up to the wide spot in the road where Chessington told her they would stop at to wait for her. She sat for only a moment and watched as Chessington and Gurlig reformed themselves into the solid figures they should be and walked over to the cart.

"That's the most amazin' thing I ever seen." Gurlig stated still wide eyed, "I sure could a used that a few times in the past. No doubt 'bout it!"

Chessington smiled, "I'm glad you liked it. You may not like the next part though."

"Why's that?" Gurlig asked.

"Because Violta and I have to change you to not look like you." He explained.

"Huh?" Gurlig wondered, "Ya mean I gotta look different? They ain't comin' after us? I say we outrun 'em."

"No," Violta disagreed, "the rest of us will be easy to spot. With you still you, we cannot be sure others would not recognize the description forwarded along. They may have someone sent ahead to Bollantoda with our descriptions waiting to arrest you and now us."

"I see," Gurlig replied, "so you two gotta do this, huh?"

"We do," Chessington replied, "but you'll know everything that's going to happen."

"Okay," he conceded, "how's it work?"

Chessington took a deep breath and explained, "I can't do it. She has to, but I have to supply her with energy and direction. She sends energy into you in various places and part by part, bit by bit, you will change into something that isn't even human."

"Like a animal?" He asked, his nose wrinkling up and not concealing his distaste for this.

"Well yes, pretty much." Violta concurred. "You can help decide what it is you would like to be."

Gurlig thought for a minute. Seemingly stuck as to what animal he would like to be. Finally, he thought about it and decided, "Hows 'bout a dog. Like a huntin' dog. A Bloodhound!"

Chessington looked at Violta, "Sure, it's as good as anything else I suppose. What should we change first?"

"I would think the muzzle," Violta stated, "and work out from there."

"He won't be able to talk anymore if we change his mouth first." The boy Wizard stated.

"Hold on," Gurlig questioned, "I can't talk no more? Why not?"

Violta answered him, "Because you will have no human mouth, lips, or human tongue. You cannot form words with a dog's mouth, only bark and whimper."

Gurlig thought a while longer, "I ain't got no choice, do I?"

"Not really." Chessington replied.

"Alright," he nodded, "go 'head."

Chessington filled the thought of the muzzle of a bloodhound in his mind and Violta did the same. He channeled his energy through the Doltist so he could not be detected by the evil entity who he felt from Chiloe after the battle outside of Marroda. She funneled the extra energy from Chessington into Gurlig and watched his mouth and nose extend out to take shape. Next, they covered the exterior of it with dark brown fur. Gurlig touched his nose to feel how it was. Disbelief from before was transformed into a sense of shock.

"It looks good." Violta looked it over deeply and studied every inch of it. "It looks like a real dog's muzzle."

"What next?" Chessington asked, letting Violta call the shots.

"Ears," the Doltist replied, "then the eyes, and head. After those, we will work down."

Gurlig growled, looking down his body.

Chessington read his thoughts, "Of course, your body will have to change." He paused a moment, "Yes, all of you."

Gurlig whined softly.

"He's not happy about this." Chessington explained to Violta, "He's afraid he's going to be laughed at or pitied."

"Sorry Gurlig," the small Doltist gave him a hug and kissed his check in sympathy, "we will reverse this as soon as we can, I promise."

It seemed to calm him slightly. They finished off the head one part at a time and studied him carefully. Gurlig's neck was next followed by his general body shape and covering. Chessington could not believe what he was seeing, a dog with a man's arms and legs.

Gurlig was visibly disturbed as his clothing fell off, and he was as exposed as any other animal would have been.

They changed his arms next, left first and then the right, and last of all his legs. They checked each part of his body, head, and limbs to make sure each and every square inch was giving the appearance of a bloodhound approximately four years of age.

"I believe we have done it." Violta sighed, "I suppose the good news is you will be riding in the cart with Sir Ghalkin, Preda, and me. You are absolutely adorable, Gurlig."

Gurlig seemed to scowl a bit, not being happy in the least. He took three steps and wobbled down to his haunches. Trying again he could not seem to get the knack of walking as a dog. He had the right front and left rear legs moving forwards together while the other two were doing the opposite, but he could not figure out why his balance was so bad.

"I believe he needs a tail." Chessington laughed.

"Oh yes," Violta grinned, "I suppose we only figured to change the features he already had and not the ones he did not have to start with. I am sorry, Gurlig."

Chessington funneled more energy through Violta as she made a tail protrude out from behind Gurlig in exactly the perfect style and color to match the rest of her creation. Gurlig again stood, this time finding it much easier to walk, even trotting for a moment before jumping himself up onto the back of the cart and lying down on top of a pile of blankets they had used when they were sleeping out of doors.

"I suppose we wait now." Chessington stated, looking up the road in the direction of Derenta.

"I suppose so." Violta looked up into his eyes and smiled a little smile at Chessington. Working her way under his arm and snuggling close to his chest, she wrapped her arms around him and closed her eyes content for the moment.

Chessington was at a loss as to what to do. He had no experience with women and found himself with his arms held out approximately shoulder high trying not the touch her for fear of getting in trouble for doing the wrong thing.

Violta took his left arm and placed it down around her waist. "Relax, you will be fine. We have a little time without having to move. Gurlig looks to be asleep, and I like this."

The Wizard, young and lost, kept his hand and arm where it was placed. Stiff as a board and uncomfortably enjoying every second he was spending with her.

Chapter 9

The six crested the hill to see their cart up ahead. Violta and Chessington were sitting in the front with their backs to them huddled close together. This surprised no one. They had shown all the signs of infatuation with one another, and none of the adults figured this would be an odd arrangement. Except for the dog who was curled up in the back of the cart, they actually expected it.

Pulling along side of them, Vastion asked, "Is that," he hesitated a second, "Gurlig?"

Gurlig looked at the group and whined a bit. Then he laid back down as if giving up.

"Yes," Chessington replied, "it was his idea to be a bloodhound. Violta and I were discussing how he could be an asset in this form. Better hearing and smell most notably, but also he could aid Bansinghaim in foraging and tracking, and I can communicate with him by going inside his thoughts now that he's an animal."

"It sounds all well and good I suppose," Vastion added, "but I'm sure he can't wait to get back to normal."

Chessington agreed, "He's a bit anxious, yes."

At this very moment, the precinct chief and four guards also pulled up next to them. "And why were your young friends not with you last evening?"

Ghalkin smiled and turned to Chessington and Violta, "This would be the chief of the precinct where Gurlig was held. I am sorry, Sir, I do not recall being introduced as of yet?"

"Chief Modinay," he replied, "and you never answered my question."

"I see, yes." Ghalkin returned, "Our younger friends here discovered that our dog had gone missing. They took the cart and went to find him. We told them if they did or did not find him, we still had a schedule to keep and to meet us on this road around this time no matter what."

"I see they found it." Modinay observed, "I suppose they found Gurlig as well, and he's under a blanket in the cart or hiding in the surrounding areas. I'll have to check under the tarps and blankets you understand."

"Of course," Ghalkin stated, "help yourself."

Modinay dismounted and walked up to the side of the cart. Gurlig stood up, growled, and showed the hackles on the back of his neck. Modinay pulled back, "He doesn't appear to like me very much."

Chessington looked at Gurlig, "Down Maldo, down!" It was the first name the boy came up with in the hustle of the moment, "Come up here and let the chief look under the tarps."

Gurlig gave a slight growl and walked to the front of the cart with Chessington and Violta. Preda slid down from Vastion's horse to take her place on the cart at the center of the bench and pet Gurlig's ears. She loved animals and saw an opportunity to play for the first time since the castle.

Chessington dropped down as well and resumed his place on his horse tied to the rear of the cart with Gurlig's, which Sir Ghalkin had ridden replacing it. Modinay removed the tarps to see barrels of water, flour, and a smaller one of sugar, changes of clothing, shovels and picks, and various other items normal for travelers to carry, but no Gurlig."

"All appears in order." Modinay helped Bansinghaim recover the load with the tarp, throwing the lines across, "Let's check the woods surrounding this area first, and after we do, if all turns up well, I'll return to town convinced you've told the truth. Anything less and I wouldn't be doing my job."

Vastion nodded, "We completely understand."

Modinay instructed the guards to proceed back into the trees at the edge of the road and go into them for at least one hundred yards to both sides.

"If all goes right you'll be on your way in only a few moments." The chief reassured them. "I understand your position, and if nothing turns up, you have all been very cooperative. Your friend Gurlig was truly annoying by disappearing back at the precinct though. I can't figure out how he did it. The cell was locked, he was there, and then gone. No one opened the cell door, and there's no window to squeeze through. It's a complete mystery."

Just at this moment, one of the guards was spotted running back to the group with an arrow protruding from his front and screaming as loud as he could, "There's hundreds of them! Go quickly, they're coming, they're coming!"

Bansinghaim and Malden helped the injured guard get into the back of the cart as arrows started to come closer and closer to the group. Grey-faced soldiers started appearing from the trees, and all mounted instantly.

"Follow me back to Derenta!" Modinay ordered.

"No, "Vastion yelled back over the confusion, "it's too late for that! Follow us to Bollantoda. Derenta is or soon will be lost, trust me."

"How do you know this?" Modinay asked, extremely suspicious now.

"I'll explain later," Vastion urged his mount down the road, "for now just follow. If you return, there's a good chance you'll be killed during the invasion."

"Invasion!" Modinay screeched, "Why would anyone invade Derentia?"

"Long story," Vastion replied, "just ride."

They rode swiftly for the better part of half an hour. Finally, not wishing to push the horses any harder, Vastion called the group to a stop. Then turning to Chessington he asked, "Can you go back and see how it looks back there."

"Certainly Sir." Chessington slumped over to do as he was asked creating a new disturbance with Chief Modinay.

"What is he doing?" he asked, "I doubt this is the best time for a nap."

Bansinghaim looked to the poor lost Derentian, "Another long story."

Chief Modinay pulled his sword and stated very authoritatively, "Then tell me this story. I can't wait to hear it."

Bansinghaim pulled his sword as well, placing it to Modinay's throat, "You don't have numbers to back you up any more. I would suggest replacing your sword in your sheath."

"Holding a weapon to a Derentian officer is an offense, which carries hanging with it!" Modinay stated.

Malden laughed, "Good luck findin' a rope that strong."

Bansinghaim gazed at the Librarian, "You're next."

"Both of you sheath your swords." Vastion commanded, "Where would we run to?"

Both men did as they were told to do, looking at the other the entire time.

Chessington popped back up in his saddle, startling the chief and to a much lesser extent Malden and Vastion, "They aren't behind us. They've concentrated on the town, and I don't find any up ahead either until you get north of Bollantoda."

"And how would he know that?" Modinay asked.

Bansinghaim started to say something but Modinay stopped him, "I know another long story. I hope we have time to explain these things later."

"It really cannot hurt to tell him at this point." Ghalkin rationalized, "Otherwise he will just turn us over to the local authorities at Bollantoda, and I am quite sure he believes also we have had something to do with this invasion."

"I got this." Malden pulled his horse up next to Modinay's and started with formal introductions as to each member of the party. Describing how the castle at Phenderia City was overrun in the same manner, the fleeing from their own country, and the invasion of the Chiloes into Derentia. He explained about Chessington and his new found abilities, their desire to stay ahead of the Chiloes, and the need to climb Mt. Bollantoda. He purposely left out Violta and her heritage back at the Woods of the Doltists or the real identity of the dog being the man he was after in the first place. These stories would be for a later date.

"Pretty far fetched." Modinay smiled.

"Ya think I could make somethin' like that up?" Malden asked.

"No," the Chief answered. "so I suppose I'm your prisoner now."

"We have no need for a prisoner." Vastion reassured him, "However, we can't have you talking to others in Bollantoda either."

"How about if I go back to Derenta, and you keep heading to Bollantoda?" Modinay inquired.

Vastion shook his head, "Because as much of a nuisance as you've been, I can't send you back there to die."

The guard in the back of the cart started to speak, but very weakly, "Sir, they weren't normal men back there. They had no emotions, didn't even look like they had a thought to them. They would just kill you and that would be that."

"So we give up?" Modinay appeared helpless, "Just let them win."

"Not exactly," Vastion added, "we live to fight another day. There's more to this story than just what we've shared at this point, but I think it best you understand what you've already been told before we tell you more."

"I'm bound by my oath as a law man to serve my country." The chief stated.

"You're of no use to your country dead." Bansinghaim knew what he was thinking, "I watched as my friends in the Castle Guard all fell to the Chiloes. I will live to fight them again, but thousands against a handful isn't really much hope."

"Bollantoda will fall also then, am I correct?" Modinay wondered.

"Yes," Chessington answered, "at this very moment they are about four days from being in place to do just that. We have less than that to get to Bollantoda, find a guide for the mountain, and be gone before it happens."

"I see," Modinay nodded, "and we can't warn anyone?"

"No," Vastion told him, "it would just slow us down and risk getting us caught as well. Our best chance for the people not taken yet is to continue on and rescue them at a later date. It's really our only option."

Violta was kneeling next to the critically wounded guard in the back of the cart. He had blacked out after his speaking to his supervisor. She looked up slowly to tell Modinay, "He does not have a lot of time left, Sir. The arrow was in his lower left lung. After the bumpy cart ride, it has created more damage. Chessington and I have thoroughly checked him over, but we cannot help him. He has just lost too much blood, and it is pooling up inside of him."

"I see." Modinay looked at his man lying on the cart, "Is he in much pain?"

Violta offered her reply, "No, that much Chessington can do without being detected. He has only a couple of minutes left."

After watching his fallen guard breath his last and fade off into death, he turned to Vastion to wonder, "May I stay with your group? I can be of service with the sword as well as help you through the country. I served in Bollantoda in my youth, and it hasn't changed much since then."

Vastion looked one by one to the others, seeing them all agree, he answered, "We'll be happy to welcome you to the group."

"I feel I should give my apologies for forcing you to leave your friend Gurlig behind." Modinay offered, "I was only doing my job, and he did rob a store."

"Oh, I'm sure Gurlig will turn up soon." Vastion grinned.

Gurlig added with a bark of his own.

Later down the road, after putting quite a few miles on, Vastion called for another rest for the horses and decided the group should take this opportunity to have lunch as well. All looked around lost at the realization their cook was no longer able to make their meals for them.

Modinay looked around at the lost group, "You act like you've never stopped for lunch before."

Ghalkin straightened himself up and looked directly at Gurlig, "We don't seem to have our cook with us any longer. Gurlig did most of the foraging and all of the cooking."

"Surely one of you knows how to cook?" The Derentian wondered.

All eyes instinctively turned to Violta. "I doubt you would enjoy what I would cook." She replied.

"She's right," Bansinghaim agreed, "I'll give it a go before that happens."

"One of us has to give it a try." Ghalkin admitted, "I guess I will see what I can do. Gurlig showed me a few things when Vastion and I were with him in the hills above Lorning. My, that seems like ages ago."

They all stopped for a moment to rethink what had happened. It had been fifteen long days since the castle had been invaded back at Phenderia City. In a little over two weeks, each of them had experienced a lifetime's worth of excitement.

"How could all a this be just a couple a weeks?" Malden somberly stated.

Vastion looked to the rest of the group, "It feels like ages ago since then. We have come a long ways though, mostly from the help of Chessington."

"I was granted certain advantages, Sir." Chessington added in modesty, "Any of you would have done the same."

"But it was given ta you, boy." Malden stated, "Whoever it was out there decided you were the best man fer the job. An' ya come through real nice so far. Ain't a one a us that'd be alive right at the moment hadn't ya done somethin'."

"I will be starting small." Ghalkin interrupted, "Gurlig showed me how to make a flat bread we can wrap cooked bacon inside of and eat as we go. I will make up the flat bread and cook the bacon. We can all make however much we want after I do. Does that sound acceptable?"

"Fine," Vastion agreed, "we do need to keep going. So it might help speed things along. Chessington, maybe you should take this time to scout around. You'd said the last time Chiloes were north of Bollantoda, but if I remember right, the only thing to the north of Bollantoda are mountains until you get north of that. Then it's just cold dry flat ground all the way to Iclania."

"No," Modinay added, "the areas directly north and east are flat lands, which only leads up into Iclania. Once you get to the border, it's only about two hours to Filu. It's a tiny fishing town on a large bay. In half a day from there, you can be in Bontu where most of the ships come in from the mainland. That's the warmest port in Iclania."

"Scout up through there," Vastion was thinking hard, "I had never realized there was anything but mountains that way. I guess it's good to know the lay of the land first hand."

"Alright." Chessington left himself immediately to go up the coastline and into Iclania.

Preda was seen nodding off and trying to stay awake, but she was just too tired. She finally succumbed to her basic need for more rest than she had received lately.

"This is going to get worse before it gets better I'm afraid." Vastion looked at the small girl, "We'll all be in the same boat as her if we don't stop soon."

"We'll be in a worse boat if we do stop." Malden reminded him, "That army a Chiloes ain't gonna wait fer us ta refresh ourselves 'fore they attack."

"I can help." Violta offered, "I'll show you. Do you have about half an hour, or did you want us to be going before that?"

Vastion wrinkled his brow wondering what she had in mind this time, "I suppose we do. Why?"

"I have never done this before," the small Doltist explained, "but I can use myself as a conduit for energy to be moved into you as you sleep. It takes about half an hour for the equivalent of a full nights sleep for you people."

Vastion, as well as the others, were intrigued to say the least. "What would you need to do?"

Violta walked over to the sleeping girl and placed her palm on Preda's forehead. Immediately, Preda's face changed from tight and frowning to happy and contented. "That's it." Replied the Doltist.

Modinay was questioning everything he was seeing again. "Why do you believe she can do this? I'm not doubting her. I just don't understand."

"Yet again," Bansinghaim answered, "long story."

"More than half an hour?" Modinay asked.

"Bansinghaim looked at Malden, and they both smiled, "Yes, that one is more than half an hour."

After the required half hour, Ghalkin announced lunch was ready for the group. Violta woke Preda, who was now wide awake, refreshed, and sent her on her way to lunch.

"How do you feel, Preda?" Ghalkin asked, hopeful this could be a great benefit to the group.

"I feel great!" She was wide eyed and full of energy, "Can I have a bacon thingy like you said?"

"Certainly." Ghalkin took one of the pieces of flat bread and wrapped three strips of bacon in the center of it. Then he handed it to the girl.

"How does it make you feel?" Vastion asked Violta.

She shrugged "I feel fine. I just sit there and allow energy to flow through me. It's pretty boring really. At least I was chatting with Chessington while we waited."

"How's he doing?" Vastion asked.

Violta sighed softly, "He was around the bay Chief Modinay was talking about up in Iclania. I saw the Chiloes already in the town there."

Vastion looked concerned, "And the area between here and there, all full of Chiloes as well?"

Violta actually blushed slightly, "I did not really notice. I was talking to Chessington at the time."

Vastion smiled, "I hope he wasn't as distracted as you were."

Bansinghaim had just finished his meal deciding to ask Violta, "Would you be willing to sit while I rest for half an hour?"

"Absolutely." The Doltist stated, sitting herself back down on the tail end of the cart next to where Bansinghaim was lying down. "Do we have another half an hour?" She asked Vastion.

"I would think so," the General answered, "but afterwards, we need to press on to Bollantoda. Maybe tonight when we camp, you could catch us all up on our rest."

Most of the way through Bansinghaim's nap, Chessington returned to himself. He sat up and spotted the General to announce, "Sorry, I was gone so long, but Violta told me we weren't leaving yet, so I went further out. It appears the only area of the island not occupied already is where we are now, the town of Bollantoda, and the mountains, besides, other than the Woods that is. They show no sign of trying to get too far into the mountains either, and as I said before, Bollantoda will fall in about four days."

"So we're going to be trapped in the mountains once we get there?" Vastion asked.

"Technically, yes." Chessington answered.

"Why technically?" Vastion prodded.

"Because," the boy Wizard replied, "after seeing the mountains from the cave to the northeast, there's a trail running straight towards Bontu letting out about thirty to forty miles from the city."

Vastion asked, "How do we get from the mountain trail thirty to forty miles in open ground in occupied territory and get around in an occupied city?"

"I don't know, Sir." Chessington admitted.

"Great," Vastion sat down on the side of the cart as Bansinghaim snored, "we'll be stuck in the mountains. I thought Queen Rhyshena told us we needed to get off the island before winter set in?"

"Who?" Modinay asked, completely lost.

"Part a that long story we owe ya." Malden put his hand on Modinay's shoulder. "Should a seen what we all had ta trust in the last couple a weeks."

Bansinghaim awoke smiling and refreshed, "That was the best sleep I've ever had!"

"Really?" Vastion asked, "How did it feel?"

Bansinghaim clasped his hands together and laughed, "Fantastic! I didn't dream or toss or know anything that was going on. It was like I blacked out and woke up feeling great. I don't usually fall asleep so fast either, but I was probably too tired to fight it and just gave in to sleeping."

Violta looked at him and added, "No, I calmed you down instantly, and you drifted off in seconds. I actually had to move your tiredness aside and bring the sleep on."

"Really?" Vastion wondered, thinking of a way to help as they rode, "Could you do this in a moving cart as well as a stationary one?"

"I don't see why not." After thinking about it a little more she added, "I don't see how it could be any different."

Vastion smiled, "Would you mind trying as we go then? We each take turns sleeping as we ride on, and you make us refreshed faster than we normally could ourselves."

"I may as well." She agreed, "I'm just sitting on the cart to begin with. Who's first?"

Vastion looked at the group, "Start with Prince Palton and then Sir Ghalkin. The poor boy needs his rest, and if Ghalkin's going to be the new cook, he needs to be fresh before he cuts something off or burns himself."

Prince Palton tied Calynor to the rear of the cart and laid down next to Violta. Within seconds he was fast asleep.

"Absolutely amazing." Modinay stared, "This is getting to be more than I can take in for one day."

The group started down the road again proceeding on to Bollantoda, the last free city on the Island of Mosa. The trip was extremely uneventful and good time was made, stopping every half hour to change recipients of Violta's rejuvenating abilities. After Sir Ghalkin was rested, Malden followed with Vastion after him and Modinay last.

Violta was able to ride next to Preda for a while after her duties were completed. The two talked as they usually did on the bench, commenting about things on the road as they passed by and Preda informing Violta what certain things were, which she had no way of knowing.

Finally, after four hours of straight riding General Vastion ordered them to pull off, asking Sir Ghalkin to make dinner. They stopped to set up a nice area to eat as Ghalkin built the fire and started mixing the flour and water with the sugar and baking powder for some dumplings to go with a pheasant mixture he was seen starting to heat over the fire in a large pot.

Modinay was staring in complete bewilderment. Malden sat next to him and started to ask, "Ya seem pretty lost."

"Just when I think I'm ready to accept this," Modinay reasoned to the Librarian, "something new comes along to make me feel like I'm stuck in a bad dream."

"Ain't nothin' the rest a us ain't had ta deal with already." Malden reassured him, "What's got ya stuck this time?"

Modinay, puzzled and confused, turned to Malden and stated, "He keeps asking the dog about how to cook dinner!"

Malden roared with laughter and could be seen rolling on the ground at the former precinct chief's feet.

Chapter 10

The traveling party continued on after dinner had been cleaned up and put away. Palton was the one to have found the creek off to the left of the road approximately thirty to forty yards and was playing with the rocks along side Preda who was piling up mud and forming it into shapes and objects only she could decipher as to what they were.

Vastion and Ghalkin looked on at the children with Violta and Chessington a few feet back, smiling as they watched. Gurlig waded through the edge of the water getting himself wet from his belly down. The sun was setting and the group was calming down for the evening, still not tired enough to sleep, but conditions too dark and hazardous to ride on until morning light.

Vastion broke the silence looking at Ghalkin and stating with his practical thought, "Let's get a good bath in here, change clothes, and wash the old ones out. Then Violta can take turns refreshing us all again, and you can make us some breakfast just before first morning light, which will help us get to Bollantoda before sunset tomorrow evening."

Ghalkin nodded, "That sounds wonderful. We would be a full day ahead of what we planned leaving the Woods of the Doltists. We could hopefully be into the mountains a good two days before Bollantoda is taken."

"If," Vastion amended, "we find a guide the first day we're there and convince him to start that day. Even starting the following morning might be difficult for a guide to just stop and leave for a couple of weeks at the drop of a hat."

Modinay overheard them talking to add, "I know it was a few years ago, but there was an older man of about fifty then, closer to sixty five now I would imagine, who would go back into the mountains for days on end. His wife would get awfully mad and scream when he'd return, but after a few more weeks he'd just leave again, not tell anyone, and get the same treatment from her upon returning. It was quite a joke throughout the town when I lived there."

Vastion thought a moment, "Do you remember where he lived?"

Modinay nodded, "I remember. There aren't enough people in Bollantoda to miss one, and they were fairly loud. We were asked to go out and quiet her down a few times. I'm sure I could take us to the house still."

Vastion smiled and looked at both men, "I guess we start there. This must be one of those things that's supposed to happen."

"What?" Modinay looked as puzzled as ever, "Will someone fill me in, please?"

"I gotcha." Malden took the precinct chief back to the cart to get fresh clothes for their bath at the creek, explaining certain things along the way. At various points in the conversation, Modinay was seen turning sharply and appeared to be more confused than before he had been updated. They made their way back to the water where the pair of females left and headed with their change of clothing upstream and slightly around the bend. Violta thought this was silly, but she respected the customs of the humans none the less.

As the men bathed and washed clothing, hanging the wet over the low branches of small trees and bushes, they discussed with Modinay about Violta, Queen Rhyshena, and the Woods of the Doltists.

Modinay asked, "How do you know for sure this queen's on our side?"

Malden smirked, "Cuz she pulled us outta the fire a couple a times already an' helped us get tagether 'fore we entered Marroda. If she wanted ta turn us over, she'd a had plenty a chances 'fore this."

"All we'd ever heard of the Woods is the strange happenings going on in there." Modinay confessed, "No one respectable ever went in that I know of."

"Yeah," Malden agreed, "that's pretty much what we thought in Phenderia too. Gurlig was scared ta death from what Vastion an' Ghalkin told us 'bout when they was in there."

"That is true." Ghalkin reaffirmed, "He would not allow us to get out of sight of the open territory to the west, and he slept outside the tree line more afraid of the woods from what his drinking mates had told him than from the Chiloe army."

"It's all so much to take in at one time." Modinay summarized, "I have to say though, after the small girl put her hand on my head and I slept for what you people say was about half an hour, I'm willing to try to believe."

"That's all ya need." Malden grinned, "Stay long enough, an' you'll be as much a believer as us."

"I have no reason not to." Modinay agreed, "From the sounds of it, I have no country to go home to, and no family even before this happened, or even a king anymore to be loyal to. You have a very convincing way of telling me I have two choices, and the other one is worse than this one."

"Kinda the same mess we're in." Malden agreed.

As the last of the men returned to the cart, they found the girls already there and talking about things they had remembered from before this adventure. Violta was talking about how her mother and sister would leave in the mornings on most days and return back at sundown. She on the other hand, loved to stay around and talk to the trees, gathering their thoughts and feelings.

Preda told her mostly about the farm and how it was so different from the Doltist way. The vegetables, the few farm animals they had, and even about the area surrounding the farm and what kinds of trees she knew of from walks in the woods gathering mushrooms with her mother, were not anything like her experience inside of the magical confines of the forest.

The two acted like best friends and talked like young schoolgirls would at the finer schools in the city. Giggling on occasion, mostly from a story Preda would tell about something Chessington had done, which was particularly humorous. She told of the last day at the farm, how he had taken her into town, and how he had treated her so special. How he had watched over her at the castle and in the tunnel, and how she loved him so much, afraid he was going to leave, and she would be left all alone.

Violta held her closely and reassured the girl this would not happen, even if she did not know for sure it was true with the unpredictability of the upcoming events.

As the night pressed on, Violta started giving rest breaks to each one in the party, taking just under four hours to complete this and rejuvenate everyone for the long day just ahead. Of the ten now in the group, seven needed the assistance of the Doltist girl, with Chessington able to revitalize himself as he needed, and Gurlig being able to rest in the cart as they rode having no real responsibilities any longer.

Once Bansinghaim, the last to use her services, was through, Sir Ghalkin set out the early morning meal of bacon, pancakes, bread, butter & jam as well as water. The meal was enjoyable for them as they were starting to become accustomed to this life on the road and enjoyed the previous evening of talking, relaxing, and especially the moments for personal hygiene. Many of them remarked how cleanliness was the thing they missed the most about life out from the castle or their homes.

They all took their spots on the cart or on horseback, as they had when they arrived at this camp site the night before, and headed off towards Bollantoda with General Vastion in the lead next to Sir Malden, Chessington sometimes present and other times scouting with Prince Palton on Calynor next to him chatting usually with the three on the cart Sir Ghalkin steered with Violta and Preda. Gurlig was usually seen standing in the back of the cart sniffing the air, and Sir Bansinghaim riding at the rear with Chief Modinay next to him talking about the stories they loved most to share with new found folks who had never heard them before.

The day went on rather nicely, breaking twice to eat, once a couple of hours before noon and then again about mid afternoon. Chessington finally reported they were only twenty minutes outside of Bollantoda and the town had no idea of what would be only a few days away.

"I suppose it's for the best." Vastion told the group as they stopped for their now usual plan of what will be their best idea upon entering the town, "Nothing we can do to change it, and there's really no escape. If we warned them, it would just cause pandemonium for the two days they have left until the inevitable."

"Yeah," Malden added his agreement, "I hope when this is over, I got somethin' ta say 'bout things. We could get some real imaginative ideas 'bout the punishment. Anyways, what ya got fer a plan once we're inside the town?"

"It's early enough in the day still to look for this Gentleman's home." Vastion answered, "What's his name?"

Modinay reflected a moment, thinking back to those days, "It was Rodinel. In fact I'll never forget it. She would scream it as loudly as she could every time she was angry with him."

"Sound like quite a pair to deal with." Vastion sighed.

Modinay remembered the days, "Oh yes, they could be quite a handful to deal with."

After a few more minutes, Ghalkin announced their late luncheon was served and guided them over to where the food was stationed on the back of the cart. Gurlig stood at the back of the pots overseeing the food as it was dispersed out to the individuals.

Modinay seemed to think it was quite hilarious having a dog who would oversee the food and never appear to have much interest in stealing a bite, "This is the strangest band of outcasts I've ever seen in my life. A man asking a dog how to cook, a girl who by the way is mostly made from vegetation and can condense our need for sleep down to half an hour, and a teenaged boy who leaves his body to do reconnaissance work. I actually believe I'm in a dream."

"There's more." Malden offered.

"No no," Modinay stopped him short, "give me a bit longer before I'm asked to go further into this."

They finished eating and cleaned up the pots and plates as well as the other belongings, which were necessary for dinner to take place, and remounted to finish the final twenty minutes required before entering the last free town they believed to see for a while.

They looked down the hill they were on to see a very small town of not much more than a dozen streets going in either direction. This was the smallest town they had been to in the past couple of weeks and wondered how it existed.

"It a very rich farming community." Modinay stated, knowing what the others must have been thinking, "The farmers in this area are as far as twentieth or so in lineage to their farms. Many even live in the same spots, in newer homes, of course, as all of their families had before them."

"Well," Vastion stated, "it's still early enough to find this Rodinel. Let's move on."

Modinay moved to the front of the pack guiding the rest on to the house standing exactly as it had fifteen years earlier, which happened to be the last time he had been there. Brick with small windows, a door with old rusted hinges, and a woman in her mid twenties sitting on the porch. The odd thing with her was, she wore no dress; a blouse and pants just as a man would wear covering her body, and a very alluring body at that. Full figured, but extremely muscular, tanned arms and face, and very masculine in her character. Her face, however, was far from masculine. She had thin cheeks, dark brown hair and eyes, and full red lips.

Vastion rode up to the porch and dismounted, looking the woman over wondering if he had the correct home. "Excuse me, please," he opened, "we were looking for a man who lives or used to live here. His name is Rodinel. Would you know if this is the right place?"

The woman looked the group over cautiously and leaned forward on her bench, "It was," she replied, "now it's my home. May I ask how you knew of him?"

Vastion looked for Modinay to come to the front and rescue him. Modinay caught the meaning of his look and started to explain, "Many years ago, I was working here in town and knew of Rodinel as a man familiar with the mountains to the northwest of here. We were hoping to find him to guide us through them to Mt. Bollantoda, and then help us climb up most of it to a cave we need to reach."

The girl sat back on her bench and thought before answering, "I doubt he could help you now. He passed away seven years ago."

Vastion reestablished himself as the spokesman, asking further, "So you bought the house after he passed?"

"No," she replied, "he left it to me. I'm his Granddaughter, Baydowa, and if you need to get up Mt. Bollantoda, I know of the only person who can get you there safely."

Vastion's eye's opened wide, "And where might we find him?"

She stood to show her figure being more impressive than before, telling them all in absolute fashion, "You're looking at *him*."

A silenced hushed the group instantly and even the children found it hard to believe this woman was an expert mountain climber and outdoorsman.

After the pause was turning from disbelief to slightly awkward, Vastion looked the woman over and asked, "You've been to Mt. Bollantoda?"

She smiled, enjoying the shock she had caused on the group, "Yes, more than once. I know where the cave you're looking for is, but I haven't been there. It's a rough way to get to it, and quite frankly, it seems like it has a strange feeling to it."

"How do you mean strange?" The General inquired further, trying to extract as much information as possible from the only person who knew anything about this place they had been seeking since the Woods of the Doltists.

"You can't say how it feels." She described, "You have to sense how it feels. Why would this place be so important you would need to hire a guide and take small children along?"

Vastion grinned, "You're very perceptive, but we do have reasons nonetheless. Would you be interested in showing us the way?"

"Why would I want to?" Baydowa asked, "What do I have to gain from this." She placed her hands to her hips and stood her ground. The negotiations were the final part of the sale to her.

"Fifty dernos," Vastion replied, "does that sound fair?"

"Seventy five." She countered.

"Sixty five." Vastion stated.

"Seventy, final price." Baydowa offered.

"Seventy," the General bargained, "and we pay you thirty five now, ten at the cave, and the other twenty five when we get back down from the mountain. Agreed?"

"Agreed." She walked down and shook the general's hand firm and strong as Ghalkin counted out the thirty five dernos, which had been agreed upon. Vastion actually thought she could have made quite the soldier. She asked as she walked back up the steps to her bench, "When would you care to leave?"

"The sooner the better." Vastion remarked, "We do want to get on with this and be done as soon as possible."

"I have business tonight." Baydowa stated, "Once I'm done, I'm free to leave. Is that soon enough for you?"

"Yes," Vastion answered, "that would suit us just fine. We will meet you back here at what time?"

"Sun up." She told him, "Be fed and ready. The first day is the easiest, after that it will get harder and harder each day we're gone. I expect with the children and the amount of belongings we'll need to carry after the cart and shortly after that the horses are of no use, we will be to the cave in eight to ten days, and then another ten to fourteen days to return back here. Does that fit your schedule?"

Vastion smiled, "You're the expert. If that's what it takes, it will have to fit."

"Good," Baydowa started walking into the house, "I will meet you back here at sun up." They heard the door shut and figured it was time to leave here for the night.

They traveled down the street, stopped, and circled around the cart. Vastion started speaking to them as a group, "An odd woman, but she seems to know what she's talking about."

"An' how exactly would we know if she wasn't?" Malden asked.

Ghalkin addressed them all together, "I believe we have been moving on blind faith throughout the majority of these crossroads. I doubt this would have been any different after seeing our past history. Something is guiding us along. Whether it is to go through the Woods of the Doltists to meet Violta, or Gurlig wrongly accused of a crime in Derenta so Modinay was forced to join in with us. In any account, we clearly are not calling the shots."

Vastion scowled, "Why do you people keep reminding me of this?"

"I beg your pardon." Violta interrupted, "I am not a people."

Vastion could not help himself but laugh, "I apologize, my friend. You are quite correct, and I by no means meant to offend."

Violta grinned and laughed as well. The general mood being lightened, Malden asked directly, "Now what? We should get at least one night's sleep in a bed 'fore we head back out fer three weeks a harder travelin' than we've had ta this point. Good luck findin' a inn here. We'd be lucky ta get a abandoned barn that didn't leak too bad."

Ghalkin told the group, "We have enough money to have dinner and breakfast as well as replenish our cart from the last couple of days of eating. That would be about all of it though after we give her the remaining thirty-fives dernos for her services."

Vastion added, "After we leave here in the morning, they won't be of any use anyhow. We may as well spend all of them and have useful items instead of useless coins. Do you remember a good place to eat here, Chief?"

"Last I was here," Modinay replied, "there were two places, and they were next door to one another."

He moved up next to Vastion and led the way to the restaurant, which would feed them for the evening. The two Modinay had remembered were still there. They chose the first they came to and entered to a nice respectable dinning area with soft lighting and a clean atmosphere. Red table clothes and pewter goblet already sitting on the tables next to fine plates looking to be imported from Hitrenda from the thin ceramic feel to them. A large chandelier was the only lighting, but more than sufficient for the room.

The nine entered, after leaving Gurlig on the cart outside only because Preda promised to bring him something, and were seated by a well dressed gentleman of around forty with dark hair and eyes. After being given a moment, the waiter returned to recite the menu.

"Tonight we have a perfectly roasted partridge with a wild rice stuffing," he stated, "a beef roast with potatoes and carrots in a red wine sauce, and a lovely dish of fresh lettuce, cheeses, green onions, radishes, tomatoes, and walnuts served tossed in a wine-vinegar dressing."

The group was a little surprised. This town did not appear to have the sophistication required for a restaurant of the class and refinement being shown here. The pleasant surprise continued after ordering and seeing the food served. They all ate as if they had never tasted good food before. All were impressed and slightly uncomfortable, each figuring this would be their last real dinner for a good, long while. They decided to enjoy it quite immensely.

After they had finished, Vastion, Ghalkin, and Bansinghaim saw two new patrons enter since they were facing in the direction of the door. The first was a scruffy male, trying to look presentable, and the second was Baydowa, their newly hired guide. She was dressed in a beautiful black dress barely covering her shoulders and flattered every part of the already beautiful woman.

Vastion leaned over to Chessington, who was sitting next to him to ask, "Could you mentally tell Violta to eavesdrop in on there conversation. A newly hired guide sitting with a shady friend the evening before we leave for a very long trip might be of some interest."

Chessington paused for a second and replied to the General, "She's listening, and I'm hearing it through her ears as well."

"Good," Vastion answered, "just give me the points of interest if you don't mind. Should he be a boyfriend and they get intimate, I feel I have no need to hear about that."

Violta and Chessington could hear the couple talking, "That's them ya say." The man asked in confirmation.

"Yes," Baydowa replied, not sounding very happy, "see they have children and a young woman. Don't do this Thaidon. It's beneath even you."

"You don't get to decide that." Thaidon scowled at her, "You just do as you're told, or she pays for your independence."

"We've done this for years." The woman reasoned back, "Don't you and the rest of them have enough money? Are you so unfeeling you have to kidnap, blackmail, and murder, even murder children. That's a new low, even for you and those butchers."

He grinned back, somewhat laughing, "Morals from you! The village prostitute. Tell me Baydowa, how should I act? You and your exemplary high values. Do you remember when we started this? You told me you were ready to try anything that kept you in the same bed every night. Then two years ago you pull that stupid act of trying to double cross us. How did that work out for you?"

She gave him a cold icy glare and replied, "Not very well."

"Not for you anyway." He agreed.

"She has nothing to do with this." Baydowa admonished, "You keep her stolen away, and she hasn't even seen sunlight since. You're a nightmare in real life. That's why I tried to double cross you."

"You should remind yourself of that more often." Thaidon nodded smiling, "Then you might forget about useless women and children and remember to serve those who keep you and your sister safe. Now repeat the plan back to me."

Baydowa looked down at the table, fingering the utensils in front of her, "I take them out a few miles on the northwest trail, and you and the rest of the men kill them at the normal spot."

Thaidon looked her in the eyes, holding her chin up to do so, "Good girl, and if you don't do it exactly that way?"

She glared straight back at him, "Then Morhan will kill Yaughtie at sundown."

Chapter 11

The group found a flat piece of ground just outside of the town to the east after Chessington had scouted around for it as well as the usual checking for Chiloes. They set camp and turned in giving the appearance to the children of all things being well. Soon after the children were asleep, the rest of the group sat at the back of the cart to formulate a new plan for the morning.

"Modinay," Vastion asked, "do you know of anyone else who knows how to get us up the mountain?"

Modinay shook his head, "I didn't even know her. It's been fifteen years you know."

"I know," Vastion replied, "but there's always hope. Any suggestions?"

"Yeah," Malden answered, "we forget 'bout her an' do it ourselves. We at least have a chance that way. We don't know how many guys they got, what they got fer weapons, where they're hid, nothin' but we're supposed ta walk inta a trap."

Ghalkin spoke next, "Then what route would you take, how would you climb it, how do we get our things up with us, and who would lead? Not to mention any troubles which might lay in the path we do not know about. I believe she does know how to get us there. From the sounds of what

Chessington and Violta described, she wants them around just about as much as we do."

"You're asking us to get rid of them then." Vastion wondered, "We know nothing about them. We could be setting ourselves up to be in more trouble than before. We caught a few breaks with the highwaymen before Maldow, but this would be as if we were the attackers."

"Yes," Ghalkin nodded, "we need to go down a trail, with or without Baydowa, and it will be guarded by murderers. We have to go that way anyhow. Just because she is not with us, they will know as soon as we are gone, we went to the mountains. I do not want to be looking over our shoulders for them for a week and possibly more after we get down from it as well."

"That's pretty cold blooded." Bansinghaim added to his fellow councilman, "You're talking about murdering them just the same as they would to us. I understand the circumstances are quite different, but it's still killing them when another answer might work better."

"You wanna stay outta a fight?" Malden raised an eyebrow, "Ya look fer fights ever' other time! What makes this so special?"

"First off," The Royal Knight Protectorate explained, "we have a woman and children present. Second, we have enough time to consider a plan B. And third, we don't know what we're headed for."

Vastion pondered a moment, "Chessington, could you find a way of seeing what their numbers are, maybe snoop around and get a little more of an idea what we're looking at if we head up the road tomorrow with Baydowa?"

"Yes Sir." replied the Wizard, dropping off immediately.

"Violta," Ghalkin asked, "could you tell us what he sees and hears, please."

"Certainly," the petite Doltist answered, "he seems to be trying Baydowa's house first."

"Logical," Malden nodded his approval, "the only real place ta start I guess."

"He's inside," she informed them, "I see four, no five men sitting at a table drinking."

Gurlig whined, sighing heavily at the thought of drinking with other men.

"I doubt you'd want to join them." Bansinghaim told the dog.

Violta continued, "I see three other men, and Baydowa serving them more hard spirits. Now she's going down a set of stairs, and we see another woman a little younger than Baydowa, but not nearly as toned or masculine."

Vastion chuckled to himself, "That would be tough for any woman to duplicate."

Malden agreed, "She can get yer attention though."

Bansinghaim nodded, "That's very true."

Violta shook her head, "I see men all agree on some things out here."

"Yeah," Malden confirmed, "we're good at it."

Violta went on with her dialog for the group, "She's explaining to her sister she has a plan to get rid of the men, and they can be free or die trying. She will not let children die for them. Besides, they both agree this has gone on long enough, and they will be free either way after this trip. For now the younger one is to act like nothing is wrong, and she will hopefully be back later if things work out well."

Vastion smiled for the first time in this discussion, "Good, this could work out well for us then. She wants them gone. We don't want to have them around either, but the one thing still left unknown is what is she thinking?"

Malden asked, "Do we let her take us a half mile inta the mountains an' then tell her we know all 'bout it?"

"No," Ghalkin answered, "she would have too many questions we could not answer just yet. I do agree, however, we should go ahead with this plan as it is thus far."

"I'm not sold on that just yet." The General told them, "It still comes down to us being led towards a slaughter whether we are aware of it or not."

Chessington sat back up in his body and looked around at the group assembled, "Miserable people there. They were rude and disrespectful to Baydowa and even each other. She really hates it there. You can tell."

Gurlig let out a howl and stared at Chessington intently.

Chessington relayed on to the group, "He says we should find a way to reduce their numbers before the confrontation on the trail. Like trapping a creature when you're in the wild, but more permanently."

Vastion wondered, "And how would we do that from behind. They'll be ahead of us the whole time."

Chessington explained, "He and I go now to get ahead of them and set a couple of simple traps to get rid of three or four of them. Then we return to the group just before we go to Baydowa's at sun up."

Ghalkin looked at him, "The two of you can do that?"

Modinay turned away from the group and spoke mostly to himself, "Fantastic, the dog has a plan. Of course, he does. Why are we bothering to discuss this? Let's just ask the dog."

Malden laughed loudly as the rest of the group tried to hold back what Malden could not.

Bansinghaim stated coolly, "He's a very gifted dog."

"I see." The former precinct chief nodded, "I guess I'm ready as ever for this. Why is the dog gifted?"

Vastion looked at Chessington and told him, "You take him and go on ahead. Do what ever you need to and return as quickly as you can." Then turning to Modinay he explained, "The dog is Gurlig."

"I see the resemblances." Modinay mocked dryly, "Anything else?"

Vastion continued, "After Chessington helped Gurlig escape from your precinct, Violta joined them outside of Derenta to give him an appearance that would fool you."

Modinay laughed, "That it did, but I thought the boy couldn't do too much without alerting your enemy about it?"

"He can't," Vastion agreed, "but Chessington could aid Violta, and I don't even pretend to understand how it works, so with his boost in energy, she could transform Gurlig without the Chiloes knowing about it."

Modinay's head fell into his hands.

Malden confirmed Vastion's explanation, "He's right. That's exactly how it happened."

"I believe you." The ex-Chief admitted, "That's why I'm so confused. I'm believing in the fact a boy Wizard and a vegetation girl can transform a man into a dog and then converse with the dog to gather a plan."

"Technically," Bansinghaim corrected him, "only Chessington can converse with him, because Violta can't read our thoughts from these types of trees."

"Now what could I have been thinking." Modinay asked himself, "That just goes without saying I suppose."

"Hey," Malden put a hand on the Chief's shoulder, "believe me, we do know what it sounds like. Vastion had the same problem right after we first met back up. He's good with it now though. You will be in a while as well."

Modinay shook his head back and forth with a blank expression, "It's just all too strange, but it's all too true as well."

Violta interrupted, "Chessington and Gurlig are at the first spot to trap them."

Vastion wrinkled his brow, "Already?"

Violta nodded, "Chessington bent time a little, and they can move in a different dimension then we normally do. It is a little hard to explain, and he can only do it in short bursts with a person or two with him. The amount he can take with him is limited; otherwise, he could do it with the whole group."

"It's very late," Vastion reminded them, "I would guess we have about four or five hours until we need to be at Baydowa's house at sun up. Violta, could you give rest to us and communicate fully with Chessington at the same time?"

"I was before," she answered, "but I would have to stop to tell you if he wanted to say something to you or you to him. I have to ignore all things outside of me and go into my mind for both. That is how I can help you sleep while I talk to Chessington."

Vastion nodded, "Let's each take a turn resting until Chessington and Gurlig return. Then we'll head to Baydowa's house, but I think the rest of us not resting with Violta should figure out exactly what to do when the attack comes on the trail."

Malden laid down in the back of the cart and waited for the girl to lay her petite hand on his forehead. Meanwhile Vastion, Ghalkin, Bansinghaim, and Modinay tried to figure out a plan to defeat the attackers without tipping off Baydowa.

"I think," Vastion answered, "we should do pretty much the same as the last time. Let Ghalkin shoot a couple and reduce them even further. Once he does this the odds could turn to our favor especially if Gurlig's traps work to eliminate a few of them to begin with."

Modinay was not as optimistic as the General seemed to be, "It's hard to take a plan which uses words in it such as *if* and *could*. It makes for a lot of adlibbing at the final attack."

Ghalkin threw in, "We could see how many of them Gurlig's traps take out, then stop and form a plan just before the attack."

"What about the guide?" Bansinghaim wondered, "If we create ripples in the plan she already has without filling her in, she could abort her plan and in an attempt to save her sister simply turn us over to the attackers. She might figure living to fight another day is preferable to waiting for the outcome. If we start killing her gang, she might get concerned the head of the murderers would think it came from her. The biggest concern for her right now is her sister, and she'll do anything to help her. She's already shown that."

"Very good point." Modinay agreed, "Also, if we do win and eliminate all of the gang, we would have to return to this town to rescue her sister. I doubt she'll just keep going with her sister being held by someone who has been given orders to kill her if things go wrong. We'll lose our guide anyways after the last bandit falls."

"I feel we're wasting another day then." Vastion replied, "We'll only be a single day ahead of the invasion of Bollantoda."

"One day or ten," Ghalkin told him, "it seems once we take to the mountains the Chiloes are not an issue for a while. Once we head from the mountains to Bontu in Iclania, then we can concern ourselves with them again."

"You're probably right." Vastion agreed, "It is hard to head into the mountains and not have any idea of how to get back out of them."

"Things seem to right themselves." Bansinghaim added, "I agree with Ghalkin. Something's moving us into the correct positions to succeed. I certainly don't want to get lazy and rely on these forces, but I think more is going on here than we know about."

Malden joined the group, "Who's next?"

"I'll go." Ghalkin stood to move over to the cart, "How are Chessington and Gurlig doing, Violta?"

"They are headed to the third trap site." She updated them, "The first two are complete. They hopefully will be on time."

Ghalkin took his turn as the other three men informed Sir Malden on there plan for the morning.

He thought about it for a second or two to add, "It has a lot a holes in it, but I doubt that could be helped under these kinds a circumstances. I got one question though, after we get back an' get rid a this guy who's holdin' the sister hostage, how 're we gonna convince the guide ta take us back ta the cave in the mountain top? She's gonna wanna get her sister set up an' looked after considerin' she's been a victim fer so long."

The other three looked at each other a moment, "I suppose we'll have to level with her. Tell her the truth." Bansinghaim reasoned, "I don't know how else we get her to come away from the town."

"If we do that," Vastion added, "she won't let her sister stay behind. We'll have two more to the group instead of just Baydowa."

Bansinghaim shrugged, "Maybe she's meant to join us as well. All things considered, it seems to point that way."

Vastion showed his concern on his face as well as in his voice, "I'm not happy about adding two more people and losing a full day besides."

Modinay stated as a mater of fact, "Do you see a different solution coming to light, General?"

"No," Vastion admitted, "and that bothers me also."

The men started setting up the pots and pans necessary for the breakfast Ghalkin would start cooking as soon as he awoke. Bansinghaim checked the horses and Malden joined him checking the cart as well. Vastion sat thinking over and over about the plan, or rather the lack of a true plan, trying to find something to streamline any part of what they had talked about. Modinay replaced Ghalkin on the back of the cart as Ghalkin started to pull out the ingredients for breakfast in preparation to make the meal.

After Modinay had finished his rest, Vastion took his turn, followed by Bansinghaim. Once the large knight had rested fully, they all started to file in for breakfast while Violta went to get Preda and Palton to start their day. Preda noticed Chessington missing as well as the absence of Gurlig who she really enjoyed after he had been transfigured.

She looked at Violta to ask, "Where are Chessy and Gurlig?"

The Doltist smiled, "They have been doing a few things tonight but they are almost back."

"Oh." The small girl stated, and headed off for the back of the cart the group had come to know as the place the food was laid out at after it was ready to dish up.

True to Violta's statement, Chessington and the bloodhound returned just before breakfast was completed. Ghalkin served Gurlig a plate of food and Chessington seated himself down between General Vastion and Sir Malden.

"Do you feel pretty secure these will help?" Vastion asked the boy Wizard.

"I'm sure they will, General." Chessington answered him, "They all seem to be traps Gurlig had used for animals in the past, but now we just made them bigger with the exception of one he used for deer. I had a little help conversing with a few new friends as well."

Malden wondered, "There's people out there?"

"No," Chessington admitted, "Three bears, two deer, a family of skunks, and a moose."

Malden laughed, "When'll I get used ta this stuff?"

"How would they help?" Modinay asked.

Chessington replied, "With lifting certain things, and I asked if they could help by making sure all of the men I had described stayed on the trail and none of them could turn around to come back to town."

Modinay looked at him wide eyed, "And they agreed? How would they understand not to attack us?"

"Oh, they understand." Chessington admitted, "I set images of us in their minds as not to harm and images of the gang of thieves as those to keep on the path."

Modinay asked, "Why don't you just have the animals attack the gang as they ride out?"

"Because," he explained, "these men are dangerous not only to us, but they wouldn't think twice before killing one of them either. It's our fight, not theirs."

"I see your point." Modinay revealed, "It really wouldn't be moral that way."

"My thinking is getting to you men I see." Violta smiled to the group, "You see animals a little differently now."

They all pitched in and broke camp getting the supplies put back and ready on the cart they were quite confident they would not have for much longer.

After mounting up they headed towards Baydowa's home a few blocks away. She was already out front and added a few items the others were sure were simply for show and mounted up on her own horse.

"Are you ready?" She asked.

Vastion moved up to be riding next to her and confirmed, "I believe we are. Lead on."

They started down the trail which at the beginning was as wide as two carts and resembled more of a seldom used road than a mountain trail. Vastion signaled for Malden to come to the front with Baydowa while he returned back to be next to Chessington.

The General leaned closer to the teen, "Can you pop off and see how your traps are doing?"

"Yes Sir." And he was gone.

Malden was trying to talk to Baydowa to keep her from checking back to see Chessington looking asleep on his mount. This would cause too many questions they were not ready to answer as of yet.

Chessington popped back, "The first trap is about five minutes ahead. It killed one man on the spot leaving seven to continue on. We need to slow down a little though, they haven't reached the second trap just yet, and they lost some time deciding to go on after the first one."

"Will we see the effects of your trap as we ride by?" Vastion asked.

"No," He replied, "they cleaned up the mess by throwing the log off to the side of the road and moving the body fifty feet or so back into the trees."

"Good friends, I see." Vastion added, "How soon until they get to the second one?"

"They should be there in about ten minutes." The Wizard stated, "We need to really slow down though. We'll catch up to them before they get to their third trap otherwise."

"Alright," Vastion nodded, "I can slow us down." He moved up to Baydowa and explained, "We seem to have a problem with the cart. Let's hold up for a few minutes, so we can fix it before it becomes a real problem."

Baydowa sighed her concern, "Alright." She stopped, not at all happy at the delay one bit. She had to be at a certain place at generally the correct time or they would think she was not being honest again.

She watched Vastion, Bansinghaim, Ghalkin, and Modinay caring for the cart. After seeing the better part of an hour roll by she finally went back to see how the repairs were going.

"Are we about ready?" Her impatience was showing on her face and in her tone, "We're no where near as far as we need to be to get to the site of the first night's camp."

Vastion smiled, "I believe we're ready."

"Good," She exclaimed, "Wake the boy and let's get moving."

After Chessington returned they all remounted and continued on down the road. Chessington leaned over to Vastion who was again riding next to him and informed him, "They are done with the final trap. There are four left and they still think they can use the element of surprise to defeat us. I'll need to leave one more time to see how they're grouped after we pass the area of the third trap."

"Can you explain the traps to me?" Vastion asked, "It seems we have the time."

Chessington stated, "Sure, the first was easy. We stood a log up next to a boulder and attached a trip branch at the bottom. When a horse tripped the branch the log fell on the first man knocking him off his mount, crushing a good part of him."

"That would take some luck to hit the right spot." Vastion added.

Chessington disagreed, "Not the way Gurlig showed me to set it up. It would only not work if you knew it was there."

Vastion asked, "And the second trap?"

"That one required more work." Chessington admitted, "We dug a hole straight down the middle of the path, more like a trench. Then we filled it with pitch and water, lots of pitch. The horses weren't ready for the change of footing and fell. The horses were fine, no harm to them, but one of the men was crushed under the weight of his horse, and another was killed by landing directly on the top of his head. Both died instantly."

"And the third trap?" Vastion asked.

"This one needed a little help." Chessington grinned, "Do you remember the bears I told you about?"

"Yes." Vastion remembered.

"Well, I asked the biggest one to stay back about thirty yards or so," he continued, "but to roar as loud as he could after they reached a certain point. Gurlig told me a bear roaring would spook horses every time. It did and they reared up, knocking two more off. One man fell under the feet of the horse behind him, and it trampled him to death, while the other thrown man only broke his left arm just above the wrist."

"So we have four men left," the General summarized, "and one of them has a broken arm."

"Correct." Chessington agreed, "the last I saw they were headed on and stopped at a spot where there were rock formations close to the road placing two on each side, but the one on the side with the man with the broken arm is busy trying to use a couple of sturdy branches to get the guys arm straight and tied up."

"How long until we get to them?" Vastion wondered.

"I would guess half an hour." Chessington answered.

"Can you let me know when we get to the last spot where a dead man is off to the side?" He asked.

"Yes," Chessington nodded, "That's only about twenty minutes ahead."

"Good." Vastion went back to be deep in his own thoughts as they rode, quiet and introspective. He thought of how exactly to reveal certain things to Baydowa and how to make her believe he was first of all on her side, and second how he knew the things he knew."

Chessington pulled along side and closer to the General, "Alright, he's off to the right side after we turn the next bend up ahead."

Vastion straightened and called ahead to Baydowa, "I believe we need to stop and have a discussion as a group."

"It can wait for an hour or two," Baydowa quipped harshly, obviously consumed in thought and reflection, "then we can stop for lunch."

"No," Vastion pulled the group for a stop, "We stop and talk now."

Chapter 12

Baydowa pulled into the group glaring at General Vastion and feeling the pressures of needing to move on. She knew what would happen if one of them were left alive to return back to Bollantoda and her sister Yaughtie. She absolutely had to have her vague plan work or her sister would pay.

"What is this stop about?" Baydowa asked, the anger showing on her face.

Vastion took a moment and sighed heavily, "We know what's ahead."

Baydowa, being caught completely off guard, asked, "What would be up ahead?" Trying to salvage her plan through innocent appearances and deception.

"We have reduced their numbers from eight to four." Vastion continued, choosing not to waste the time arguing with the guide, "We set up a few traps which killed four of them already, and we know they're set up around the next bend."

"How could you have known?" Baydowa asked.

Modinay answered for them, "They have ways that would take too long to explain, but in truth they do. Besides, you know already by what he says that he does know."

Ghalkin added, "We also know you had a plan to do the same thing. Like you, we have no plan to harm your sister, or let anyone else harm her."

"How could you…" Baydowa was panicking, her mind spinning and scrambling.

Vastion finished the information part of this discussion, "Tell us your plan."

"What plan?" She was still disoriented. Finally, after seeing no other option, she leveled with them. "Fine, I was going to get them to kill only the ones of you who were the fighters. After that I would turn them against each other. They seem to be at a point where Thaidon is being challenged for leadership from Baidon, his younger brother."

"Ah, a family business." Malden added.

Baydowa continued on, "They've been fighting for a few months. The group appears to be split four for Thaidon, four for Baidon, and Morhan back at the house not taking sides. I was going to have them fight it out between themselves here in front of you and your friends. I would not have allowed them to hurt the children or the lady, whether you decide to believe me or not."

"We do." Vastion noted, "We know you don't like doing what you do. For now we need to make a plan to kill them and not us as we turn the next bend."

Baydowa, getting her thoughts about her, stated, "That depends on which of them are left."

Chessington spoke next, "The one you were at dinner with last night is dead. He's off to the right a few yards behind a large rock. The other three are behind us off in the bushes in the same way."

She went to confirm what Chessington had told her and found Thaidon, dead and bloodied, exactly the way Chessington had stated. Returning to the group, she asked, "How exactly did you know that? You couldn't have done it yourselves. That would have been impossible."

"We have our ways," Vastion told her soothingly, "but at the moment we need a plan before they get more suspicious. Can you describe each member of the group to Chessington here?" Pointing at the teen.

"I can." She answered, "There's a man with very dark eyes and a thick mustache, and a long scar on his left side just under his eye. That's Baidon."

Chessington left momentarily and reopened his eyes, "He's up ahead on the left side of the road."

Baydowa seemed skeptical but continued on, "Jinto has green eyes, light colored hair and a brown button up shirt with a big hole under the pocket."

"He's alive too." Chessington answered, "He's the one with the broken arm."

She looked at Vastion, "He's on Baidon's side. How about a man with no hair and really large ears?"

Chessington searched and returned again, "He's dead, he was the first to die."

"And a man with a full beard and no mustache?" She continued.

Chessington did not need to leave this time, "He's up ahead next to the man with the broken arm on the right side of the trail."

She nodded, "Those were the ones loyal to Baidon. What does the other man who's next to Baidon look like?"

Chessington left.

Violta picked up for him, "He's short, stocky, and has really large arms, bushy eyebrows and almost no neck."

"Quite a looker." Malden added.

Baydowa nodded. A bit confused the small lady was answering for the teen boy, "That's Renwahl. He was loyal to Thaidon. What plan do you have?" She asked looking to Vastion. She had already determined he was their leader.

"It seems they think they have the element of surprise with them." Vastion paced as he talked, "We should let them think that for a while longer. Ghalkin, can you get behind on one side or the other and eliminate two of them just as we round the corner, before they show themselves?"

Ghalkin thought a second, "I am sure I could. Which side?"

Chessington volunteered, "The right side would be easier. There's a large rock formation twenty feet behind the two on that side."

Vastion looked to Chessington, "Follow him and return as soon as he's in place. You and Violta need to change Gurlig back, and then we'll head in."

Bansinghaim shook his head, "Five fighting men against two, that's not very good odds."

Malden laughed, "Yeah, fer them."

Ghalkin left through the woods with Chessington leading him to the appointed place. Violta picked it up from there, "They're moving like Chessington and Gurlig did last night. He has Sir Ghalkin set up behind the rocks and is returning himself.

Chessington appeared through the brush, "All set, General."

Baydowa wrinkled her brow, "Sir? General? Who are you, and how do you do these things?"

Vastion smiled, "A conversation for another time, I'm afraid. For now our day is full, and we do need to get this over with. Violta get Gurlig back to normal."

The group watched as piece by piece, Gurlig transformed back into himself standing and smiling at everyone as he reappeared. Chessington made sure his clothing was appropriate as his body transformed, and Violta giggled at his insistence. Modinay and Baydowa stared openly as the bloodhound became the scruffy man, but they did not say a word.

"Ahhh yeah," Gurlig sighed, "much better. Hope I ain't gotta go do that again. That's embarrassin'!"

Modinay stared at Gurlig, to which the former drunk replied, "I didn't do it."

Modinay still stuck for words, simply replied, "I believe you."

Vastion, acting as if this was just another day, instructed to the entire group, "Let's mount up and proceed. Chessington, as we get to the corner verify for me that Ghalkin hit his two marks."

Chessington nodded, "Yes Sir."

The General rode next to Baydowa, and Gurlig took the reins of the cart as they continued on to the inevitable meeting ahead. They rounded the corner and saw the rock formations Chessington had told Baydowa of earlier.

Violta informed General Vastion, "Sir Ghalkin hit both marks perfectly, General. They were dead instantly."

"Alright then," Vastion nodded, "let's get this over with."

They proceeded forward and stopped as the two remaining stood, arrows to the ready, and watched as Bansinghaim sliced open the stomach of the short stocky man, leaving Baidon to stare openly at the large group amassed in front of only himself. Ghalkin stood, arrow notched and ready to fly as he saw the only man left of the attackers jump over a large rock behind him and was last seen streaking away back in the direction of Bollantoda.

Baydowa turned her mount and started to follow, afraid he would reach town and warn of what had happened here. She knew what would happen to her younger sister, Yaughtie, should Baidon be allowed to return to the house.

"Stop," Vastion ordered her, "Yaughtie will be safe. Trust me."

Baydowa stopped her mount and looked puzzled at General Vastion, but before she could ask yet another time of how exactly he was so sure of this, she heard the familiar sound of bears. This time though they were attacking.

Vastion turned to Chessington yet again, "What's going on up there."

The boy dropped off and left himself. Violta gave narration to what Chessington saw, "There are two bears mauling Baidon and another one watching them along with other woodland creatures just observing. They have killed him and are now getting disinterested with him since he is not moving any longer. Chessington is telling them he appreciates their help and he considers them as good friends. They can take the bodies if they would like, and we will return to our town and be back to pass through later. They are returning the pleasantries and taking the body as they retreat into the woods."

The group stood in shock and disbelief. They stared at each other and waited for Chessington to return each one thinking about how Baidon had met his death. None of them would miss him, but it would be a horrifying end for a normal human being.

Chessington returned to the traveling party to announce, "You're more than likely glad you didn't see it. They were quick and to the point."

Vastion grabbed a hold of himself mentally to ask, "Now, what is our plan for back at your home?"

* * * * * * *

It had been nearly a week since the attempt to poison Lord Maldifren had been tried, but the Emperor refused to leave his chambers or to eat. Paranoia was taking hold in his brain. He, with the aid from an outside force, was thinking nonstop about how close he had come to being killed by his eldest son all in a power play. He tortured himself over how he had been so careless, so aloof, so trusting. It shocked him it had never happened before. If they could do it so could someone else.

Thank goodness Pazlin had intercepted the plan and stopped it in time. He had butted heads with his old teacher, but he knew now he was the only one he could truly trust. The experience had humbled him. It had made him quieter and more introspective. It was completely quiet when the knock came to his door.

Lord Maldifren paused before asking, "Who is it?"

The old voice of Pazlin returned, "It is I, Your Majesty, Pazlin."

Maldifren's face lifted, "Come."

The old man walked through the door and sat across from the Emperor. He waited for a moment and stated, "There is unfinished business needing your attention."

"Most of it can be handled by my advisors." Maldifren replied, "There is not really anything which only I can decide. Besides, I have not had the stomach to return to my duties just yet. They will have to understand."

Pazlin asked, "When do you see yourself returning? After Mosa is secured? Before the excursion is to take us to the Phanthow? Are you waiting until it is too late and the moment will pass us by?"

Maldifren chuckled a laugh of superiority, "You could not understand what I have to deal with. I may never leave this room. I do not need to see anyone but you, and no one else will need to see me. I have no use for others."

Pazlin stood, "I see you feel staying in here will keep you alive."

Maldifren smiled a contented smile, "Exactly, you can inform me of events that are of concern to me, and I will tell you my decisions for you to carry out."

"And what about your people?" Pazlin asked, "How are they to feel the Empire is doing without seeing their Emperor?"

"Not of my concern," the Emperor smiled, "I have you here to be my champion, and I need nothing else."

"Are you concerned about another attempt on your life?" The old Sorcerer asked.

Maldifren stood, walked over to his desk, and took up a piece of paper, "Absolutely, but I have figured out how to remedy most of that. Read this and tell me what you think."

155

Pazlin knew before hand exactly what it said. He had placed every word into the Emperor's mind, but he read it again anyway to give the appearance of seeing it for the first time. "You have ordered the entire royal family executed. Why?"

"To keep myself alive." Maldifren answered, "Every single one of them has a map to the throne, and unless they are all eliminated, I am not safe. It is them or me, and it will not be me."

"You have your military staff in here as well." Pazlin added, "Are they also a threat?"

"After the royal bloodline is eliminated, they would rule next." Maldifren explained, "It will just be you and me, and after that goes into effect, I will have no reason to doubt anyone. You are the only one I trust anymore, Master Pazlin."

Pazlin smiled to his Emperor, "We will rule well, Your Majesty." Then he turned and left the room.

* * * * * * *

The group stopped just around the corner from the house they had meet Baydowa at the previous evening. They pulled in close together with all eyes on the General.

"Chessington," Vastion asked, "go check the inside. See if it's just the one man and her sister."

"Yes Sir." They had started getting used to seeing him drop off this way and were less and less disturbed by it. Within moments he had returned. "The man seems nervous, checking the windows and pacing around. Yaughtie is still locked downstairs. She seems to be unharmed."

Baydowa looked visibly relieved, "I don't know how you do what you do, but I've seen enough to give this a chance. The best way is to have me sneak in the back while someone keeps Morhan occupied at the front of the house. I kill him, and we set her free. Then I will be happy to guide you wherever you wish after setting her up and making sure she's okay in a few days."

Vastion started to explain further, "That's another thing you should be told. We will need to leave tomorrow morning."

Baydowa refused, "Out of the question. My sister has been locked up in that basement for two years. She has to be taken care of first. Surely you could wait a few days to seek your treasure or whatever it is you want up on that mountain."

"I assure you we aren't after any treasure." Vastion went on, "We're staying ahead of a foreign army which is taking every town on the island and sending the town's people away to the south. If we stay, all of us, including you and your sister, would fall to them and be taken prisoner. She would be free in the mountains but not here."

"How close are they?" The guide asked.

"Tomorrow we know they will still be getting ready outside of town," Vastion answered, "after that we just don't know."

Baydowa was trying to think quickly. It was true she had seen enough to know these people were genuine about what they had said up to this point. "Then I will go with you in the morning as long as Yaughtie comes as well."

Vastion smiled, soft and grateful, "Absolutely, but first we need to get her out."

Baydowa, Bansinghaim, and Modinay walked to the back of the house from behind the street and through the grounds of the home behind Baydowa's. Chessington was overseeing the grounds and reporting back to Violta. Ghalkin had his bow ready, with General Vastion, and Violta to his right in that order. Gurlig stayed behind at the corner with the children, and kept the mounts ready just in case something went awry.

Violta passed Chessington's information on to the General, "He sees us and has an arrow pointed at us through the open window in the front."

General Vastion quietly motioned for the three to stop, "Morhan, we've come for the girl. You can give her to us, or we can take her. It's up to you."

Morhan screamed back to the street, "I'll kill her, I truly will! I ain't afraid ta kill a girl, see!" An arrow flew directly at Violta too fast for her to move away from. The tiny Doltist was struck through the chest and pinned to the fence behind her.

Ghalkin and Vastion turned to see her stuck, but heard the door slamming to the house. Morhan walked behind the human shield of Yaughtie across the front porch. Knife to her throat.

"Can you get a shot?" General Vastion asked his fellow councilman.

Ghalkin explained, "Not really, she's covering too much of him."

Morhan yelled to the two in front of him, as the three from behind appeared out the front door, "Everyone stop! Drop all your weapons or she dies!"

The group saw no other options. They knew he would do it, and they knew it would be quick. They lowered their weapons to see his arm pull away from Yaughtie and watch him fall dead to the ground.

Baydowa ran to her sister, who was still adjusting her eyes to the daylight. The rest ran to Violta. Chessington was the first to appear at the site of the small Doltist. She had the arrow stuck into her chest and coming out the back of her into the fence.

Violta put her hands to her hips, "Would you all stop staring and get me unattached from this fence!"

Vastion paused a second, "Aren't you hurt?"

"I only look like a human," she explained, "remember. I have no internal organs and no blood, just sap. I'm more closely related to trees than any of you. Now please, get me off of this fence!"

Bansinghaim pulled the arrow first out of the fence and then out of the woman. She straightened her dress and fixed the hole in her outfit where the arrow had gone through in both the front and the back. After which they watched her walk calmly over to Baydowa and her newly freed sister.

"I ain't never gettin' used ta this." Malden shook his head.

158

Baydowa was speaking to her little sister, who appeared to be in her early twenties about three or four years younger than her sister, "It's over, we're free of them Yaughtie. I have to tell you to trust me though. These people want to get out of here tomorrow morning and head up Mt. Bollantoda."

General Vastion moved up to them, "I'm afraid it's worse than that. We need to leave now."

"No," Baydowa replied, "she can't be hurried so much."

Yaughtie looked at her sister and replied, "I'm okay. Whether we leave tonight or tomorrow won't make any difference. I've slept on the cold basement floor for so long just being out and in the fresh air is a treat."

"It's my fault we need to leave so soon." Chessington admitted to Yaughtie, "I killed Morhan. I was reading his thoughts, and he was seconds from hurting you. I had to do something and I filled his lungs with sand. I had to move his arm back first, so he didn't cut you while falling."

Baydowa wrinkled her brow again and exclaimed, "You did what? I've seen many strange things since you people came to my door, but how could you fill his lungs with sand when you were asleep in the back of the cart?"

Chessington tried his best to make the two women understand without the aid of knowing from the start, "I have certain abilities like leaving myself to spy elsewhere and seeing others thoughts. I can do those without our enemies detecting our whereabouts, but what I did with the sand in his lungs is most definitely traceable. They now know where we are, and I'm certain they will speed up their attack on the town."

"They want you that badly?" Baydowa asked.

Vastion answered for him, "Yes, they do. Take ten to fifteen minutes to get anything you need on the back of the cart from the house, then we have to go into the mountains."

The two women went back into the house to retrieve anything they could not live without: changes of clothing, extra boots, and extra mountain gear. Chessington made a second cart to carry the extra items as well as the newest member of the party. Gurlig drove the cart using his horse and another which was in the stable off to the east side of the house.

After only ten minutes, the sisters returned to place their belongings into the back of the new cart and get themselves into position to ride off with the group they had known nothing of just one short day before.

Chapter 13

The trail wound around the foothills of the mountain range, bumpy and narrowing as they moved onward. After the first twenty minutes past the failed attack site, the trail narrowed down to a point where the cart could not turn around without help except in a handful of places. No one was interested in turning back around as there was nothing behind them to go back for. Ahead would be the only direction to keep this group of twelve safe any longer.

Chessington had been out of body searching around the area for Chiloes and others who might not be a welcome sight. He finally returned to report to General Vastion, "I see no sign of anyone else around us for miles and miles except back at the town. The Chiloes are forming their lines around the city and are actually at the beginning of the trail at this very moment. They have orders to take the town in the morning, but they aren't coming into these mountains."

Vastion wondered, "That makes no sense to me. They have to think of this area as a viable escape for us. Are you sure they felt you back there?"

"They had to have." Chessington answered, "If they have the ability, what I did was definitely on the list of things which are traceable."

"I don't care why they ain't chasin' us," Malden added, "at this point we need ta feel safe fer the first time since the Woods."

Baydowa looked puzzled again, "Could someone explain to us what is happening, and how you people know and do what you seem to be doing?"

Vastion looked at the sky and pondered how best to answer, "We seem to be far enough away from the Chiloes and Bollantoda to stop for the evening. We've all had a pretty full day and a good rest at the beginning might just help keep us fresh. Gurlig and Ghalkin can start dinner while the rest of us try to make our two new members believe what we have to tell them."

Modinay sat next to Yaughtie with Baydowa beside her. He was still trying to understand things as well. If one thing being a law man had taught him, it was to listen to as much information as you can. After the introductions were completed, seeing them find it hard to believe they were among royalty, the story began. Chessington started with the foreign men coming to the farm house and being asked to leave after getting unruly.

Then Bansinghaim described how the same men tried to assassinate the Prince, Eltiph, and himself, only to have one of them escape and to return to the farmhouse, kill the farmer and his wife, and set fire to the home.

Vastion told them of what had happened to Ghalkin and himself on their journey east of Phenderia City, and how they had met Gurlig, all the way from sobering him up through the finding of Jissar and the traveling through and around conquered towns.

Malden explained to them how the Prince, Chessington, Preda, Bansinghaim, and himself had fled through the tunnel system under the castle, how they had traveled through the Woods of the Doltists, and afterwards on to Marroda where they met back up with Ghalkin, Vastion, and now Gurlig as well.

Chessington described the battle outside of Marroda and how they had been thought to be dead by their enemies. After which he told of how they had fallen back into the Woods of the Doltists to regroup and see what would be next for them. There they were instructed to have Violta come with them, and he described a bit about how the Doltist community lived and what they were, but also how the energy was a part of them just as it was a part of him now.

Vastion took them through Maldow and the troubles with both the highwaymen and then the town's folk afterwards. He described how things went in Derenta and about Modinay becoming the newest member before themselves.

"And I believe you already know what happened from there to this point." Vastion finished. "Any questions?"

Baydowa started to say something and stopped. Then thinking again she asked, "So now you need to get to the cave in the mountain, but then what?"

Chessington answered, "Then we check the book again. I have to go there to find something, something I'll need to know or have in the future."

Yaughtie, who had been relatively quiet up until this point, asked her sister, "Why do you believe them? This is absolute lunacy. We go from murderers and thieves to a group of insane people, who are mostly foreign, and they believe in magic and ghosts. We need to return home."

"I've seen enough to believe them and their far fetched story of magic and ghosts." Baydowa replied, "Chessington saw us last night when I told you I had a plan. He also saw ahead on the trail this morning and told me things he couldn't have possibly known. We all saw Morhan drop dead with no one around, and he conversed with bears to kill Baidon."

Chessington interrupted, "I didn't tell them to kill him. They did that on their own. They've actually been following us ever since we entered the trail."

Yaughtie looked at him, "Of course, you say that. How can we prove it?"

Chessington grinned, "I know a way."

After a few seconds three brown bears started to appear over the ridge to the right of the trail they were on. Walking slowly and methodically they approached the camp the dozen in the party were staying at.

Chessington met them at the edge of their camp and mentally conversed with them for about a full minute. After which he returned to the center of the group with the biggest of the three in tow.

"He's curious about you." The Wizard told them, "He's going to smell each of you and then be on his way. He's curious as to which smells are from which bodies."

The bear moved up close to each of the petrified members and smelled them closely, matching an aroma with a person. Once he was done, he looked at Chessington, who grinned and held back a laugh, only to return to his friends and the three could be seen lumbering just as slowly as before back into the forest they called home.

Violta smiled a slight smile and caught Chessington's eye. "He is right you know."

Chessington blushed a solid red from the neck up.

Vastion asked, "What was that all about?"

Chessington answered, "He said we were all too clean smelling, and it wasn't natural for us to be this washed."

Violta smiled and told him, "Tell them the rest."

Chessington sat quietly, not wishing to elaborate.

Violta, hands behind her back, bouncing up and down on her toes while grinning, finished for him, "He told our good Wizard here his *mate* smelled differently than the rest of you."

Chessington embarrassed, corrected her, "He didn't use the word *mate*."

Violta looked indignant, "He most certainly did. It was not a word, but it most definitely meant *mate*."

Bansinghaim smiled, "Careful boy, whichever way you go with this, you'll lose at some level."

The group was lighter in spirits now and Yaughtie now had her proof Chessington was what they had said. Dinner was served and they had a relaxing meal for the first time in a long while.

* * * * * *

Pazlin paced back and forth in his study waiting for Grastock to arrive as he had communicated to him to do. He was troubled slightly and feeling confused as his number one Adherent came through the door.

"You called for me, My Master?" Grastock greeted.

"Yes," Pazlin stated going straight into his reason for calling him, "I am sure you felt it, too, but the Wizard I saw die on the Island of Mosa still lives. I have no explanation how, but he most definitely does."

"I felt him too, Master." Grastock reaffirmed.

Pazlin continued, "I am thinking of sending Phosting up from Phenderia City to catch him once he comes out of those mountains. He could be to the northern side of the range by morning." Pointing to the map he had laid out on his desk.

"Master, why do you not believe he is still in Bollantoda?" Grastock wondered, "He could feel there are no adherents close and make a stand in the town keeping it safe for a while."

"No," the old Sorcerer disagreed, "he knows more than I have given him credit for. He knows he could not hold the town for long by himself, besides, he would have done that somewhere along the line before this. There are too many towns between Maroda and Bollantoda for him to have just decided to make this one his final stand."

"So he is just hiding from us?" Grastock asked.

"That," Pazlin noted, "and somehow either he realizes we cannot go into those mountains, or someone is helping him."

Grastock looked confused, "I thought no one with ability could enter them."

"Actually," Pazlin explained, "only we from this side of the Great Beyond cannot go there. There seems to be five places we have no ability from the energy at on the western side, two on the Island of Mosa and three on the mainland. The other on the island is the forest known to them as the Woods of the Doltists."

Grastock was still confused, "Why, I find it unimaginable I could not find energy somewhere to manipulate into how I choose?"

"It was one of the safeguards My Master, Rustaph, placed when creating the Great Beyond." Pazlin clarified, "You remember the story. It was at the same time he gave them fertile land."

Grastock was starting to understand, "And he erased us from their minds."

Pazlin sighed, "No, I did that. They would have found out just how weak we were and attacked us for our land. They had many more people, especially men, after the two great armies were killed by my Master and Feachen. I did it to help save us. The rulers in those days were stupid, self-serving, and arrogant. The West wanted to enslave us. Take us to do their labor for them. That was why Feachen killed my Master. Rustaph was the only one great enough to keep the West away. Feachen was stupid and violent."

"It was good you were there, Master." The foremost Adherent praised.

"Yes, it was, Grastock." Pazlin admitted, "We stand poised to return the favor now. The first shipment of slaves from Phenderia should be arriving within the month. The beginning of the new era is starting."

"And Lord Maldifren?" Grastock asked.

"He is as good as dead." Master Pazlin seemed to sneer, "After three thousand years of manipulating those idiots, it is almost over. He is the only one left now of his line, and he will not be much longer. The best part is, it will seemingly be by his own hand. The fool will hang himself before sunset tomorrow. His mind is a mess. He is completely withdrawn, and he has no way to recover. I will step in, no one would dare challenge me for the leadership. I would kill them if they did, so my plan is finally in its proper stages after all these years."

Grastock could see Pazlin sliding back to an earlier memory and deciding to redirect the conversation, he asked, "And as to the Wizard on the Island of Mosa, My Master?"

"Ah, yes," the old Sorcerer pondered, "our friend the Wizard. Well, a wizard has never been a match for a sorcerer, history has proven that. Phosting will wait him out to the north of the mountains, but you made a good point about Bollantoda. We will send Narrol there. He is with the front line army attacking anyhow. We wait at both sides and see what happens."

* * * * * * *

The group awoke refreshed and ready for further travels once the morning came. Once breakfast had been served, eaten, and cleaned back up again, the party continued on down the trail with Baydowa leading next to General Vastion, Chessington and Prince Palton riding behind them, and the older cart driven by Sir Ghalkin with Violta and Preda riding along after them. The second cart driven by Gurlig with Yaughtie and now Malden as riders followed with by Sir Bansinghaim and Chief Modinay to the rear.

The weather was slightly drizzling for the first time in the little more than two weeks they had spent on the run. Clouds had concealing the sun ever since the later part of the previous night.

The ground, being dry from the past weeks of clear weather and sunshine, soaked up the light amount of water landing over it almost as quickly as it hit the ground. The slight dampness was most refreshing as the temperatures from the last few days were going up as they will at the beginning of summer.

The mood of the travelers was refreshed and light as well. Chessington reporting every hour news of the Chiloe Army and how they were in fact taking Bollantoda as they rode, but had no interest in going after them into the mountains.

"I would guess," General Vastion theorized, "they won't come into the mountains until they can't find Chessington in town anywhere. It'll be quite interesting to see what they plan on doing. It really wouldn't take a brilliant mind to come into these mountains to look for him."

"They stay away from here like a cat next to a lake." Chessington told him, "Like they're afraid to enter. Even when they attacked the towns on this side of Derentia they came up from Phenderia and not anywhere near the mountains."

Baydowa asked, "Why do you need to get to the cave in the mountain so badly. Why can't we just get to the coastline and catch a ship for the mainland. It would be much easier to stay hidden where there are more people and more areas to hide."

Vastion answered her, "Queen Rhyshena specifically told us to do things the way the book told us. Right now it says to go to the cave in Mt. Bollantoda. When we get there, it will tell us our next step. It could be here on the Island or to go to the mainland. It could even possibly be doing neither of those things and going in a completely different direction."

She laughed, "We're taking directions from a book which changes? I must be as much of a lunatic as you, but since I see no way out otherwise, and you did most of the rescuing of my sister and me, we'll go along. And incidentally, I also know many other trails in these mountains. I can make sure you have the quickest path to your next step. Not necessarily the safest, but most definitely the quickest."

"I'm not as much of a thrill seeker as I once was, dear lady." Vastion admitted, "Safer might be better than quicker."

"That depends on where you have to go." The guide stated as a mater of fact, "If you choose the wrong town, there is no safe way to go."

"I guess that's a discussion for a later time after we've been in the cave." The General conceded, "How much longer should it take to get there?"

Baydowa thought for a brief moment and answered, "That can also depend."

"You mean on the weather conditions and such." The General replied.

"That too." She answered, "Now it's your turn to think I'm crazy. I've been to the big mountain seven times. Each time you can see the cave entrance, but each time it's in a different spot."

Vastion laughed after a second of contemplation, "Of course, it would be."

They remained silent and smiling, laughing at the newest far fetched reality they had to ponder. A wizard with special powers, a book with a mind of its own, and now a cave entrance which moved from place to place along the side of a mountain. Vastion was astonished this was not easier to understand after the past travels he had to endure.

Baydowa turned to Vastion much more softly than before, not as a hired guide, but as a person making conversation to pass the time, "What do you expect to be the outcome of this?"

General Vastion thought about it. He had not allowed himself to think past the day or two they had to worry about at a time. He then stated in return, "I suppose to defeat the Chiloes, regain Phenderia for ourselves and the many Phenderians who are held, and to go back to the way things were. I'm not sure they can be the way they were though."

A few hours passed, and they stopped for a late lunch after putting quite a distance between themselves and where they had started in the morning at first light. They had taken only one small break at mid morning and were all delighted to stop for a considerable time. Gurlig and Ghalkin set out to find something fresh for lunch. Modinay and Yaughtie built a strong fire together and set a few things close to it, having gotten wet over the travels of the morning. Vastion listened to Baydowa describe how the afternoon trail was to be. Sir Bansinghaim and Prince Palton looked after the horses, and Preda followed them not really helping so much as staying with her friend the Prince. Malden sat next to Violta and the seemingly sleeping body of Chessington, listening as the Doltist told him what Chessington was finding in the surrounding areas and back at the town.

Violta was relaying to him, "The town fell in less than an hour."

Malden responded, "Not surprised. It wasn't all that big ta begin with. 'Re they comin' inta the mountains?"

She thought for a moment and then answered him, "No, they seem to be stationing their men in defensive positions. They don't seem to be coming after us at all. Besides, with the entire Island controlled by them, excluding these mountains and my Woods, they should not have any more places to go to."

"I guess that'd be right." The Librarian stated, "Their work here must be close ta done. 'Re the people still bein' marched south?"

"Yes," Violta confirmed, "they are not pushing them too hard, and they are making sure their health is taken into consideration. Some are not completing the journey, however."

"Ask Chessington ta see where they're bein' driven too." Malden asked her after realizing the gravity of her last statement.

She replied, "That would take a while, even at his speed. He would need about two hours to get back to your capital city and probably much longer to go further south. By then he would have to hunt for them. He would not have any idea where they are unless someone told him exactly."

"I see." Malden replied, "Still, it might be something he could do after dark tonight while the rest a us slept, providin' we're all safe an' sound without any chance a getting' inta trouble. He does come in quite handy at times."

She giggled, "Yes, he does, and he also agrees he should scout around the entire island during the night. Tonight, he'll head south and try to find the population and see what's happening to them."

"Good," Malden nodded, "that could help somehow. If nothin' else we still consider ourselves as leaders. We should at least know where our people are."

Chapter 14

Chessington roamed the southern end of the Island. At the present he
was around Plangibra, an inland town known as a center for lumber from
the hills to its northwest. The town was empty not even the conquering
army was seen anywhere. He searched further to see mostly rats
confiscating food, which had been left behind, and scavenger birds such as
hawks, sea gulls, and crows picking at the dead soldiers littering the ground
where they had fallen weeks ago.

He found himself becoming more and more angered with his enemy
and their complete disregard for others and their lifestyles. His mother, as
well as Uncle Fein and Aunt Rishna, had taught him to be respectful, and it
would take him far in the world. The evil mind he briefly touched outside of
Marroda was disrespectful of everything even those of his own countrymen.

He could never forget the feel of his mind. The arrogance, hatred, and
destruction it desired, were everything he had been consumed with to end
in evil and wrong intentions. This nightmare was horrific, families uprooted,
towns left to rot and decay, but worst of all were the lives which could
never be recovered.

He saw nothing to make him believe any human life existed in the town
of Plangibra. Nothing looked to be inhabited. He decided to press on to
Rajule, just northeast of Lake Baktu. It had been a town of fair size, being
the commercial hub for a very rich agricultural area. Once finished there, he

would need to return back to his group in the mountains of eastern Derentia. He had just enough time.

As he traveled around the lake, he saw a group of Derentians who had stopped to rest for the night. Each was sleeping under a blanket and each had their own pillow as well. From what he saw, they were able to stay in families as they were traveling, but it looked like cattle more than people. None gave the appearance of abuse, but it was still a horrible sight to have to take in. He hovered close to the ground. Guards stationed around the sleeping mass waiting for tomorrow's march. He studied the Guards to see the energy had them held in its clutches. They required no sleep, just as he and Violta, but they had no thoughts or emotions unlike themselves. At one time they were real live men capable of everything others could do. Now, they were little more than puppets of a single puppet master, ready to follow whatever they had been directed to do. He felt some of these men were hundreds of years old, a few over a thousand, but how long had they actually lived? Had they been like this all that time or did they have a personality before the evil master had taken their liberties away.

It was all too sad. He could simply not bare it a moment longer. After turning northward and heading for home, he opened his mind to Violta to give him some comfort after the past evenings revelation.

* * * * * * *

The rains kept coming, usually slow and drizzling, but occasional cloud bursts made for this to be the most trying day to this point. The development of the rains made the traveling sluggish and dreary for the better part of the second day in the hills. The group was for the most part quiet, resolved to just following the trail and winding around the feet of the smaller mountains on their way to the primary. The clouds were heavy and low, making it impossible to see Mt. Bollantoda from here, even though on a mostly clear day, Baydowa knew from experience, it would be visible. The tracks of the carts were getting deeper as the ground softened and the horses needed to rest more often from the effects of the excess pulling.

During one of these rests, Baydowa and General Vastion sat discussing, while Modinay, Ghalkin, Malden, and Bansinghaim looking in on their conversation.

Baydowa was notifying the General as well as the others, "Either late tonight or early tomorrow, we will have to leave the carts and proceed on horseback. I would guess shortly after that, maybe even by tomorrow late afternoon, we will have to set the horses free and hike the rest of the way."

"We knew it was coming." Vastion sighed, "How close will we be to the mountain when we abandon the horses?"

"At the foot of it." The Guide stated, "We will be climbing after that. Gradually at first, but it will get steeper in spots."

Malden asked, "How long ta hike ta the cave?"

She laughed, "It depends on where it is on that set of days."

The Librarian chuckled, "Why da we bother. It could change seconds 'fore we get ta it an' have ta hike fer two more days ta get in."

"It could." She answered, "I've never seen it move, but we could chase it around forever I suppose."

Vastion looked back to where Chessington, Violta, and Yaughtie were sitting with the children, "Chessington, come here please."

Chessington stood and walked to the leaders, "Yes Sir?"

The General asked, "Could you scout ahead and tell us about the mouth of the cave and where it would be today?"

"Sure." Then he sat and dropped off in his now familiar fashion.

Violta moved up to sit and report back as to what was being seen by her new boyfriend, "He sees the cave opening, but it is not the real opening. It is an illusion, and yes it moves from spot to spot, but the real opening is high up and well concealed. He is going in it and seeing a lot of space to the back of the cave, with a single tunnel winding downward and to the back side of the mountain. He believes it to be around fifty miles of winding tunnel, no light, water in four places to drink, and much more friendly to the carts, horses, and the children than this way would be. The turn off for it is just up ahead about eight to ten miles and is quite grown over with brush, but the carts can go over it with some difficulty."

Ghalkin smiled, "Plan B?"

"I think so." Vastion answered, "Do you know of this trail, Baydowa?"

"No," She replied, "I must admit, I thought I knew every trail in all of these mountains, but never one to the back side of the big mountain."

Chessington popped back into himself, "It's well hidden and it really doesn't want to be found."

The guide stared at him, "The trail itself didn't want to be found."

"Yes," the young Wizard confirmed, "it needed to stay hidden all these years so others couldn't find it and go up to the cave. That's also why the tunnel inside the mountain is so long, to discourage people. The good news is, after we enter the cave and get around the first corner, I can do anything with the energy I please completely undetected."

"Good," Vastion smiled, "but how do you know that?"

Chessington grinned, "The cave told me."

Malden was the first to speak after the long pause, "Course it did, how stupid a us. Boy, ya ever think 'bout lyin' ta us? Just tellin' us we wouldn't understand er somethin'."

"Do you want me to?" Chessington smiled.

"Guess not." Malden replied, "We'll just keep gettin' off balance."

"How long from the turn off to the tunnel entrance would you guess?" Vastion asked the teen.

Chessington thought about it and answered, "A full day's ride, I'm sure. The trail isn't as good as this one is until we get inside the mountain. Then it's beautiful, like a new road would feel."

"Gurlig has lunch almost ready." Vastion was talking to the whole group now, "After we're finished, we'll all pitch in to keep going and hopefully tonight will be our last outside in the rain until after the cave."

The group ate quickly, none of them enjoying the constant raining or the dampness of all of their clothing. Things were cleaned up and reloaded onto the respective cart it had come from with the proficiency of ones who had done this many times in the past. As they remounted, Chessington rode up with General Vastion and Baydowa, so he could tell them of the trail he had seen when scouting around.

They reached the turn off after only a little under an hour, but took the next forty-five minutes cutting the growth away so the horses and carts could pass through. Violta understood the need for destroying the brush and bushes as well as a smaller tree, but was not happy it had to be done this way.

Once on the next trail, the brush cleared away and the horses could plod their way through the mud and mire with just slightly more effort than they had on the previous trail. They had moved on down the new trail for almost an hour when General Vastion called for them to stop.

"Look up ahead." He asked the ones closest to him as to not startle it, "I've never seen anything like it."

The entire group had all pulled up to see the beauty and oddity standing off approximately thirty yards in front of them and to the left in a clearing eating tall grasses. It was mostly a mountain goat, but it walked on two legs as much as four. Its head was larger and the horns were not curled around in a circle like the ones they had seen before. Now, looking closer, they saw another full sized one and a baby, assuming this to be a family.

Chessington started to explain, "The female one says there are others like them, mostly on the eastern side of the great mountain. She also tells me they have no reason to harm us and we none to harm them. She understands we are curious, and they are new to us, but they are harmless so long as we continue on our way."

General Vastion agreed, "That, I'm sure, is wise advice. We need to continue on anyways."

They moved further down the trail and spotted more animals, which were not exactly normal to their standards as the group knew. Bears standing on their hind legs and arms almost scraping the ground as they walked. Porcupines with their quills much longer and arrowhead tipped. Deer with enormous antlers and rough fingers instead of hooves. But, by far, the most odd to the group was a single wolf with a shorter snout, hands and feet like a man, and walked erect as a man would.

Chessington told the group these creatures were indigenous to only this mountain and were all quite peaceful, coexisting for thousands of years, each and every one of them herbivores, and none to be meat eaters as their ancestors had been.

Violta explained further, "They are the same as we Doltists are, only slightly different because of certain circumstances. The energy in our woods is more in touch with the vegetation than the animals there and evolved us to what we are. Theirs must be more in tuned to the animal life. Core energy close to the surface of the ground or even exposed in certain spots, expels constant energy which changes things as it sees fit over time."

The group seemed to trust she knew what she was talking about, none being able to dispute anything she had to say. Chessington would have been the only other one there to have been able to know anything on the subject, and he figured she was right. He could see how it had happened this way.

Yaughtie leaned over to her sister, "I don't doubt for a minute any more."

Baydowa stared at the small lady claiming to have come from another species altogether, "I just wish the strangeness would stop. I need a break from thinking like this for a little while."

Bansinghaim interjected to their conversation, "You'll get used to it."

They camped for the night with only an approximate six hours left to their traveling out in the wilderness. General Vastion gave Chessington the task of scouting for Chiloes in the mountains and to see also about the towns to the north, mostly on the Iclanian coastline facing the Straight of Mosa. They may need to get to one of those towns as a way to get to the mainland after leaving the cave.

The tarps were fashioned into tents and the group slept three and four to a tent for the evening on a high spot, which was less soaked than the rest of the area around and harder than the group had felt on previous nights. Preda was ecstatic at sleeping with the two sisters and not having to be with the men for a change.

Chessington did the scouting he was asked to do but conversed with Violta every minute he was out working.

How did you know we were meant to be together? Chessington finally asked her after two hours of them saying nothing in particular.

Violta, preferring the direct, answered him, *I felt it. Did you not feel it too? We clicked together from the first time you entered the Woods, and I realized you were for me after you left to go to Marroda. I felt emptier after you left the Woods. I actually was sad for the first time in ages. I guess I did not feel complete any longer. Once you returned, I was happier than I had ever been in my life. I waited at that part of the Woods the entire time you were gone just hoping to see you again.*

Chessington felt the excitement too, *I guess I was the same way. You were so different and still you were the most beautiful creature I'd ever seen. As a wizard I can see your thoughts and feelings as well as your physical appearance, and I can't find anything I don't like. Does that make sense?*

Perfect sense. She was thrilled this was coming out, *What happens in your culture next then?*

Chessington laughed in his head, *Normally the male, or me, would go see your parents and tell them of his intentions. Once I'd done that, the families would get together to discuss things about the wedding and then a priest would give a ceremony for the couple to be joined. A ceremony would be performed, and they would be married for the rest of their lives. Not all do it this way, but the proper people do. How would Doltist join together?*

We just live together. Violta stated, *We have no need for ceremony. If two wish to be joined, than you join together. It really does not take a third party to make it alright. If the two say they are joined, then they are, and they are joined for life.*

Chessington thought hard, *It's an awfully big step.*

177

Violta replied, *Yes it is, and in our case it would be for a long, long time. I would expect to live for at least hundreds of more years, and you control how long you should live.*

That's all true. Chessington agreed, *Would it bother you if I took a little longer to think about this? We are up to our eyeballs, as my Uncle used to say, in other things at the moment and being joined together would give us only a few more privileges than we already have as a couple.*

Violta whispered just a bit, *I can think of one thing we could share if we joined.*

Chessington was definitely not ready to discuss this with her. His shy upbringing was not even close to ready to converse about the subject of marital relations.

Violta laughed as quietly as she could when she felt the deafening silence coming back at her and saw the slumped over form of her boyfriend blushing to the roots, still seemingly asleep.

* * * * * * *

The group of twelve awoke early the next morning in preparation to start the internal assent to the cave at the top of Mt. Bollantoda. They did take time for a breakfast, however, it was hearty, due to the demands the day would hold. The General decided to start the meal before sunup, have a fast lunch in the late morning, then rest and eat as they wanted with Chessington able to give them the creature comforts they all desired from before the journey once they were all safely inside of the cave.

The rains were harder than ever and the wind was increased as well. The horses would be, for the most part, climbing the gradual slopes for the better part of the afternoon. A long hard day could land them at their destination before they stopped to make camp for the night.

As they pulled out from the campsite, they all formed into the traveling ranks they had been set into the previous two days since the arrival of the two sisters. Chessington was his usual in and out, scouting ahead as well as around for signs of any abnormality.

After a long morning of travel, which lasted for five hours with only two short rests for the horses, they stopped for the speedy lunch Vastion had told them of at breakfast. It was quick and to the point. Chessington scouted ahead and reported back the opening of the tunnel was only a couple of hours away, and they looked to be a little behind schedule, but with any luck they could still have the relaxing evening just a little later than they had originally thought.

Violta decided to converse with Queen Rhyshena, updating her as to the events getting them this far. After the formal report had been given, they talked as a mother would to her daughter. Violta opened, *He does love me. I can tell. It's just so different with a human. He's so slow.*

And he always will be, Violta. Her Queen returned to her, *It is an adjustment you will have to make. He is what he is, and you are as you are. If you changed, he might not find you as desirable as he does now.*

Violta thought about it a moment, *This will be so much work though. Can I really be happy if I have to work so hard to please both of us?*

I believe a better question is, would it be worth having if you did not have to work so hard. The matriarch was getting to her, *He is working, too. On these kinds of matters it is very difficult to see the work the other in the relationship is doing, but it is always far easier to see what you yourself have done. You will find many times when you do not think things are fair, neither will he. Ask yourself this, is he worth the work?*

She thought about the question posed by her queen, and answered confidently, *Yes, he is. I know we belong together, and I want that more than anything, but there is so much work to get us both as a couple thinking close to the same level.*

It sounds like you already have your answer. The Queen noticed, *Now is the challenging part.*

I know. Replied the small Doltist, realizing she was hopelessly in love, *Thank you, Your Majesty.*

A warm feeling was sent to Violta from all those miles away, and afterwards the connection was gone. Violta sat thinking to herself about the boy Wizard who had turned her around from the inside out. She knew he would be slower, less able to see things than she could for a while. She also knew she could not go on without him as her mate. This thought hurt her, but seeing herself without him was not an option. She knew she had to be patient, and they would be together always.

At the same time the young Wizard was out of himself scouting around the area close to the entrance of the tunnel. He already knew it was safe. He more or less wanted some alone time to think. He had a large responsibility to eleven others as well as every person west of the Great Beyond, but it all seemed to pale in comparison to what was at the front of his mind, Violta. She was so beautiful, so vibrant, and most of all caring. She was also pushy and forward at times, but he even admired those qualities about her. Physically she was adorable, whether in her Doltist form or her human one. He found himself thinking of her whenever he was allowed small moments from the reality they were all in. Was this love or the infatuation he had heard Uncle Fein and Aunt Rishna talk about at the table during meals?

He knew he was in over his head, and he needed to speak to someone. He had no way of knowing for sure if Sir Malden had any experience in this matter, but he had a bond with him from the past few weeks and decided to seek him out.

Chessington returned to himself and stood from the place he had been seated behind the group eating to sit next to the Librarian on a fallen log, which was still hard enough to keep its form before decomposing.

"Do you have a second, Sir?" Chessington started.

"If I can eat at the same time?" Malden said with his mouth full of the dried meat and cheese they were all fed when not stopping long enough for a formal meal. "What's on yer mind, boy?"

Chessington waited a moment before speaking as softly as possible, knowing just how well Violta could hear, "It's about women, Sir."

"Ah," the Councilman nodded, realizing also why Chessington was speaking so low, "not my strongest subject, but I'll do what I can. Go on."

"You see, Sir," Chessington moved a little closer, "it's Violta."

"Well ya didn't have ta say her name fer me ta know what ya meant." Malden stopped eating and made eye contact with the teenager, "We all been seein' how you two been actin'. How da ya want it ta go?"

"That's my problem," he admitted, "I don't know. I'm sixteen years old with more responsibilities than I had ever dreamed I would have, running for my life from someone I don't even know, and with all those things to think about, I'm wondering if I'm in love."

"Sounds like ya got hooked, son." Malden stuffed another piece of cheese in his mouth followed with six to eight rams head peas. Trying to talk through it, he stated, "I ain't sayin' ya two wouldn't be perfect, cuz ya would, but I ain't the one that's gotta do it. Why da ya think its love, boy?"

Chessington sighed loudly, "I find myself not listening to her words, just staring at her, and I guess because even back at Baydowa and Yaughtie's house when she was hit with that arrow, that's when I did what I did, not because he was going to kill Yaughtie. I knew she was alright, but I felt I needed to do something. I did the same thing back at the castle with the soldier who would have killed Preda."

"Yer a good kid, Chessington." Malden slapped the back of his shoulder blade in friendship, "I think ya need ta just not try so hard. If it's right, it'll come ta ya. Ya ain't gotta go lookin', but ya do have ta keep yer brains available fer this strange journey we're on. If ya don't, we may not need ta worry 'bout you an' her bein' together."

"Should I talk to her about this?" He asked.

Malden shrugged, "Yer smart, kid. You'll know."

"Thanks Sir." Chessington drifted off to go scouting again and once again more to be alone.

Chapter 15

They reached the opening to the tunnel at the southern base of Mt. Bollantoda about an hour after noon. The entire group huddled into its opening seeking the shelter from the rains which had tormented them for the past three days and night. The tunnel was easily twice as wide as the carts and even though the riders on horseback still rode two abreast, they could have set another along side of them. It was tall, leaving around six feet of space between the rider's heads and the ceiling of the route to the cave. Lined in solid rock, the walls were rough and moss covered in most spots, as was the ceiling, but the floor was much more of a gravel and sand mixture, as smooth as glass, but still easy for the horses to grip with their shod hooves.

As they turned the first corner and daylight disappeared, Chessington asked the General to have the group stop in the nearly dark cavern they all were nestled in.

"Sir," the Wizard stated, "I have a few suggestions of things I can do to make it both easier and quicker to get us all to the top."

General Vastion raised an eyebrow, "Such as?"

Chessington first produced a light glow running one foot wide in a continuous strip across the center of the ceiling, illuminating the entire tunnel as far up the path as they could see. "It goes all the way to the cave at the top, Sir."

"Very impressive." Vastion nodded.

Next Chessington was going to do something he had read about but never tested. It should work just fine, but just in case he walked past the group and started to bring in energy. They all watched as he started moving slowly at first, and then he disappeared around the corner. As he disappeared, they noticed now the ground was moving and turning up new ground to replace what had just been sent uphill. Soon they saw the ground stop and reverse itself, seeing Chessington moving back closer to them.

"That's pretty good, boy." Malden commended, "Can ya do it all the way up?"

"Yes," Chessington beamed, "I can. Also watch this." He produced twelve chairs, each very soft and ornate, three sets of hitching posts for the horses, and two sets of bracings for the carts. "Shall we continue?"

Bansinghaim, Modinay, Ghalkin, and Gurlig unhitched the carts from the horses and tied them to the bracings on the floor of the tunnel. Malden, Baydowa, Vastion, and Chessington tied the horses to the hitching posts, and Violta and Yaughtie took the children to their seats to wait for the others.

They arranged the chairs in a little more than a half circle so all could be in touch with each other for the trip up the inside of the mountain. They sat down waiting for the Wizard to start them forward, excitement flowing through the group at the anticipation of this new unknown perk.

Chessington explained, "You'll feel the ground start to move slightly at first and then gradually faster until we reach the speed we'll stay at. The ground under us will be moving, that's true, but should still be solid enough for us to walk around and stand on and do other things. I guess that's it. We should be to the cave in about two hours."

They all found a seat and waited in anticipation for the movement to start. Chessington drew in energy and redirected it to the ground. The chairs, hitching posts, and braces for the carts all started moving, very slowly at first. The group could not really feel it except when it gave the appearance of the walls moving downward instead of them and the floor moving up. A breeze started from the motion of the group, but

Chessington took care of it by moving the air around them to the same speed as the floor. After a full three minutes of working, he turned his attention from his wizardry and focused back to the group once again.

"There," he announced, "we're up to speed. The corners are gradual, and I've tipped them up a bit so we shouldn't even feel them. You might have a tendency to think you're losing your balance if you're standing, but it's not you; it's the ground." After he had given this information, he sat between Violta and Yaughtie very pleased with himself being able to make things more comfortable for everyone.

Yaughtie turned to him, "How come you didn't tell us you could do this?"

Chessington replied, "I'd never done it before. I figured I could, but just in case, I didn't want to look stupid if it didn't work."

Yaughtie smiled, exposing her full charm, "I don't know how you could feel that way. You can do so much! I think it's amazing how you can be who you are and still be so humble." She held eye contact, "It's so sweet."

Violta took Chessington's hand in hers, "He is, isn't he."

He was not sure why, but the young man, inexperienced with women, found himself uneasy about the current situation. He enjoyed holding Violta's hand, however, and looked at her more closely. She was so beautiful.

Yaughtie, trying to gain his attention, inquired, "I'm sure I couldn't understand it, but could you explain to me just how you can do this?"

He turned to see her and noticed her face was fair and smooth with deep blue eyes and soft red lips. Her blond hair resting down over the front of her shoulders in soft wavy curls. She was nearly as full figured as her older sister, but unlike Baydowa, Yaughtie knew how to flaunt herself as a young woman.

If I make my breasts bigger and show them off more will you look back at me? The Doltist girl shot into Chessington's mind as a warning.

Chessington's head whipped back to his girlfriend instantly, *I was being polite. She asked me a question. It would be rude if I didn't answer.*

Violta, still threatened by the newest member, replied, *I see. Then you should answer her question, by all means. I would hate to think of you as rude.* Standing up and releasing his hand she walked sternly back to the horses and disappeared from sight.

Yaughtie smiled a coy smile and asked again, "Would you tell me, please. I would find it fascinating to hear from a wizard about such things."

Chessington furrowed his brow and started to stand, "I should go check on Violta. I'll explain it later, if that's all right."

She touched his hand as he stood, "I don't pretend to know her as well as you do, but as a woman there are times when it's best to let some things be. I'm sure, after a little time, she'll be ready to talk about it."

He sat back in his chair, "I guess. I just don't understand women at all."

Yaughtie just smiled and kept holding his hand. Smiling all the while as if she were enthralled with every word he said.

Violta heard everything. She sat in a ball between two of the horses. This was so different. Why did she have to come along? Things where going wonderfully before her. Oh she knew what she was doing, and she was good at it, too. He kept staring at her. Why would he stare at her? Was it the hair, the eyes, the breasts? How could she know? Chessington had learned to seal his mind from her when he did not want her to see in. Now he was talking to that tramp and ignoring her! What could she do?

She thought a moment. He seemed to enjoy her looks mostly from what she could read of him. She supposed she would have to fight fire with fire. After drawing in a tiny amount of energy, she formed her hair a little longer and with a touch more curl. Next, she lightened her eyes to be more of a light greenish blue, and finally she looked inside her dress and added just a small amount to her breasts. Checking to make sure things were as she had wanted, she stood to rejoin them.

Seeing him with his hand holding Yaughtie's, she took his other hand and held it firmly, smiling and staring deeply into his eyes, holding her arms close to push her breasts together for the full effect.

Chessington noticed she was different and somehow softer than when she had stormed off. He also noticed her eyes were lighter, or had he just not paid full attention to them before. He stared back at her for a full minute noticing every detail, every hair, and every curve. She was breathtaking. He leaned closer, his lips trying to touch hers, but this was not to be the time of their first kiss.

"You never told me how it came to be that you could do all this." Yaughtie interjected.

"Huh?" Chessington snapped back to reality, "Oh, I'm sorry. I forgot where I was in our conversation."

"Oh, it doesn't matter I guess." Yaughtie smiled at him, "So long as you know." She stood and walked back over to her sister seeing she had planted a seed and would now see what direction it would grow.

* * * * * * *

As the group reached the top of the inside of Mt. Bollantoda, they saw a large table, set for eleven, filled with a minimum of forty different types of foods from roasted meats to delicate desserts. They all turned to Chessington and gathered around him first to show their gratitude at this wonderful break in their less than proper travels, and then seated themselves happily at the table. The cave itself was enormous, easily larger than five of Uncle Fein's barn put together. There were a couple of rooms back at the castle Chessington had seen which were larger, but they were for extremely large gatherings.

He set in next to divide the section next to the wall to the right of the cave entrance into six fairly large bedrooms. Placing beds, nightstands, standing closets, and oil lamps for each person in the group. He followed by making smokeless fireplaces in each to put out a respectable amount of heat, and finished it off with a thick plush carpet covering the entire cave.

Once finished with the living quarters, he fashioned a stable with an individual stall for each horse, fresh hay, and two large troths, one for water the other for oats, hay, and grasses with plenty of carrots set off to the side.

Next, he produced more food as well as a separate room to store it in. Hanging meats such as corned beefs, cured hams, and dried fish were placed there. He produced barrels of ale and wine, and fresh milk for the children kept cold in a special room he personally removed the heat from. He stored eggs, fruit and vegetables, and a tub of butter in there as well.

Once the requirements for the group had been handled, he started in on the leisure activities for them to use to occupy their time waiting for him to do what he had to do. He made arrows and targets for Sir Ghalkin. Fine dresses for the women as well as Preda, with scores of shoes and jewelry to try on. For all to enjoy, he made decks of playing cards, chess and checker boards, dice, and a throwing game using different colored balls about the size of a grapefruit and a hole in the dirt two feet across and in a perfect circle.

Last, he formed a lounging area full of sofas and overstuffed chairs with the book of maps he had recognized from the book store back in Derenta.

He had furnished the cave as would make any resort jealous. Then he did what he was sent here to do. Returning to the books he had read from previously, he sat on one of the sofas and started to open The Book of Past Times. He had not seen Malden come from the table to sit next to him, "Those the books?" He asked in reverence.

"Yes Sir." Chessington nodded still staring at them.

Malden leaned over to get a better look, "First time I seen 'em all. Better start readin'. May as well see what the next step is."

Chessington opened it up and turned to the last page as he had done before, the last time being at the Woods finding out they needed to come here. He read aloud so Malden could hear as well:

Chessington the Twenty-ninth,

This is the cave Maldo the first stumbled into when first he discovered the energy and its uses thousands of years ago. You remember the story from this book, and now you are a part of it as well. Your reign as a wizard is told in these pages now and forever, but you have need for more before your story is completed.

"Kinda figured we wasn't done yet." Malden interrupted.

This evening you will have a visit from the Shade, just as you had back at the castle except this time you will be fully awake. You will proceed with him to the back of the cave and into a corridor, which will seal itself off once you are received inside. For this first visit, you will bring another with you, but choose wisely to whom it will be. This first visitation will be about your enemy. Choose someone who will understand the need to study them from a historical aspect as well as a geographical one. After you return from this first part of the teachings, look again to this page for your next set of instructions.

The two looked at each other with a silent understanding communicating between them. It was between two men, Sir Malden and Sir Ghalkin. Chessington knew they would both be excellent choices as well as intrigued by the opportunity. He already knew the right one with no disrespect intended for the other.

"Sir," he asked of the Royal Librarian, "would you like to be the one to come with me?"

Malden grinned from ear to ear, "Absolutely boy. This is the chance of a lifetime." He clasped the hand of the boy and went off to get his particular area ready for when he returned from the newest quest he was included in.

Preda came and sat next to him. "What did it say?"

Chessington, still slightly overwhelmed from the reading, smiled at his cousin, "Not as much as I had thought it would, but enough for now."

She perked up and asked, "Can you read it to me?"

"Well, I suppose I can," he replied, "in fact I'm sure I can. I think it might be a better idea though if we all gathered around and I read it once instead of eight more times individually. That could get very old very fast."

She smirked, "Yeah, I suppose."

They called the others over to hear the words they had all traveled so far to hear, some more than others, and after the short reading, he read it over again knowing once he left, there would be no one left who could do so. He explained how he had asked Sir Malden to join him on this first part of his teachings, and how he had thought between the Librarian and Sir Ghalkin, but being able to choose only one, he felt compelled to make the choice he did.

"I cannot say I am not jealous," Ghalkin admitted, "but I do understand. Besides, I was hoping to spend some one on one time with His Highness. We have not been this preoccupied with things since the absence of his parents. I do need to remember my first and foremost duty to Phenderia."

Chessington turned to Violta after this, "Could I speak to you privately, please."

She beamed from the inside out and stayed quiet as he led her to the back of the cave and around a bend to be completely private.

Bansinghaim shook his head and announced to the group, "That boy has it something bad."

Preda, not following, asked, "What's Chessy got? Is he sick?"

"Love sickness is all." Modinay answered, "She has burrowed in deep, and I doubt she'll ever come out."

"They make a good match." Vastion added, "It's completely natural for them to fall in love I would suppose."

All in the group felt the budding romance, and all were very happy for the couple.

All except one. Yaughtie stood, making for the room she shared with her sister, who was following her only a few steps behind.

Chapter 16

Evening came with the group staying awake to see the Shade come for Chessington and Malden. Each had placed their belongings, if they had any, in their designated bedrooms for the stay at this major stopping point in their journey.

Chessington had just finished two large bathing areas off to the front of the cave overlooking the beautiful Derentian Mountains to the north. It was still raining outside, and the group felt even warmer and comforted seeing what they could have been stuck riding through. The rains were falling harder than they had in any of the last few days with snow accumulating at this elevation at the entrance to the north jutting out a good fifteen feet into the open.

The group was in the lounging area Chessington had produced earlier in the day, but all were anxious as well as apprehensive about the visitation which was to come. Gurlig, Bansinghaim, and Modinay were playing cards at a table with ale mugs sitting to the side. Bansinghaim was also put in charge of Gurlig not over doing it at the General's request. He did not wish to have the need to sober him back up for a second time after what they had gone through back at Lorning. Vastion, Baydowa, and Yaughtie were discussing the last few years of torment at the small town of Bollantoda for the women. Each telling of what had happened to have the group of killers get a hold over them. Ghalkin, Violta, Palton, and Preda were seated together talking about things they had remembered from before they had all met. Sir Ghalkin telling of the day Palton had decided to flee out the window for an early morning swim in the cold pond behind the castle.

Chessington and Sir Malden sat talking as Malden was very nervous about the upcoming meeting they were to have with an actual spirit.

"How's he communicate?" The Librarian asked the boy, "Ya said he don't talk an' has no hands ta write with."

"Mostly I asked yes or no questions." The teen answered, "He has a way of leading you along and you get the point. I was always sure I understood what he was saying."

"I gotta admit, kid," Malden opened up, "I'm nervous 'bout this."

"You won't be after we get in there." Chessington reassured his friend, "He's not at all scary or spooky like you'd think from what everybody says about spirits. I felt it was more strange talking with my Uncle back in the unused room at the castle. You'll see."

Almost on cue, a form started from the back of the cave and emerged towards the group. It was a dark shade of gray but not solid. It had arms and a head, or a spot where those should be, but it appeared to be only a floating robe like you would have seen a priest wear. It came towards Chessington, and the Wizard stood in acknowledgement of him, and then to everyone's surprise, it spoke.

"Chessington the Twenty-ninth," the Shade addressed him formally, "who have you chosen to accompany you for this session in the betterment of your arts?" The voice was definitely male, not as deep as Bansinghaim's, but a man's voice nonetheless. He spoke in an accent none there could place, seeming very foreign and very ancient.

"Sir Malden," Chessington stood straight and tall as he spoke, a little startled himself at the voice of the Shade in front of him, "Royal Librarian to the Castle in Phenderia City and Royal Councilman of Phenderia." He figured the propriety shown by the Shade should be used for him as well.

The Shade remarked, "You have chosen wisely. Come."

The Shade turned and headed back towards the rear of the cave from where he had come from with Chessington following him and Malden slightly behind the Wizard. The rock wall at the rear of the cave split open to produce a doorway approximately four feet across and nine feet high leading into a room of glowing light no one could see deep into because of the glow given off by the intense glow inside. The three walked through the entrance and a few feet into the room, disappearing from sight as they were consumed by the light. All were mesmerized as they watched the rock shift and twist to reseal itself in effect closing off the room to any outside influence.

"I'll be!" Gurlig stated after a long silence had lingered through the ten left behind, "That's the best yet. Ain't no body never ta believe that."

Sir Bansinghaim standing next to him continued his thought, "I'm not sure I believe it, even after seeing it happen."

Baydowa showed her concern, "Are they alright?"

"I'm sure they are." Violta answered, "It would seem consistent with other dealings we have heard tell of back in the Woods. Although, try as I might, I cannot mentally connect with Chessington in there. There is a high amount of energy at that end of the cave, so that could be why."

General Vastion gave a final thought to what they had all just witnessed, "Whether they're fine or not, they are in there. I doubt at this point there would be anything we could do about it either way."

"I also doubt I'm going to be able to sleep for a while." Modinay stated still staring at the rock wall, "Bansinghaim, Gurlig, shall we get back to our game. We could stand here staring for days and it might not change a thing."

They all dispersed, Sir Ghalkin and Violta taking the children to their rooms and getting them into bed, then retiring as well themselves. The three returned to their card game, while the sisters and the General sat to discuss more of what had just happened.

* * * * * * *

Malden was afraid to speak for the first time in his life. The Shade had taken them into this glowing room, sealing it after they had entered. He saw no walls, no ceiling, and most disturbingly of all, no floor. They were supported, he just could not see how. The glow was easy to see through from the inside. He could see the Shade and Chessington as clear as day, but nothing else.

The Shade broke the silence, "In this place you will lay your bodies down as your spirits will continue on their path. After we arrive at the Tribunal, you will be restored your speech. I will introduce you each to the Tribunal as well as introducing them to you. They already know you, but this is proper and respectful of the three. Now please, lay down your bodies and proceed with me."

Chessington and Malden felt a soothing calmness overcome them as their bodies lay down on a floor area they could not see. Instantly they closed their eyes and found themselves rising up through the top of their heads, releasing themselves from their bodies and seeing their forms lying still and motionless behind them as they drifted behind the Shade and away from themselves.

They followed the Shade through a tunnel of light, which showed no distance, coming after an indeterminable amount of time to a room with walls and a floor but a ceiling made up of swirling energy. Around the room were shelves upon shelves of books, some seeming older than time while others looked fresh and new.

Three men sat a table. A tall man, muscular and dark, sat in the middle, giving the presence of someone demanding respect. He had dark eyes and square features to him, thin lips and a square jaw line, with dark straight hair seemingly not combed, but not unkempt either.

The man to his right was shorter and seemed younger in appearance. Dark hair and eyes also, but a rounder face and softer features than the man in the middle. He was not as toned in body as the other, but he too was physically fit.

The third looked completely different from the first two. He had a round head with sandy brown hair curling on top. He was looking to be a man of around thirty years of age, but age apparently meant nothing here. His eyes were blue and soft. He smiled unlike the others, and his face had rounded cheeks, which were red as a man who had drank alcohol would show after years of abuse.

The Shade spoke to the Tribunal, presenting the two guests, "My Lords, Chessington the Twenty-ninth, Wizard of the West, and Royal Wizard to the Monarchy of Mosa.

The Tribunal stood, making both of the newcomers feel strangely important. Walking over to them, the man seated in the middle before moved to the front to greet Chessington personally, "This is the new Wizard we have waited three thousand years to have surface. I am glad to finally meet you. You do not yet realize how much we are all glad to finally meet you." He had a calming voice, soothing to the nerves the two outsiders were feeling, but spoke with confidence and authority as well.

The Shade turned next to Malden, "May I also introduce, Sir Malden, Royal Librarian to Phenderia, and Councilmen of the Royal Phenderian Council."

The attention shifted over now to the older of the two brought before them. With the same man greeting him as he had greeted Chessington, he stated, "Royal Librarian, the title speaks volumes about your character, Sir. We are honored to have you join us."

The Shade moved next to the dark haired smaller man who had been to the leaders right, "Falsdor, exalted Adherent of the Eastern Kingdoms, trained by Rustaph himself, Loyal in Spirit to the Forces of Eutheria."

The two outsiders stared at him in awe from the announcement, failing to know why they revered him, but knew he was important all the same.

The Shade moved over now to the man who had been to the left when they had come in, "Feachen the Twenty-eighth, Wizard of the West, Royal Wizard to the Monarchy of Mosa, and Loyal in Spirit to the Forces of Eutheria.

This had caught Chessington by surprise. He had read about Feachen, but had not understood why he had suddenly disappeared. It was also strangely disturbing to have the exact same introduction himself as had Feachen.

The Shade next floated over to the man who had been in the middle, "Rustaph the Great, Last Great Sorcerer to the Eastern Kingdoms, Loyal in Spirit to the Forces of Eutheria, and Leader of the Tribunal." Following the final introduction the Shade faded out and was gone, leaving the five remaining spirits as the only ones left in the room.

Rustaph spoke to all left present, "Come, sit, we have much to teach and much more to answer."

Chessington and Malden spotted two large chairs, which had not been present when they had come in the first time. The now five chairs were placed equidistant from each other in a perfect circle, showing no advantage of placement for any of the men. They were of fine quality and comfortable, both men noticing even though there bodily forms were not with them, they still felt things and noticed the comfort of the chairs.

"Please," Rustaph began, "you both have questions. Feel free to ask anything you would like. We are here to answer."

Malden started, "We was told we was comin' here ta find out 'bout our enemies, 're you with us or them?"

Falsdor leaned forward to answer his question, "Although, it may appear we are on your side, we are firmly on the side of justice and freedom. Your enemies wish to carry out a plan, which has been in the works for approximately three thousand years. We are trying to undo a great wrong that was committed then, and except for one twisted mind with power unparalleled in your world behind it, things would not have been as bad as they have turned out to be."

"Ya must be in government." Malden answered, "I didn't make any sense outta that."

Falsdor explained in simpler terms, "We are on your side so long as you try to champion justice and freedom. Should you become greedy or evil, we will look for another to give support to."

"Okay," Malden nodded, "I got that one."

Chessington spoke next, "Feachen the Twenty-eighth, what happened to you? You were the last Wizard on the Island of Mosa, and then you just were gone?"

Feachen rose to go to one of the shelves lining the room. Producing a book from the massive volumes stored there, he replied, "That is a long story, and it might better be explained from having you both read this book."

He handed each of them the same book and telling them to start. They read the front cover, which in an old style script had been hand written, *The Dialog of History*. They turned to each other and waited only a moment before they opened the book with each reading from the beginning and after what seemed to them as many hours they both completed together and stared in awe at the three before them.

"This all happened?" Malden asked to whomever wished to answer, "Just the way it says?"

Rustaph replied, "Yes. The books in here are written by History itself. They are unable to lie. They just write as it happens. They can assess the moods of the people they are written about, but they read those from the actual persons, and not having any judgment in the matter, they simply explain how things really were."

"So nobody wrote this book." Malden had a hard time clinging on to this knowledge. He always believed a book was as smart as the writer, but without a writer how could you have a book?

Feachen helped a little, "The books in here are the almost complete collection of History itself. History happens, and it is stored for the ages here. We knew this would be the proper place to bring you to understand exactly who your enemies are. Mind you, your enemies are not an Empire. Your enemies are just a few people. The people of Chiloe are just as devoid of freedom as the people of Mosa now are. They are ruled by an Emperor who is a puppet for Pazlin, as you have read already. You also see now, Pazlin is finding no use for Lord Maldifren or having someone even to be the Emperor other than himself. Pazlin is your real enemy. His Adherents are strong, one or two of them stronger than yourself, Chessington the Twenty-ninth, thus far. The one you destroyed near Marroda was the weakest of his Adherents. The rest have much more ability."

"Ya *said almost complete.*" Malden wondered, "Where 're the rest?"

Rustaph smiled, "There are only three missing, and they had been sitting in a cold lonely room for three thousand years."

Chessington's eyes widened, "My books?"

Rustaph nodded, "Yes. This is why words change and speak to just you. This is why you need to keep checking them at certain points in your journey. It is also how we help you."

"You're the ones then who keep moving us the right way." Chessington figured.

"No," Falsdor amended, "we have access to the same knowledge. As History speaks to you, we see it as well. Knowing your plan, we can shift slightly certain events, place thoughts and roadblocks in the path of your enemies or even yourselves, and help you to see what is correct and not to argue with yourself when something seems unreasonable to you but has to be done a certain way anyhow."

"So what's next?" Chessington asked.

Rustaph almost laughed, "We would have no idea. After you leave here, you will read your spot in The book of Past Times again. After that, we will all know what is next."

"So you're wingin' it, too." Malden summarized.

Feachen smiled, "Yes, yes we are."

The Shade reappeared and took Chessington and Malden back to their physical bodies, allowing them to rejoin with themselves. He spoke only once before opening the rock wall to send them back to their friends, "I will return for Chessington and another chosen one two evenings from now."

They looked back into the glow one last time and stepped through the wall to see their friends waiting for them on the other side.

Neither one of them saw or heard the rocks move back into place as the Shade sealed the room off, returning the cave to the way it had been for centuries.

* * * * * * *

Pazlin sat wondering to himself, seated in his overstuffed wing-backed chair in his personal study reflecting on the many events he had his hand in. Mosa was taken and complete. Only a few more of the civilians to ship back to the East, and it would be time to attack the mainland itself. In three or four short months the invasion could begin. He suffered less casualties than he had predicted. The Westerners were fools and inept. They could not make a stand at any of the battles they faced, and every human belonging to the military on the entire island was now dead. Farmers and city dwellers posed no threat, only the last Wizard could disturb anything he had yet to carry out, and he had hoped he would try. That way he could be pin pointed down to a spot with Pazlin's Adherents killing him once and for all. It disturbed him the Woods of the Doltists and the Derentian Mountains could not be his, but after he discovered the Phanthow, he could change that.

He was less and less concerned about Maldifren than he had been in the past. With him being now the last of his line, executing all of his relations to the third cousins, no one would be left of royal blood after he had Maldifren convinced to kill himself.

He had just given the orders to send more troops to the West and stage them on the Island of Mosa. He could invade from there much easier than from long distances away. He already had Balstass and Clostig doing his preliminary work in the larger kingdoms of the mainland, Balstass in Hitrenda and Clostig in Bodash, leaving Grastock as his only Adherent left in Chiloe. Things would be moving forwards quickly from here with everything going well. Nothing could stop the plan he had spent nearly his entire lifetime organizing and implementing.

He still felt uneasy, and he could not figure out just exactly why.

Mark L Porter

Chapter 17

They sat around in the lounging area all speaking at once, trying to talk to Malden and Chessington at the same time. The two being sought after were still dazed just a bit after rejoining their group moments before. They sat with glazed looks to themselves and looked simultaneously at each other. Then busted out in the loudest and most heart felt laugh they had felt in years.

"They've gone mad." Vastion smiled, "Are you two going to explain or just hold us in suspense for a while longer?"

Malden, feeling a great sense of relief after returning, announced, "Yer right. I'm off ta bed."

Vastion and Ghalkin seated him right back down and after another bout of laughing attacked the two, Chessington answered, "It was the most intense thing I've ever done and the most calming."

Vastion looked puzzled, "How do you put those two opposites together? You can't be calm and intense."

"Yeah ya can." Malden smiled, "No way ta explain it, but ya can."

Ghalkin started asking next, "Could one or both of you please explain what went on in there?"

Chessington sobered himself first to answer, "Well Sir, after the wall sealed itself back up, we were instructed to lie down, and the Shade helped us come out of our bodies much like I explained happened to me back in the Castle Library the same night I met the Shade the first time."

"Alright," Ghalkin replied, "why did you need to do that?"

"I would have no idea, Sir." Chessington answered.

Malden took it a step further, "He really wasn't askin' so much as sayin' that's how it's gonna be. We laid down cuz he said to."

"Then what did you do?" Vastion asked.

"Then we followed him to a room with three men in it." Chessington continued, "They were very imposing figures, but at the same time made us feel as equals. They were all men who had lived at the same time approximately three thousand years ago, and all were either a sorcerer or a wizard."

"What's the difference?" Ghalkin asked.

Chessington defined, "A wizard, such as what I'm supposed to be, comes from the kingdoms west of the Great Beyond, and a sorcerer comes from the eastern side."

"Alight," the Royal Tutor understood, "continue, please."

Chessington thought for a second to remember where he had left off, "The three men there were called a Tribunal. One was the last wizard before me, and the other two were sorcerers from the same time as him. Actually in life they killed each other trying to stop others from being killed. They explained the one I felt after the battle outside of Marroda was actually another sorcerer from their time. He has now turned into a vindictive and evil sorcerer who's turned his own kingdoms, now called an empire, into something far worse than what he's done to us over here so far."

"Worse how?" Modinay asked, "Things seem pretty bad out there."

Malden spoke next, giving the boy a break from the questioning, "Seems this guy don't care 'bout anythin' except conquerin' the world. After he was the last sorcerer standin' after the creation a the Great Beyond, he started schemin' 'bout how ta use the East ta take over the West."

Vastion shook his head, "He hasn't had the opportunity to do that for three thousand years?"

"Nope," Malden answered, "he was left with not a lot ta work with after the big battle. Three-quarters of a million soldiers an' leaders were wiped out that day, all by two a the three guys we just met, too."

Ghalkin wondered, "So how do we know these three are really on our side?"

Chessington added, "Because they wiped out each others armies as a defense to save the civilian population of the sides they represented. The leaders were all too greedy, and it was the best they could do at the time. It seemed to them to be the lesser of two horrible choices they had to make at the moment."

Malden helped finish the story, "Ya see, at the time the East had all the farmin' land an' the West had all the people. The leaders a the East raised their prices up ta where the West couldn't afford ta pay 'em. The West got a huge army together, 'bout twice the East, and stood on the doorstep ta the East where the Great Beyond now is."

"The West has wonderful farm lands." Modinay replied, "Why couldn't they grow their own food"

Chessington explained, "We do now. Rustaph, the greatest Sorcerer of the East, turned the land over and over giving the West better top soil during the creation of the Great Beyond. Before that the West was mostly rocks and dry dirt."

"Alright," Ghalkin said, "continue please."

Malden picked up where he had left off, "After Rustaph tried ta reason with the leaders a the East ta give in 'fore the West slaughtered 'em, he tried ta reason with the Western leaders an' they, havin' the advantage, didn't see why they should negotiate. They tried that 'fore an' the East wouldn't do nothin'. Well anyways, the one leader a the West decided ta attack, an' Rustaph, feelin' responsible fer the East, made the Great Beyond, but the entire army a the West was killed durin' the shiftin' in the ground. Then the Wizard a the West came in and made sure the East couldn't attack the West by killin' all their leaders an' soldiers with a storm."

Vastion wondered, "So all that was left was the three you saw in the room back there."

"And Pazlin," Chessington told them, "he was an Adherent to Rustaph just like the other man, Falsdor, who is in the Tribunal."

Modinay seemed confused, "I'm not really following. How many were left now?"

Chessington gave a quick summery, "Feachen, the Wizard to the Western Kingdoms; Rustaph, the Sorcerer of the Eastern Kingdoms; Falsdor, the First Adherent to Rustaph; and Pazlin, the Second Adherent to Rustaph."

Vastion nodded, "Those were the only four left out of three-quarters of a million people?"

"Yep," the Librarian agreed, "until Rustaph tried ta stop Feachen from killin' all a the Eastern Army. He was too weak from creatin' the Great Beyond ta fight back an' got sucked inta what Feachen was doin'. Falsdor, tryin' ta help his Master, got sucked in as well. The three a 'em died on the spot an' Pazlin was the only guy left."

"So our greatest enemy right now," the General summed up, "is a three thousand year old sorcerer who hates the West because he believes we killed his Master and sent the East into hard times."

"Yep, pretty much." Malden nodded.

Modinay asked, "What do we do now?"

"I read in my book again, and it tells me what to expect next." Chessington supplied, "The Shade told us he'd be back tomorrow night. What time is it here?"

"Shortly after noon," Bansinghaim answered, "Three days after you went into the rock wall."

Malden's eyebrows rose, "Seemed like 'bout ten ta twelve hours."

Chessington replied to his friend, "Time has no meaning in there."

"So I see." Malden agreed.

Vastion, being somewhat impatient, asked Chessington, "Shouldn't you read your special part of the book again?"

"Oh, yes!" Chessington stood to go get it. Walking into the area of the bedrooms he and Preda shared, he opened a drawer. Removing The Book of Past Times, he came back to the group to read aloud:

Chessington the Twenty-ninth,

Your first lesson went exceedingly well. We are well pleased with the knowledge Sir Malden and yourself have now obtained. We now, however, have need for you to continue with the second part of your learning agenda.

The next lesson you will undertake will entirely pertain to Geography. You will need to have knowledge of where you are going and where others should be coming from. You will study with Rustaph himself as to the lands you are familiar with as well as those you are not. You will learn of maps, which are not invented, trails others do not know of, and other oddities no Westerner, or Easterner for that matter, has any knowledge of; although, in some instances you will not remember those until the need presents itself.

Again you may choose one amongst you to accompany into the glow. Choose wisely, for this individual will be responsible for guiding you not only through these mountains and on throughout the Island of Mosa, but must understand the entire system of paths and trails for the remainder of your journey.

After this lesson has concluded, return to this page for your instructions to your third and final lesson to this part of your quest.

"It seems you have a decision." Vastion concluded, "We have two guides and only one may go."

Chessington thought, "I believe I have three choices, Sir. Baydowa, Gurlig, and yourself."

Vastion shook his head, "No, I'm not a guide. I'm many things, but not a guide."

Gurlig shot up from his seat, "I ain't goin' in there! Ain't no way ya gonna get me inta that hole in the there wall an' have it lock me up. She can do it. I ain't goin'"

Baydowa looked somewhat glassy eyed, "I'm not sure I'm right for this either. I just met all of you. True, I'm a very experienced guide around here, but this sounds like an extreme amount of study. I can barely read to begin with."

Gurlig stepped in again, "There ya go. I can't read nothin'. She got me beat."

Chessington looked the young woman softly in her eyes, "I believe you're our best bet. I can help with the studying and the reading, but you'll more than likely be our guide for the rest of this trip. You're going to need to know this. Besides, I have certain advantages to help you remember things."

"I have to tell you, I'm a bit scared." Baydowa replied.

Malden looked at her solidly, "It ain't so bad. Actually, it's real nice. Trust me, you'll wonder why you were nervous after ya get there."

"I suppose I have no choice." She smiled, but only to cover her nervousness. She faked a smile and retreated to her bedroom with Yaughtie following her, concerned about her newest challenge.

Chessington followed her as well, telling her somewhat of what she could expect, also explaining he could not always be positive of what to expect either. She relaxed partially, but stayed on edge for quite some time to come.

Yaughtie smiled a sincere smile of gratitude at his concern over her sister and left it at that.

* * * * * * *

After the group had all turned in for the night, Violta silently walked into the bedroom Chessington shared with Preda. She saw him lying on top of the covers and worked her way under his arm. He was out scouting, unable to hold her back.

What are you doing? The boy Wizard asked her in her mind.

I missed you. She replied, *I missed not sharing our thoughts. I missed not being able to see or hear you. I especially missed your touch.*

It was only three days, he reminded her, *and you knew I'd be back, but I guess I understand. Even though it was only a few hours for me, I suppose I've been spoiled by hearing you whenever I please.*

Violta smiled, *You missed me too?*

Of course I did. Chessington admitted, *You said before, we were meant to be together. I think of you as part of me now.*

Really! The Doltist girl beamed inwardly, not being able to hide it from Chessington.

Of course, he again told her, *I enjoy our time together.*

Like you enjoy having Yaughtie talk to you? Violta questioned, *She is trying to take you away from me you know.*

I doubt that. Chessington laughed at the notion, *Why would she?*

Because you're a catch, Chessington the Twenty-ninth! She nearly screamed at him, *But you listen to me. You're my catch, not hers.*

Yes dear. He answered back, *I don't think I'll have any trouble being reminded of that.*

Good, she stated, nuzzling into his chest a little harder, *I wish you were here. Where are you at the moment?*

On my way to Loglistin. he told her, *It's a shipping town on the southwestern shore of Phenderia. I might be back a little after the rest of the group gets up. It's pretty much as far as I can go and still be on the island. It's the last place I have to look.*

Are you close? Violta asked.

I'm actually very close. I should be there in just a few seconds. I only saw two bands of civilians being marched south, a group of Iclanians and the other was Derentian. I do see now there are a lot of Chiloe soldiers, most are either guarding the shipyards or larger buildings. They seem to be loading the people onto boats. I assume to be sent back to Chiloe. The book Malden and I read suggested to the option of Pazlin using our people as slaves there, but it never came right out and said it. I would guess because they haven't actually been turned into slaves yet.'

Why do you say that? She wondered.

Because, he explained, *the book is written by History itself. It can't write it until it happens. If Pazlin thinks it or tells someone about it, History can write it down as a thought or a potential future, but it can't call it fact until it happens.*

What was it like meeting the people of the past? She asked.

It was exciting. He admitted, *Kind of like the first time you get to be with the adults when you're a child. They knew so much, and they were so hopeful for us. I don't think they hate Pazlin, but they most definitely don't want him to succeed.*

Violta held his hand, even though he was not there to hold hers back. She wanted to kiss his cheek, but felt it would be lost on his shell of a body without the real man inside of it. She loved talking to him mentally, but she really wanted him to be there with her.

He, too, was wishing these nighttime scouting trips would end. He now felt he could stop going south to see where the people were going off to, but starting after this next meeting between himself, Baydowa, and Rustaph, he would start scouting to the north and see what shape the deserted towns along the Iclanian coast line were in. They would certainly need to get off the island at some point. He had better find out what condition those towns would be in.

After a few hours Gurlig and Malden awoke to sit together in the lounging area. Once there they started talking amongst themselves, trying to stay quiet in respect of the others still sleeping.

"I hear yer from Lorning." Malden started off with to the companion he really did not know very much about as of yet.

"Well, that's the last spot I called home." Gurlig answered him, "I also lived a little in Hostin, Ultipera, Velso, Tarint Mosa, Drinblock, Rajule, and Lodlin, but I was born in Plangibra."

"Huh," Malden chuckled, "so was I. My Dad was a noble, but he disgraced the family when I was just a kid, an' my Grandparents brought me up."

"My Dad was a drunk." Gurlig offered, "He'd go out an' slap me 'round fer a while 'til he got bored with it an' then usually passed out. My ma left cuz he'd beat the tar outta her too, an' one day she ups an' goes an' I ain't heard a her since."

Malden nodded, "We sound a lot alike. The family never talked 'bout my Dad. Mom wasn't gonna say nothin', an' the only things my Grandparents ever said was stuff I wasn't allowed ta repeat. The servants around the house told me a few times they would catch him with some a the serving girls and chamber maids. I guess one day Ma caught him with a servant, trousers down a course, an' she told Grandpa. Even though it was his son, they found out he got her pregnant. Dad flew off the handle and slap my Ma an' beat Grandpa hard 'fore three servants could stop him at Grandma's request. She had him thrown out an' the pregnant girl, too. We never saw 'em again."

Gurlig stopped short in his thought, "How old was ya then?"

Malden thought, "'bout five I guess, why?"

The former drunk asked again, "How old is ya now?"

"Forty-nine." Malden's eyes lit up for a second, "You ain't thinkin'.."

Gurlig nodded, "I'm forty-three. My Dad's name was Danstirk, but guys called him Danny."

Malden stopped talking. If what he thought was coming together, he had to think about this for a while. This was his father's name as well, and Plangibra was not a town, which could have two with such an unusual of a name in it.

Gurlig looked him over, "You an' I,.. we could be, .."

Malden stated with a large grin to his face, "Brothers, half brothers, but still brothers. Whoa man an' I thought yesterday was the biggest thing I'd have happen in here."

"So my Dad was from high class?" Gurlig asked.

"A Duke actually." Malden clarified, "The Duke a Pallin. I was until I got to be a Councilman, then I dropped the Duke stuff and was called Sir Malden. The posts vacated. I guess you're the next in line."

"I ain't no Duke!" Gurlig laughed, "I'm just a drunken wood cutter vagabond."

"The way I sees it," the Librarian confirmed, "an' it's my job ta clear up this stuff, since I ain't got no brothers 'er sisters, you got the bloodline. I ain't the Duke no more, so here ya sit, Gurlig, Duke a Pallin. Course yer land all got taken by the Chiloes, but ya still got yer title."

Gurlig slunk back in his sofa. Malden could see he was thinking about this. He looked out into the room to see General Vastion and Sir Ghalkin coming out into the open.

"Have a seat." Malden asked the other two councilmen, "Ya gotta hear this."

Malden explained about how he and Gurlig were related, and the two smiled and congratulated the pair on finding each other and having family after all these years of not knowing.

Sir Bansinghaim heard the story as well as he joined the group, "Well Gurlig, I hope you're more intelligent than your brother. He likes to let his tongue get him into trouble."

"Yer talkin' 'bout bein' intelligent?" Malden remarked, "The only thing I could see you bein' interested in readin' would be a menu."

The large knight kept talking to Gurlig, "As you can see, he really hasn't much intelligence at all. He's small and slow, and I will teach him manners one day."

General Vastion changed the subject, "I'm very happy for you both. Tonight, we'll see if Chessington can put something special together to celebrate."

Gurlig announced, "I'd appreciate that, Sir. Man, I just can't believe it. I got a brother, an' I'm a Duke."

Violta moved out of the bedroom area with Preda and Prince Palton beside her. She came and sat next to Sir Ghalkin, who she was rapidly seeing as a father figure, to tell the group, "Chessington has figured out where the population has been taken."

They all turned facing her, "Where?" General Vastion asked.

"Loglistin," she answered, "they are all marched there where large ships have been taking them presumably back to Chiloe. Chessington believes they will be taken as slaves by Pazlin and used to be labor for the Chiloes."

"Sounds like what we read 'bout in the History book yesterday." Malden agreed, "That Pazlin hates the West. He'd take a lot a delight in seein' us all killed er conquered. The guy's got a real twisted brain."

"I see nothing we can do in the immediate future." Ghalkin added, "Although, it will be tough times for the people until or if we can do something about it."

"I'm bettin'," Malden continued, "he's gonna try ta take the mainland as well. I doubt he just hates Mosans. He'll try ta wipe out the whole West."

"I doubt he's already taken the mainland." Vastion strategized, "Bansinghaim said they saw ships from the mainland back at Marroda, and we would have seen trade come to a stop before they invaded us."

Malden stated, "Guess it stands ta reason the mainland has ta be wonderin' 'bout us then. They ain't seen a ship from us fer three weeks."

Sir Ghalkin agreed, "They should be able to figure it out. But how could they figure out they would be next."

General Vastion put everything into perspective, "There's really no way to warn them, and all we can do is stay on the path we have to stay on."

The final members, excluding Chessington, came from the sleeping area to join the rest of the party. The trio of Derentians; Modinay, Baydowa, and Yaughtie, sat in the final chairs to complete the circle, which they had placed them all into.

Malden looked to Baydowa, "Ya ready for yer trip this evenin'?"

"No," she answered with a grin, "but I doubt it matters if I'm ready. I'll be alright, I'm sure just very nervous."

"You'll be fine." Yaughtie told her sister, "You've done far harder things than this before with the gang and all. They were horrible. It sounds like these gentlemen are friendly."

Malden agreed, "She's got a point. The Tribunal is tryin' ta help us out here, an' you're a very important part a getting' us all through it."

Chessington finally came around the corner after his late night scouting assignment, "What did I miss?"

Malden smiled, "A lot."

He sat next to Sir Malden and listened as he explained how he and Gurlig found out about their blood ties. After the others dispersed, he also asked Chessington to explain a bit more about the current state the civilians were in and if there were anything he could do about it.

Chessington told him he could, but it would not be the best thing for the big picture. He could free them until Pazlin felt him. Then the entire quest they were on would be doomed to fail.

Malden figured as much, but had to ask. He always felt the people should come first. It was hard for him to understand putting the people's needs first meant letting them be sent into slavery.

After Malden left for breakfast, Chessington sat thinking alone on the settee wondering about how things might transpire after they left the cave. The rest was necessary for the group, both mentally and physically, but soon they would need to be on the move again. Not knowing in which direction they were to go bothered him. He wanted to know so he could scout ahead until he felt a small hand grab onto his.

"Chessy," Preda sat up on his lap, "can I sit here?"

He smiled and all of his other concerns faded away, "Of course you can. Are you enjoying it here?"

"Yes," she stated as a fact, "but I would like to stop moving all the time. Do we have to keep running around?"

Her cousin held her a little tighter and answered, "Yes, we really do. I think we will for quite a while, too. Just enjoy staying here for a few more days, and after that it'll be sunny most of the time, and we'll be traveling again. You and Violta will ride with Sir Ghalkin, and you two can talk all you want."

"I like her." Preda beamed, "After you marry her, am I going to live with you guys?"

Chessington smiled and stopped for a second to recompose himself, "I don't recall asking her to marry me yet."

"Everybody says you're going to." His cousin told him, "Why wouldn't you. She's really nice. I like her a lot, and she asks all sorts of stuff about you, so I know she'd say yes."

"It sounds like you want me to." He replied.

"Yes," she answered, "I think it'd be the best thing that could happen to us."

Chessington realized just then his relationship with Violta affected others, too. Preda would need to be his responsibility for many years yet. Would Violta be the best female roll model for her? Could she handle life in the outside world of humans for the rest of her life? Would he have to move himself and Preda to the Woods instead? Would it be the best thing for his cousin? He loved Violta, but maybe too much. Would it be the best decision for everyone, including her?

He had to think like a man about these things now. He had obligations to other people. Would a marriage to Violta work out over time for everyone?

Chapter 18

The celebration for Sir Malden and Gurlig lasted deep into the evening. The two told stories of their childhood to the rest of the group, both understanding places and moments from their childhood only they would understand being someone who had grown up in Plangibra. There were certain people each knew of, shops both had been in during their upbringing, and officials who they had both remembered as well.

The feast itself, supplied by Chessington, was of many of the foods the two men loved most, and in the case of Gurlig, the beverage.

Baydowa sat quietly at the end of the long table the Wizard had produced for the occasion still thinking about her role in all of this. She had to be a guide outside of her area. This made her extremely uncomfortable. She finally walked over to Chessington to ask him, "What if I'm not the right one for this?"

Chessington sat with concern but confidence, "You are. Look at this group. What do you see? I see a mismatched group all the way from a drunken wood cutter, a being from a culture most have never heard of, and going all the way up to the future King of Phenderia."

"I see leaders," she replied, "many leaders. Leaders who are born and raised to do just this. I'm a girl from the mountains of Derentia. I'm not special. I'm not someone who can be in charge of something as important as this. I'm someone who likes my mountains and stays in them. After the last few years, I'm not even sure I like other people. Most want to use others and then forget about them. I don't know any of you well enough to put this kind of trust in you. "

"Alright," Chessington acknowledged, "let me explain something to you. When I was nine my Mother and the rest of my family were killed by a plague. I went to live with my Aunt and Uncle until they were murdered while my cousin and I were away a few of weeks ago, and the home I'd known for the past seven years was destroyed by fire. Then we're sent to stay at the castle with the reigning Prince of Phenderia nonetheless. After only a couple of days to let it sink in, I was shown by spirits I'm going to be the next wizard of the western world. At the same time I was sent to help certain people escape an invading army who wants to kill them, and I have been trying to stay a step ahead of them ever since. I can't practice my new craft except in a few places, or I might put the lives of everyone I now hold near and dear in peril. Oh yeah, and I'm taking orders from a book. I doubt that sounds much like any leader has ever had for an upbringing before, but I really didn't have much choice."

"But maybe I do." She explained.

"And what would that choice be?" The maturing young Wizard asked, "You could never leave these mountains. You might find it alright for a while, but I doubt you'd enjoy it forever. What about Yaughtie or the other people you've met. Do they deserve to be slaves to an evil madman? I think you'd always wonder if it would have been different back when you had the chance to change it."

"You seem to understand me a bit more than I originally gave you credit." Baydowa admitted, "I would have regrets, but what if I fail, and we all die from my decision?"

"You worry too much about failing." Chessington stated.

"Because that's what I have done in the past." She answered, "My sister was a hostage for more than two years because I couldn't get her out."

"What could you have done differently?" He asked.

"I don't know." She was getting more and more confused, "I could have told someone or done something."

"Or maybe the right thing to do was to wait until someone came along to help you." He offered, "Maybe you did the right thing. She's alive and free! You kept her alive. You did everything you had to do to keep her from getting killed."

Baydowa remained quiet a while, and Chessington was smart enough to let her be for as long as she wanted, but remained close by to still help her through this. She finally turned her head back to him and agreed, "I will still go with you, and I'll do whatever it takes to see this thing through to the end. You're a bit more than you seem, and you seemed like quite a bit to begin with." She leaned over and kissed him on the cheek, stopping as he retreated slightly, blushing from every pore on his being.

They both spotted the glow at the rear of the cave, standing up to advance towards the imminent meeting between the two of them and the Shade. He stepped forward out of the glow and came closer to them only to state, "Chessington the Twenty-ninth, has there been one chosen amongst you to accompany us in this portion of learning?"

The Wizard replied, steadfast and strong, "I have. Baydowa our guide. She will learn with me about where we are to go and the places we need to know about."

"You have chosen wisely again." The Shade commended, "There is one other among you who has need of joining us."

The room was stirring and all inside were nervous. No one had seen this change coming. The Shade turned towards the table.

Chessington asked, "Who am I to choose and for what purpose?"

"This one is not a choice." the Shade stated, "This is a person who has the sole purpose on this journey to be here for this moment and important moments yet to come. This individual shall be of the utmost importance, and without which, you would all be certain of failure. I am here to have Mistress Yaughtie proceed with us to be a valuable part of this lesson."

219

Yaughtie was shook to her very core, "Me? I could certainly be of no use to them in the study of Geography. I know very little about places and such."

"It is not for the purpose of your learning about such places." The Shade told her, "It is about your personal make up and design, however."

"Excuse me?" The young girl asked.

"You are the key to everything in this lesson," he replied, and as a sense of finality, he ended it with, "and you are to join us."

She stepped out from behind the table and stood next to her sister. The Shade turned to face the section of the wall the glow was coming from and disappeared inside. Chessington followed, with Baydowa and Yaughtie reluctantly stepping through as well. The remaining nine watched as the wall closed back up and sealed itself shut, just as it had the first time.

Violta stood and excused herself, walking rapidly to the room she had not used up until this point.

Bansinghaim noticed and remarked to the table, "It'll be a tough few days for her until they return."

Malden agreed, "He's in fer a rough go once he gets back, too. She's a jealous little thing. Not that I don't think she's got reason, but that boy's got it bad fer her, too."

Vastion stood to go see what he could do, but Sir Ghalkin was already ahead of him moving to see how he could comfort her.

* * * * * *

As the rock wall closed behind them the three entering where instructed to lie down, just as Chessington and Sir Malden had been instructed the time before. This time there was a slight difference though as Chessington and Baydowa escaped from their bodily confines, but Yaughtie did not. They waited as the Shade removed the clothing from the younger sister's body and carried the nude sleeping form of Yaughtie to the next room ahead.

Baydowa jumped over to her sister, "What are you doing? What are you going to do to her?"

"She will not be harmed or abused in any way." The Shade explained. His tone was calming, relaxing, and reassuring to both Baydowa and Chessington explaining how this was necessary to the purpose for why they were here.

Their spirits followed the Shade into the next room through what seemed to Chessington as the same corridor he and Sir Malden had gone through the last time. They entered a room not as large as the one before, but on a table was a three dimensional map of what Chessington believed to be the West, East, and area of the Great Beyond between the two. The Shade lowered the body of Yaughtie down onto it as the other two watched it consume her. The Shade moved back, and just as before, he faded away from sight to be done with his business here.

Chessington and Baydowa watched as Yaughtie was lifted up and floated around above the table seeing the map itself draw around her, landing on her, and affixing itself to her. You could see the girl was still nude, but the map wrapped itself so tightly to her skin, she appeared to have one massive tattoo from just below her neck to in some spots down to the middle of her left thigh. They both could see the curvature of her body was perfect in the complimenting of the map as certain curves and features showed the ending of one place and the beginning of another.

"It goes beyond that even." Rustaph announced his arrival to the room, "She has had moles and freckles on her from birth representing cities and spots you may need to go to. She has been made to be the one and only personal legend for this map and your quest."

"Why?" Baydowa wondered, finding the courage to ask for the sake of her sister, "Why couldn't paper or a book work just as well or even better than this? I find it highly irresponsible to do this to my sister."

"First off," Rustaph explained further, "it's perfect. It will be concealed for the most part. The only ones to know of its whereabouts are the people in your group. Secondly, with Chessington's mind as precise as it is, after this experience, and by the time you return to your friends, he will mostly have no need to see it again. It will be part of his mind, and he will never forget it. Third, it leaves you as the guide as the only other person who will have any need to consult her body on a regular basis. Trust me, the men of your group are of the highest integrity, they will not ask to look at it unless they truly have a need to. And fourth, this is her purpose. You have all heard if one of you fails you all fail. This is her part. Her body has been made through centuries of the right two people getting together to create the perfect genetic match for this map, which has been here for more centuries than I have."

Baydowa looked at her sister, "I see this is quite the unexpected turn. I doubt she will be pleased after finding out what she is used for."

Rustaph moved to a bookshelf, which had not been there before when he was explaining things to them. He removed a book and placed it next to Yaughtie, sitting in a chair at the same spot which appeared as he was lowering himself onto it.

"Alright," the ancient Sorcerer began "Mt. Bollantoda is here." He stated, pointing to a large mole on Yaughtie's right breast. A varicose vein, they both understood as they saw her, represented the path they had taken all the way from Phenderia City, on the lower part of the same breast. He looked her over in all the visible areas he could see, but it seemed to be the only vein exposed at the surface of her skin.

Baydowa placed her finger close to a mole just to the west of where they were to ask, "Is this the next place to go? The vein doesn't seem to be near there, and you said moles could make for spots we needed."

"You are very perceptive." Rustaph smiled, "I believe you could be right, but that is up to History. You might need to go there, but you may need to go elsewhere first. Going straight there, might be the wrong move just yet, or it may not. Chessington, since there are no names of the places on this map, what town would you expect that to be from your memorization of the maps you have seen?"

He looked close, seeing it to be on the western edge of the island close to the middle and just above the River Lostanda. Chessington deduced, "I would say it has to be Drenne. Correct?"

Rustaph agreed, "That it would. It does not mean you should go there just yet remember, but it is very likely."

They spent hours on the front of Yaughtie's body, studying the mainland and paying close attention to the freckles and moles, which seemed so unimportant just a little while ago. Chessington placed a name to every one of them, a town, a river, as well as mountain ranges. They learned of areas above the Northern Glacial Limits and Islands in the southern Ponican Ocean, some islands not having been discovered as of yet.

Chessington noticed a large mole on an Island, "Where is that Island? I don't believe I've ever seen that one on a map before."

Rustaph agreed, "I would doubt if you had. No one has officially discovered it yet."

"No one lives there?" Baydowa asked.

"Not necessarily," the ancient Sorcerer replied, "but people who make maps have never heard of it and returned to tell others. The one thing you cannot afford to do throughout all of this is assume."

He stood and returned the book to the bookcase, removed another, and sat back down. He had Yaughtie lifted up slightly from the table she had been lying on and turned a quarter turn to her right, leaving her left side straight up.

"Now we shall move on to areas you have not seen a map for." Rustaph continued, "This will start the portion of your learning about the Great Beyond."

He handed the Wizard the book and instructed him to open to the first page. Chessington opened as instructed and saw the most northern edge of the western border inside of the Great Beyond.

Rustaph showed Baydowa the area on her sister representing this page, "This spot is all high mountains. The path you will need will be found at one of the southern areas to it." He moved down to Yaughtie's hip and located a series of freckles, which represented the trail they would need to get from the Western Kingdoms to the Eastern Empire. "Here is the only passable trail through the Great Beyond. No one has ever tried, but it can be done."

Baydowa laughed, "That's good to know. As a guide I'd find it ridiculous to go down a trail that couldn't be done."

Rustaph grinned, "You also have to understand, just like here and the Woods of the Doltists, the Great Beyond has larger amounts of energy because of the turning of the ground. Higher amounts there than anywhere else you could ever find. So high in fact the animals and plants that have strayed into there over the years have changed from what they once were to a more mutated version of the same species. You may discover some things there you might find strange and very out of the ordinary."

"Will it hurt us?" Baydowa wondered.

"Not for the amount of time you will be there." The Sorcerer answered, "These creatures have been in there for years, some ever since the creation of the mountains."

"Her entire side here at the Great Beyond has almost a purple color to her skin." Chessington noticed.

Baydowa remembered, "She's had that ever since she was born." Pointing to spots on her front, she added, "She has spots of purple in these small areas also. Mom thought it was strange at first, but it never seemed to bother Yaughtie, so we all just forgot about it."

"Look at the Island of Mosa again." Rustaph turned Yaughtie back to her original position, "Notice the two purple spots on the Island?"

Chessington felt odd looking intensely at the sleeping girl's right breast, but did as he was asked, "The two spots are the Woods and this mountain range."

"Correct," Rustaph agreed, "because those purple regions are where you may practice your energy and not be detected. By the same token it is also where your enemies cannot go. I made that revision at the creating of the Great Beyond. As I was dying, I felt Pazlin's mind. It seemed unnaturally aggressive. In hindsight I am very glad I did this. It will give you pockets of relief from the Chiloes should they become a nuisance again."

Rustaph turned Yaughtie face down this time to expose the areas of the East. This map covered her entire back from her shoulder blades to the very top of the back of her thighs. Starting still on her left side and going almost all the way to her right side, stopping just before her body curved back around to the front.

There were mostly areas of freckles with only seven discernable moles to look at and consider, one the size of Chessington's finger tip directly at the top of her right buttock.

Chessington asked Rustaph, pointing to it without actually touching it, "Is that our final destination?"

"That would make the most sense," Rustaph nodded, "That is Ruderrac, the Capitol City of Chiloe. It would also be where Pazlin lives. I am fairly sure whatever you will need to do will ultimately end with confronting him."

Rustaph took a third book from the shelves and placed it in front of Chessington, "Here are the most current maps of the Eastern Empire. The two of you need to study it extensively before you leave. Chessington will have to commit this to memory as he has the Western Kingdoms. After that, the Shade will return to take you back to your physical bodies and to redress Yaughtie before you go back to your group."

Baydowa commented, "You act like you're going to leave us."

Rustaph stood, starting to move towards the wall, "I am. You are not through here yet, and you do not need me for the rest of this. It is just studying the book and the map." He turned to look directly at Baydowa, "And in answer to your questions from before you came in here, if you were not the right person for this task, you would not be here." With this being said, he disappeared through the wall and out of sight.

"You know I feel awkward studying your sister like this, don't you?" Chessington apologized.

"I can tell." Baydowa replied, "I know he's right about this. It's strange, but seeing it on her body like this and seeing the maps in those books, it has to be as he said it is. She's a walking map of the world."

Chessington started to study from the book naming places and having them both find them on Yaughtie's back and buttocks. They studied for what appeared to them to be six or seven hours. Convinced finally Chessington had both the books and Yaughtie's body committed to memory. They sat waiting for the Shade.

He appeared very shortly thereafter, bringing the corridor leading them back to their bodies as well as Yaughtie's clothing. Chessington used the energy to hold the girl up while Baydowa redressed her completely.

The Shade awoke Yaughtie from her sleep and moved the rock wall open to reveal the people from the cave coming from their bedrooms as they could see out the cave entrance it was sometime in the middle of the night. They just were not sure which night it was the middle of.

Chapter 19

Yaughtie seemed quieter and more at piece with herself after the trip she could not remember having. Baydowa took here back into their shared bedroom and told her of what had happened, but more importantly she told her why. Yaughtie felt oddly alright with her role in this excursion. She understood, from the way her sister explained it, about some of the abnormalities to her body, especially the purple birth marks.

Chessington was trying to explain to the rest of the group, with the exception of the children still sleeping, just what had happened and why once they were inside of the room with the Sorcerer Rustaph. He told of what had transpired from the Shade and the sense of shock they both felt as Yaughtie was undressed by him and placed upon the map. He tried his best to give the complete picture of how the map wrapped itself around the form of Yaughtie, adhering to her body, which had to be the perfect match for this particular map. He explained how she had been studied and how they had learned a great deal about certain things; especially, places they would have to experience. He explained further about places where he could practice his craft undetected and how the purple tinted birth marks would show them these locations. He explained about the moles and freckles and how Drenne was a definite mole and a place of some value. All in all the group sensed the personal nature of this new revelation, remaining quiet. Each of them not knowing exactly what to say.

General Vastion started to ask, as his body showed a growing amount of uncomfortable restlessness, "Is Drenne the next stop for us then?"

"We don't know really." Chessington admitted, "Rustaph did warn us of not trying to skip stages or get too assuming about things. We have to do what the book says, the way it says, and most importantly, when it says."

"Okay," Malden asked, "I'll be the one ta ask it. What if we gotta see the map? What if Vastion er Ghalkin has ta know where we are er where we're goin'? You gonna draw one? Doesn't seem too practical in our culture ta put a map someplace we shouldn't have any business lookin'."

A hush dropped over the meeting until a voice came from behind the majority of the group. It was Yaughtie. She had heard what Sir Malden had asked and answered definitively, "Then you will look at the map. My goodness, I'm not a schoolgirl. I know it isn't exactly the best situation, but it's the one we have, and quite honestly, I'm fine about this. At least I know my role in this. A lot of you, and I mean no disrespect, aren't really sure what your purpose here is."

Vastion stood and reassured the young woman, "I assure you, it will only be when necessary, and then only the ones who really need to study the map."

"I'm fine about it, honest." Yaughtie smiled, "Most of you should see it. You have much too much to do and knowing what lies up ahead could be of great value to all of us."

Violta stood next to her, "Coming from a culture where we never wear clothing to begin with, I had an awkward time understanding your tradition of staying covered up. I do understand it is important to humans. Yaughtie is being very mature and understanding about having to put aside certain customs."

It could have been the energy influence inside the cave itself. It could have been the conversations Violta had with Sir Ghalkin while they were gone. It could have been the sleep in the glowing room which had affected Yaughtie or a combination of any of those things. Whichever it was, the two hugged, smiling at one another, and realized they had to set their differences aside for the sake of the group.

Chessington breathed a sigh of relief. He could see how Violta had been mad at her, but was more impressed with her than ever at her ability to see reason in the face of jealousy.

Vastion, feeling the need to move past talking about Yaughtie and her embarrassing role, decided to ask the fairly new Wizard, "You were gone eight days while we all waited. What's the next step. We're all pretty antsy about getting on with this journey."

"As usual," Chessington replied, "I check my book for the newest message. Everything until now has suggested there is one more trip to the room for at least me." He stood to go to his bedroom to retrieve The Book of Past Times yet again. After returning, he sat with them all waiting impatiently for him to read:

Chessington the Twenty-ninth,

It is time for your last lesson at this mountain. There will be other lessons later at other areas for you and your companions as well. For now we will concentrate on this one.

You again will choose one amongst you to follow you and obtain knowledge. This time you will further your studies in your skill of the energy. You will learn new uses, different ways to conceal under certain situations, and be able to practice under the tutelage of a wizard as should have been his duty, and your right, to apprentice before his untimely passing.

The Shade will come for you and your guest again tonight. Choose well, and return to these pages once you have returned. You have much to learn; although, I will advise you this. You will be gone to you what seems to be an undeterminable amount of time. To your friends left within this cave, however, they will count twenty-seven days until your return. On the next day following your return, you will all leave here to continue upon your journey. Set them up well before you go. They cannot leave here before your return.

"Twenty-seven Days?" Vastion exclaimed, "What are we to do here for twenty-seven days?"

Malden leaned back, "Remember when we all thought we was gettin' too tired from runnin'."

"Yes." Vastion remembered.

"Well," the Librarian replied, "we all wished we could stop an' take a break. Guess what, ya got yer wish."

Sir Ghalkin nodded, "He is right in a strangely obnoxious way. We have been here approximately two weeks already, and we have almost one month more to rest and relax, but also to do things we did not have the time for in the past month. Sir Bansinghaim and myself can start instructing the Prince and Preda once again. Chessington can leave some books for General Vastion, Sir Malden, and Modinay. Also, Violta and Gurlig can discuss plants and such and their values."

Chessington stopped him a little short, "Violta should be the one to come with me. I know she's valuable to you as well, but she's more understanding of the energy than anyone else here. She's the most logical fit for this lesson. Besides, if I have to spend twenty-seven days with only one of you, no offense, but she's the one. I would have chosen her even if she had no ability with the energy to begin with."

She came over and held him tightly around the waist, trying not to show the tears she had forming in the corners of her eyes. Everyone watching, even Yaughtie, felt happy for the young couple. He wrapped his arms around her shoulders and held her tightly to him as well.

"Oh, he is good." Bansinghaim approved.

"An absolute natural." Malden agreed.

She looked up into his soft brown eyes and smiled, softening them even further. After a smile was placed on her lips, she turned to Sir Ghalkin and for a reason only they knew of, she hugged him as well.

They all retreated to the lounging area where Gurlig brought them a hot spiced drink and a soft cheese and bread tray during which they discussed certain items the remaining ten of the group would need. Everything they might require such as food and water, parchment and ink, toys for the children, books for all to study, and feed and materials for the horses and carts. Bansinghaim, Modinay, and Gurlig were going to spend time creating a removable canopy for each of the carts, which could be used to keep things covered and have a need for privacy as they traveled down the trails. Yaughtie volunteered for Ghalkin and Vastion to study the map, each of the men insisting Baydowa be included.

Chessington and Violta approached Ghalkin, Malden, Baydowa, and Yaughtie about watching Preda. She had always been cared for by either one or the other of them, and since they were both going away for almost a month, she had to be cared for by the group. Of course, they all agreed, understanding exactly how hard this was for her cousin to have to do, but he knew he had to. She could not come along, and he must go.

After a few hours the children came out as well. Preda ran to Chessington and grabbed him around the waist. He hugged her tightly back and felt odd that he noticed she came up to the same level Violta had, only Preda would still grow taller. The three of them moved to one of the sofas and sat themselves down, the small girl between her cousin and the new female figure in her life.

"What did you do while I was gone?" Her cousin asked, putting his arm around her shoulder and drawing her closer to himself.

"Violta and I played mostly." The younger girl looked at Violta and smiled, "She taught me some games Doltist kids play. She also said I was a little taller than her." Preda grinned, proud she was growing up. "We played dress up, and she stayed in our room with me at night the whole time you were gone. Palton and I studied some. Sir Ghalkin said I can read very well for my age, and he let me write you a letter on real parchment. Here!"

She thrust a folded piece of paper at her cousin and watched him unfold it. He started reading from it, "I love you, Chessy. You are the best cousin ever. Love, Preda." The S's were backwards and there were a few capital letters in the middle of the words, but it brought a smile to Chessington's face.

Preda grabbed it from him, "Read the back, too."

He looked at the back of the paper and read, "Marry Violta soon. I like her."

Chessington blushed and Violta started giggling as well, "I had nothing to do with that." His girlfriend stated.

"Nope," Preda admitted, "that was from me, and Palton helped me spell that part."

"I'm glad you like her, Preda." Chessington told her. The smile dropped from his face as he started to tell her what he had to say, "Actually, I know I just got back, but…"

"You have to leave again, right?" His cousin finished for him.

"Yes," he confirmed, "it should be the last time for a while, but I'm not sure. I don't have a lot of say in what I have to do any more."

"Violta and I'll be alright." Preda added, "We like to do girl stuff."

"Well actually," he continued, "this time she has to come with me. We have to study more about the energy together. We're going to be gone for a very long time. Twenty-seven days to be exact. We asked the rest of the group, mostly Sir's Ghalkin and Malden, but also Baydowa and Yaughtie, to take care of you."

"I want to stay with you though." Preda hugged her cousin tighter.

"I know you do," Chessington replied, "but not this time. We have all of today. After we get back, we'll be going again, and you and Violta can sit on the cart and have girl talk all you want."

Preda liked talking to Violta. She would talk and listen to her for hours and never get tired of her, "I guess, but I want to spend the rest of the day with you both."

Chessington looked at Violta, to which the Doltist replied, "Of course. That is what I wanted to do today also." They all sat a while longer and talked of the things they would do after breakfast.

In the bedroom of Baydowa and Yaughtie, the two sisters sat on the edge of their beds discussing what had gone on lately and how they needed to study during their time waiting for Chessington and Violta to return.

"You seem to be taking this very well." Baydowa stated, "I think far better than I would have."

"I doubt that." Yaughtie smirked, "You know you'd do the same if it were you. Really now, in the grand scheme of thing, does it really matter if a few men see me for the potential good coming from it. It feels kind of nice to be needed after sitting in a basement for the past two years."

"It is a very detailed map." Baydowa continued, "The way your body shows the areas is truly remarkable."

Yaughtie laughed, "I haven't even seen it myself yet."

Baydowa's eyes widened, "Really, you haven't thought to look?"

"Oh, I've thought about it." She answered, "I'm just a little scared to see it."

"It's a magnificent work of art, Yaughtie." Her older sister stated, seeming to have a slight admiration for her situation, "You have to see it."

"Will you stay with me while I look?" She asked, placing her hands on Baydowa's arms before she could stand to leave.

"If you would like me to." Baydowa agreed.

"Please." She stood to unbutton the bodice of her dress top, after taking a deep breath, not knowing what to expect. She folded her top down and unhooked her corset, laying it across the bed. She looked down at her breasts and stomach seeing the map of the West present on her skin. She saw the Ponican Ocean down most of her right side and the Island of Mosa mostly across her right breast.

"See," Baydowa smiled, "you're beautiful. Each freckle and mole is a certain place in the world, and those purple birthmarks are areas where Chessington can use the energy without the Chiloes knowing about it. Your left side is the Great Beyond, an area of huge mountains and was created three thousand years ago by the man we met to study this map. Past that on your back is the lands of the Chiloes. We'd call it the East. It's bigger than the West or the Great Beyond."

Yaughtie looked her front up and down seeing places she knew nothing of. After a full minute of silence, she smiled to her sister, "It would explain a lot about why I've had so many things on my body all these years. How much is on my back? You said the East was a lot bigger than the West."

Baydowa stood and started out of the room, "Just a moment and you'll see." She went out to Chessington and asked, "Could you make a floor mirror for Yaughtie. She's trying to see the map, which seems very difficult if it's on your back."

Chessington laughed and produced a very ornate and tall floor mirror with flowers and leaves carved onto the frame.

Baydowa picked it up, carrying it back to her room to show her little sister. Placing it on the floor in the middle of the room, she announced, "There, now you can see for yourself."

Yaughtie turned her back to the mirror and saw the breathtaking artwork, which was now her back. Seeing it not stop at her waistline she lowered her dress further, then further, then decided to let it fall all the way to the floor. Stepping out from her dress and undergarments, she turned to look herself over in the mirror. Studying the map on her back, she stood there speechless, unable to comment, only smile.

"It's amazing, isn't it?" Baydowa asked.

"Absolutely!" Yaughtie answered, "Oh my, I feel so different, like I'm another person now. I always saw the lines of freckles," pointing to her hip, "and wondered why they were in such a line that way."

"That's where we have to travel through the Great Beyond to get to Chiloe. I can see why, after looking you over more, how a flat piece of paper with this on it just would not be the same." Baydowa explained, "And look at the vein on your right breast. It shows where the group started, and Rustaph said it would grow as we traveled along showing where we've been."

"I'm going to have a long vein showing through all over my body?" She seemed annoyed at this, "I don't want an ugly line running from my front around to my back!"

"Who's going to see it?" Baydowa reminded her.

"A lot of these people!" She replied, "I don't want them seeing an ugly vein running around on my body!"

"It doesn't bother you they can see other things," Baydowa laughed, "just a vein?"

They both laughed at how it sounded while Yaughtie stood in front of the mirror a while longer looking at her new appearance.

Over at the lounging area, Ghalkin, Vastion, Bansinghaim, and Malden sat discussing how they were all stuck there for another four weeks. Each understanding, but also trying to get a schedule for the time they could have to prepare for the upcoming travels.

Vastion opened the discussion still thinking about what would be their course after leaving the mountain and setting out, "Drenne sounds like the long way around to me. I understand if it's what the book says, then we must, but if we need to get to the mainland, I could find much faster ways from the eastern shoreline than the west."

"I'd bet that's what the Chiloe's 're thinkin', too." Malden stated, "I know when we were lookin' fer that escaped assassin, we didn't try west. You an' Ghalkin went east, an' as it turned out, so did he."

Bansinghaim added, "He's right you know. It wouldn't do us much good to go the fastest way possible just to end up getting caught or killed."

There was a hush for a moment before Ghalkin stated, "Once Chessington returns, we will need to have a very thorough list of what we will need to get by until we can get to the mainland and a place to obtain some local currency. Then we will have to find an area where he can produce more without being detected."

"But where will we land, where would the closest place for Chessington be, and what nation's currency would that be?" Vastion wondered, "Before that I would be asking where will we get a boat and further more who knows how to sail one big enough to hold twelve people, nine horses, and two carts, which are fully loaded?"

"Ain't you a ray a sunshine." Malden quipped, "Ever' one a those questions we don't have an answer for. An' ya know what, we won't get an answer fer 'em fer at least twenty-seven days an' maybe longer. 'Bout all we can do is get ourselves ready mentally ta know every option we think could happen. So let's list those instead a bringin' up things we ain't got a chance a knowin'."

Bansinghaim shook his head, "How could you possibly be in politics. That could easily be the most annoying of all the rants you've had on this trip."

Ghalkin kept it moving in the right direction just as if they were back at the castle in the Council Chambers, "Yes Bansinghaim, but he is right. I truly hate to say it, but we need to study the map."

"I agree." Malden nodded, "Knowin' that map backwards an' forwards could be the difference in getting through er not. We get Chessington to make a few copies a current map books fer the four a us, plus Modinay an' Baydowa, and we study 'em 'til our brains fall out. We need ta know those books as well as the boy does without havin' his advantages."

Vastion had to agree, "After we know the books, we can study Yaughtie and see the places which are significant and find the places we really need to understand."

"That sounds reasonable except," Ghalkin proposed, "we should study Yaughtie first with the books and then take notes as to which places are more significant than the others. If we do not see a reason to study say Waston for instance, we should spend our time looking at areas with higher amounts of freckles and moles. After we find those out, we can study independently away from her until we would need to refresh ourselves on the places she locates on herself."

Malden concurred, "That makes the most sense ta me. Awkward as it may be, it's also our best option."

"I see Chessington over by the kitchen area." Vastion stood as he spoke, "We should ask him about those books, as well as a few others we've all mentioned, so he can make them available before they go."

"Might be nice ta have a proper send off." Malden added, standing as well, "I know all a us 're gonna miss those two fer the next four weeks."

Vastion slapped him across the shoulders and smiled, "Absolutely, old sport, absolutely."

Chapter 20

The going away party for the young couple was coming to an end. They all knew the Shade would be there at any moment to take them away, but this time for much longer than he had before. They would be gone for twenty-seven days, after which time the entire group would be on the run once again and headed for who really knew where.

They all were feeling happy still and enjoying the company of one another, none of them choosing to realize it was all about to change. They each had their plans for when the couple would be away. The leaders and guide would study the maps and trails, Ghalkin and Bansinghaim would continue their studies with the children, and the others all had side projects they were looking forward to doing. None had the possibility of getting too bored for lack of things they could do.

Malden stood to make a toast, "Ta preparin' fer better times ta come."

All agreed and toasted to the group's success cheerfully understanding this time was well spent celebrating their group's commitment to each other. Tomorrow would start the work.

Gurlig brought the last piece of the celebration to the large banquet table, Chessington's favorite dessert, blueberry pie. Three of them to be exact.

Yaughtie cut the three, placing the pieces on plates, and then instructing Preda on whom to serve each piece. The little girl took delight in being included, smiling at each member as she took them their dessert. After all were served, they started eating and a hush fell over the cave, which had been consumed with the voices of each person engaged in a private conversation just moments ago.

Bansinghaim looked to Gurlig, "Best pie I've ever had! Where did you learn to bake like this?"

Gurlig smiled, "I worked fer a baker fer two years in Tarint Mosa."

"Who was that?" Vastion asked, knowing a bit about the town in which he was reared.

Gurlig looked down the table at him past Baydowa and Modinay, answering, "Hamblin, over by the Tarint Bridge."

"I remember going in there as a kid. He made these cookies out of the left over pie crust with cinnamon sugar baked on them. He just gave them away to the kids who would come in. He was a round happy fellow."

Gurlig nodded, "Yep, he liked ever'body, an' ever'body liked him, too. If ya don't like a baker, ya gotta look at yerself."

Vastion asked, "How come you only worked there for two years?"

Gurlig looked back, "Cuz he died. He never married, an' so he didn't have nobody ta give the shop ta. So the city took it. Turned it inta a home fer folks with no wheres ta go. After that I left fer Drinblock."

"He could bake." Vastion added.

"Cuz a his secret was the temperature a the ovens." Gurlig admitted, "Gotta be just so, er it don't turn out right. Anybody can bake, but ya gotta know how ta get it ta bake even an' let it get flaky."

The group was talking amongst themselves again when the Shade reappeared from the glowing room at the rear of the cave. Chessington and Violta stood, giving each in the party one last hug goodbye, then left through the opening. They all stared at the rock wall as it closed up to consume their friends one final time.

A silent hush fell over the table as they all sat missing the two who were gone. Each one of them thought to themselves about how the next few weeks would go.

Modinay breached the silence, "I suppose we should think about starting our studies. I'll clean this up and then turn in."

Malden offered, "I'll give ya a hand."

Without the guests of honor, the party seemed to hold no meaning anymore. The group having the current reality hit them, even though they knew it was coming, turned the general mood somber. Each stood, cleared their own plates to the wash tub area, and turned in quietly for the night.

After the Cave was cleaned the entire group went to bed to await the new day and the tasks, which were to be fresh and new, in the morning.

* * * * * * *

The Shade took them into the small glowing room just as he had twice before. Instructing them to lie down and relax as they shed their physical bodies.

Chessington appeared from himself to see Violta as she had looked back in the Woods of the Doltists, a soft mossy green skin, which hid none of her features. He noticed her small form, petite even for a Doltist, hips and breasts giving no indication of anything masculine about her. He looked her over admiring her form from a short distance away. She returned his look with an appreciative smile that soothed him, having to force themselves to look to the Shade patiently waiting for them as they took their time.

They passed through the tunnel of energy to sit in the same room Chessington and Baydowa had studied in, or so Chessington believed. He could not be sure if it was the same room or merely an identical one, and it really made no difference.

Seeing he and Violta were alone with the Shade already leaving them, they sat on a sofa of soft cushioned fabric. Chessington put his arms around her shoulders, and she nestled under his arm with her head against his chest.

"Do you think he will come soon?" Violta asked.

"I wouldn't know." Chessington smiled, gazing into her soft eyes and forgetting much of anything else.

She met his look and gazed back, as their lips moved closer, neither realizing this was the first time they had been truly alone since they had met. His lips touched hers, and they softly kissed a short kiss, then pulled back slightly in recognition of the step they had just taken.

Chessington's mind was swimming. He did not know what to think after their first kiss. Should he kiss her again? Should he wait a while? Should he say something? Having no experience prior to this with a woman, he felt out of his element.

He had, however, dropped his guard and let her see his thoughts, "You should do what you think best." She replied to his thoughts. To which he immediately closed himself off from her abilities.

She laughed at the situation, "If it makes you feel better, I have no experience with males either."

He gave a puzzled look, "But you said you've lived for over three hundred years. Certainly in such time there had to have been a male in the Doltist community who took a liking to you?"

"Sure," she replied, "I've had a few who liked me, and even a couple who liked me enough to try, but I never kissed them. I never feel strongly enough about them."

He met her gaze again, "But you feel strongly enough with me?"

"My goodness," she smiled, "Chessington the Twenty-ninth, where have you been! I have told you repeatedly, I want you as my mate. How could you not figure I wanted everything that went with it, not just holding hands."

He sat for a second, thinking about what she had just said. He still was not sure he knew what he wanted. He knew he liked the kiss, and he would very much like another. He also knew he was confused about a lot of his emotions. He wanted her very much. From what she had just said she wanted him too. He also knew from some of the other boys he had seen with girls, there seemed to be a difference between wanting someone and loving someone.

"You are wise beyond your years, Chessington the Twenty-ninth." It was the rounder form of Feachen the Twenty-eighth. Chessington had remembered him from the first meeting he and Sir Malden had been invited to. "You must learn about emotions and how they can sway your decision making abilities. Should a situation arise where you must choose between a close friend and the betterment of your quest, you must have a clear head to understand the consequences of your actions."

"Will I need to make a decision like that?" The Boy asked him.

Feachen shrugged his shoulders, "You may or you may not, but in either case you must be prepared for it. Energy is not as much ability as it is judgment. You have a gift and with it a responsibility. Abuse it and you may find yourself as bad off as Pazlin appears to be at this moment."

"How will I know?" He wondered aloud.

"You will know." The ancient Wizard nodded, "You have been raised correctly. That was important in you being the one to complete this task. Your mind is sharp and clear, but as happens sometimes, you think of how something is effecting only the situations at the moment. The confrontation at Baydowa's home for instance. You thought quickly, but what you did served to alert Pazlin you at least, and possibly your friends, were still alive and running free on this Island. How would you have done better now since you have the gift of hindsight?"

Chessington knew this. He had thought about it constantly after it had happened. "It would have been better for me to have waited. If Violta had been hurt, as I had feared at the time, the moment waiting wouldn't have changed anything. Yaughtie was securely surrounded by my friends, and there really should been no need for me to have done anything in that situation except make sure he couldn't harm anyone. I should have reminded myself of Violta's internal make up and realized she would be fine."

"You have figured it out for yourself then." Feachen praised, "You are ahead of most your age in this as well. Learning to put aside hatred and ego for the betterment of the group, and in this situation the world, puts you at an advantage even Pazlin has yet to learn."

"I didn't say I could do it if I had to." Chessington revealed, "I just said I know I need to."

Feachen smiled, "Knowing what to do is always the first step in changing the process. Now, let us study. We have much to cover, and you must practice everything until it becomes second nature for you."

The teacher turned to pull three identical books from a shelf, which appeared only as long as Feachen needed for it to and then faded from sight. The old Wizard walked to the opposite side of the room to sit at a table with three chairs placed around it, setting a book in front of each chair.

Violta and Chessington sat, each behind a book, and saw them open to the same page in each.

Feachen started his lesson with the statement, "We will start with the teaching of how to detect others who are using energy. It will be very important for you to know where Pazlin and his Adherents are at all times. They will be heading for you as soon as you clear these mountains. Sometimes you will not be able to avoid them, but usually you will."

Violta looked at the page in her book, which was written in her native Tistenesse, a language having been the written language for the Doltist community since their inception thousands of years ago. "Did History write these as well?"

Feachen answered, "Not directly, but History has a hand in everything that happens. It places ideas into our heads and pushes certain situations together, but in the end we still have the freedom of choice to do what it suggests or not."

"So," Chessington summarized, "we would be better served following intuitions and our hearts on most occasions than trying to out think ourselves."

"Oh my yes," Feachen replied, "very much so. That is most of the reason you have all gotten this far. General Vastion could have decided to ignore Queen Rhyshena when they were at the edge of the Woods of the Doltist. You could have stayed away from the room under the castle after your dream with the Shade. And you could have not chosen to take Modinay with you, but you all listened to your instincts and your heart over your heads at those moments and trusted yourselves."

"Why do we do that?" Chessington asked.

Feachen laughed slightly, "Animals already know to follow their first instincts, and yet humans do not understand how they have survived for centuries without humans around to save them. Humans feel a need to be in charge. How many times have you been given a choice and your first thought is to do it one way, but you convince yourself the other choice is better only to find out you were wrong?

Chessington thought, "Quite often, I would guess."

"Because," the old Wizard replied, "the first thought was placed there by History itself, and the second thought was your freedom of choice. In most instances it really is not terribly important, it is just a small choice, but now your choices are much larger. You need to think with your feelings and your heart first but separate from your emotions as you do."

"That seems easy until you have to do it." The boy acknowledged.

"Absolutely." Feachen agreed, "Now to continue with our lesson. To detect the whereabouts of others using energy you must first go to the core of the energy and become part of it. Right now you know how to use the energy, but you have no concept of being part of it. It is an enormous feeling. You could get very lost if you get turned around. This is why we have learned to tether ourselves to our bodies before we go out to find where the energy is being used."

"How would I tether myself to my body?" Chessington wondered.

Feachen answered, "The same as you do when you leave yourself to go scouting for General Vastion and Sir Malden. You leave a trail of energy behind you, which you can recognize and follow it back."

"But if I'm traveling inside of energy," He asked, "how can I tell mine from all of the other energy already there?"

"First of all," Feachen reminded him, "what is energy and where is it?"

"It's everywhere." Chessington remembered from The Book of Mysticism, "Everything with mass, no matter how small or large, is made up of energy."

"Correct," Feachen agreed, "so when you leave your energy behind you, after you leave your body, you still know yours from the rest that it is around, correct?"

"Yes," Chessington understood, "so the energy below the surface is no different than the energy on top?"

"Not exactly." The Wizard taught, "The energy on the surface is mostly at rest, the energy below is much more active. You need to set a more solid trail for yourself to return, but it is the same basic principal."

They practiced having Chessington send himself down into the energy a few times and then return. After they had practiced for a while, Feachen showed him how to go and look for energy moving back up and follow it to the surface, but not quite all the way, or he could be detected doing it by the one or ones there. Chessington was told at the battle outside of Marroda, when he was feeling Pazlin trying to locate another body to inhabit after the destruction of Dainthin, he was inadvertently made very vulnerable. A proper Wizard could have cut him off from behind and separated him from his body back in Chiloe.

He told them if you do get cut off from your body, you have two choices. First, you can try to find it by going back below and through the energy, but that could force you to get very lost and take forever. The second choice is to go around on the surface and travel the way Chessington does on his scouting missions, but that takes a long time as well. He explained if Pazlin had become disconnected from himself at

Marroda and he chose to go above ground back to his body, it would have taken him roughly six or seven days to return if he went directly there.

Feachen told Chessington to go under and look for passages to the surface. Since time has no meaning, he would be to his destination at the same second he entered the underground energy. The boy left to explore underground and traveled through the energy to where he spotted a light from above. Going upwards he found he was at the surface, in a warm climate, mostly sandy and completely uninhabited in appearance. He saw the occasional cactus and the wildlife appeared to be mostly of lizards, snakes, and insects larger than he had ever seen before. He noticed no people and saw no clouds, only a hot burning sun scorching everything under it. Taking it all in, he retreated back into the energy and followed his trail back to Feachen and Violta.

"What did you see?" The old teacher asked.

"I saw a land full of large snakes, lizards, and insects where the sun was extremely hot all of the time and nothing grew from the ground except cactus, which I had remembered from a drawing in my books back at the farm."

"You were at the southern edge of the Bortegestian Desert." Feachen told him, "You saw the greatest desert known to this world. Energy is very strong there, but the heat and sun's constant rays have made it uninhabitable to humans."

"That's past many hundreds of miles of ocean and more land as well." Chessington was amazed at how quickly he could be to another part of the world.

"Around one thousand four hundred miles from here." Feachen explained, "Every spot in the world is as easy to get to as that one and all are instantaneous. There are the two points on the Island of Mosa, three on the mainland of the West, all of the great beyond, and seven places in Chiloe. We use them as short cuts, and after a while of practicing and getting familiar with them, you can decipher which passages are which. With even more use you can figure out how to move at the same speed through the surface using the passages to get yourself close and then following the surface energy as fast as the underground energy to get anywhere instantly."

"How long would it take to learn that?" Chessington asked eager to be competent enough to travel at this speed.

"I would imagine after two or three months of exploring the underground, you would be able to find all of the shortcuts." Feachen thought further, "Maybe another month to master traveling fast on the surface."

"Should I start exploring now?" Chessington asked.

"I do not see why you would not." Feachen advised, "I have matters to discuss with Violta as well. Remember, time has no meaning where you are going. You will return at approximately the same time as you leave. The only difference is the amount of time you spend on the surface before submerging back underground again."

Chessington, anxious to learn this new skill, left and started traveling through the underground leaving Violta with Feachen.

"Now," Feachen turned to the young Doltist girl, "you may have the most important assignment of the group."

"How do you mean, Sir?" Violta wondered.

"You have the job of keeping him mentally alert and ready at all times." He revealed, "Young Chessington has all of the abilities, but anyone who has been given great powers has also been given great responsibilities. It is always a temptation to wizards and sorcerers alike to try to use there use of the energy to their own personal gain. This has a fine line it involves."

"I understand." She stated, "He can do certain things for himself, but not if they infringe on others rights as well."

"Exactly," Feachen agreed, "this is why you two were pushed together. Who would be better to understand the responsibilities of having certain abilities than a Doltist who uses her abilities every day to keep her entire species safe from the outside world?"

"Is that why I was chosen to come on this quest?" She asked, "Was I to be the stabilizing factor for the Wizard?"

"Mostly yes," Feachen nodded, "it is also why you love each other and are meant to be together. It is because you are so closely intertwined you actually are the absolute compliment to the other. You were formed that way over time, just as much as Yaughtie was designed by her genealogy to be the perfect compliment to the map. You were meant to be with him before either of you were ever born."

"So we will live happily forever?" She asked, very hopeful this would mean her life was going to be a little easier after all of this.

"As like anyone else," Feachen replied, "you will get out of it exactly what you put into it."

Chessington took this instant to return to the little room. Excitement brimming from his face as he appeared tired and exhilarated at the same time.

"I visited briefly from here to a farming community in the northeastern part of Chiloe, and everywhere in between." Chessington told them, "It was terrible to see how they live there, but the odd thing to me was they don't realize they're being mistreated. They do what their ancestors have done for generation after generation. Women are grossly abused and men are basically slave labor which is run into the ground. There are no pets or colors, even the plants seem drearier. There's no recreation or enjoyment, they just work for twelve to sixteen hours a day and then do it again the next day. Children have their future decided for them by the age of eight where one test decides if you'll be a farmer, a soldier, or in the higher workings of the government."

"It sounds horrible." Violta exclaimed, "Why has History not pushed to change this sooner?"

"It has many times," Feachen revealed, "but it has never gotten this far. The short distance you and your friends have made it is farther than anyone before you has gone on this quest."

"But it seems we have so much farther to go?" Chessington said in amazement.

"You do," Feachen agreed, "but most quests never made it to the part where the right people believed enough to try to do anything."

"What would be next then?" Violta asked the old Wizard.

"Next you will rest together for a while." Feachen stated, "I must go and prepare for your next lesson, but you both need to be alone for a while and realize just how closely woven you two really are."

"When will we see you again?" Violta wondered.

Feachen grinned and started to fade out, "When it is the proper time. Until then you must allow yourselves to open up and become mentally joined. The Doltists are correct, young Chessington the Twenty-ninth, you do not need to have a ceremony or a priest to be joined. If it makes you feel better, once I return I will join you both together as man and wife if I feel you both are sincere about it at that time." Then he turned himself away and was gone.

Chapter 21

Three days after the departure of Chessington and Violta, the group had their daily routine down. Gurlig had breakfast ready and on the table at seven, the children would study with Sir Ghalkin from then until lunch, after lunch Sir Bansinghaim would teach Prince Palton about horsemanship and combat training while Yaughtie was showing Preda how to sew and cook, and after dinner the study of the books and maps began. Yaughtie would disrobe, leaving Vastion, Ghalkin, Malden, Modinay, and her sister to study from the books using her body as the study guide. After an hour or so of this, they would all retreat to the lounging area for an evening of discussions before they would all turn in.

While some were doing their normal daily routine, Malden would spend most of his day reading and rereading the books Chessington had left behind, mostly The Dialog of History they had read together while they sat before the Tribunal. He had now completed it for the third time, each time picking more and more information out of the great book. He knew tomorrow he would read it again. It was an obsession for him. His desire was to know and understand every facet of his enemy in case he needed an understanding of the many hows and whys of the Chiloe people's mindset, but mostly the mind of their enslaver, Pazlin. It made him want to consume even more. He had to fully get inside the Sorcerer behind all of the turmoil befalling the West and even before then the East.

Modinay, Gurlig, and Bansinghaim had a rough shell made for one of the carts, which could be easily broken down to fit inside and flat on the back of it, but they had a few areas to work the bugs out of yet. With twenty-four days to go, they still had plenty of time.

Yaughtie was sitting next to Preda showing her how to sew together squares which would eventually form a blanket. They were talking about things they remembered from before these hard times. Yaughtie was telling her about a time she remembered from when she was just a couple of years older than the small girl.

"My mother sat me down and showed me exactly what we're doing here." The young Derentian woman recalled, "She showed me on squares just like you have, and we would sew them together until it was taller than I was. Then we made another one just like it."

"I have to make two of these?" Preda asked.

"Of course," her teacher explained, "we have to put some stuffing on this one, then we put the other one over the stuffing, and after that we sew it closed around the edges."

"And then we're done?" The little girl wondered.

"Oh no," Yaughtie continued, "after we get it so the stuffing won't fall out, we have to sew patterns in the middle. The first pattern I made was of a flower with long pedals with little flowers all around it."

"So it'll look pretty, right?" Preda grinned.

"Yes," Yaughtie agreed, "but also to keep all of the stuffing in place. If we don't stitch the middle, every time you pick it up, the insides will all fall to the bottom. If we stitch it up in the middle, it all stays where it should, and the blanket will be warm all over and not just at the bottom."

"Oh," Preda understood now, "I always though it was just to make the blanket pretty, but that makes sense too."

After a moment of silence, Preda turned and asked as children will sometimes do, "Does it bother you to have the men see you naked?"

Yaughtie thought a moment, not wanting to be misunderstood, "I suppose it would be if they were just looking at me to see me, but they aren't. They have a need to see what's on me, not me personally if that makes any sense. It's just different. There's respect involved, and sometimes we have to be uncomfortable for the group so we all can beat our enemies, like this Sorcerer Pazlin."

"Did I stitch this right?" Preda stated unfazed by her friend's answer to her question. Preda had the understanding of a child. Adults were the ones dwelling on certain things while children are given the ability to let them go.

Yaughtie looked over and saw she had gone too deep into the square she was sewing and bunched a bit of fabric up making it wrinkle just a bit. "You have a very good eye, Preda. If we pull this stitch out now, we won't have to pull more out later." She pulled her needle off of the line of thread the child was using and pulled out the stitch. She handed the needle back to her after she had rethreaded it, and then showing her how to fold over the edge of her squares so the line she was sewing would have a better look to it.

Preda looked up to see the massive Sir Bansinghaim showing the much smaller Prince Palton about hand to hand combat and how to get the advantage even against a much larger opponent.

"Now," the large knight was instructing to the much smaller boy, "if someone should attempt to pick you up and carry you off, I'm going to show you something you can do to slow him down and maybe even try to get him to leave without you. First, take your first two fingers on your right hand and stick them out along with your thumb."

The Prince held up the three fingers his friend had asked him to.

"Good, now using your thumb as a guide, pinch hard right at the soft spot on the base of my neck." Bansinghaim lowered himself down to the Prince's level waiting for the sting in his neck he had told the child to do.

"Ow!" Bansinghaim played it up only slightly, the Prince had pushed quite hard, not knowing his abilities yet, "Now, with any luck he would drop you. What do you do next?"

"Run away." The boy replied.

"Not yet, Your Highness." Bansinghaim replied, "At your age he would just recover and chase you down much wiser than before, figuring you would try to hurt him again. Rather than run, while you have him surprised and reeling from the first sting of your attack, since you're on the ground, you're going to kick as hard as you can at either of his kneecaps, forcing them backwards and breaking his leg, making it impossible for him to get back up." He laid on the floor and demonstrated in slow motion what he wanted the Prince to do. "Now you try, please."

"I don't want to break your leg, Sir!" The young prince stated.

"No no," the large teacher grinned, "You'll kick at my hand pretending it's my knee."

"Oh, okay." Palton laid on the ground on his side just as Sir Bansinghaim had shown him. He raised his leg and kicked at Bansinghaim's hand.

"Pretty good," his instructor nodded, "but you'll need to do it faster, sharper, and a lot harder. This is a grown man. You will probably only get one shot. After that he'll adjust to your attack and being larger and stronger, he'll just hit you until you stop putting up a struggle."

"But I'm the Prince?" Argued Palton.

"He won't care, Your Highness." Bansinghaim explained, "All he knows is, he's supposed to take you to someone. All you need to understand is, he could do anything at any time, and the longer you let him be in charge, the better are his chances of taking you."

Palton kicked again at his friend's hand. Each one was critiqued by his teacher until he had a stream of sweat running off of his forehead from the exercise.

After around one hundred kicks, Bansinghaim agreed he had it down very well. Seeing the boy getting a workout, and being a bit hungry himself, he wrapped his massive arm around the boys shoulder, and they headed off towards the kitchen area.

Meanwhile Sir Ghalkin, General Vastion, and Baydowa were studying the books of maps they each had been given before Chessington left for his most recent lesson. Baydowa was looking over a map of Hitrenda, seeing how the towns were all very close together and none were of much size except three. The port towns of Bowenda in the north and Lienda to the south were two of the three largest cities in the kingdom. The capital city of Slenda on the main river of the country, the Valdo River, would be the largest city they knew of in the West. She saw a never ending series of lines, too confusing to study to the point of memorization, signifying the roadway system of the country.

Since they were studying the roads of the mainland, Sir Ghalkin told them both a story he had heard while learning about negotiations as an apprentice. "It seemed Hitrenda was the most influential and wealthy nation in the West as they still are to this day. They had more of everything and all of it could be sold for the right price. Once, approximately three hundred years ago, the King of Valdo hired a company from Slenda to design and install a system of roads for them matching the quality of the originals back in Hitrenda. After the completion of the job from the company, a job I might add which took seventeen years, the King of Valdo decided they should not have to pay because Valdoans were superior to the working class Hitrendans; therefore, it would be an honor for the Slendan company to do the job for free."

"Are they really that arrogant?" Baydowa asked a bit shocked at the nerve of the Valdoans.

"Oh yes," Sir Ghalkin reassured her, "they still are too, and for no real reason. The King of Hitrenda decided to amass his army on the Valdoan border and invade for the first ten miles of Valdo. Valdo, having only a token army since they are grossly under populated, had no other choice than to surrender. During the treaty negotiations, the Valdoans were forced to pay all amounts to the private company plus ten percent, and the Hitrendans pulled back five miles keeping the first five as a reminder to the Valdoan government they were hardly as superior as they seemed to think they were. The border has stayed the same to this very day, and the two have coexisted ever since."

"But shouldn't a King know better than that?" The guide wondered.

"My dear," Vastion added, "as a rule, Kings are the worst at wanting everything their way without giving up anything in return. It seems to be how they are. Palton's father was never like that, thank the good Lord, but your King, rest his soul, was horrible at thinking of himself first and others later. We ran into an entire town held hostage by highwaymen robbing and murdering at will much like the men you were faced with. Your King would not spare the men to rid this problem because he had an attempt on his own life five years prior and just simply would not allow men to leave to go keep the peace."

"What do you mean *rest his soul?*" Baydowa asked.

"I am not sure, of course," Vastion admitted, "but the first thing the Chiloes wanted to do after invading Phenderia was to assassinate the royal family and all of the high ranking government officials. We all just happened to be spared because of events, which when added together, kept us out of their hands."

Baydowa staring at the pages and pages of maps said for both of the men to hear, "This would be so much easier if we knew the route we were taking. How much easier could it be if we already knew the order of the towns we had to go through?"

"I would suppose," Ghalkin suggested, "we could connect the dots on Yaughtie and see roughly how we should be headed. There might be a few side trips the book could throw in our way, but generally I do not see why we should not do just that."

Baydowa and Vastion looked to each other each one coming to the same conclusion after the revelation by Sir Ghalkin. Baydowa turned to the General, "I'll get Yaughtie while you two get Malden and Modinay, and then we'll meet up in our room."

"Absolutely!" Vastion stated as he rose to do as she had just suggested.

The four men entered to find Yaughtie face up on her bed, already in the proper fashion for what she had to do. Her top exposed, as they would have no need for her below the waist on this occasion. They would track the path to the trail of freckles on her hip through the Great Beyond and then discuss the trail before continuing on into Chiloe.

Malden sat at a small table next to the bed the group used when studying the map. He had his book of maps, a quill, and a small cup of ink ready to mark his book to the straightest paths corresponding with the moles and freckles on Yaughtie's body.

Looking at the large mole on her right breast, Vastion stated, "We already know from Chessington, we will probably have to get to Drenne. We all assumed once there we would need a boat to get to the mainland."

Modinay noticed, "We have two choices then. One, we start at the northern most mole and work our way south to the trailhead in Bortegestia, or two, we find another port town and figure we need to head north to those moles above it. We already know the last place we need to be on this side of the Great Beyond is in Bortegestia and the trail on her hip in the southern part of the country."

"Logical," Malden agreed, "let's find the names a all the towns corresponding ta her moles an' freckles, an' then we can look an' see how many er on the coast."

Starting in Bodash, they located Resota, Osendan, Peggat, Kolgatga, Alagapa, Vologa, Rikipo, Odiccu, Sippshu, Whildo, Ingu, Ordent, Perllia, and Dorga. Below there in Ghalacadia they located only five towns, Daping, Whillshow, Gindo, Hinguta, and Horgling. Still further to the south in Hitrenda, they located the capital city of Slenda, but also Goenda, Makawa, Leacoupawa, Illenda, Glivda, Crelda, Khlenda, Podowa, Dollawan, and Boge north of the capital. Then the trail turned to the east through Betowa, Skewa, Talawa, Vowa, and Keyana. Afterwards it led to Valdo as they located the town of Leotot before getting to Great Valdo City and turning back south to go through Yantot and Dretot before crossing into Bortegestia. Once there they would enter Relafelg before going to their capital city of Gestiafelg. Continuing on, the trail kept moving south to Loopafelg and Wagafelg before heading to Lake Felg and the lake towns of Ashagafelg and Gogafelg. The final place, which there was only one single mole left before the trail of freckles inside of the Great Beyond, appeared to be Chepafelg.

Once naming every town represented by a mole from the young woman's body, they noticed there were only two coastal towns on that list, and both were in Bodash. Dorga at the southern most point of the Bay of Stoga, and what they believed to be Peggat, a small town on the coast approximately seventy-five miles south of the capital city of Kresh. The group decided Dorga made better sense to start at, but Peggat would be less noticeable if they were being chased.

The list appeared to flow from north to south with two noticeable turns to the east, one from Slenda to Great Valdo City, and the other from Lake Felg on to the Great Beyond. They studied the map Malden had marked up. The trail was easy to see once it was put on paper, but as they had all seen it on Yaughtie, it looked very disjointed and random. Now, with the map matched up to the corresponding towns and cities, it was as plain as day.

"We start at Dorga," Vastion stated. It was so obvious now, "you may redress, Yaughtie. We should study from Malden's book tonight and commit this to memory. Soon we'll do the same with the Great Beyond and Chiloe. We shouldn't need to see Yaughtie's map so often."

"Guess we start studyin'," Malden stood and left to the lounging area. Others being more proper, thanked Yaughtie and complimented her for her understanding and reason before heading to study with the map book.

* * * * * *

Emperor Pazlin sat in his throne room overlooking the crowd of men who had amassed for Lord Maldifren's funeral. Seeing it filled with dignitaries and high ranking officials from some of the closer regions to the capital as news and information certainly had not traveled as far as the outlying areas pertaining to Maldifren's death as of yet. He did notice some of their representatives who were living in Ruderrac from all regions had attended, and soon all of these people would realize how little the new Emperor needed them.

Grastock, standing to the right of Pazlin, looked out as well, "Emperor, shall I do away with them now?"

"No," Pazlin stated indifferently, "I'd like to watch them squirm as I tell them about upcoming events. This is my dessert after three thousand years of playing their games. Believe me I wish a few from the past were still here to torture instead of this worthless lot. I could bore you with stories of jackasses who thought they were far superior to me only to find themselves jumping off of a chair with a rope around their neck much like Maldifren did."

Pazlin waited fifteen more minutes and nodded for the doors to be sealed and the guards to stand at all doors and windows. "Dear guests," he started off with a gentle tone and a smile, "we are here today to remember the legacy of our departed Emperor, Lord Maldifren. I should like to tell you a few things I know personally about him."

All stood and were quiet as the ancient Sorcerer sat at his new throne and spoke to the crowd. "He was an idiot." Pazlin remarked to the shocked looks from the men's faces in the crowd before him, "He had no ability whatsoever in concerns of government. He could barely lace his boot in the morning without help. He had the worst temper I had ever seen, including all of his ancestors, who also where complete idiots. I and I alone have ruled this great country for three thousand years, unified it, governed it, built it up from the abysmal state it was in after the great war with the West, and I alone am solely responsible for the future conquering of the West which lay at our feet."

"Even as we speak my army is in complete control of the Island of Mosa, and we will use it as a launching area to take the West, country by pitiful country." He stood and paced across the front of the raised area his new throne centered. Placing his hands behind himself, he spoke while appearing to think out loud, "I have seven Adherents, each more powerful than any of you. With them I can rule this expanding Empire and know more than it would be possible to know through you."

He paused a moment to let all grasp exactly what he was saying to them. Stopping his pacing and turning to face them all, he completed his thought, "I am enjoying this moment, telling you how little you are all worth to me. You should now realize what is coming. I am relieving you of more than your duties. I truly see no use for any of you. You would make terrible farmers, and the military is now run by me. I could have you all sent to prisons, but that would mean I would have to feed you all and clothe you. Honestly, do you think I need such things on my mind? I should say not. No, I believe you are all very expendable even to keep you around would be cumbersome. You would require things I would rather give to the military or the procreation houses, so I will be releasing you into the air, and no one will miss you."

He started with a man in the front who had been the Royal Liaison to the First Prince. He looked at him and instantly all around watched as the man of around fifty-five disappeared into the air around him.

A quiet shock sped through the room followed by a panic of rushing bodies trying to break through the guards who had them all sealed in. Like shooting birds in a cage, Pazlin took great delight in extinguishing the life of each man present one by one. As the room cleared, one was left, a representative from the region of Ekla. He looked horrified as he awaited his demise, "Why are you doing this?" The man stated frantic of his fate.

Pazlin, with Grastock next to him, sent him to his destiny and remarked after he was gone, "Because I can."

Pazlin then turned towards the door with Grastock in tow. They had more important things to deal with such as to return to his study and start the plans of the invasion of Bodash.

Chapter 22

Chessington and Violta had spent days together. Days filled with talking, cuddling, studying, practicing, and intimacy. They where becoming the compliment of each other. Chessington was the power and raw force needed to work the energy, and Violta the stabilizing factor needed to keep him grounded and solidly focused.

They were as close to being one person as there could possibly be. Following directions in their studies to the letter and making themselves work through practice and repetition. Chessington would do something, and the petite love of his life would keep him directed as to what he was doing. Some of these processes were far more complicated than anything he had done in the past. Some were basic things done together to achieve a certain outcome. Others were completely new to the Wizard and required more persistence before getting things just the way they needed to be.

They knew also the energy alone would not make them complete. They had to be one person, one soul, and of one mindset. They were achieving this required intimacy, the kind only found through love and mutual respect. They were finding they could never say they were done studying this, as it would be an ongoing challenge for them until the day, far off in the future, when they would parish from this realm and reside in the next.

Chessington had just finished studying the mechanics of how to statue, a way to hold someone captive by removing their ability to move most of their bodily awareness, even closing down the innermost part of the mind filtering energy through. This could be very valuable, but also dangerous to the wizard or sorcerer trying to immobilize another with the ability. If the person you were dealing with was quick enough they could trap you inside, close the exits, and essentially trap the attacker in their own mind leaving them helpless to finish what they had first tried to do. After which the one now trapped could be dealt with in numerous ways. It seemed to Chessington, the most crucial part was to get in and immobilize your victim as quickly as possible, and then retreat just as quickly before the victim knew what was happening. With practice he could trim the time down to less than a single second.

The beauty of this lesson would be your victim could not run away or fight back, but they could listen and speak. Once they were trapped, they would be completely at the mercy of their captor. The interrogations could begin, and the interrogator could do as they saw fit. Chessington would be merciful. He would not expect Pazlin or any of his Adherents to do the same.

"This is a lesson which has to be precise and quick." Violta explained to her boyfriend, "If something turns out wrong, there would be no way for us to help you. You have to practice on me."

Chessington appeared shocked she would volunteer for such a thing, "Are you sure? I would have complete control of you. This is, you know, how Pazlin and his Adherents keep all of the Chiloe Army in line."

"You have to practice it." Violta looked deep into his eyes, "I doubt I would have any problem with anything you would do to me." She hugged him around the waist and looked mischievously up into his eyes, daring him to do it.

"You would give me that kind of power over you?" Chessington asked.

Violta grinned, "I would, but I would not suggest you should ever allow me to return the favor. I know what I would have you doing." She kissed him softly on the lips, and as he held her tightly, it happened, "You tricked me, Chessington the Twenty-ninth!" She laughed hard; although, the only part of her moving was her mouth and tongue, her eyes were even stuck staring straight ahead.

"You told me to." He replied, "Besides, if you knew it was coming, it wouldn't have been a true test for me now would it?"

The frozen Doltist girl thought about it, "You are right. It would not. Now what?"

"Now I need to go inside your mind and find out what parts of the brain go to what parts of your body."

He laid her down on a soft floating pillow perfect for her size and shape, and he moved into her mind. "Can you still hear me?" He asked.

"Perfectly dear." She replied, "Remember you need to find the parts controlling motor functions, speech, and reason."

"I think I've found where the speech is." He sent a message to the spot he had found and listened.

Violta spoke as plain as day, "Chessington loves me, and I will be happy to wait as long as it takes for him to completely commit."

"Hey!" she screeched, this time of her own accord, "Stop that! I would not want to wait too long, dear. Besides, you know I am right."

"I know what I heard." Chessington smiled, "You'll wait as long as I want."

Next Violta found herself sitting up and standing, "I see that you have located the motor skills."

He laid her back down and proceeded on, "I think I just have reason left then." He found it after minimal searching, and asked a simple question, "If you could think of one reason to wait for us to join together as man and wife, what would it be?"

She knew he had her this time. He had bypassed her ability to lie or stray away from the truth. She had to answer to the best of her ability even if it served her not to, "I would wish to wait just because you are not ready yet."

He asked another question, "Is this the only reason?"

She answered softly, "Yes, I know with all of my heart we belong together. All of this could be stronger with our commitment to join together. Call it what you wish: joining, marriage, becoming one; we are meant to be together. I wish for it sooner because I know it is what should be. Why would I wish to wait for it when it is right in front of us? I love you. I always will, and every second we wait is one less second we could be joined together as one. You talk about being committed to this quest first and foremost, but I know in my heart you would be stronger if it were us instead of you working on this. It is what this whole lesson is about. You allowing me to be the part of you you do not already own, and me practicing being your, I mean our, feminine side."

Chessington was dumbstruck. She made so much sense, and he knew she was right. She had said it truthfully, and he believed she would have said it exactly the same had she not been under his influence of telling the truth.

He removed himself from her mind and released her from the crippling effects of his lesson. She sat still on the pillow he had provided for her when she was helpless and immobile, watching him lower himself to one knee before her.

He looked to his hand and concentrated energy into a ring, a solid gold ring as petite as the finger it would rest on for hundreds of years to come. The sides she noticed had many trees engraved on it with hearts in their branches and sparkling colors of reds and greens. The images were so interconnecting, it appeared to be alive. The trees appeared to move, and the hearts appeared to float through the design as if they could move around the ring. He looked up into her face, the most beautiful he had ever seen, to ask, "Violta, most enchanting of all creatures ever to set foot on this world, the love of my life and the future of me, would you please do me the honor of marrying me as soon as we may be?"

Violta, sitting in quiet disbelief of this moment now actually happening, answered, "Yes Chessington, oh my dear, yes! As soon as we can, we will be, and I will love you forever."

They held each other for a few moments longer only to hear from behind Violta, "Congratulations to the both of you." It was Feachen the Twenty-eighth, "You have now completed what you were brought here to do."

Chessington looked confused, "I thought I was brought here to understand the uses of the energy better."

Feachen grinned, "That was the tool of the lesson, but the lesson itself was for you both to realize you needed to be completely committed to one another for the strongest outcome of your quest. This is one you had to learn without a book, and your future bride said it so well, *that all of this could be stronger with your commitment to join together.* As soon as she said it, it became perfectly clear to you, did it not?"

Chessington thought back to the moment his heart softened. He understood it was about them and not only him, "Yes, that was it. She made me realize I didn't need to think as I was raised to think. My place isn't to be the provider and protector. She can do all that for herself. I have to think as a Doltist would. We are a team and not two individuals."

Feachen nodded his agreement, "You both will be each others biggest asset in the future. Rely on each other, and you will be stronger than Pazlin himself."

Violta asked, as impatient as ever, "When are we to be married?"

Feachen laughed and smiled at the happy couple, "When you return to the cave, I will follow instead of the Shade. As a wizard, I have the authority to marry. I will perform the nuptial ceremony and then return to here. Remember, you will need to leave the following morning from the cave. Look to the book at your special page once you are outside at the base of the mountain and in search of a direction to go."

Chessington was happier than he had been for a long time. Looking at Violta he held her close and stated, "I'm going to have a wife."

"Yes, you are," she replied, "and you will be a husband. My husband forever."

* * * * * * *

Pazlin sat in his personal study in long distance conference with each of his Adherents simultaneously. Grastock, his number one Adherent, was seated next to him in the spacious study, while Rostic, his second Adherent, was in charge of the affairs on the Island of Mosa with central command coming from the castle at Phenderia City. Phosting, Narrol, and Pritt were also on the Island, the first two, numbers three and four respectively, were overseeing the Derentian and Iclanian relocation, but were also actively looking for the Wizard who had escaped into mountains almost seven weeks before. With Pritt the lowest ranking Adherent left after the murdering of Dainthin, all he could do was to oversee the loading of the civilians onto ships at Loglistin. Number five, Balstass, was laying the groundwork in Slenda for their overthrow, and the number six adherent, Clostig, was getting things ready in Bodash for the first invasion of the mainland.

Since all detested each other, this meeting had no informal chit chat, which usually happens in the beginning of these types of events. All focused in and waited for their turn to speak once spoken to.

Pazlin started the conversation, "Clostig, how are things going in Bodash?"

"Very well, My Master." Clostig stated, confident he had all of the right answers, "King Rupath has his guards running around the country side. They see nothing coming just as it was in Phenderia. I picked another farmer close to the capital city, murdered him, and burnt his home. It seemed to work so well the last time. I figured I should not change a thing."

"Good," Pazlin agreed, "Westerners see fit to champion every farmer and civilian who has something go wrong. It is their downfall I suppose, caring."

"It seems to be the outcry amongst the locals that justice needs to prevail." Clostig continued, "It is all so humorous really, as if a King should waste time about one farmer."

Pazlin moved along. He asked now for the current information of Hitrenda, "How are things in Slenda, Balstass? Have you worked your way into the government yet?"

"Yes, My Master." Balstass replied, "I have taken the form and voice of the King's First Advisor. He should be easy to manipulate, very simple minded. He spends most of his day listening to the minor squabbles of the local businessmen here. I should have him convinced very shortly the Hitrendan Army needs to invade Valdo. With the majority of the Army settled on the eastern border, our Army will walk straight from Ghalacadia south to their capital virtually untouched. By the time they realize they are out of position, we will have the fortified positions and the warehouses of their weapons."

"Perfect," Pazlin smiled, "the Hitrendan Army is the only one in the West even remotely close to our own. With them out of position so badly, and unable to call them back quick enough to make any discernable difference, the rest of the West will be a walk through. Do the Westerners on the mainland seem concerned about what is happening on the Island? How much do they know?"

"They know something is wrong there," Balstass answered, "but all they do is keep sending ships to investigate. When it does not return they send another. They have no idea what is going on. I would guess because they have no idea we exist."

Pazlin laughed, "My genius three thousand years ago appears to be paying off now. They cannot see us coming if they have no knowledge of us. Pritt how is the evacuation of the new slaves coming?"

"The final ship should be leaving here in two weeks," Pritt announced, "a full week ahead of schedule. All of the civilians are here in town and kept in the pens. Even the pens are emptying out, and the final few thousands will be heading to you soon. We are loading ships as fast as they land here."

"Very good, Pritt," The ancient Sorcerer was getting very pleased thus far, "after the population there is sent off, I want you to go to Peggat on the Bodash coast to prepare for the same task there."

Pritt, feeling very pleased with himself, replied, "Yes, My Master, it will be an honor."

Pazlin moved to the three left on the Island of Mosa starting with his leader who had returned to the castle in Phenderia City to oversee the operations from there, "Where is my wizard, Rostic?"

Rostic stated with brimming confidence, "He is still hiding in the Derentian Mountains, My Master."

"Could he have slipped out without you knowing about it?" Pazlin asked.

"No, My Master," Rostic replied, "if he had set so much as a foot out of the range, he would be spotted by either Phosting or Narrol. They have so many traps set around the mountain range they see every deer and bear coming out. The second he appears they will tell me, and I will relay it to you."

Pazlin thought a moment, then ordered, "Kill him on sight. No warning, no tipping him off. Strike fast and hard. Do not give him a chance to retaliate. We have no idea what his ability is, and we have already lost one Adherent. Kill him and any and all around him. Then bring me the body. I want to test it myself this time. I was far too underestimating of his ability the last time, and I will not make such a mistake again."

Rostic replied, "Yes, my Master. He will die the moment we can touch him. Phosting and Narrol will both do the honors."

"Good," Pazlin agreed, "then we have nothing more to discuss. Go about your duties and report to me as necessary."

Pazlin released the communication lines which had been open leaving the six abroad to return to their individual assignments.

"Master," Grastock asked, "with Maldifren dead and you firmly in control here, could I be used better in the West as well?"

"You would definitely be an overwhelming force there," his Master praised of him, "but I have a special task I need you to look into. My

Master, Rustaph, had ancient maps from his personal library along with many books which described and explained many things about the Phanthow. Upon his death the location of it was lost with him. He had not planned on dying on that day, and he never told me of its whereabouts. I have traced some of the clues down to certain areas and even a general area of where, but nothing specific enough to find an entrance to it. In three thousand years I have figured it must be in the old kingdom of Stulla in the far northeastern corner of Chiloe. I have located it to the town of Brantag thirty miles inland. The town does not exist anymore, and it would be hard to find since about twenty-two hundred years ago a massive tidal wave disintegrated the town and killed everyone in it."

"Would not the library have been destroyed as well, Master?" Grastock wondered.

"No," Pazlin answered him, "my Master was very wise. He took no stock in placing his important structures above ground for reasons such as the tidal wave but also thieves, fires, animals, and storms. No, he would have made it underground using rock supports and walls. He had infinite power to move whatever he wished. He would have made it indestructible from outside forces. The question is, how deep and where in Brantag would he have put it? Any marker at the surface would have been washed away twenty-two hundred years ago. You will have to find the library and then report back to me."

"As you have ordered, My Master," Grastock bowed as he stated, "so shall it be done."

Pazlin remembered as Grastock was walking towards the door, "First, I believe I will have you accompany me to the individual governors of the outlying areas. One of them may decide to have future ambitions since the Empire is changing. I do not need someone creating discontent or hope out there. We will be removing them and assigning all power to me personally."

"As you wish, My Master." Was Grastock's only reply.

Mark L Porter

Chapter 23

Feachen the Twenty-eighth picked up the ornate wooden case Chessington had been staring at ever since it had appeared behind the Wizard who had been teaching him his lessons. He knew it held something of great importance. Something which should be revered and carefully handled. He just had no idea what it was. He did understand the case held something containing pure energy itself, something holding a greatly concentrated amount in a small area. He figured now was the time he would find out about it. He was right.

Feachen stood in front of the couple to be holding the long flat case towards them, "This is something you must have with you at all times. It will be your greatest and most powerful defense, but you may never use it first, only when attacked and no other possible solution is readily seen. Do not be anxious to use it either. It is of the utmost importance you understand the immense responsibility this weapon requires. As you use it, it will drain you of your stored energy. Should you become completely drained, you would disappear into nothingness and lost forever. While using it, you will be doing the exact thing to your enemy you are doing to yourself, draining their stored energy. The only difference being your energy will be draining at half the speed as the one stuck with the blade. With that being said, it is my duty and privilege to give to you Umniague BeVotasia, which translated means *The Sword of Veracity*, so named because only a wizard of sincerity may carry and brandish it. Not just any wizard, only the wizard or sorcerer who it chooses, and then it chooses you for life. Should another try to use it other than yourself, it would consume them, forcing the sword to drain them into nothingness. After your life has extinguished, it will return to our realm to wait for a time, if it should occur in the future, where it will be needed again."

Chessington opened the case and studied the most ornate sword he had ever laid his eyes upon. The handle made from pure energy straight from the core of the source itself and was of a white metal harder than steel. The blade was from energy also, but not solid. The entire blade was transparent in appearance as glass would look, but held no substance. The handle and blade had what they thought at first to be engravings which had been colored in at some point in time, but after further study, they both realized the ornate engravings were moving as if alive!

Chessington started to reach for the sword and stopped, "What if I'm not the one to have it. You said I could be consumed by it, disappear into nothingness."

"Like so much you have seen, if you were not the one to have it," Feachen explained, "it would not be here."

He reached for the sword handle, anxious and nervous at the same time. He touched it with the tip of his fingers as he went to cradle the pommel in his right hand. At the very moment he made contact with the sword, it started to glow an iridescent blue tint. He watched the blade as it glowed to see the moving figures stop to stare at him. He saw the horse and the snake, the lion and the owl, but the most dominant figure he saw looking at him by far was the dragon.

Violta saw the look in Chessington's face and started connecting to him mentally as they had done so many times in the past. *Are you alright?*

Yes, he returned to her, *they seem alive, and yet that would be ...*

Impossible? They both heard the Owl state, *Have you not learned by now, just because things go against the conventional wisdom of your day, it does not make something impossible. Your friends have had to learn this, and yet you still need to be shown.*

The Dragon spoke next, *He is a product of his upbringing. We cannot expect him to accept everything the first time he sees it.*

Who are you, Chessington asked of them, *and what is your purpose there?*

The Dragon explained, *We are the characteristics of the keeper of the sword. We are the five main elements which make you distinctly you. I myself represent your spirit, the side of you seeking enjoyment and adventure, but also your will and desire.*

The Owl stated next, *I am your wisdom, the part of you which craves knowledge and study. I am an enormous part of your makeup and design, but I am smart enough to realize the other aspects of you represented here are of equal value to keeping you strong.*

I represent your bravery and courage. The Lion spoke next, *I am the one you will call upon when faced with adversity which is imminent. Should you ever truly have a need to use this sword for your defense, I will come through strong and fast, and we will fight together as one.*

I am your reason and artful side. Explained the snake, *I will help you decide when to attack and when to wait, when to retreat and when to forge ahead. I will advise you on many occasions as to your best course, but I am just an advisor. You must ultimately make the decision for yourself.*

Finally, the Horse spoke to them, *I am your determination. I will be the one to give you strength should you start to lose the will to continue. I will help you to go forth when it may appear all is hopeless and lost. I will be your drive to keep you on task and to make sure you see this through to the end even though you are tired and wish to rest.*

Once again the Dragon spoke, *What Feachen the Twenty-eighth has explained to you is all true. You may never use us to attack; however, you may use us to kill once the battle has been started from another, and you have no other recourse. Should you choose to use us, remember, we can as easily kill you as we can your enemy, so be completely sure you know your limitations and weaknesses before you enter into battle. You are the only hope of defeating Pazlin and keeping the West free as well as freeing the East.*

Feachen held now a leather sheath, very plain and very unsuspecting, "This is the scabbard to carry your new weapon in. It is made plain as to not draw attention to the sword itself, but the moment you hold the handle in your right hand, it will fall off of the scabbard and come to your service. Upon returning, you may show the sword to whomever you choose, it is of no matter, but they must understand that for them to touch it with or without your permission would mean instantaneous death."

"I believe I can remember that." Chessington found his heart racing as he placed the sword in the scabbard, tying the cover to his back. "I will get to know and understand it so it knows Violta and me as well as it can."

"Good," Feachen smiled, "you are starting to understand the importance already of your bride. I feel we are finished with your studies here. It is time to return and have the ceremony you both must have with your friends to join you together in marriage."

Chessington felt a sense of anxiety washing through him. Nerves along with a feel of suddenness coursed all throughout him realizing this was the moment he would always remember as his wedding.

"Shall we have you both rejoin to your bodies for our return to the cave and your friends?" Feachen had already brought the tunnel leading back to their bodies, and they walked through to rejoin themselves to their physical forms.

Chessington asked Feachen one last favor before opening the rock wall to see their friends again, "Could you wait for one moment, please?"

"Certainly." Feachen answered him.

Chessington turned to his soon to be bride, holding her tightly and kissing her solidly on her lips. After what seemed to them as an instant but more in the span of half of a minute, they parted and held hands, with Chessington exclaiming, "Alright, we're ready."

Feachen turned to the rock wall and started the process of opening the doorway back to the cave and the rest of the traveling party.

* * * * * *

The excitement of the return of Chessington and Violta was all the ten left behind could think of. It was the morning of the twenty-seventh day, and they would all be rejoined together to become the group which had entered this cave nearly two months ago. They all knew tomorrow morning they would be leaving to continue their quest, rested and mentally prepared to return to the fast paced and dangerous lifestyle they had been doing for the two and a half weeks leading up to their stay here.

"Wonder when they're gonna come poppin' outta there." Malden stated. He had become very close to Chessington recently and very much felt odd with the boy not around.

"I'm as anxious about it as you are." Sir Bansinghaim replied, "Truth be known, no one knows except the Shade who keeps taking him in and out of there. I do know this though, I'm ready to leave this place. At first it felt like a retreat, almost a vacation. Now it feels like a prison. I believe if we weren't getting out of here tomorrow, I would go mad. It makes me want to go to sleep just to hurry it along."

"I understand that one," Malden agreed, "but I bet we're ready fer another one within a month a leavin' here."

Bansinghaim laughed, "I'm sure you're right."

General Vastion was trying to preoccupy his mind waiting for them by studying and restudying the mapped out routes they had taken from Yaughtie's body. The trail seemed difficult after they came out the other side from the Great Beyond. It headed northeast, then southeast towards the capital of Ruderrac, but there was a circle which formed to the east of there with no way of knowing which direction to take afterwards. He was not as puzzled with the map of the Great Beyond. It seemed quite clear. Once they entered the trail represented by freckles on Yaughtie's stomach and hip starting at Chepafelg in Bortegestia, they went about two thirds of the way, and then it appeared they turned north to an enormous lake called Restoration Lake. After visiting the lake they returned back to the original trail and finished their journey to Chiloe coming out of the mountains into the area known as Grostil.

With Baydowa looking over his shoulder, they would talk to each other about time frames and the logistics of traveling on certain terrains as opposed to others. Neither, of course, knew whether the trails in the Great Beyond were passable with carts or even horses for that matter. First they had to get to Chepafelg and enter the trailhead, and it was more than likely months away from now. Still, it is better to be prepared for a future dictating success rather than be too negative about their situation.

Preda sat on Yaughtie's lap waiting very impatiently as well. Prince Palton sat next to them watching the rock wall intent on willing it to open as much as waiting for it to. The young woman watching them had tried her best to see if they would like to play or study, but neither child was in the mindset to do so. She figured this might be the last quiet moment they had outside of sleep, so she sat quietly.

Sir Ghalkin, Modinay, and Gurlig were busying themselves with loading certain items onto the carts they would not have need of for the remainder of the stay there, trying to get a jump on the process which would take place in the morning before heading to the tunnel at the rear of the cave taking them back down to the base of the mountain.

"Do you think you will need your large soup pot?" Modinay asked of Gurlig who was the unofficial, yet assumed, chief of the meals and food preparation.

"Naw," Gurlig answered, "I ain't makin' no soup here. I got ever' thin' made I'm gonna make 'fore we get out inta the open again."

"And your large spoons?" Ghalkin wondered.

Gurlig thought just a second, "Better keep 'em. I still got a few meals ta serve yet."

All heads turned simultaneously to the rock wall as it split open to reveal Chessington, Violta, and another man only Sir Malden remembered from before. All rushed the wall seeing their friends emerge out from it and noticed the smiles on their faces and the look in their eyes.

Baydowa saw it first, the ring on Violta's small finger, "Does that stand for something?"

Violta brimming with excitement could hold it in no longer. The short amount of time she had seen them was still far too long to have waited to share her news with her closest friends outside of the Woods. "Chessington and I are to be married!"

The group was ecstatic as they hugged and congratulated the happy couple. Chessington was shaking hands and being slapped on the shoulder by every male member of the group while Violta was hugged and swarmed under by Baydowa, Yaughtie, and even Preda, who dashed for the small Doltist instead of her cousin. Each staring at the ring on her finger as the hearts and trees danced along throughout the circular exterior of the ring.

Bansinghaim noticed first the large sword strapped to Chessington's back, "Very nice sword, boy. May I see?"

Chessington gripped the handle feeling the blade fall out of the scabbard while General Vastion, Sir Bansinghaim, Modinay, Gurlig, and the Prince were looking the sword over, Sir Malden and Sir Ghalkin were more intensely observing the makeup of the sword. The handle was like no metal they had ever seen before, white and as hard or harder than any metal they had ever heard tell of. They could tell by looking at it, the sword was of vastly superior quality, but something about the blade caught their eye. They could not figure out why at first, then both realized, with Sir Malden speaking first, "They move!"

Chessington had figured there would be some explaining to do, "Yes, they're alive as well. Each animal represents a part of me and my character. They will aid me if I ever need to use this in a battle."

Sir Bansinghaim's eyes widened, as he laughed, "I for one would not care to be your opponent."

Chessington told the short version of the rules for the sword, "I basically can only use it if I have no other choice, and it's really to defeat wizards and sorcerers more than folks without the ability to use energy."

Feachen stood quietly as the group reacquainted themselves, but also knowing the time constraints of how his being there worked. He had to push slightly, "Shall I do what I came here for?"

Violta shed a single tear and smiled, "Everyone, this is Feachen the Twenty-eighth, last Wizard to the West before Chessington. He has the authority to marry, and we are going to have our ceremony."

Baydowa and Yaughtie looked shocked, as Baydowa told the small Doltist, "You can't have it now. You have to plan these things. You'll need so much!"

Violta smiled, "All Doltists need is a mate. Everything else is extra."

Yaughtie reprimanded her, "Well you're among humans now, so you'll need to know how we do things. First, you'll need a dress, a long white flowing dress, very ornate and beautiful. What kind of dress do Doltists usually where?"

"Well," Violta replied, "we do not. Doltists have no use for clothing. It inhibits air from flowing to our bodies."

"Oh my," Baydowa exclaimed, "no. You have to have a wedding dress."

Yaughtie added, "And white shoes plus the proper jewelry. You know like necklace, bracelet, earrings. Your hair will have to be styled. My, we need to take you to our room, and it's bad luck for the groom to see the bride! Chessington, turn your back."

Chessington turned around for the women who had taken over the situation until the four females had gone leaving the men to whatever they had to do.

Malden stared at the women as they turned to disappear around the corner to the bedrooms, seeing Violta overwhelmed at the fuss made for the occasion, "Ya better have yer part done when they come back. They look serious."

"What do I need?" Chessington wondered.

"I was married before." Modinay volunteered, "She passed away many years ago, so I married my work after that."

Ghalkin looked genuinely towards him, "I am very sorry."

"It was over fifteen years ago." He stated, "Believe me, I've had time to adjust. We were only married for three weeks, and it was arranged on top of that. Chessington and Violta actually love each other. It's very different."

Chessington was concerned he would not make his obligations, "What do I have to do? I thought I just had to stand there and speak when spoken to."

"Pretty close," Modinay replied, "but you will need a couple of other things. First, you'll need a best man to stand up next to you when the ceremony is going on."

Chessington looked at Sir Malden, "Sir, would you mind?"

Malden beamed from ear to ear, "Mind! I'd be honored, boy. Guess I need ta stop callin' ya boy while I'm at it. You're gonna be married."

The groom turned back to his Derentian friend, "What else?"

"Well," Modinay answered, "just one I could think of since we're way out here. You need a wedding ring."

"I just gave her a ring." He replied, rather caught off guard.

"Yes, you did," Modinay agreed, "but that was an engagement ring. Now, you need a wedding ring. It should compliment the engagement ring, but not overpower it."

"I see." Chessington thought a moment, closing his eyes. He pictured what he wanted in his head then held his hand out and produced it. It was the same size as the first, but with stars and hearts instead of trees and hearts like the first one. The stars moved to show the patterns of movement constantly in motion. They would circle the ring occasionally going out of sight and reappear back again.

"Anything more?" He asked.

Modinay thought, "No, out here there wouldn't be. In town you would have a few more commitments, mostly dealing with your groomsmen."

Baydowa came out of the bedroom area staring straight at Chessington, "I need three things, and you're the only one who can do it." She said very excited at the thrill of the moment.

Chessington put the ring in his pocket and asked, "Alright, what do you need?"

Baydowa stated without taking a breath first, "Violta needs a bouquet of flowers to carry."

Chessington thought a moment, "Any particular kind?"

Baydowa answered quickly, "Red roses with a touch of baby's breath and a soft handle so the thorns don't hurt her hands."

Chessington produced the flowers, twenty-four soft petal roses, deep red at the center with a softer red on the tips. He added the fragrance he had remembered from his Aunt's roses back at the farm and gave them a compliment of white baby's breath.

"Oh, they are beautiful." Baydowa admired, "Now, she needs a ring for you to wear."

He produced a plain golden band and handed it to Baydowa, simple yet perfect to his comfort and personality. Anything more ornate would not seem like a ring he would have liked.

She held it in her left hand with the bouquet, "Most importantly, she needs a white dress, beautiful and long flowing, with beadwork around the bodice. Low cut at the top, and ribbons circling the waist. We'll also need a veil, sheer and soft, with beads throughout the netting, a necklace, bracelets, and earrings."

He thought about it and pictured the dress in his mind. The difficult part was to picture it without Violta in it. If she were in his thought while making the dress, he would also make a Violta as well. That could be awkward.

He held out his arm and the beautiful dress appeared draped over it with the veil appearing in his hand, jewelry held in his palm. He held out his arm and wordlessly handed the set to Baydowa to take back for approval. More Yaughtie's approval than Violta's, he was sure.

Baydowa turned to scamper back into the rooms, but first told the group of men, "You'll all need to clean up and wear more formal attire. Oh, and Chessington, Preda, Yaughtie, and myself will need formal gowns and jewelry as well, and make this place more like a wedding hall! It looks like an old dusty cave." She disappeared into the rooms to leave the men dumbstruck and wondering.

Prince Palton headed over to the front area first, "I'm first to the bath." He announced.

Vastion, still reeling, stated, "He'll make a good husband one day. I'm second. I certainly don't want to have all three of them scowling at me if I don't."

Ghalkin added, "I'll be third."

Before they could get the order straight, Yaughtie poked her head around the corner, "Sir Ghalkin, Violta would like a word with you."

Ghalkin turned to Modinay and Chessington, "What in the world could she want with me at a time such as this?"

Modinay grinned, "I don't think I'd wait too long to find out."

Ghalkin nodded, "I believe you could be right." And he also disappeared back into the rooms.

Once in there he saw Violta in her dress, hair curled and framed around her face with just a hint of color to her already tanned cheeks, asking the other three women if they could have some privacy.

He held his breath a moment at first, then stated, "You are beautiful from head to toe, my dear. A sunset would be jealous."

She ran up and hugged him tightly around the waist, "It is all moving so fast. During what seemed like this morning, I had no idea this would be happening, and tonight I will have a husband."

"How are you holding up, dear?" Ghalkin asked, looking into her eyes, genuinely caring about her mental state.

"I am okay." She replied, "It is just so fast paced and all. I want to do this, but I will be so happy tomorrow, or next week after it gets to be normal. I really do not like being the center of all of this."

"It will be over soon enough," her friend reminded her, "but for now enjoy it. It would appear Yaughtie and Baydowa have things well under control. I doubt you will need to lift a finger."

Violta smiled, "That is true. Oh, thank you. I knew you would know the right things to say." She squeezed him tighter around the waist.

"If this is all you needed, I should return to the men and prepare myself." He started to head back out, but she stopped him before he could get away.

"Wait," the little voice broke slightly as she spoke, "they tell me I need to have my father walk me up from here to Chessington during the ceremony. Since my father is not here, and would never understand such a custom of making a fuss at a joining, I would very much be honored if you would take his place. Would you feel alright with this, please?"

He smiled and this time he hugged her first, "It would be my privilege. I could think of no higher honor."

After which he left the room, unable to speak. She saw the other three women return to the room after he was seen leaving and knew she would have more priming, receive more information as of what she was expected to do during the ceremony, and continue to be the center of attention. How to walk up the aisle, how to stand, how to speak; these women had a rule for everything it appeared.

Her mind connected to her future husbands and wondered, *Is all of this necessary?*

She heard him return back to her thoughts, *It seems to be for them, and from what I remember from the few I went to, it seems pretty authentic. I will sure be glad after it's over though.*

How are things going out there? She inquired.

It will all be ready soon. He reassured her, *I have a few more trousers and formal shirts to make for the men, and then I start on the cave. It should all be ready within ten minutes if Yaughtie and Baydowa would stop thinking of more things we have to have.*

They are dears. She smiled at the thought of their efforts, *I feel lucky to have them here.*

I suppose so. He agreed, *I just want to get this through.*

It will be soon enough, dear. She explained, *A wise man just told me to enjoy it. Everything is taken care of.*

He chuckled to them both and replied, *Sir Ghalkin is right I suppose. I will try.*

I will see you soon, my love. She ended.

At this point he knew it was happening, and he was going to be married.

Chapter 24

The cave was transformed into the closest thing Chessington could remember to a church, with the aid of Yaughtie and Baydowa to remember certain things which were missing. The rug was changed to a deep crimson with gray trim around the edges and small gray accents throughout the interior. A long bench with crimson back and seat cushions sat towards the front for the comfort of the guests viewing the ceremony. Candles floated in mid air illuminating the area with soft tones of flickering light every few feet apart. Flowers circled the group, turning this part of the great cave into a small sanctuary for this sole purpose. There was a long rise in the floor which had Feachen standing in the middle facing the bench, with Chessington and Malden standing to Feachen's left and Preda to his right all turned half way to see the back of the room where Sir Ghalkin and Violta would appear from the system of rooms.

The guests as well were turned to face the back, all awaiting the same sight. The men were dressed in tan trousers with white shirts and gray belts. Baydowa was wearing a deep blue dress which was low cut and very flattering to her figure, with a white ribbon running throughout the dress going under in spots and reappearing again elsewhere. Yaughtie had a yellow dress with no sleeves, a small train in the back, and low cut as well with a short slit in the front starting just below the knee. Preda had enjoyed telling Chessington just exactly what she wanted, with Yaughtie's help, and stood very proud in her small pink dress, ruffled from the waist down, and having embroidered flowers from her shoulders to her feet in accented white.

Chessington, being told he had to look different from the other men present, although he was not quite sure why, appeased them for the sake of his bride. He wore black trousers with a gray shirt and crimson belt. The most noticeable difference from him and the other men was the overwhelming presence of Umniague BeVotasia strapped to his back. The women did protest this, but Chessington knew the great sword would be a part of both of them and should be present at such an occasion. It was the only thing about the wedding he insisted upon, and the women found his reasoning acceptable after a brief disagreement, letting it go quickly.

Then it happened. She appeared. The small form standing next to the distinct and slender presence of Sir Ghalkin. She was smiling a nervous breathy smile through her white beaded veil, red tumbling curls wrapping around her face to frame her jaw line perfectly. Her dress was dropped down off of the shoulders and appeared to be held up by her breasts and the tight fabric around her waist. The beadwork, had it been done by hand, would have taken months of constant work by professionals had Chessington not produced it in an instant. The train fell a good eight feet behind the small girl forming in a rounded circular appearance as she walked slowly to the front. Her hands shaking through her white gloves, trying to hold the roses still, yet unable to conquer her emotions.

Chessington had remembered the two dozen requests the women had made to get her dress perfect, although now as he saw it on her, he was admitting to himself the wait and the fuss was well worth it, but currently it was time to proceed.

The pair stopped at the front a few feet from Chessington, Malden, and Feachen. All stopped as the quiet consumed the makeshift wedding hall. Every eye looking at the petite beautiful bride.

Feachen, having performed hundreds of these throughout his mortal lifetime, asked for all to hear, "Who so giveth this bride to be taken in matrimony?"

Sir Ghalkin stated clearly, "It is my great honor to say I do, with the aid and approval of someone else." He then backed away, smiling at Violta who had no idea what was going on.

The tiny bride felt another small hand take hers from the opposite side. She turned to see Queen Rhyshena's spirit standing next to hers, transparent and luminous, but there all the same.

"How...," The small Doltist started to ask, but was cut off by her Queen.

"It would appear your future husband is getting very good at certain ways of the energy." The elder Doltist smiled back to her military leader.

Violta whipped her head back to see Chessington reach out his hand, waiting for her.

She hugged the loose form of her Queen and started towards Chessington. He took her hand, and she looked to see Baydowa and Yaughtie completely in tears, seeming to know nothing of this surprise.

Feachen only waited a moment for the Queen of the Doltists and the Royal Tutor to the Prince to take their seats before continuing, "It is true, I have not known the happy couple before me as long as you here have, but I do know what the realm beyond here knows. Chessington the Twenty-ninth and Violta of the Doltists have been brought together for a purpose. A purpose we will all understand as events unfold further. My time in your realm is almost past, and I am honored to have this be my last act upon the realm I first was shown any knowledge of. It is now time to proceed.

"I will ask each of you to answer the exact same questions with a simple *I will.*" The Wizard instructed.

Turning his head slightly first to Violta, he started the actual ceremony, "Violta, will you profess your love, respect, and unity to Chessington. To act as one with him, to aid him in times of need, and to always hold him as your most important obligation until such time as one or both of you ceases to exist in this realm?"

Violta smiled at Chessington, intentionally staying away from the sight of Yaughtie crying not even six feet away, to state clearly, "I will."

Feachen then turned to Chessington as the group looked on. Baydowa and General Vastion seated together with their hands holding between them. The fondness they had shared as the leaders of this expedition since they had entered the mountains had grown into a mutual admiration and at the present time into a budding romance of all its own.

The ancient Wizard smiled at his next in line and continued, "Chessington the Twenty-ninth, will you profess your love, respect, and unity to Violta. To act as one with her, to aid her in times of need, and to always hold her as your most important obligation until such time as one or both of you ceases to exist in this realm?"

Chessington, without a moment's hesitation, agreed, "I will."

Feachen smiled and stated to them both, "Would you each hold your symbols out for the other?"

Violta took Chessington's ring from Preda who had carried it in her palm tightly from the moment she had been given it, as Chessington did also from Sir Malden.

They held them out as Feachen instructed Violta to speak first. To make this part flow more smoothly he formed the words in her mind she was required by human customs to recite. She looked up into his eyes and spoke soft but clear, "Chessington, I give you this ring as a symbol of my love for you, complete and whole, with no foreseeable end. I will place it on your finger as a reminder of our commitment and unity, for all to witness, we belong together until such time dictates. I do this willingly and without any reservations and will love you each and every day of our lives together, even if parted by circumstance."

Now it was Chessington's turn, "Violta, I give you this ring as a symbol of my love for you, complete and whole, with no foreseeable end. I will place it on your finger as a reminder of our commitment and unity, for all to witness, we belong together until such time dictates. I do this willingly and without any reservations and will love you each and every day of our lives together, even if parted by circumstance."

Feachen then stated in a booming voice, joyous and invigorating, "I now pronounce you as husband and wife. Chessington, turn and kiss your bride."

The moment their lips met Umniague BeVotasia shot an iridescent blue light from one end of the cave to the other as all present converged on the newly married couple before them.

The women, including Violta, were seen staring at the rings, which now where joined together as well. The stars shooting through the trees, with the hearts dancing a vibrant deep red as they proceeded around the special ring, each of the two parts being completed since the other was now connected.

Feachen the Twenty-eighth patted the couple on the shoulders, smiling as well, congratulating them on their new life together, which was beginning at this very moment. He also stated his goodbyes and reopening the rock wall, he disappeared inside of it to return to where he now belonged.

The group celebrated from this moment, around two hours after noon, until early evening. After which time, General Vastion announced they should think about going to bed shortly within the next couple of hours since the morning would start the continuation of their journey, and they needed to be refreshed.

"He's right ya know," Malden agreed, "I fer one ain't gonna be sad ta leave here. It was great fer a while, but let's get this goin' again."

Baydowa looked at Chessington, "Does your book say anything about when to be out from this cave except just *in the morning?*"

"No," he stated, "we just needed to leave the morning after Violta and I returned from our lesson."

Bansinghaim asked to quench his overwhelming curiosity, "Have you learned much more than when we came here?"

Chessington seemed quite confident in his answer, "Oh yes, more than I knew existed before I came here. Each trip into the other realm showed me more than I had ever expected to learn. I learned about our enemy and why they are the way they are, but maybe more importantly what they hope to achieve from this war. I learned about some of the locations we have to deal with in the upcoming days and even a few of the things we should expect when we get there. I have been taught about traveling with the energy, and I learned the most important part was Violta and I are one being, just two sides of it. It's going to take a little longer yet to understand what all of it means, but I think we're going to be much more useful and efficient in this quest than either of us could have been before we married. Believe it or not, the entire purpose for us to learn in there the last time was simply a test to have us fall in love further."

Bansinghaim chuckled, "You two were truly pushed together by the cosmos."

Violta added, "I think we would still be in there if we had not gotten it yet. The whole lesson was just to get him to ask me to marry him."

Yaughtie sighed the sigh of a hopeless romantic and turned to Preda, "How would you like to sleep with Baydowa and I tonight. Since it's our last night here, we can have an evening of just us single girls."

Preda, seeming serious, agreed, "We have to stick together, huh."

"Yes, we do." Yaughtie answered, clearing the way for the newlyweds to have an evening alone.

Baydowa smiled, "You two start without me. General Vastion and I need to study the maps a little more."

Preda seemed disappointed, "But you guys have already studied the maps a whole lot."

Yaughtie stood and took the small girl by the hand, "We'd better go and start having fun. She'll be with us very soon I'm sure. Let's see what hasn't been packed away yet and take something to eat back with us."

Preda dashed to the kitchen area to start looking for some of the sweets which had yet to be packed away or eaten.

Vastion started to stand, "Well, Baydowa, we should start studying then. She sounds like she would like to have you there."

"I believe you're right," she agreed, "let's start." They left to go to the lounging area and opened the book of maps they had written their notes into.

"Wonder who they think they're kiddin'." Malden laughed, "They ain't studyin' no maps."

"Be nice, Sir." Violta grinned, "I think it's adorable."

"Well," Sir Ghalkin announced as the voice of reason, "I believe we all have something needing to be done. I for one am going to go and finish my personal packing."

The entire group rose to go back into their rooms. Each filing off and disappearing into their own separate bedrooms for the final time in the last two months.

* * * * * * *

Chessington was up early his first morning of being a married man, watching the sun rise from the ledge protruding out the front of the cave towards the north. He was thinking of the night he and his wife had spent together, the first of far too many to count he hoped. The others had just wrapped up the loading of the carts, and he would soon be returning the cave they had lived in for the past couple of months to the way it had looked for all those years before they had gotten here.

"Enjoying the view?" The familiar voice of Violta asked as she wrapped her arms contentedly around his waist and squeezed as hard as her limited strength would produce. He turned to face her and leaned down for a kiss for the first time this moment.

"I'm happy for today." He admitted, "Yesterday was nice, but I'm very glad it's over. I didn't really do anything, but I feel mentally tired for the first time since I found the energy. I am looking forward to the next thousand or so years together."

She laughed, "We'll see how you feel after a few years are behind us."

"Just the same I'm sure." He kissed her a final time and then took her hand, leading her back to the rear of the cave where the exiting was about to take place.

Everyone was ready to depart. The horses were tethered to the hitching posts, the carts were braced into their floor brackets, and most of the others had already taken their seats. Chessington turned back to the cave and released each and every individual item back into the air as it had been prior to their inhabiting it.

He saw each member ready for the trip down the mountain, getting comfortable for the long ride taking them back to daylight and the foot of this great mountain they had traveled inside.

Before getting seated next to his wife he announced to everyone there, "While in training, I learned how to speed this up considerably. So don't let the time it takes confuse you. We will be there very shortly, but please do not stand up for any reason from this point forwards until I tell you to.

After speaking, he sat down. Then he stood back up. "Alright," he announced again, each thinking he had forgotten something to tell them, but to their shock and amazement he simply stated, "We're at the bottom."

They all looked confused and quite puzzled. Sir Bansinghaim walked around the corner to see daylight.

He reported surprisingly back, "He's right. We're at the bottom!"

Malden tried to talk through his laughter, "Good one, boy. I bet we looked pretty ridiculous."

Violta grinned, "He would not let me tell you."

After the carts and horses were placed and mounted, Chessington opened his book for the reading:

Congratulations Chessington the Twenty-ninth,

You have done very well in learning what you were sent here to do and to acquaint yourself with Umniague BeVotasia. This extended stay was important and necessary as I am sure you can now see. Your knowledge is greater, your gifts of the sword and map are vital, and your marriage is immeasurable to the cause you now go forth to champion.

As you have all guessed by now from the map, you are headed to the costal town of Drenne to the west. Travel through the mountains as your enemies cannot come in to harm you inside of this range. Be warned, however, the instant you emerge from the protection herein, you will be spotted. Even if you think you have taken every precaution, know this, you will be found by your enemy as soon as you emerge.

You will be faced with a battle the very second they see you with orders to kill you and all who are with you. This is all I know, other than there are two Adherents looking for you to come out. I would be amazed if they do not try to kill you together rather than separately. Make your plans before you set foot out into the open. Should you reach Drenne look to this page and see what will await you further.

"That sounds bad." Malden summarized, "Then what?"

Chessington finished, "Then I have to fight them I would imagine."

Violta corrected him, "We have to fight them."

Sir Ghalkin wondered, "I mean no offense, Violta, but how would you be able to help?"

She replied to her friend, "Feachen explained to me, together Chessington and I would be more powerful than Pazlin himself."

Ghalkin seemed confused, "Meaning?"

"I would have no idea," she explained, "but it was how he explained it to us. I would imagine we will find out then."

General Vastion added his thoughts on the matter, "I'm afraid what you're suggesting is extremely out of the question. You two will be fighting a pair of fully trained Adherents without any aid from us. Simply out of the question."

Malden saw the logic behind what Chessington and Violta had proposed. Maybe it was because he understood after going into the other realm what did and did not seem logical any longer. Maybe it was because he felt compelled to stick up for the boy, but for whichever reason he said it anyways, "An' what would we do ta help? We stick our noses out there an' we turn inta liabilities they gotta look after. I think they'll have their hands full just stoppin' the two goons they gotta deal with. Besides, other forces 're drivin' this. Since when did we start gettin' ta be in charge?"

Sir Ghalkin agreed, "He is right you know. It would seem our purpose for stopping for the past two months was solely to gain more power, be it intellect, energy, or resources for what is to come. I know you and Bansinghaim are fighting men, but how would you fight them? They would serve you both along with the rest of us up on a plate and feel no remorse or regret whatsoever."

"Alright," the General agreed, "but this is very unnerving for me. Let's go on and ride to Drenne and hopefully some better plan will come to us before we need to use it."

"May I suggest one more thing, Sir?" Chessington asked.

Vastion sighed, "Absolutely."

The Wizard explained his plan, "Baydowa, can you take us to Bostichi?"

"Certainly," she agreed with the utmost confidence, "but we need to go to Drenne. That would be two hundred miles in the wrong direction."

"Exactly," Chessington nodded, "if we appear close to Drenne, they'll look for us there after the battle."

"But if we appear two hundred miles away," Vastion saw the logic in the plan Chessington was proposing, "and close to the Iclanian border, they will search there and the ports to the east instead of bothering around Drenne and the western side of the island."

"Won't that take us another four or five days to get to Drenne though?" Modinay wondered, "Through very open territory also I might add."

"We duck back into the mountains and travel back to Drenne through these hills." Chessington finished, "That way they never see the rest of you. So all they will really know is Violta and I are still alive and moving around. They could still be thinking the rest of you are dead. Let's keep it that way."

"True," Vastion saw the logic, "better to spend five extra days traveling than to get in a hurry and not make it at all."

"I'd vote fer that." Malden stated, "Let's try it Chessington's way."

Chapter 25

It had taken the group traveling north three days to circle around the base of Mt. Bollantoda and another two to get to the northern edge of the range overlooking the plains heading on to Bostichi. The trip had been easy with Baydowa knowing a perfect trail to met up to after the first day and a half from the exiting of the cave. They had seen more breeds of unexplainable wildlife close to the big mountain, but after a day's ride to the north of it, and closer to the northern plains, they found to them what were more normal and unaffected animals and plants.

Chessington kept his abilities to himself after leaving the cave. He knew the Chiloe Adherents could not come in to get him, but he was fairly sure they could detect where he would be if he opened a channel of energy flow to create anything. He conversed with his wife constantly as they rode. Appearing to be silent as the ride was taking place, but all the while talking mentally about anything and everything from their current love to strategizing about the upcoming battle.

I am still fairly unsure about my roll in all of this. Violta confided to him, *I remember he said to keep you focused and to aid you, but I have no idea what that could really mean.*

I'm sure we'll figure it out after we have some practice. Chessington tried calming her a bit, but truth be known, he was nervous about the events closing in on them as well. *I think I'll scout ahead and see how close we are to coming out of here.* He dropped off for less than thirty seconds. Being much faster now once he had been trained properly as to leaving himself to go out ahead and returning to report aloud to Vastion, Baydowa, and Violta, "Do you see that hill up ahead?"

Baydowa nodded, "Yes, it's no more than an hour away."

"Once we crest the top of it," the young Wizard notified the leaders, "we will be looking at the northern plains below us."

Vastion stopped the group calling for a break for lunch, even though it was still a good two hours from mid day. Gurlig started his routine of building a fire, foraging, hunting, setting up, and cooking all jumbled together to a schedule only he really knew. Sir Bansinghaim, Sir Ghalkin, and Modinay went to help as well.

Malden assisted Yaughtie with the Prince and Preda while Vastion, Baydowa, Chessington, and Violta sat discussing the best way to combat the forthcoming attack the newlyweds would have to defend against.

Vastion opened, "We still haven't come up with anything better than the original plan you gave the first day out of the mountain."

Chessington admitted, "I don't know how any strategy could help us. All it's going to come down to is us against them. Violta and I are just going to have to out match them energy for energy and hope they aren't as good as we are."

"It leaves a little too much up to dumb luck for me." The General stated, "I like to think and plan for every situation imaginable before having to do it to the death. It will be to the death you know. I realize you killed one of them before, but you will have to go out and do it again, and this time with two of them. One of them isn't going to stand still and wait his turn while the other one gets to play. It will be two attackers against one and an assistant who has to remain safe while you battle."

Violta admitted, "He would be right. I have no attack of my own."

"Ya suppose they know that?" Gurlig interjected from the fire he was building.

"What was that?" Vastion turned to the cook.

"Does they know she ain't got no powers?" He added.

The group looked at Chessington for the answer, "I don't see how they could. They don't even know about her. Pazlin saw me at Marroda, but Violta was still in the Woods then. What do you have in mind Gurlig?"

"Ya comes out tagether," he explained, "both a ya shootin' what ever it is ya all shoot. They feel it comin' outta her too an' divide up ta covers their backs. That way ya got one on one ta start with 'til ya all figure out how ta kill 'em."

Bansinghaim nodded, "He's got a point. If she's a decoy, you can move more freely against one and then the other. Can you do that, boy?"

Chessington thought about it for a moment, "I could have Violta sending a constant stream of energy at the one who feels weaker. Then while I'm dealing with the stronger, she could be kept safe inside of a defensive cage so to speak. After I defeat them, I release her, and we return."

Vastion added, "Great, now let's figure out what could go wrong with this plan."

Chessington stated, "Two things I can think of. She couldn't move out of it. It might also be should I get too weak, so would her bubble, or it could do the opposite and stay strong after I die That could hold her prisoner forever or until a stronger person came along to release the energy."

Violta asked, "I would still be able to feed you energy though, correct?"

"I can't see why you wouldn't." her husband thought, "The energy of the two of us can flow freely in and out of the bubble. It's just their energy that couldn't, at least that's what the books say."

"Why haven't we used this bubble before then?" Vastion asked.

Chessington answered, "Because it takes a lot of energy to keep going for a long time, and it's highly traceable. Besides, it would have to be moved with the group constantly, you could never pass through it until I made it disappear."

"I see," the General admitted, "and you could do this and fight at the same time?"

"I don't know why not." He replied.

Violta thought of something they had never thought of before, "Maybe you should check with your sword, dear."

"Oh," the young Wizard realized, "I hadn't even thought of that."

He held onto the handle of his great sword, Umniague BeVotasia, to feel it free itself from the scabbard and come to his conscience. He felt the snake and the owl come to the front both in equal partnership.

The owl started the advisory session, *Everything you have assessed is correct in theory; however, the best laid plans have a history of going awry from extenuating circumstances.*

I understand. Chessington replied, *Unfortunately, I cannot predict extenuating circumstances.*

No, the snake agreed, *but you can watch for them. In my experience the side who adjusts to the unforeseen first usually wins the battle.*

Chessington thought about this for a moment, *Do you see another way?*

The snake answered for all of the animals, *No, just prepare yourselves for the obvious and the unforeseen. Preparation is always the best weapon in battle.*

Chessington remounted his sword to his back, looking to the rest of the group, which now included Gurlig, Sir Bansinghaim, Sir Ghalkin, Sir Malden, and Modinay along with General Vastion, Baydowa, and Violta. He informed them, "They agree with our plan, but advise us to be prepared for anything that could possibly go wrong."

"Sound advice." Vastion agreed, "Will they help you out there?"

"If the circumstances allow them to, then yes." Chessington answered.

Violta explained further, "He can only use the sword if it's in defense. He can't draw it first. If he pulls it out, and he has other options, he may get another animal than the lion and the dragon come to the front. It could waist valuable time in a fight such as I expect this to be."

"There's too much unplanned here." Vastion still worried, "I don't like it."

Violta placed her tiny hand into his, "There is just too much we have no way of knowing. We are going to have to do it this way and find out as we go."

"At least ya got the element a surprise ta a small extent." Malden interjected, "Ya know it's gonna happen taday, that's more 'en they got."

"An'," Gurlig finished the thought started by his half brother, "they think ya all got no clue, but ya do. They're gonna be a little shook up when ya all turn an' fight back right aways."

"They're both right." Bansinghaim added, "They couldn't really know much about you both either."

Modinay asked to Chessington, "How do you see the battle going?"

"I really couldn't even begin to guess, Sir." He admitted, "I see it as the first side to make the first kill having the advantage."

Modinay agreed, "I would suspect you're right. Here's my thought. One of you, probably Violta, fake your death. After the one attacking her turns to come for you, open the channel back up to attack him from behind. It may not kill him, but it will definitely keep them off guard. If they're too busy thinking defensively, they can't devote their energy to attacking you both."

"Makes sense." Bansinghaim agreed.

"That it does." Vastion nodded, "Many battles have been won by just that. Confuse your enemy and hit them trying to change their tactics."

"I believe we need to head out of here then." Chessington stood, "You all should still be safe from the top of the hill up ahead if you choose to watch."

Sir Ghalkin admitted, "I am not sure I could take the stress."

Bansinghaim added, "I wouldn't dream of missing your work, boy."

In the end, Bansinghaim, Vastion, Modinay, Gurlig, and Baydowa decided they should for their own sake watch the upcoming battle, while Malden, Ghalkin, Yaughtie, Prince Palton, and Preda would stay behind.

The larger of the two groups rode ahead to the hilltop ready for viewing the field ahead of them down at the bottom of the grade the couple still had to descend. Chessington figured out approximately two hundred feet before they would be out of the energy shadow of the mountain range so the Adherents could see them clearly.

"I guess it's time to find out." Chessington looked at his bride of less than a week.

She took his hand, and they walked on foot leaving the horses behind as to not subject them to any of the battle and make them an uncalculated casualty. The five remaining said nothing as they disappeared around a corner and out of sight.

* * * * * * *

Phosting opened a communication line to his Master back in Chiloe finally giving him the report he had desired for over two months now. "Master, the boy Wizard has been spotted coming out of the north end of the range he has been hiding in, and he has a small girl with him."

"Good." Pazlin sat up feeling the intensity of the fight about to take place, "Contact Narrol and meet before you do anything. Make sure you two are united. Also do it fast. Dainthin played around with him and you see how he ended up. Use your wits, and I will expect your favorable report soon. Kill the girl as well, but kill the boy Wizard first."

"Narrol has already arrived, My Master." Phosting announced.

"Then do it now." Pazlin resituated himself in his seat, "I expect this victory. Do not disappoint, Phosting."

"We will not, My Master." Phosting replied as he cut the line to the conversation.

* * * * * * *

The young couple had just stepped down onto the area of the plains which started leveling out flat and clear at the base of the mountain range. Chessington stopped to look back at the top of the hill they had just descended to see the five outlines of their friends who had decided to come to their battle and at the very least support them with their presence. Sir Bansinghaim, General Vastion, Modinay, Baydowa, and Gurlig could each be identified even at this distance by some of the subtle differences making each of them special. Baydowa of course by her long flowing hair and curved figure, Modinay was slightly shorter than the other men present, Bansinghaim by contrast was by far the largest there, and General Vastion had the posture and heir Gurlig lacked. He then turned to his wife, kissed her softly, and smiled.

"What was that for?" She asked him.

He just smiled and replied, "I have to have a reason to kiss you now?"

She giggled slightly, feeling the nerves he was feeling also, "Well no, it was very nice though."

"Shall we go on?" He asked her, pointing to a spot just ten feet ahead of them, "That would be where they can see us again. I suppose I'm as ready as ever."

"Alright," She took his hand, squeezed it, then letting go again she exhaled, "I'm ready, too."

The pair stepped out the ten feet Chessington had indicated, but nothing happened. Stepping out another thirty feet or so, they felt it.

"Chessington, over there!" Violta pointed to two robed figures standing fifteen feet to their left. They turned to see them, one taller and thinner than the other. The taller of the two matching Chessington in height, but considerably thinner. Chessington separated himself from Violta by approximately twenty feet and surrounded her in the energy bubble they had discussed. He pushed energy out of it towards the shorter of the two robed figures, feeling he had less ability than the taller one.

The shorter of the two was thrust backwards falling hard to the ground only to arise and fire energy of his own back at the small girl inside of the protective bubble.

Chessington felt a thrust hitting his chest now noticing the taller one which was left for him to fight. Chessington corrected his error of neglecting to account for him and pushed his energy back, feeling the pain he was dealing out to his enemy by the way his body was contorting. He would have him defeated shortly at this rate, but was distracted by the constant watch he kept over Violta.

She had stood her ground and was funneling energy into her husband at a rate which would not overload him, as she knew had happened on a much grander scale to the Adherent back at Marroda, but fast enough to keep him sharp and on top of his abilities. She could gage his level by the bubble around herself as well as by linking to him mentally. She could keep him strong for hours, and she knew it should not take too long.

Suddenly she felt him weakening faster than before and was trying to keep up with his need. She watched him manage his attack, but he was faltering, weakening, even being overcome by the dark pair who was now ganging up on him in teamwork instead of dividing to become easier to defeat. Their plan was not working. They both fixed a shield between themselves and Violta, keeping the energy Chessington was sending from her from hitting its intended targets. She could do nothing but watch him fade and slowly lose his energy. The Adherents appeared to be winning.

She then thought of their last hope, and sent the message to his mind, "Chessington, grab the handle of Umniague BeVotasia."

Chessington reached behind his head and took the sword by the handle, seeing and feeling the lion jump instantly to the front with the dragon right beside him and the horse steadying them both with his presence.

Chessington found the strength to right himself as Violta was filling him back up with the energy he would need.

He stood tall facing first the shorter and less able of the two, to thrust the sword into the chest of him and hear the taller laugh.

"You feel you can defeat us with human weapons?" Phosting smiled, "You waste your time! You grow weaker by the second as we dominate you."

But Chessington and Violta both knew he was not growing weaker from the battle with the two Adherents. It was the sword making him weaker and weaker with every second he held it inside his opponent's chest.

She tried keeping her flow of energy going into him as fast as the sword was thrusting it out, but she just could not keep up. She watched as Chessington weakened and the shorter Adherent faded out into nothingness.

Chessington, absolutely exhausted, fell to the ground unconscious. Violta held in her bubble could not go to his side. Umniague BeVotasia lay inches from his unresponsive fingertips.

Phosting walked over next to the limp body of the Wizard, "I am sure my Master will be glad to trade the life of a mid level Adherent for the life of the Wizard of the West. Narrol will not have died in vain as did Dainthin."

Bending down to use the sword of the unconscious Wizard on its owner, he grasped it tightly to raise it over his head, screaming at the touch of the sword. He felt the lion and the dragon consume him and found himself unable to release it. They attacked internally at the Adherent striking hard at his core, making him feel the wrath and pain of taking the sword which was devoted to only one master. Phosting was not this master.

Violta watched as the taller Adherent screamed a horrible cry of pain and anguish until the moment he faded from existence. The Battle was over. Certainly not without its casualties, however. Chessington lay unresponsive and unaware upon the ground with Violta trying to send him little bursts of energy to get him to a level where she could awaken him, all the while still stuck inside of the bubble she could not get out of without his aid.

She saw the group of five running at breakneck speed down the side of the hill towards the area of the site of the great battle just moments before.

Vastion reached the girl first, "Is he alright?"

Violta cried through her tears of mixed joy at the outcome and concern for her new husband, "He will be. I do not know how long it will take, but he is in there and responding slightly to my probing. It is a bit difficult to explain, but there is a certain area, if it is completely depleted, it has to be brought back slowly. Feachen taught me how to do it once when Chessington was searching the energy region, but it is a slow and precise procedure."

Baydowa sat, "Then we will be quiet and leave you to your work."

The five sat staring first at Chessington and then back at Violta repeatedly for the better part of an hour. Finally, Chessington twitched.

Bansinghaim stood up, "He moved! His hand moved. Violta you're doing it!"

"I know." The exhausted Doltist woman had worked and fought through so many barriers and obstacles, she was exhausted herself from this massive effort, "Just two more details, and he should be awake."

Sure enough to their great delight, Chessington opened his eyes, weak and tired from the battle which had nearly destroyed him internally, "How did it go?"

Bansinghaim smile, "You won! They're both gone. Faded away and assumed dead, but you both have some healing to do."

"Violta," the conquering Wizard looked to see her still entrapped in her bubble, making her freedom from it his first priority, "you're alive."

She ran to his side the instant she was freed. Looking down onto his face and seeing him unconscious just from the slight amount of usage he needed to free her. She dove back into his mind and found the necessary adjustments required to set him right for a second time.

He awoke for her once more. This time his head lay on her lap as his friends sat all around, "We need to get back up the hill before another one comes after us. With these two gone, Pazlin will be searching for us again, and we are in the open here." He took his great sword from the ground next to him and returned it to his scabbard. The animals, unhappy with the foreign touch of the Adherent, relaxed as they felt their true and rightful master back in control of his weapon.

Bansinghaim carried Chessington while Gurlig picked up Violta, as they headed back into the protection of the foothills in front of them. They all looked around to make sure no one had followed them back.

Chapter 26

Modinay, Vastion, Bansinghaim, and Gurlig each took turns carrying their injured friends up the long and sometimes steep grade on their horses leading back to the camp. Seeing the remaining five jump at the site of their return, concern evident on the faces of the ones left behind, they could see the two being carried were alive and Violta was even somewhat smiling. Chessington, having his eyes opened and blinking, appeared to be the only ways to tell he was even awake. His body was limp, unable to move, and although it had no visible wounds and his clothing did not appear to be torn or abused as in a conventional battle, it was nonetheless easy to see his pain. His face gave off the appearance of exhaustion. He caught the sight of his small cousin and smiled as he saw her.

"Chessy!" Preda screamed as she ran to meet Gurlig who was now holding him in his arms, tears running down her small face, "What happened?" She had been quiet the entire time the others were gone. Her cousin and now Violta were the only living relatives she had any knowledge of, and they had to return safe even though at the age of seven, she knew it could have turned out differently.

Violta, having more strength, explained, "He will be fine, sweetheart. He is just very worn out right now."

Bansinghaim, still excited from the spectacle he had just witnessed, stated, "It was incredible! It seemed to start just as everyone had talked about! I'm sure it was far more intricate than it appeared from our vantage point, but it was quite the sight to behold!"

"It was very intricate actually," Violta continued, "and I do not propose to know as much as the others who were out there. They started by sneaking up to our left side, pretty much the way we talked about; although, we did not take advantage of it at first. Before they really knew what was happening, we were attacking them, and they set up their counter attack. I really could not do anything myself. It was all Chessington. He set me up in my bubble and held an attack, which seemed to come from me to the lesser of the two there."

"They took the time to let you do all of that?" Modinay asked.

"Not really," she explained, "all of *that* happened in the blink of an eye. Chessington was beating the stronger one for the first part of the battle, but they set up a shield against my attack and pretty much ignored me afterwards. Somehow they figured out either I was far weaker, or I could not move from my spot, or both. I guess we will never really know now. They did know Chessington was the strongest one out there. It very much made them uncomfortable. I think it hurt their egos to find someone with more ability than themselves. They appeared to be very pompous about anyone who was not like them, even condescending. Once they set their shield up against me, they started draining Chessington."

She stopped to catch her breath, still tired and recovering from the mental healing she had performed on her husband. She would occasionally look over to him, still deeply concerned about his physical health. She noticed he was listening to her story of their recent events. He would look into her small face and smile at her, just getting her attention for an instant, and then she would smile back. The group was patient with her, allowing her all the time necessary to regain her strength.

After a full minute of thinking and recuperating, she continued, "They thought they had him, even after he took his sword out. They even laughed at him for using human weapons on them. The taller one was laughing at a Wizard using such a weapon on an Adherent. The lesser one found out soon enough the sword was more than he could take. He disappeared shortly after Chessington stabbed him in his chest, draining the energy from him at a much faster pace than we had ever considered. That left the stronger one standing over Chessington who was unconscious after the defeating of the shorter one, with Umniague BeVotasia sitting next to him and myself trapped in the energy bubble unable to leave it."

She stopped for another chance to catch her breath. The group, even the ones who had witnessed it, hung on every word from the small woman who had seen it so closely. Most of them thinking this was the worst possible place for her to stop her recount, but they waited patiently realizing they really had little choice.

Finally, she finished her telling, "He had us. He could have finished Chessington off with his own ability, but he tried to take the sword for himself. He just smiled, looked at me, and picked up the sword. I believe he knew I was an imposter at this point and would have stabbed Chessington first if he had gotten the chance. He was a dark creature. His soul felt cold and alone. They both did for that matter. It had to have been horrible for him once he touched it. The pain on his face for those few seconds it took for him to disappear completely had to be the worst thing I could ever imagine. I know we had to kill him, but that was awful."

Vastion smiled, "It's all over now at least for a while. The next step is to get you two on the road to recovery and head back through these mountains to Drenne and find our next set of instructions. It was a great victory, but this isn't even close to over yet."

Sir Ghalkin looked in earnest to them both, "Are you expecting a full recovery for the pair of you?"

Violta answered, "Yes, I should be fine within twenty-four hours. He is going to take a bit longer. I should imagine at least a week until he has returned to the way he was before this all happened. How long will it be until we should be out in the open again?"

Baydowa thought, calculating the distance they needed to travel, "We should be in these mountains four or five days. We'll start by skirting the foothills on the northern side here before we go deeper into the range. Then we follow the river to see the plains heading to Drenne. Once we get there, it will take a full day in the open to get to Drenne. I've never been there, but I've studied maps my grandfather had when I was a little girl. I know how to get there."

"We'll wait the extra time it takes." Vastion decided, "I for one wouldn't step out of these hills if that young man is less than one hundred percent."

"Same fer me." Malden added, "He's our only real hope. Ya need ta get better, boy. The West needs ya too badly."

"I'll be fine, Sir." Chessington reassured him, "Violta has already told me how these first couple of days are going to be."

Violta looked shocked, "I did not *tell* you. I strongly suggested, and you have to admit, I am right."

"I never said you weren't." He replied, already getting his wits about him and keeping his bride happy. He sat up to lean forward, his elbows on his knees, resting but finding himself eager to move or walk. He knew it could not be today, however.

Violta looked at Vastion and Baydowa, seemingly unfazed by what Chessington had said and moving on, "I believe it would be better for him to stay here for the rest of today and tomorrow rather than moving him right away. He cannot even walk yet."

Vastion stated with absolute finality, "Then we don't move from this camp until the day after tomorrow too much is riding on his health and well being. Besides what he has to offer us and the West, he's also our friend. We'd wait if it were important to any of our members."

Bansinghaim picked up the exhausted Wizard carrying him to the cart doubling as his infirmary for a while. Violta and Preda followed closely and would remain by his side until he was at least well enough to walk again. The two remained quiet, hoping Chessington would rest, but he seemed to have caught a second wind and took more delight in talking than in resting. After close to twenty minutes, he had to give in to his need for rest. He could feel the energy flowing through him slowly and wondered how he could be so weak after the effects of the battle. It shook him a bit to realize he was this vulnerable, and he had still more Adherents out there wishing him dead, some with more ability than himself. He also had realized he had placed Violta in serious danger out there. Should he have lost, she would have been lost as well.

Ghalkin asked in a low voice, knowing full well how Violta's hearing was, and not wishing for her to hear him, "She looks almost as tired as he does. Why is that? Was the furnishing of him with extra energy so exhausting?"

Baydowa explained to the ones who stayed behind, "After the two Adherents were defeated, Chessington was in terrible shape. He was unconscious and barely breathing. I believe he would have died if she hadn't nursed him back. It took her almost an hour to get him back to being conscious, and then he had to release her from the bubble and lost consciousness again. She worked on his mind or soul or whatever it was she had to do for almost another half an hour before he came back again and was healthy enough to even be carried."

Vastion added, "She was far too modest. Her aiding of Chessington's energy seemed to be the only real reason he was stronger than the other two. She may not be the one with all of the ability, but she is vital nonetheless. He would have died without her. There's no doubt in my mind."

"Well, we'd better get the camp set up." Gurlig announced to whomever would listen, "Guess we're gonna be here a while, so I'm gonna rustle some good stuff fer dinner. I think I saws some squink weeds just back up the trail a ways. They'll patch him up good if he'll eat it."

Ghalkin remembered the squink they had before when it was just the three of them trying to meet up with the others after the invasion, "I remember them. They were invigorating. Rather tasty as well if I remember correctly. Would you like another set of hands for the harvest, Gurlig?"

"Sounds good ta me." The woodsman admitted, "Extra hands 're always better."

Modinay went as well, curious about what a squink was, asking them both if a plant could really make so big of a difference. The group left behind heard Sir Ghalkin sing out the praises of the weed as they left, also mentioning something about green tree snake.

* * * * * * *

Pazlin finished his search for the two he had sent out to defeat the Wizard, not being able to locate anything except a high concentration of expanded energy where the battle must have taken place. He was angered by the fact he had obviously lost two more Adherents, but even this would have been easier to swallow if he had known for sure the new Wizard of the West had died as well. With the mountains so close, he could not be sure if the Wizard was not just hiding again inside of their protection. He had to treat the situation as if he were still running around the Island of Mosa ready to ruin his hard fought and intricate plans.

He had plans for both Phosting and Narrol after the defeating of this Wizard, now he would have to move others to where he needed them. If only he had not killed Maldifren yet, he could have left himself to attend to some of these things, but now as Emperor he was forced to stay behind. The very reason he had never wanted to be the Emperor for the past three thousand years was now the exact reason why he was stuck in Ruderrac. It made him hate the boy Wizard all the more.

He called for his lead on the Island of Mosa, "Rostic, where are Phosting and Narrol? Have they reported back to you since the battle?"

"No Master," Rostic reported, "I have not heard anything from them in days. I knew nothing of a battle."

"It would seem most likely they have been defeated by the Wizard, but I need to know if the Wizard was defeated as well. They found him and a small girl exiting the mountains just south of Bostichi. They must be heading north to what used to be Iclania." Pazlin's patience was short. Rostic knew he had to do something or face a taste of the wrath his Master was ready to dole out to whomever was closest.

"I shall move myself to Bontu." The second Adherent stated, "I will personally take care of him when he tries to escape the Island. It is the only port close to Bostichi we have not destroyed for military reasons."

"Good," Pazlin agreed, "this time take nothing for granted. Treat him as if he has the same abilities as myself. I know he does not, that would be absurd, but treat him as such and you will not fail me. Go, do it and report back."

He stopped his communication with Rostic and immediately opened another line to Grastock. Finding him northeast of himself around the town of Gobatu, Nullowa, he asked, "Have you progressed in finding my Masters library?"

"I have a few clues to follow up on." Grastock reported, sensing his Master being of an ill mood, "Only one looks fairly promising. The others are more than likely false, but I need to follow through on them also."

"What is your firm clue?" Pazlin wondered.

"It seems an old town was known of ten miles or so to the west of Theowa, Nullowa. It would be in the old kingdom of Stulla, and it has a local legend stating some of the old town was buried by a mudslide before the tidal wave destroyed the area."

"Good, follow up with this one first." Pazlin ordered, "Do any of the other leads warrant my knowing about?"

"Not unless they should show more promise than they seem to at this time, My Master." Grastock answered.

"Fine then," Pazlin stated, "I feel I should notify you that Phosting and Narrol seem to have found the Wizard of the West and gotten themselves killed for it. I have no idea if they happened to kill the Wizard as well or if he escaped back into the hills in Derentia, but Rostic is going to see if he is trying to escape the island up in Bontu."

"Could he be headed back to the western shore to be inconspicuous?" Grastock wondered.

"No," Pazlin answered, very confident, "he needs to get off of the island before it is too late. He has to go to the mainland. If he gets there before we cut him off, we could have a hard time finding him in so much area. I will order Pritt to station a few ships around the southern end of the

Island just in case they do spot another ship coming from the back side of it."

"As usual you know more than I, My Master." Grastock stated, not convinced this was the best course for them to take. This Wizard had killed three Adherents already. As one of the five remaining, he did not want to have to go looking for him himself; although, out of loyalty to his Master, he would do it. He did know better than to oppose his Master openly.

"Good of you to agree with me, Grastock." His Master praised.

"Thank you, My Master." The Adherent acknowledged before he cut his line of communication to return to his appointed task.

Pazlin sat thinking in his usual chair as he was once again alone with his thoughts. The plan had been for Phosting to remain on the Island with Pritt, freeing up both Rostic and Narrol to head to the mainland and infiltrate Ghalacadia and Paldost, the two most powerful kingdoms after Hitrenda and Bodash where Balstass and Clostig were respectively. Now he had Rostic waiting at Bontu, not even positive he would find the young Wizard there, and Pritt at Loglistin finishing up the evacuation of the islands inhabitants. He could not take Grastock from his search. It was far too vital for his finding the Phanthow, and as a result he was reduced to four Adherents working the West. He would need to forego any infiltration of Ghalacadia. He simply did not have the man power necessary to place someone there. He would, however, place Rostic in Paldost if the boy Wizard had not shown himself within three weeks at Bontu. It would leave Pritt in charge of the base operations at the staging areas on the Island of Mosa. This made him feel depleted, having to use his lowest Adherent to manage the generals and the troops, but he saw no other option. Pritt was not experienced enough to infiltrate, Clostig and Balstass were already inside in their kingdoms, and Grastock was out of the question.

This Wizard was making three thousand years of planning, positioning, and hard work a shambles. Pazlin wished he could personally meet him face to face to make sure this child playing a man would feel his punishment first hand. He just simply could not spare the time from his work to eliminate this problem personally. It lay under his ancient skin much like a splinter or a boil nagging at his mind constantly. After three thousand years of having his way with no one even close to being able to challenge for his power, he found now he had an adversary, but he would never allow himself to admit this Wizard of the West was worthy of being called an adversary.

Chapter 27

They broke camp after nearly two days in the northern foothills of the Derentian Mountains during a beautiful sunrise seeing them wake up refreshed and ready to go on with their journey. Breakfast had been served at first light, and now with the cool of the morning still present, they mounted and set off to the west in order to fulfill the requirements History itself foretold of them. Vastion, the uncontested leader of the group, was in the front next to Baydowa, the guide and woman he was finding himself growing more and more fond of by the day. Behind them were Modinay and Sir Malden discussing the political similarities and differences between the old governments of Phenderia and Derentia. The first cart appeared to follow with Sir Ghalkin driving as it also had Preda on the front bench with him while the back carried Chessington still resting but able to walk again for close to the past twenty-four hours. Riding in the back, mostly making sure her husband was recovering and not exerting too much energy, was Violta with her hands folded on her lap and one eye continuously watching the Wizard she so dearly loved. The second cart had Gurlig driving with Yaughtie sitting, the pair discussing foods and outdoor life mostly. While completing the group and taking up the rear guard were Prince Palton and his Royal Champion Sir Bansinghaim both discussing swordsmanship and fighting tactics. It was true the large knight could not do much teaching as they rode on each day, but he could still verse the boy on things they could practice later.

The General was asking how he should expect the day, and afterwards the rest of this trip, to proceed to his guide, "So today we will travel further back into the mountain range, and tomorrow if all goes accordingly, we should be shortly before lunch to the beginning of the River Lostanda, correct?"

She smiled, flirting with her new interest, before agreeing, "We should. It's mostly downhill and should be fairly easy to follow. There's really only one part I was told where the carts might have some difficulty getting through, but it shouldn't be too bad. This is why we took this trail. It's a full day's ride longer, but we can get the carts through. The other way is even a little tight for the horses."

"We seem to have the time." Vastion added, "I'm not going to push the pace any. Chessington still needs time before he pokes his head out of here if anyone is looking for us. Hopefully, we threw up a feasible enough diversion to keep them on the eastern side of the island anyways."

Baydowa looked up ahead at the waterfall cascading through the far off hillside. She pointed and smiled hoping her admirer would see the beauty in front of them. Vastion stopped the party so all of them could behold the splendor nature had placed before them. Each of the adults had realized now just how much they were missing and exactly what they were fighting to keep. There freedom and the freedom of every person in the western kingdoms were riding on their success. Each region had untold beauty, special features, and breathtaking sights. For people to miss out on these things or to be disallowed to enjoy them was the most basic act of tyranny imaginable. People needed to work, whether free or enslaved, but enslaved was working without hope. Free you had the hope to continue on and ensure yourself, as well as your family, life had the opportunity to get better.

This was just the uplifting moral support they all needed to boost their spirits and drive them on towards the next phase of their trip. Everyone smiled at the sight, welcoming the view. The group had rediscovered the purpose for their drive to succeed, and they had their souls refilled to the brim.

Chessington reached across the cart to hold Violta's tiny hand. Choosing not to break their gaze at the beautiful scene, they just watched as the water flowed endlessly over the rocks only to land in the pool it had made for itself countless years before.

"My, that looks inviting!" Bansinghaim stated, eyes never leaving the sight of the spectacle. "I would imagine it could be quite refreshing."

"That it could." The General concurred, "I'm just afraid if we stopped there, we'd never start up again."

Sir Ghalkin agreed with the General, "We do need to keep going. After all we did just start out after two days of rest."

"Valid point, old sport." Vastion nodded to his friend, "Let's continue on."

Ghalkin had thought back to the last time he had been called *old sport* by the good General. He was sure it had been months ago at the least and maybe even clear back to the trip before this catastrophe erupted, and more than likely all the way back to Lorning.

Ghalkin had not thought about Lorning, Tarint Mosa, or Phenderia City in weeks. Everything they were going through at the present took center stage in his mind every moment of every day. What had happened to Haldiston, his daughter Jhulida, Ditena, or Carinoa the serving girl who had cleaned up Prince Palton's mess in his study all those months ago? He found himself wishing they had been taken as slaves, because the alternative to this was far worse. How were they fairing? What sort of slave had they become? Where women from the Island of Mosa sent to those procreation houses Malden and Chessington were taught when studying Chiloe? The thoughts of these injustices ate at his core, and he knew he could not dwell on these probable scenarios of which he had thought, or it would eat him alive from the inside out driving him mad if this situation was not resolved soon.

Violta saw the pained look to her friends face. She felt the need to ask, "You seem hurt. Are you alright?"

"Physically yes," the councilman replied, "I was just reminiscing about people I remember from before the invasion. People some of us know, some are family even, but mostly I found myself hoping a horrible situation was true."

"Oh my," the tiny Doltist remarked, "why would you hope for the horrible?"

Ghalkin looked her in the eyes, "Because if the horrible occurred and they are all prisoners enslaved by a concurring empire, then they are still alive with a chance for us to save them yet. I remember the story General Vastion told of a sergeant in the Phenderian Army who was tortured by being left to die with an infected leg wound and loss of blood. If someone had known earlier, he might still be alive. Quite possibly less one leg, but not less his life."

"I believe you are a good leader, Sir." Violta expressed, "You still care about your people even after they are thousands of miles away, and you are running for your life."

"Thank you, my dear." The Royal Tutor smiled directly at her, "You have helped me. We are going to get them back are we not?"

This time Chessington sat up a little, encouraged by the caring and concern Sir Ghalkin had shown, "I believe we will, Sir. They seem to win a few, but we're winning in a couple of spots as well. Once we get to the mainland, we can start the journey to finish what they started."

"I believe we will, also." Ghalkin agreed, "I just hope we can save all or as many as possible."

* * * * * * *

Riding had gone well on the first day and so far on the second as well. The group was in site of the headwaters of the River Lostanda for which they would follow for the next three days down to the plains holding a straight dash from the mountains to the harbor town of Drenne, the final destination for this leg of the quest they were on. Being midday all of them were excited to see the landmark to the front. General Vastion decided to call a stop and allow each member to rest for an extended lunch. The horses stopped at a fairly level spot next to the north bank of the mountain river, which was really no more than a stream at this point, seeing it only a few feet across and not believed to be more than three or four feet deep.

"I remember the last time we stopped by a river. We all decided to bathe and swim." Violta smirked, "I also remember the women had to go around the bend, and the men had the water at the camp site."

"I recall that," Vastion agreed, "but I also remember you decided to go upstream. We didn't push you out."

Baydowa turned to her new interest, "Well, I believe if Violta is correct, the men need to go away for a while. We'll let you know when we're ready. Now go, we'd like to get undressed."

The men knew they had been bullied away, but none found it serious enough to argue about. They took a change of clothing and some lye soap and headed upstream to clean themselves for the first real chance since leaving the cave.

"I now see why I remain single." Bansinghaim laughed.

"Ya sure that's the only reason?" Malden ribbed.

"Oh, come now," Vastion smiled as he took another glimpse of Baydowa before he turned to go around the corner and out of sight, "I believe the women are right on this one. We are men, and we should take the chivalrous approach."

"You do realize she has you." Bansinghaim grinned back at his friend and fellow councilmember.

"Who has what?" Vastion appeared shocked.

"Baydowa," the large knight stated as he pulled his chain mail off to get ready for the stream, "she's gotten inside you."

"I have no idea what you're talking about." Vastion stated as he removed his boots.

"It won't be long I'd wager." Bansinghaim kidded his friend.

"What won't be long?" The General asked, starting to get slightly annoyed.

"Before you're in the same situation as Chessington here." He pointed to the young Wizard sitting on a rock trying to remove a sock, which had gotten soaked from the walk over to the stream area where they were to bathe.

"Keep me out of it if you don't mind." Chessington replied with a small laugh, "I'm not taking sides over something like this."

"Malden," Bansinghaim chuckled aloud, "is the good general heading down a dangerous path towards matrimony?"

"Two thirds down the isle already." Malden had just gotten in and found his face contorting to the extreme cold of the water, "Holy cow, did this water thaw yesterday er this mornin'?"

"I believe you're all just making a mountain out of a mole hill." Vastion tried defending himself, "Tell them, Ghalkin."

Ghalkin remained quiet, walking into the water and finding it as cold as Malden had expressed.

"Ghalkin!" The General asked a second time.

"Malden is correct." Sir Ghalkin stated, "This had to have thawed this morning. Throw me the soap, so I may try to have the feeling of my body return as soon as possible."

Vastion reached for the soap, "You get the soap after you tell them they're wrong."

"I cannot do that." Ghalkin admitted, "I do not believe they are; therefore, just pass me the soap before I lose consciousness, please."

Vastion tossed him the soap, "You know you're all mad. I'm a career military general. A woman would complicate things. We're just finding it nice to work together on this journey, and that's all."

Vastion entered into the water to find neither Malden nor Ghalkin had exaggerated one bit. He stood adjusting himself to the temperature as all eight of the males heard the sounds of multiple females screaming at the top of their voice.

Modinay, Gurlig, and Chessington had not gotten into the water yet and ran at breakneck speed back to where the girls had started their bath while the remaining five in the water swam the short distance around the bend to see what the problem was.

They all seemed to cover the short distance at roughly the same moment to see five very large wolves lining the south bank of the stream a few feet from the women and ready to pounce on their prey trying to get out of the water on the northern side of the bank.

Bansinghaim ran to his horse from the waters edge to retrieve his broadsword with Prince Palton following to do the same. Ghalkin speeding out of the water as well found his bow and quiver in time to notch the first and let fly, finding its mark directly in the face of the lead wolf hoping it would turn the others around. It, however, did not.

As Vastion, Malden, and Gurlig were helping the girls out of the water and up the bank, Modinay grabbed his sword while diving into the water behind Bansinghaim and the young Prince. The wolves were much more wild than any of them had ever heard tell of, growling and holding their ground. It seemed the pack felt their territory had been violated. Since the wild animals saw the four women as food, with food being scarce for the past few months now, they found a need to stand and fight even though they had no chance of winning against the men swinging at them from the edge of the water as they fought from the bank. Finally, Ghalkin found a clear shot at one of the two Prince Palton had attacking him. He saw the boy doing his best to hold back the large canines, but he was not winning his battle just staying even to them. The arrow found its spot in the larger of the two's chest, and the wolf fell instantly into the water creating a wash over Modinay's face, blinding him for the moment. The group on the north bank saw the wolf who had been concentrating on him dive into the water for the kill, but Bansinghaim's sword came hard and swift to the ribs of the attacking beast.

After the Prince had finished with his adversary, and Ghalkin had shot the final wolf Bansinghaim had been toying with, they looked around to see all combatants safe and sound.

Malden, still nude, as were most of the others except Gurlig and Modinay who were only short of being the same by one or two pieces of clothing, looked around asking the group, "Where's Chessington?"

They ran upstream to see him fallen over around the corner and face down in the mud, unconscious and not responding.

Violta ran to his side, asking Gurlig to turn him over so she could better see his face and mostly his eyes. Gurlig, as gently as he could, complied, and then he backed away.

She probed his mind looking for what had happened finding out he must have tried using his abilities to save the women being attacked. She started crying as she worked at his side. No one spoke. No one moved. She dove into his mind to find the area he had extinguished was the same as the one she had repaired only two days prior. This time it was worse. He had not recovered completely from the first battle. Now since he had tried to use it again so soon, he had done more harm than the first time. It had come in like it was supposed to, but he lost control of it right from the start, and it had taken control of him. He lay motionless, unconscious, and breathing erratically from the devastating effects of his efforts gone awry.

"Carry him to the back of the cart." She ordered to anyone who was listening, "This is going to take a long time to fix."

After Sir Bansinghaim had placed the young Wizard in the back of the cart after Gurlig and Modinay had cleared a spot to lay him down, Violta asked Yaughtie to help her and the rest to go and let them work. Yaughtie's only job was to alert Violta if she seemed to labor her own breathing while she was inside of Chessington's mind. "I have to stay strong, or he cannot be fixed. If I get too weak myself, I will be no good to him. If all is well with me, my breathing should be slow and steady, as you humans are when asleep. Should I start breathing harder, you will need to tell me, so I can come back and return to being more calm. Do you understand?"

"Yes," they all were concerned for both the Wizard and the Doltist trying to revive him, "I can do that."

"Thank you," Violta stated, "time to go in. Tell Preda I will let her know as soon as I get out?"

"Absolutely." They young woman answered.

Shortly after Violta had gone in, Yaughtie was intensely concentrating on Violta's breathing as Baydowa walked over to her sister with her fresh clothing. Yaughtie realizing for the first time in quite a few moments she was nude still, laughed, and took the new dress from her sister, giving her the same instructions as Violta had just given to her, asking for her to watch the small woman as she dressed.

After only around five minutes, Yaughtie had to bring Violta back. Her breathing had started to labor, and she could feel the small body of the Doltist tensing up without relaxing.

"He is going to take a lot of looking after." Violta returned to admit, "He will live, but it is going to take some time. We did not just go back to where we had been after the battle. He is further down now than ever. The scars in his mind will need careful nurturing and guidance to heal correctly."

"Do you know how?" Baydowa wondered, "Can you heal him completely again?"

"I can," she confirmed, "but I am going to have to ask you both to watch my breathing in shifts, and it could take days where as before it took hours; although, I see no disadvantage this time to riding on the back of the cart as I go in. The bumps he will go through will not be felt, and we should get out of these woods if the wildlife is starting to get desperate enough to attack humans."

Baydowa apologized, "I'll be leading up front with the General. There are a couple of places on the trail he'll need to know about, and I'm the only one who has ever seen the maps of this trail before."

"She has a good point," her sister agreed, "but I'm sure Malden, Modinay, and even the Prince can take turns. I don't know about you, but after this little memory in the stream, I'd like as many fighting men around you and Chessington as we can get."

Violta nodded to them both, "A good plan. I am going back inside of him for a while. Baydowa you take the information to General Vastion and the other men, and Yaughtie I will need you to watch me."

Yaughtie asked almost sheepishly, "Do you want me to dress you while you're away?"

Violta allowed herself a small grin, "Yes, I suppose so. I would hate to offend someone with my body!"

All three saw the humor in her words, but Baydowa retrieved some of Violta's clothing, which she had taken out before her swim and brought them back to Yaughtie, seeing the Doltist had already gone inside of her husband's mind.

"I can't imagine being so calm with your husband so hurt and unconscious." Baydowa remarked, "She's incredibly strong. What an inspiration."

"So are you." Her little sister replied, "You were strong for me all those years I was a hostage. You did whatever it took to keep me as safe as possible, and I've yet to say thank you once. I hope you know how I adore you. I wish I was as strong, but I'm not."

"You have your moments." Baydowa informed her, "You withstood the torment they dished out, keeping you in the basement, never seeing sunlight for years, and through it all you kept your sanity. I would have been a mess inside of the first month. You are a truly amazing woman as well, and don't you ever sell yourself short again."

They hugged long and hard, both realizing they could now be the sisters they had wanted to be for so many years now. They could share things with each other and tell their hardships if they needed. The adversity of their prior situation, as well as this one, made them closer than ever.

"I need to inform the General about Chessington." Baydowa finally stated to keep from becoming even more awkward in this situation, "I'll be back soon to spell you. Would you like me to send Preda back to keep you company?"

"No," she answered, "I would like to be alone with my thoughts for a while I guess. Besides I need to dress her. I'll see you soon."

Baydowa left finding the General and explaining the situation to him first, waiting for him to see what he wanted to do with the information.

He looked out at the somber group getting things set for the upcoming meal. Realizing they would need lunch shortly, he announced, "Baydowa has an update on our friend's condition."

Immediately each member dropped everything to gather around the guide had the news they all hoped would be positive.

Baydowa thought of the best way to say it to make it sound like it was not as bad as it was, "It seems Violta believes she can get him back." A collective sigh passed the lips of everyone in the group, "But he isn't going to be ready to do anything for even longer now. She told Yaughtie and me he had regressed in his recovery to the point where he would take longer now than he did right after the battle."

"How long?" Ghalkin asked"

"She doesn't know just yet." The guide stated, knowing this was not the answer any of them had wanted, "She did say we could continue traveling. He seems to be to a state where the bumps and jars of the trails won't impede his recovery. I had gotten the feeling, and I may be wrong, but it seemed he would be unconscious for a few days."

The crowd gathered around talking low amongst themselves with phrases such as *poor boy* and *how could he have hurt himself so badly* rising to their ears. They all looked at the guide as she started to appear as if she were about to speak again.

Baydowa did reply, asking them, "We will all need to take turns helping Violta. It seems someone has to keep watch on her to make sure she isn't laboring too hard, or she could become damaged like she was before as well."

Vastion spoke next, "We'll pack up and move out directly after lunch, stopping for dinner tonight, and moving along again at first light in the morning. Someone will ride the back of the cart at all times with Violta and Chessington, mostly Yaughtie and Preda. The rest of us need to be alert for the creatures of these woods. If one group of animals is hungry enough to attack a group of humans, I'm willing to wager there are others as well. Ghalkin, keep your bow and quiver with you at all times until we're out of this region, and the rest of us need to have our swords strapped and ready for whatever could happen. Any questions?"

Malden asked, "I ain't no fightin' man, but I'd be glad ta take a turn with Yaughtie an' Preda in the cart if I can."

"That would be good." Vastion agreed, knowing full well Malden had no fighting skills in him and could become a liability in a fight, "You and Gurlig should change places. It will give us one more fighting man on horseback should we need it."

"I ain't got no sword." Gurlig admitted, "What 'ld I do?"

Bansinghaim stepped towards him, "I have an extra I'll sharpen up. It's a little smaller than mine. I use it sometimes when Palton and I square off. It gives him a little better idea of what a real fight would be like. Very few men use as large a weapon as mine."

"Come, my brother," Malden slapped Gurlig across the shoulders, "I gotta get ya used ta my horse. He's almost as crotchety as I am."

"Poor horse." Bansinghaim replied, lightening the mood slightly.

"Alright," Vastion agreed, "let's have a quick lunch and then try to make time before we might need to stop and let Chessington heal again."

The group dispersed, heading off to complete the tasks each knew from experience they needed to accomplish before they were on their way again.

Chapter 28

They all settled under their blankets, Modinay and Vastion taking the first three hour shift of guard duty, with Ghalkin and Bansinghaim to relieve them afterwards, and finally Gurlig and Malden taking the last shift before the group would continue on. The day prior to this had been hard, starting out positive and turning sour after the attack of the wolf pack happened and the resulting relapse of Chessington into his unconscious state. Violta lay next to her husband where she had yet to move from for the better part of the last ten hours. Yaughtie and Baydowa took turns every two hours to relieve the other while watching to make sure the small Doltist did not harm herself during the healing process of her husband.

The ones asleep stayed close to the fire, refusing to spread themselves out to become an easier target and more area the guards would have to keep watch over. Finally, the sun rose in the east, and Gurlig pulled double duty as guard and cook with Malden aiding him in preparing for breakfast. Starting at first light gave him the extra time to prepare a full meal, feeling it would probably be the only real meal they would get for the day. If they rode hard, they might find themselves overlooking the plains late tomorrow.

Gurlig was preparing the potatoes and instructing Malden on getting some ham and cheeses cut into slices and placed on sliced bread. Then stacking these in the special box, which remained cool constantly which Chessington had provided them with before leaving the cave.

"We'll get some taters an' milk gravy with some chopped sausage in it, plus some fruit," The woodsman seemed pleased with himself. "That should get us down the road a ways."

"I got lunch then." Malden stated, "We just gotta stop a short time, an' then we're off again. I hope this day gets that boy up an' around some."

"Ya never know." Gurlig added, "He could be gone a while yet."

"I know, an' Violta says he ain't real close ta comin' out either." Malden looked over to see Yaughtie pinching the bridge of her nose, tired as the rest of them, but still watching her friend Violta as she lay helplessly next to her husband, trying her best to revive and cure his mind from the damaging effects of the days before.

The two cooks for the morning saw the camp waking up, slowly at first, but then straightening up the blankets and getting everything placed properly for their departure as soon as breakfast could be cleaned up.

Malden walked a plate of greens and pine nuts over to the cart as well as a plate of potatoes and gravy with an apple off to the side, "Here ya go. She said anythin' yet?" He asked Yaughtie as she nudged Violta back from her task, seeing her start to breathe a little harder.

"She hasn't said yet." Yaughtie answered, her hair strewn all over the top of her head and her dress wrinkled from how she had laid as she watched the small girl work. "But it is time to bring her out anyways. We can ask." Yaughtie touched the small woman's arm, and Violta returned, catching her breath as she did so.

Violta took the plate specially made for her and answered him, knowing he had asked before she had come out, "He is coming back. My best guess would be tomorrow or the next day, and then we had better be where we need to be to stop for a while because the second he regains consciousness we have to stop for a long time."

"Wow, he really did it good." Malden stared at the boy of which he had grown so very fond. He knew the importance his health and well being had to them all, being the only thing now to save millions of lives.

"Yes he did." Violta took a bite, trying to finish quickly and return to her work, "We all should have guessed he would have. He knows he can stop certain situations faster and better than anyone else here. He even could have saved the wolves if he had his abilities."

"I suppose the only good news is we still got a shot a ever'body bein' just fine." He stated, "That's all that really matters."

Yaughtie saw the softness to the gruff demeanor of the small and hunched looking man. She knew his expertise was in books, not people, but he cared so much for his friends and their wellbeing that she bent over a bit and kissed his cheek.

"You're a sweet man." She added.

"Don't ever tell nobody," he pointed a finger to her face, smiling all the while, "an' even if ya did, they wouldn't believe ya."

He turned and went back to Gurlig dishing up the remainder of the plates for the group and handing them out.

"You like him," Violta smiled, "don't you." She worded it as a question but stated it as a fact.

"Maybe a little," Yaughtie admitted, "but I doubt he could ever find me as someone suitable for a councilman who helps rule a kingdom."

"It amazes me," Violta added, "how humans make things so difficult."

They both laughed in spite of themselves and finished their breakfast with each knowing how important it was for Violta to return to her work.

* * * * * * *

The group had just started again after the quick lunch Sir Malden had made during the morning, making it easier for them to eat and get on their way again. They were traveling down the trail holding the River Lostanda on their left, now widening out to between fifteen and twenty feet from one bank to the other.

Baydowa turned down a side trail, which headed to the north and west a bit taking them away from the river and deeper into the woods, seeing the trail narrow rapidly to almost the exact width of the carts with which they traveled. Vastion and Baydowa took the lead with the Prince in front of the first cart Sir Ghalkin was driving seated next to Preda and holding the unconscious body of Chessington, his wife Violta, and Sir Malden watching the breathing of the small woman as they rode on. The second cart driven by Gurlig seated on the bench next to Yaughtie, who was trying to get a moments sleep as they traveled, followed closely by Sir Bansinghaim and Modinay as a solid pair of fighting men prepared for an attack from behind.

As they had barely started down the new path, the branches of low trees were scraping the riders and carts while they squeezed through the center. Only being able to see the person directly in front and behind each other, the confined conditions making the group edgy and nervous as they slipped by. They rode on tired and constantly watching the bushes for signs of danger coming through to attack. They only waited for thirty minutes before a strike came.

A very large grizzly bear was standing in the middle of the trail having General Vastion and Baydowa stopped and pausing for the attack. Vastion knew the situation had to be handled very carefully. Sharp shredding claws and powerful strikes made it the most deadly of the creatures in the forest if provoked.

Gurlig stepped down from his spot to the rear, moving to the front of the procession, "Careful, she's got a cub 'round here somewheres. She's just pertectin' her little one. Don't go forwards, just let her take her time an' she can get away."

"I think it would be prudent to at least draw our swords." Vastion stated, "If she does come at us, I'd like to have something to keep her off of me. Baydowa, you go to the back and have Bansinghaim and Modinay come up."

"We're already here." They heard Bansinghaim say, "Now what?"

"Gurlig?" Vastion asked, hoping he still knew more about the beast blocking their way.

"She's gotta either go back, attack, er we gotta go back." The woodsman informed the men, "She looks like she hungry too. That ain't gonna help."

"Getting the carts turned around here would be next to impossible." Modinay added, "We could just leave them here and take the horses with us, leaving the carts for her."

"That might be worse for us." Vastion replied, "Without all of our things, we'd have to survive on our own out here. That could be tough for a dozen people in a woods filled with hostile animals and Chessington unable to be revived just yet. How's she looking, Gurlig?"

"She's gettin' more agitated as we stand here." He was looking directly at her, not breaking eye contact for so much as a moment as he spoke to the brain trust next to him, "She ain't ready ta attack just yet, but she ain't too far off neither."

"Any idea how long?" The General asked.

"When she stands on her hind feet she'll start chargin'." Gurlig stated, "Then ya got the time it'll take her ta come from there ta here, that's it."

"Not a good timetable." Vastion stated nervously, "So do we just wait?"

"Ya could try backin' up just a little an' seein' if she goes back." Gurlig suggested, "If she thinks we're leavin' she might go get her cub, and we can run through quick like."

"Okay," Vastion stated, "everyone back up just a few feet."

The group backed away from the angry mother only about six feet but enough to make it shown they were retreating. Then fate reared its ugly head.

The cub the mother had been protecting, for whatever reason, popped out of the brush at this very second next to Vastion's boots. The mother reared back on her hind legs and charged the four men standing next to her baby.

The three armed men had their swords ready before the angry bear had much of a chance. Bansinghaim stood directly between the wild animal trying to enforce her maternal instincts and the road carrying the entire traveling party, horses, and carts as well. He also unwittingly stood between the mother and its cub lying under the first cart looking at a spider who had caught its attention.

With the main focus of the enormous beast centered on Sir Bansinghaim, while Modinay and Vastion proceeded to aggressive positions to the right and left of the bear respectively. They stabbed at her sides repeatedly seeing no other option available to saving their group.

The massive animal fell with blood pouring from the wounds. Modinay's sword had hit her lung on the right side as Vastion made a hard slice through the throat. The beast quickly was silenced by death. The cub, heartbreakingly, moved to lie next to its slain mother, waiting patiently for her to take command of his shortly spanned life once again.

The sight of the orphaned bear cub was horrible for them, but the other sight they had in front of them affected them harder still. There was Sir Bansinghaim lying on the ground with blood coming from his right arm and chest area attempting to stand from the spot the attacker had left him.

Vastion and Modinay ran to his aid looking at his wounds, the large knight fighting back the pain in a gallant effort to appear tougher than he needed to be.

Soon the others were around him as well. Even Malden and Violta took a moment from their nursing of Chessington to see what had happened to the large protectorate.

Violta studied the wound telling the others, "He is lucky. The bear did not get much except the muscles. Another fraction of an inch and he would have bled to death almost instantly."

"I feel lucky." Bansinghaim quipped, making light so the others would not worry as much, "It'll heal, and I'll be able to boast about it at the pubs one day. Are you alright leaving Chessington right now?"

"Yes," she answered, concentrating on the shoulder and thinking what she should use to bandage the arm and chest, also what plants around them could help as a poultice to aid in the healing process, "he is stable now. I just need to go inside him to keep it going forward. He will not regress again unless he is conscious and moved around too much or tries to do something like he did before."

She studied his wounds further, noticing his ripped chain mail bent inward and gouging into the exposed area of his wound on his chest. "Can you walk?" She asked.

"Only one way to find out." The large knight, with the assistance of Vastion and Malden, hoisted himself to his feet. "A little dizzy, but I'm up."

"Good." Violta looked down at the small cub, licking his mother's muzzle as if the rest of the world was never there. She took charge of the situation, and all listened to her as she spoke with the authority of her wisdom, "Ghalkin, Vastion, Modinay, Prince Palton, and Gurlig get the Grizzly out of the middle of the trail. Bansinghaim, you sit on that fallen tree next to the bear. After the bear has been removed from the road, we need to move the procession up until the second cart is next to Sir Bansinghaim. Malden and Baydowa get the cub into the back of the second cart."

Vastion looked puzzled, "You aren't asking us to take the bear cub along with us, are you?"

"Would you like to stay here and see what will happen to him if we do not?" Violta asked, her hands on her hips staring the great General down in a show of wills.

He knew she would never relent her stance and the bear cub was as much a concern to her as Chessington or Bansinghaim at this moment. She was not a human being. She had no more loyalty to the human race than she had for any other species. In her mind the cub was coming with them.

"Get that cub in the second wagon," Vastion, frustrated over the current situation, turned to the group waiting instructions, "and let's get this moving so we can get out of these mountains before one of us has a problem Violta can't fix!"

Violta followed Malden and Baydowa back with the cub in their arms and hoisted him into the back of the cart. She saw the confusion in his eyes and connected mentally with the small orphaned cub via the unconscious mind of her husband, *We are not going to harm you. We are going to take much care of you, however. Your maternal is not able to any longer, so we will aid you.* She had spoken to bears before in the Woods of the Doltists and knew basically how they thought and reacted.

I saw my maternal's form lying down, the cub returned, *but my maternal was not there. Has she gone?*

Yes, Violta answered, telling him exactly what was happening as animals have no concept of how to lie, *she was engaged in a battle to the death. She did not win, so now we assume responsibility for your health.*

Will you feed me soon? The cub asked, *We have seen many fallen in the trees. I have smelled them, but they smell unhealthy. My maternal could no longer find us animals to eat. She told me a small animal that lives under the water was good, but we have seen none since I came.*

Where I come from, Violta explained, *your kind eats tree parts and the coverings of the bushes, also the seeds that are red and filled with the liquids.*

I know those seeds. The cub remembered, *We have found small amounts in a few areas, but my maternal tells me they are being eaten faster now that small animals are no longer plentiful.*

Violta reached into a small barrel holding apples in it, giving six to the small cub. *Here, eat these, and we will feed you again when we feed as a family.* She knew the bear cub would have no concept of a group consisting of others outside of the family unit, so it was easier to tell him this was a traveling family unit and have him understand he now belonged to this unit.

The cub looked her in her eyes, *I had not fed since three darks have passed. Last time I did not eat for so long, the food hurt me inside, and I was not good.*

This may happen again, the Doltist stated, *but you need to make your inside used to having food each light time again.*

Alright, the cub replied, *I will eat.*

She left the cub to rejoin the group getting ready to move up and allow Sir Bansinghaim to sit in the back of the second cart next to the cub as she and another male would need to be back there as well.

The cub paid no attention to the cart moving when it was the carts turn to move up, paying more notice to the apples and his eating than being moved around on the cart. Bansinghaim laid down next to the small bear cub seeing him eat at the apples and have very little use for much else going on around him.

"I see you've found some food, little one." Bansinghaim brushed the fur between the ears of the baby Grizzly, causing the bear to sniff and smell the large knight, wishing to get to know the members of his new family. "You smell the blood, little one? It doesn't feel well either."

The cub licked the face of the large knight as the two bonded instantly. Violta saw a side of the large knight she had not seen before. He had always seemed as if animals were secondary to humans, but he treated this small orphaned cub as an equal showing him affection and kindness. He seemed to have a respect for the cub instead of a pity at its situation. It made her smile.

"He likes you." Violta told the injured knight, "He is licking your face in respect, telling you he recognizes you as his better."

"Well, I suppose it can't hurt to have a bear on your side." Bansinghaim never looked away from the cub as it licked his face, "Tell him I will not allow anything to harm him, which I can help with."

Violta addressed the cub and laughed, "He says you look odd with hair missing in spots. He asked if you were well before your body broke."

Malden answered for him, "Tell him no. This one's been broken fer years."

"I see you get mouthy when I'm unable to draw my sword." Bansinghaim told his fellow councilmember, "I will heal you know."

"Only on the outside," the Librarian stated climbing into the back of the cart holding the large pair of pliers Violta had asked him to bring back with him, "inside yer still messed up."

Violta laughed out loud.

"You think he's funny?" Bansinghaim asked the Doltist who was about to bandage him back up.

"No," she replied, still grinning, "the cub asked if you two were mated. He senses you two are closer than the others are to each of you."

"So much fer animals an' their instincts." Malden stated.

"I don't see how that could be." Bansinghaim added.

Violta, letting the conversation drop off, asked Sir Malden to bend the links in the chain mail back and out of the open wound while she went to look for some plants and roots to mash together to keep out the infection and clean the wounds before wrapping them up.

Malden started prying the links out of the chest of his friend and within ten minutes he was able to help him off with his metal shirt which looked odd off of the barrel-chested man who lay underneath it.

"I'm bettin' she wants yer shirt off too." Malden stated, "So long as we got ya up, let's get that off as well. I doubt ya got much use fer it anyways now that its got a giant hole in it."

They pulled it off over his head just as Violta returned with all of the ingredients she would need to patch his arm and chest back up. She took out a small bowl and crushed the roots into paste, adding the leaves, and mashing them together as well.

As soon as she had Bansinghaim wrapped back up and lying down, telling him to get as much rest as he could, she moved back to the other cart and probed softly into Chessington's mind to see where he was at in his progress before going up to the group who had decided to use this opportunity to have a quick snack, ensuring they could ride on until night fell once it became too dark to continue on for the day.

Vastion saw her coming, standing to ask before she had even sat down, "How are they all?"

"Bansinghaim will be fine." She started explaining to the group, "He should have total use of his arm but not for a few weeks at the least. The cub has taken to him very well. He recognizes Sir Bansinghaim as his better and would follow him anywhere he goes. Chessington seems to be progressing even without my help, and I may need to slow him down from progressing so fast, or he could awaken while we are still in these mountains. We would have to stop wherever he wakes up at for at least a week and more than likely two."

Vastion looked worried, "We can't spend two weeks in these trees. We've been attacked twice in two days. At this rate we'll need to fend off these poor animals at least ten more times and probably more. I wonder what could have disturbed the food chain so badly that the animals are out of their normal routines."

"We cannot stop outside of the mountains. That would be worse." Ghalkin stated, "I believe we may need to take our chances on a dead run to Drenne and make a home there for the time Chessington needs to recover."

"The Chiloe Adherents can see us out there." Baydowa interjected, "We'd be sitting ducks to them."

Ghalkin continued, "We have been before. For the entire ride from the Woods of the Doltists to the Derentian Mountains, we could have been seen. Granted there were other people around, and they thought we were dead, but we may have to hope they will be looking elsewhere. We can make a fast run to the town before we stop."

"Sounds risky," Malden added his opinion, "but we know the animals er gonna attack. I say we do it Ghalkin's way this time an' take our chances there."

"I agree." Vastion concurred, "These animals are hungry and see us as meat. I think we need to get out of here as soon as we can."

All had to agree as they finished the food they had been snacking on and returned to their places ready to ride towards the end of this trail and on to the town of Drenne.

As Yaughtie climbed onto her place on the second cart, she glanced at the back, "Oh Malden, look!" She pointed to the blanketed Sir Bansinghaim, sleeping soundly from the events of the past hour's events and the concoction Violta had given him to sleep, but the most noticeable thing about the back of the cart was the grizzly bear cub sleeping with his head on the stomach of the large knight as he lay there.

Chapter 29

The band traveled as fast as the trail would allow them in these hills with the winding and twisting turns mountains can bring on from the quick changes in terrain. Never once did they see a squirrel or a field mouse, no sign of a garter snake or even a salamander. All smaller wildlife seemed to be unexplainably absent from this lush green forest, which usually saw the likes of such animals flourish.

They had made it to the ghost town of Stonata, an ex-logging town upriver from the capital city of Lostanda approximately seventy-five miles or so. They had passed the town of Plittow, which lay on the far side of the river approximately fifty miles earlier in the day. Seeing no signs of life there, they were left to assume the cover of the mountains from the Chiloe Adherents had worn off, and they were highly exposed once again to their enemy.

Vastion led the group into a barn, which looked to be in very good condition and, more importantly, would cover them for the night, concealing their location for one more day.

"Let's set up in here." The General dismounted once inside, then asked Violta who had just returned from keeping Chessington from awakening as he had wanted three hours earlier, "How is he?"

"He is trying to wake up still." The young bride of the unconscious Wizard answered, "Is this where you want to stay for the next two weeks, General?"

"Not especially." He admitted looking around, "Do you think you can keep him down for one more day? Not even a full day really. We're about eleven hours from Drenne, and then we can be completely out of these woods."

"I can do that." She replied very confidently.

"How much do you know about the Adherents and how they operate?" Vastion asked the small Doltist.

"A little I suppose." She was not actually sure how to answer such a question, "Why?"

He proceeded to ask her, "Would we be better off riding in the darkness of night rather than in broad daylight?"

"It should make no difference to them." She stated, "They search with their feelings. They only use their eyes for things right in front of their faces. If anything, we would be the ones disadvantaged by traveling in the dark, not them."

"Alright," He decided, "we stay the night here. First light tomorrow, we dash on to Drenne and let Chessington come out of his rest."

"Should we have him come out right away?" Ghalkin wondered as he unloaded a large tarp to spread out for the sleeping area, "If the next step is to flee once again, he would be at a serious disadvantage."

"What do you propose?" Vastion asked the Royal Tutor.

"We get to Drenne," he explained, "read the next step out of his book, and afterwards decide if bringing him around is the wisest choice."

"That'd work 'cept fer one part." Malden corrected, "Who's gonna read the book?"

"We are unable?" Vastion asked the Librarian.

"I couldn't 'fore." He told them, "The boy showed it ta me, an' I had no idea what words they was makin'. He saw it perfect, but I couldn't do it."

"Interesting," Vastion thought, "I think we should try it Ghalkin's way again, but we may need to wake him if we need it read."

Bansinghaim walked over to the group with the bear cub in tow, who followed the large knight everywhere he went. He added just one thing to the plan, "I would suggest we travel into town and stay inside somewhere like this, but very close to the docks."

"That would be extra traveling." Vastion corrected, "I think it might be better to get into town and immediately find out our next step."

"I would agree," The Royal Knight Protectorate nodded, "if we don't need to wake Chessington. If we do, and then need to be off again, logic would tell us that we're sent to a port town to get off of the Island. If we do need to leave, it would have to be by ship. Ships are at the docks."

Vastion saw the wisdom in what he was saying, "And the warehouses by the docks would be a short distance for him to travel, having just come to consciousness."

"Right," the knight agreed, "then he can lay still and rest while the ship is out to sea."

Malden laughed.

"What's so funny now?" Bansinghaim asked the much smaller councilman.

"If I didn't know better, I'd swear that bear hit yer head." He explained, "That was actually smart."

"My friend here will be taught to eat you when he gets older." Bansinghaim stroked the fur between the cub's ears as he talked to his friend.

"It was a compliment, ya idiot." Malden scolded.

"How could I have missed that?" Bansinghaim grinned.

Gurlig came to the General with another slight problem, "How ya want me ta cook?"

"I beg your pardon?" Vastion sounded a bit awkward at the question.

"Well, I could go ahead an' clear a spot an' make a nice fire," Gurlig explained himself, "but this place 'ld fill up with smoke pretty fast."

"Can we break through the side of a wall close to the fire?" Ghalkin asked.

"Not without everyone watching to see someone's here." Vastion answered, "The smoke would be a beacon that there are people here."

"I can do cold food 'til we gets ta the sea." Gurlig added, "Kinda warm taday anyhow."

"I think that would be best." Vastion agreed, "Between all of us, we should be able to out think our opponent. I'm not very happy about being out in the open plains tomorrow, but we really have no choice."

Ghalkin shook his head, "None which I can see."

Gurlig set out a spread of sliced ham, cured beef, cheese, bread, and fruits. The buffet table was a nice change from the eat and run style of the past week. They opened the main door to the barn and took in the sunlight in full summer bloom, which was still a good three hours from setting. The group decided to spend an evening in the style they had grown to favor when back in the cave. The same groups stayed together with either studying or playing. Many hours had been passed at the cave in just this manor, and all had forgotten how much they missed it.

The evening turned to night, and the group turned in to be ready for the mad scamper across the plains which would come at the first light of the new day. Everyone still finding comfort in sleeping close to one another, blankets not necessary even in the early morning hours before daylight and finding them still left unpacked and in the back of the carts. There were ten lying on the ground with Violta nestled beside her husband in the back of the first cart, still finding it necessary to remain in his mind. Bansinghaim found the bear cub cuddling up to him and finding comfort only there. The tranquility of the group seemed wondrous to Vastion who stood first guard. He noticed everything about each of them, but mostly he noticed Baydowa.

She looked like no other woman he had ever seen before. She was feminine and not at the same time. She had worn a dress really only the once after the first day he had seen her, at Chessington and Violta's wedding, but her figure was a very wonderful representation of the female form. Her face was sharp and well defined. Even though her sister was more rounded and cute as a woman, he could still see how they were related even though to first appearance they seemed to be far from similar. Baydowa had the full figure but athletically built. Yaughtie had a full figure but in a more traditional sense, more than likely from not exercising in the mountains and foraging in the woods like her older sister had.

All in all he found himself mesmerized by the sight of Baydowa sleeping on the ground beside her sister and Preda. He wondered what especially made her so different from the other women he had found it so easy to disconnect from after a very short time. He had no answer for himself and decided to let it go.

Turning to stare out the massive door which had been opened to try to get some air flow through the stuffy old barn, he looked down the road Baydowa had told him earlier would take them to the bridge crossing the smaller River Bodona as it drained into the much larger River Lostanda. He stared out until he felt an arm hug him from behind while he stood just outside and around the corner from the large doorway.

He turned to see her nestle into his chest and hold him tightly. He started to speak, to tell her she should sleep while she can, but she stopped him with a soft kiss. The first one was followed by another and another until they stood contented in the euphoria they were providing for each other.

* * * * * *

The band of travelers had put just under ten miles behind them as it was still early in the day. The day they would hopefully get to their long expected destination of Drenne. If all was right with their thoughts of how it would go, they would stop once in the late morning for a fast lunch and then refrain from stopping except for short pauses until they were just inside the city gates of the port town. They traveled down the bumpy highway which only a few short months ago would have been packed with caravans taking merchandise from the docks to other areas of the kingdom. Mostly to the capital city of Lostanda; although, now with the island void of its population, the highway was a single lonely ribbon of road leading endlessly into the distance.

Sir Bansinghaim had to ride his mount next to the second cart. The bear cub had attached itself to the large knight and was making quite a fuss if he were more than ten feet away at any given time. Most men would be annoyed at this inconvenience, but the Royal Knight Protectorate rather enjoyed the attention paid upon him by the young cub.

The first cart was filled will Chessington being kept still and unconscious by his wife, Violta, still nursing him mentally but not allowing him to awaken until they could be stopped, or close to it, for many days in a row. She had maintained her vigil for the past three days ever since he had tried to rescue the group from the wolf pack, which had attacked the women out of hunger while they bathed in the river.

The talking was at a low point. Most felt the pressure of riding out of the protection of the mountains. Some were just plain bored with riding another monotonous day in a row. The rest were simply talked out.

Prince Palton rode next to the first cart where two of his three best friends were, Sir Ghalkin and Preda, with Sir Bansinghaim being the third. He liked talking to Preda because she would look at him with big eyes, and with him being older, she would look up to him, something the adults did not do. They treated him with the respect of a future king, but never thought of him as a valuable part of the group. He had defended the women against the wolves, he had suggested the fountain in Marroda as the spot to meet at, and he was one of the three taken back to be read to with Queen Rhyshena. He knew it was his age. He also knew these times needed strong leaders, and General Vastion, as well as Sir Ghalkin, would be far better qualified to head this expedition than he was. These were the experiences they had already had. He did remember being told to pay attention to what was going on because if they were victorious, he would be stronger and wiser as King after he was returned to power.

Preda burst his train of thought, "Hey, what's that up there?"

Everyone heard the child and saw what she had been talking about. An enormous cloud of dust was being churned up in the distance and off to the right of the road they were heading down.

"What could it possibly be?" Ghalkin wondered.

"I have no idea." Vastion replied, "We don't have Chessington to pop up ahead and see either."

Violta answered him, "Definitely not."

Modinay broke from the line and stated, "I'll do it the old fashioned way I guess." Leaving them grinning at the thought of their dependence on the young Wizard and his ability to make life on the road so much easier for them all.

"Should we wait here?" Ghalkin asked.

"No, let's move ahead." Vastion sighed, "Even if it is horrible, we're too far out of the mountains to fall back now."

"I fer one 'ld feel better if we wasn't so depleted goin' inta a possible fracas." Malden threw in, "We got our best weapon unconscious an' our second best without the use a his right arm. Makes us a poor bet in a fight I'd think."

"Running back into the mountains could hold the possibility of living to fight another day." Ghalkin commented.

"I see your points." Vastion remarked, "Let's go forward cautiously and see what Modinay brings back."

They moved at a steady but nervous pace once again down the highway. Having only traveled a very short distance, they saw Modinay riding rapidly back to them.

"I found out what it was." The former Police Chief announced, "It seems the mutated animals from the mountains have run out of food in their natural environment. There are thirteen cougars attacking a small band of cattle, which seem to have gotten out of their pen somewhere out in a grassy field. They circled them and have them penned up. It appears that, approximately two or three at a time, they are killing a single head of cattle, eating it, and all the while the rest are taking turns watching the rest so they don't get loose before another two or three attack. Afterwards, the fed cougars become the fence line for the remaining live cattle. I believe they plan on exterminating the entire heard."

"We should be safe to pass then?" Vastion raised the question.

"Possibly." Modinay answered.

"I think we need to keep moving forward." Vastion stated, "What do the rest of you think?"

"I say pull back an' wait it out," Malden stated, "but then again, I ain't a fighter ta begin with. If they're mutated from the mountains, they could have tricks that ain't normal fer a cougar ta have. They obviously can think, formulate, an' converse with each other."

"It's thirteen against thirteen," Bansinghaim added, "We both should know we're around. I say we start through with every intention of being attacked, and if it doesn't happen, we feel lucky. Should we be attacked, though, I think having the proper people in the proper positions would be of the utmost importance."

Vastion looked to the remaining councilmember, "Ghalkin?"

"I believe we need to get off of this Island before more things start going sideways on us." The tutor exclaimed, "We have to get to Drenne before we can do anything else, and things are getting further and further out of control here. I actually agree with Sir Bansinghaim. We have five strong swordsmen, two of which are very inexperienced with Prince Palton and Gurlig, and myself with the bow. I do have over one hundred arrows after having lost a few back at the wolves, but I should be of assistance in the battle as well."

Modinay agreed, "I think you would mow down quite a few before the main pack hit our entire group. The problem I see is in our casualties. Them having thirteen, all of fighting ability, and us having basically six. It would be very instrumental for Sir Ghalkin to take out as many as he can before they get to actual swordsmen. Should they decide to double up on one of us, they could eliminate us one by one until all that would be left are the defenseless."

"It would appear the decision is being made for us." Baydowa stated looking off to the distance and seeing thirteen large mountain lions, walking on their hind legs, coming towards them from the area where the dust cloud had been.

Mark L Porter

Chapter 30

The wild mountain lions were walking slowly and methodically towards the band of travelers they saw as a threat and dangerous to them. They meandered up closer to the bands of mostly humans, spreading out and taking positions around the carts and horses, trying to make it more difficult for any to escape after the attack.

"Can you reach them yet, Ghalkin?" Vastion asked.

"Not quite," The archer answered him, "but I think I have a plan."

He shot a single arrow a short distance to the right of the cart he was standing in.

"What was that for?" Bansinghaim wondered.

"If they have mutated intelligence," Ghalkin replied, "they might feel free to come up to that line. From what Modinay told us of the attack on the cattle, they seem to have not only the ability to work as a team, but also to reason." He shot another to the left at the same short distance.

Continuing, he explained further, "If I can draw them closer, I can get a few before they come at us too rapidly, picking off a few of the larger looking ones before they get to you with the swords." He shot a third to the rear of the group, again at the shortened distance of what he was capable.

It appeared to be working, the large cats stopped a few feet from the arrow line Sir Ghalkin had placed out fifty feet from the traveling party They studied their victims cautiously pacing and seemingly conversing together.

Violta stood in her cart, "They think we're weak and have too many females to be much of a threat. They will attack from the front first towards the fighting men, and then after a few seconds, the ones in the rear will attack the women, Chessington, and the cub."

Vastion barked out the orders, "Modinay, Palton, and Bansinghaim you stay to the front with me. Ghalkin, you shoot to the sides and the rear, Gurlig you maintain yourself as the last line of the rear defense."

Everyone moved into place and awaited the forthcoming attack. It did not take long, but the animals made an unfortunate error before attacking in a move which is normally foreign to cats and could only be brought on by their mutated brains as a show of intimidation before attacking. They stood upon their hind legs and growled as a battle cry to one another. In actuality it only served two purposes for Sir Ghalkin. First, if standing they were much larger targets to find a soft spot for the kill, and second, they were stationary targets and much easier to hit. He had four pierced between the ribs, three puncturing a lung and the fourth being shot through the heart, before any advancement was ever made.

The remaining nine pulled back and growled at the archer in anger and frustration at their fallen pack members. They were seen pacing back and forth, still realizing they out numbered the fighting men and waiting to regroup before the attack. The thought of the easy kill of the defenseless members of the human party, as well as the horses, still weighing on their mutated minds as they paced back and forth in anticipation.

Vastion called back to Violta, "What are they thinking?"

Violta called out loud and clear, "They are spewing anger and hatred at Sir Ghalkin, vowing to avenge the deaths of their family by ripping the throats out of each of us. They also are closing up the holes in their ranks. They feel they still outnumber us in their fighting members versus our fighting members. This time they each have a member to attack. And some are coming for the weaker of us first."

"Ghalkin," Vastion exclaimed, "you have to watch and see which of them are coming for the weaponless and let us handle the others. As we get our battles won, we will slide over to help those who haven't."

As soon as the words had left his lips, the wild cougars attacked quick and direct. Ghalkin saw one heading for Chessington and shot straight at his face, piercing his eye socket at such a close range. The second he fired at was headed for Preda, hitting him through the chest as he jumped to get the small child sitting petrified on the front of the cart next to himself.

Gurlig had rammed his sword through the stomach of the one designated for him at first charge, not realizing the weight of the beast and having the dead carcass of the animal land directly on top of him.

Bansinghaim, even though fighting left-handed, wasted no time in decapitating his attacking mountain lion and quickly was moving next to Vastion to do the same to his. Modinay made quick work of his and turned to see how the others were doing.

The final three had decided to take the smallest warrior of the humans together and then deplete their numbers from ganging up on them. What they had not counted on was how well the young Prince could handle a sword. He easily sliced the throat of the first to reach him and kicked the second in the side of the head as it was attacking from behind. The third had assumed the small boy would be consumed with the obvious attacks of the first two and be unaware of him attacking at his blind side from the left and slightly behind. Palton had seen him, however, and whipped around to slice a strip across the cougars belly all the way through the muscle and having the trail of intestines fall to the ground where he was opened.

The final cougar paced around the boy as the men came quickly to help him. It proved to be unnecessary. The cat, feeling it was about to be cornered, sprang at the younger and much smaller Prince causing him to fall under the superior weight of the large mountain lion.

The group feared the worst as the cat covered most of the Prince lying under him until they realized the cat was no longer moving. Bansinghaim kicked the cougar who had attacked his young ward to the side, revealing the boy had fallen back on purpose, steadying the hilt of the sword against the hard road he had fallen upon. The weight the cougar had actually thought to have been his advantage, instead turned out to be his downfall. He lay next to the young Prince, sword protruding from his chest, dead.

"Check for casualties, everyone!" Vastion announced.

Bansinghaim called straight to Violta, "The Prince is cut on the upper left thigh." She was already coming over after seeing the blood herself, "He appears to be alright otherwise."

She looked at his cut and decided to have Bansinghaim carry him over to the other cart and remove his riding trousers. Meanwhile, she went to the second cart and gathered some of the plants she had carried from the mountains to use on Bansinghaim's arm and ribs to ward off infection. The white flower of the Chamomile could be crushed into a paste and the oils from the pedals would keep the infection from setting in as well as aid in the healing process. Once added to a few cranberries, the infection would never have a chance to take hold. She understood plants and their principal uses making her very valuable in these times of minor, as well as major, crisis.

"Yaughtie," Violta took over the situation, "get me your needle from your sewing things and some very strong thread. Gurlig I need a small fire, nothing fancy, just enough to kill the dirt on Yaughtie's needle. Baydowa, I need you here with me, and Modinay and Bansinghaim, you will have to hold him still while I do what I have to do."

Sir Ghalkin, talking full responsibility as his legal guardian, asked, "What exactly do you have to do?"

"I have to use stitches to bring his muscles and skin back together." She answered as everyone, including Prince Palton, was listening to what she had to say, "I am going to clean it out as best I can, rub some of the oil from my plants in his wound, and have Baydowa hold it as close together as she can. Then I can take the sterilized needle and sturdy thread and sew it back together so it has a chance of healing normally; otherwise, he stands a great chance of walking with a limp for the rest of his life. Not the end of the world mind you, but I am sure he would rather not have to. Then I will lay a poultice on it and wrap it up to heal, much like I did with Sir Bansinghaim."

"Why do you need Modinay and Bansinghaim then?" Ghalkin wondered.

"Because it will hurt," she admitted, "a lot."

"I'm not afraid, Sir." The Prince reassured his teacher, "I don't want to limp the rest of my life. I'll be as still as can be. Sir. I promise."

Ghalkin took the boys hand, "I know you will, my boy. You are a man before your time." Then turning back to the uncontested doctor of the party, he stated, "Proceed please."

"Do you want to go?" Violta asked as everyone stood around watching the boy slowly bleeding from his upper thigh, "It will be hard to watch."

To a person they each decided to stay and be with the boy throughout the entire procedure. Yaughtie brought the blackened needle over and threaded the toughest thread she could find through the eye of it, laying it on the plants to be used after the stitching to keep away the germs could cause infection.

Violta washed the cut out with some water, and the young Prince winced slightly as the water touched the sensitive area the cougar had opened. She poured a small amount of the oil into the center of the cut and pushed it together as tightly as she could.

She turned to Baydowa, "Hold this together and keep it still, please." Baydowa did as she was instructed, holding the muscle tissues together tightly, her muscles locking into place, almost afraid to move after getting it perfect.

The small Doltist started with her stitching, going in on one side and out the other of the long cut, placing three to four stitches to every inch of cut skin. After forty-five minutes, and thirty-eight stitches, she had Baydowa remove her hands. Seeing the line she had made hold, she looked pleased with her work and saw the face of the boy was sweating and mildly contorted.

She turned to Baydowa, "Take this root, it is called Valerian Root, and mash it into a paste. Then heat some water over the fire I see Gurlig kept going and make a tea out of it. Give the Prince one cupful and store the rest, at least enough for six more cupfuls, in an empty jar for later. He should be asleep very shortly after that." She finished by rubbing the poultice over the area and wrapping it firmly, making sure she had not cut off the circulation to his leg.

Yaughtie brought the tea over, and they all watched the young Prince drink it down after it had cooled for a few minutes. Within thirty minutes of drinking it, whether from exhaustion, loss of blood, or the tea, the young boy was asleep and on his way to recovery.

Vastion bent down to put his hand on Violta's small shoulder, which was actually closer to his thigh than even his waist. "What would we do without you?" He asked.

She looked fatigued, not tired so much as mentally spent, "I need to return to Chessington and concentrate all of my energy to keeping him asleep. He really wants to wake up." With this she hopped out of the cart Prince Palton was sleeping in and onto the one holding her husband.

Bansinghaim and Ghalkin were watching the sleeping form of the injured Prince contentedly lying still and sleeping after the ordeal of the past hour and a half. Gurlig joined them after retrieving the Prince's sword from the cat who had made the wound in his small leg and slicing the throats of all thirteen cats which had been slain even if the throat had already been cut.

Bansinghaim looked at the boy sleeping and spoke softly, "He fought like a man today, outnumbered and still victorious. I saw the last two he killed. He was perfect in form and technique. Even when he knew the bigger cat was going to pounce on him, he found a way to win. As the teacher I'd love to take credit for that, but the truth is, you can't teach it. You're just born with it."

"He is being forced to grow up faster than normal," Ghalkin stated, "both he and Preda. He squeezed my hand hard all throughout the stitching, but never once cried or let out a sound."

The group heard the cries of more cats in the distance to the north. Each knowing exactly what it was they were hearing.

"We had best be moving on." Vastion ordered, "The horses should be well rested. Let's get some distance between us and this place."

No one spoke. They just fell into place in their spots they already knew of and left. They for once did not stick around to clean up the fire or the dead carcasses of the mountain lions littering the plains in this spot. All knew they did not wish to have a repeat of what had just happened and pushed their horses as far as they dared with the wounded in the carts.

* * * * * * *

The traveling party finally passed through the city gates of what had been Drenne, the port town they had been instructed to get to by History itself. A passing of the accomplishment moved through the group, helping all to feel a slight sense of relief.

Vastion led the party to a side road holding on to the advantage of not being able to be seen from the plains they had just passed through for the past twelve hours, the last eight of which at a hurried and thankfully uninterrupted pace. They all dismounted and hopped from the carts to stretch their legs and twist their backs from the hard riding they had just finished.

"I had thought we would never make it here." Ghalkin stated.

"We almost didn't," Vastion smiled, "many times in fact."

"Yes, I remember." Ghalkin replied.

Violta, not wishing to waist any time, was bringing the Book of Past Times up to Sir Malden to see if he could read it or if they still had to move on further and wake Chessington to do it for them.

Malden opened the book carefully and looked to the writing on the first few pages, "Nope, it's a old language, but there ain't no way I can read it."

Ghalkin asked, "The page he usually reads from is in the back if I remember correctly. Try there first before we have to wake him."

Malden studied the back several pages, "I see the page, but all I can read's his name. After that it's just garbled up symbols I can just assume means somethin'."

"Well," Vastion sighed, "I guess we have our answer then. Let's finish this at the docks before something decides to get brave and enter the town."

Bansinghaim looked at the General, "I think we might want to admit they may already have."

Vastion nodded, pinching the bridge of his nose in relief of his exhaustion, "Valid point. Let's ride two abreast. Bansinghaim with me in the front, even left handed you're the best we've got. Modinay and Gurlig behind us, women in the carts, Baydowa you will drive Ghalkin's and Yaughtie you will do the same with Gurlig's. Ghalkin you will ride facing backwards in the last cart. Malden you ride between the two carts."

They all shifted to the arrangement the General had ordered up with the bear cub sniffing Sir Ghalkin as he rode next to him. Ghalkin did not mind as he scratched between the cub's ears and felt the soft fur of the orphaned bear cub warm on his hand.

After ten minutes of uninterrupted riding, they saw ahead of them the docks they had planned on reaching before they had to awaken the young Wizard to read the page from his book to them, instructing them as to the next step in their quest. They moved down to the waterfront and into a warehouse, which seemed to have been unloaded of all of its belongings before the evacuation of the town however many months earlier.

Violta was already regressing her thoughts to get out of his mind and allow him to awaken like he had wanted to naturally for the past day and a half. Within seconds of her leaving his thoughts, he stirred and moved out of the unconscious state he had been kept in for the good of everyone involved and opened his eyes.

Violta jumped immediately into his thoughts and explained to him, *You've been asleep for the past three days, my love. You hurt yourself trying to help us against the wolves. We are all fine; although, other things in the forest are attacking, and even though we all still have good health, Bansinghaim and Palton are scarred and cut, but they will be fine.*

I see Sir Bansinghaim. He answered her, *Where's Palton?*

He is asleep in the other cart. She informed him, *His wound is fresher, and he lost a lot more blood than Sir Bansinghaim did. I promise to fill you in better once we move on, but we need your help for something right now.*

Of course, he replied, trying to sit up and finding that he could not, *but what can I do?*

We are in Drenne, dear, she explained further, *and we cannot read the book to find out what to do next.*

Hold it above my face, please. Chessington asked her.

She complied and everyone heard her say as he mentally read to her:

Chessington the Twenty-ninth,

The trials and tribulations of the past week have greatly added to how strong you will be in the future. May the truth be told, you must further develop to become stronger still. You all will be tested harder and deeper than you have as of yet.

Now for your instructions on the next phase of your journey to defeat the ones creating havoc in the world. You will remount immediately and proceed out to the docks. A large freighter will be docked at the end of the pier six docks to the south of where you are now. That is the one you must enter. You will know which by the large side mounted doorway large enough for the horses and carts to fit through. You will also know it by the size. It will far and away tower over the remaining abandoned ships docked there. Load your animals and carts, lock them down to the cargo locks, and close the doorway tightly. Release the lines and the tide will take you out to sea.

Do these tasks laid before you as explained, and then return to read as to the next phase of this leg of your journey. As always you must fulfill these requirements before you are to read the next phase.

She returned the book to his side and watched him fall back to sleep after expending what little energy he had on just staying awake and concentrating for the brief moment.

Vastion looked at the group around the cart, "I guess we remount and move down the docks six piers to find the large freighter, load it, seal it, and cast it off."

Ghalkin asked, "In the manor we did coming here?"

"Yes," Vastion agreed, "we've come this far. Let's not drop our guard now that we're getting close to being off the island."

They all remounted and stationed themselves in the defensive positions they had maintained after entering the town gates, moving the group down the docks to find the large freighter they had been sent to find.

They did travel the six piers to the south they had to travel and saw the most enormous ship any of them had ever seen. *The Rosataphan* was painted in bold black lettering on the bow of the ship. They moved to find the freighter shut tightly with a small boarding plank leading across to a small doorway to the left of the larger doorway they were to load the carts and horses through. Modinay and Gurlig crossed over to open the loading bay hatch, and as it opened, they saw a cavernous empty hold, which would be exceedingly more room than necessary for the meager amount of two carts and nine horses being stored there for the trip they assumed to be to the mainland.

"Men," Vastion ordered, "we will get the cargo loaded and locked down as well as the horses. The women will scout the ship for sleeping chambers and general layout of the ship. Ladies, as you go through, make a mental note of where we may hold our infirmary and the whereabouts of the galley. I feel we need to get Chessington and the Prince settled as soon as possible to get them back healing and stable."

The women broke off and investigated the ship while the six able bodied men moved the carts and horses into the hold area, which must have been for livestock before this as it held enough hay and oats for them to be away for months with the amount of horses they were feeding.

After the loads had been secured, Violta came back below to tell the General they had found the perfect room to use for Chessington and Prince Palton. Also, Baydowa, Yaughtie, and Preda were fixing up the beds and afterwards would be taking an inventory of the food supplies in the galley they had found. She informed the men also, of a large storage of wood for cooking was already in place in the main cooking area. It appeared as if the ship was almost ready to pull out by the looks of the rooms and galley.

"It must have been just waiting its turn to leave when the Chiloes arrived." Modinay figured, "Obviously, the Chiloes liked the cargo and took it but didn't wish to waist any time by searching the remainder of the ship for useful items and supplies. We may be able to find some gems for our own journey after we land," he paused in realization, "somewhere."

"Good point," Vastion picked up on the fact that even though they knew they were going out to sea, they all had no idea where they would be landing, "as for now there are still more things to do before we untie this huge thing from the docks and head out. Modinay you carry Chessington, and Ghalkin you take the Prince. We'll follow Violta up to their room and get them settled. Meanwhile, Bansinghaim, Malden, and Gurlig, you three close up the hatches and dumb them up with the compound between the doors. Make sure we have no leaks in the doorways. None of us are that good of swimmers. After the doorways are secure go to the galley and get Gurlig set up to make something. We're all going to be hungry very soon

Modinay, Ghalkin, and I will get the ropes off and set us adrift. Then Violta can have Chessington read the book again, and we can start getting away from this island finally."

No one saw a hole in the plan he had just laid out before them, and all went on their way to perform the tasks they were to accomplish. The doorway was closed, tied off tightly, and sealed with the sticky compound the men found in the bucket for just this very purpose. The injured were taken up to a room having large windows for sunlight and beds screwed to the floor, as much had to be on a ship, with an area for eating off to the side closest to the door.

The three who had brought Chessington and Prince Palton up to the infirmary now emerged for the first time to the top deck of the large freighter finding seven thick ropes holding it to the dock from bow to stern. Waiting for only a few moments they unhooked all but the first, last , and very middle until Sir Bansinghaim popped his head up to notify them the hatches had been secured and they were ready to have the tide take them out to sea. Once the ropes had been removed, they stayed on the deck awaiting the sight over the railing of the ship safely moving from the dock to more open waters.

Ghalkin gave a sigh of relief as the final task had been performed from the list of things they had to do for the book, "I suppose it is time to awaken Chessington and see if we can find out where we are going."

"Alright," Vastion nodded, "Ghalkin you go to the galley and get Gurlig and Malden. Modinay you go find Bansinghaim, and we'll meet in the infirmary."

Too tired for small talk, they all just went their separate ways and proceeded to find the people they had to get to the beds of the two injured boys who were doing their best to recover from their debilitating wounds.

In only minutes they were all gathered by Chessington's bed as Violta brought him back, this time a little stronger than before.

The Prince was even sitting on the corner of his bed looking at the Wizard who was also his friend and awaiting the newest revelation of orders, which History had to give.

Exile

Chessington started his reading:

> Chessington the Twenty-ninth,
>
> Your group of fellow adventurers has performed well yet again. This is the easiest part of the trip for all except yourself. You will live on this ship for three weeks while moving north around the northern most tip of the Island of Mosa. Do not allow yourselves to be seen from the shoreline, staying well out of sight until you reach the Bodashian town of Dorga at the southern end of the Bay of Stoga. This is extremely simple. After you reach the town, read from me again and find the course you are to take afterwards.
>
> It was of the utmost importance for you to make it to this point on or before this date. Things will be set in motion which you will need to stay ahead of after this, and the three weeks you will be out to sea will be more than enough time for the healings of your Royal Knight, crowned Prince, and yourself as well. You feel it already. You are getting stronger. The energy is starting to flow more and more freely every minute you are resting. Your mind will welcome a full recovery within twelve days, well before you dock at Dorga.
>
> As always return to these pages for further instruction after you are in the city.

They all shouted great shouts of joy at the finding out of their going to the mainland. They each had the feeling the troubles were not over by any means, but the problems they had witnessed and lived through on the Island of Mosa were at least behind them. They had escaped from the nerve-racking and watchful eye of Pazlin the Sorcerer for now. They also new it would come again, but at least they would have a break as they had in the mountain cave back at Mt. Bollantoda.

Unexpectedly, they were startled by the sight of a man, tall and slender, standing in the doorway, dressed in his Captain's uniform with his sword drawn, and screaming, "What are you doin' on my ship!"

This ends book two of The Phenderians

ABOUT THE AUTHOR

Now a resident of Spokane Valley, WA, Mark L Porter was born in Spokane in 1962. Married, with two daughters and two grandchildren, he started writing in 1996. After being an active member of the Spokane Writers and Novelist group, he has continued writing with this novel as his third published work.

www.ingramcontent.com/pod-product-compliance
Lightning Source LLC
Chambersburg PA
CBHW071507260626
47170CB00002B/296